VIETNAM REMIX

Jack Nolan

ISBN: 1543031102
ISBN 13: 9781543031102
Library of Congress Control Number: 2017902246
CreateSpace Independent Publishing Platform
North Charleston, South Carolina

VIETNAM REMIX is dedicated to

Sergeant Swanson, M.P.

and all the Vietnam Veterans

who, like him, answered the call

1

3 April 1967

THE GREYHAWK SIX

Seven months before Rene Levesque emerged as Brother Andre and nine months before Mulcahey and Rosenzweig received a tray of cookies from Major Hideo Shimazu, the three PFCs gathered around their bunks in an enormous, sunlit dormitory on the third floor of the enlisted quarters at Fort Greyhawk, trying to stave-off a crisis.

Tall and pale as the alabaster statues that inhabited his parish church back in Rhode Island, Levesque coolly instructed his friends, "It is a simple matter. They lied to me and I lied to them. The recruiter told me I would be a 'translator' and I promised him three years of my life. Now they have betrayed me and gone back on their word, so I am free to go back on mine. I maxed-out the Army Latin Test and he said I had a good chance of going to language school at The Presidio. I'm not at The Presidio, am I? Now they say I agreed to be a spy, which I did not. Besides...." As he turned to face them with a perfectly folded shirt in his long fingers, the sunlight falling on his pale features from the tall windows made him appear even more cadaverous than usual. "I have grandparents, uncles, aunts and cousins in Montreal, where I spent every summer growing up, and I'm fluent in Quebecois. I can pile up degrees at McGill or Laval for three years while you guys go and spy on the Vietnamese."

1

"They didn't say 'spying,' they said 'intelligence,' and you don't know what that means any more than we do." Mulcahey was up on his toes, which still left him just shoulder-high to Levesque. "Give it a week for chrissakes. Then you can put your tail between your legs and let 'em run you outta your own goddamn country. Canada's lousy with draft-dodgers, but I bet they send deserters back and that's what you'd be, a goddamn deserter. They'll ship you back and you'll be piling up rocks at Fort Leavenworth!"

Levesque continued folding clothes, placing each item carefully into his duffle bag, as though he were quite alone. The clash of styles between the formal, unflappable Canuck and the hot-tempered Chicago Irishman had provided a much-needed distraction during basic training at Fort Campbell. When February rain had frozen into layers of ice on their ponchos or when firing M-14s from muddy pits had left them deaf, this fire-and-ice dialog supplied comic relief, the basis for their friendship. Zachary Rosenzweig, the only other Greyhawk-bound recruit in Company B, found a role for himself as a catalyst for the Levesque-Mulcahey chemistry. Rosie seemed to know how to ignite an exchange that would shatter the boredom of waiting in endless lines for food or trucks or nothing at all -- and how to tamp things down before the gloves actually came off. Their triad drew together for mutual protection once they discovered they were all headed for Greyhawk Intelligence School: college graduates who had volunteered for three-year hitches in exchange for nice, safe office jobs in the Intelligence Corps, afloat in a sea of younger draftees nabbed from small towns and city streets who were destined, many of them, for combat.

At six-two, Rosie towered over Mulcahey, so he put a hand on the shoulder of his fatigues and said, "Back off and let him think about it, Mad-dog. It's his decision what he does."

"He's not listening anyway because he knows I'm right. He's a goddamn stubborn...."

Rosie placed firm hands on both narrow shoulders and pushed Mulcahey away from the bunks, marching him to the far end of the bay. They sat on the top landing of the concrete stairway and waited for Levesque.

"I'm gonna kick his ass," Mulcahey barked into the echo-chamber of the stairwell.

"I wouldn't try it. He's got fifty pounds on you."

They both knew Rene Levesque would come their way hauling his duffle bag -- in which case nothing they said would change anything -- or without it, and they would not talk about it again so that their friendship might last for some months more, or for years, or a lifetime. Either way, the freezing weeks at Fort Campbell under the sadistic reign of their drill sergeant, along with an outbreak of meningitis that put a third of their company in the hospital and a truck accident that injured a dozen more, were their shared history. Now wearing fatigues or a dress uniform no longer seemed strange. They accepted "yessir" and "nosir" as their own jargon. And April in southern New Jersey on an "open" fort where they could come and go as they pleased in uniform or in civvies, an easy bus-ride from Philadelphia, seemed like freedom-itself. The small movie theater, chapel and bank branch that sat in a neat row across the lush grass of the parade ground might have been on any college campus, except for a group of soldiers, three abreast, marching to the cadence of their class-leader across the way.

" I AM gonna kick his ass. I mean it."

"Stop, all right? We could both bust his ass but if he's leaving, he's leaving. He's stubborn as a mule, and you know it. And it might help if you laid off with 'chrissakes' and 'goddamn'. You know he doesn't like that."

"Oh, for chrissakes! Why does he want to go ruin everything now, after all we got through together at Campbell?"

"OK. Tell me exactly how it would help to kick his butt before he leaves?"

Three other PFCs came up the concrete steps who had been at the afternoon's orientation session for their new class, ES-3-1967: The big powerhouse with the massive head was Braxton Hood,

Mark Babineaux was the red-head with the broad, cock-sure smile, and Rick Singleton was the only "colored" guy -- the term some thought respectful back then -- in the new class. Rosie was from Nashville so he at once recognized that Hood and Babineaux were from the Deep South, not a border-state guy like he was, and that soft-spoken Singleton was a Northerner. But Mulcahey had never known anyone from the South and he tried to stifle a laugh when Hood asked, "All y'all in ES-3?" PFC Hood noticed Mulcahey's smirk and had to suppress asking what was so funny -- and would this Yankee like to have his head ripped off. Babineaux quickly stepped between the two, jabbed an index finger into Mulcahey's chest and laughed, "How'd ya' like that fat-ass colonel with the Charlton Heston voice?" He boomed into the echoing stairwell an uncanny imitation of a scene from *The Ten Commandments*: " *I HAVE COME TO BRING YOU THE WORD OF GOD, MY CHOSEN DOUCHE-BAGS! YOU HAVE BEEN ELECTED ABOVE ALL OTHERS TO BRING SALVATION TO THE INDIGENOUS MASSES SUFFERING UNDER THE COMMUNIST YOKE*! Can you picture this jackass coming home at night? He kicks in the front door and shouts, *YOUR FATHER'S HOME!* and the wife and little kiddies pee their pants!" Babineaux laughed along with the others at his own skit -- while two months of basic-training "Yessir!" and "Yes, drill sergeant!" obedience made way for the return of brash iconoclasm, the natural medium of college-educated young men in America. The dancing blue eyes, gruff voice, agile wit and gift for mimicry gave this Cajun wild man every tool necessary to lead his friends, in time, to the borders of madness. For now, he said, "Let's get out of these clown costumes and go find a bar."

Rene Levesque approached back-lit by sunlight, in civvies and without a duffle bag, and said affably, "Did somebody mention a bar?"

"What did I tell ya'," Babineaux stage-whispered. "I knew there was a corpse haunting this floor!"

Mulcahey was offended: "Cut him some slack, OK? He's a friend of mine and he's had a bad day."

Half an hour later, they were nestled in a corner booth at a large, busy tavern across from the main gate, The Greyhawk Inn. Buzz-cut military and long-haired civilians blended together, some soldiers still in uniform seemed welcomed, a fancy, old Seeburg jukebox was playing "Penny Lane" and the waitress was friendly, so they ordered two pitchers of suds and settled in.

Babineaux chattered away through his big smile, "My best friend Dupree, he's the death of me, man. We grew up together in Lake Charles and he's always been getting me into shit and walking away since we're little. This time, I got a full scholarship to law school at Four Lane, that's the grad school at Tulane, and Dupree says to me, 'Let's find us some girls and get smashed'. A week later, I'm in the drunk tank over in Biloxi and have all these weird memories about how I got there. Dupree bails me out and hands me $400. 'What's this for?' I ask him. 'It's the money left from your car,' he says. 'I sold my '56 Bel Air for 400 bucks!?' I yell. 'No but we spent all the rest,' and I have more of these weird memories coming back of hotel rooms and women. So then I can either go home and hear what my father and the law dean have to say to me, up close and personal, or I can enlist and write them all letters from some army camp."

"So that's how you came to serve your country in uniform?" Hood asked, raising his glass in mock salute. "Another true-blue American patriot heard from."

"And so what are you, pro-war?" Mulcahey asked.

"I am pro-the-United-States-of-America, sir, first, last and always. My daddy fought in Korea when it was his turn. He didn't get to choose his war, so how come I should choose mine?"

Mulcahey's Hyde Park neighborhood was full of other University of Chicago men, active protesters who found ways to dodge the draft through school, teaching, even marriage or, these failing, enlist-ment to avoid a combat role. He had never met anyone who thought Vietnam was a good idea. College seemed to be a given in this group, so he blurted out, "Where d'ya go to college?"

"Clemson."

"Where's Clemson?"

Hood tilted his bear-sized head and glared at him. "South Carolina, sir."

"OK, how 'bout this," Mulcahey snapped. "Levesque, Rosie and I did basic at Campbell and we noticed all the drill sergeants were Southerners. We kicked your asses in the Civil War and now you join up in droves and you're all patriotic and pro-army and stuff. How come?"

Hood set down his beer mug and placed his massive hands flat on the table-top. "Well, here's how ah reck'n," he drawled out in a parody of Southern archetype, "Since we're all sooo stupid, it took us a hundr'd years to fig'r out we need to take over the Army so we can invade you-all Yankees and kick your-all asses and get even. Maybe that's it."

Mulcahey's response was a happy, mocking, beer-soaked laugh. Rosie put a firm hand on Mad-dog's forearm and shouted, "HEY! Isn't the Army just great for bringing us all together for a frank exchange of views? North and South...so am I the only border-state guy here who's neither one? Rich and poor...OK, so am I the only poor guy too? Christian and Jew...OH NO! Yahweh damn it! I'm the only Jew!"

"Black and white? Oh damn!" Singleton chimed in and laughter broke out around the booth.

"So, Private Mulcahey, what led you to sign on the dotted line?" Hood asked.

"Call him Mad-dog," Rosie said. "You're beginning to see why everybody does."

"I plan to be a writer...a novelist."

"No shit," Babineaux said, "You aim to be the next Hemingway?"

"The next Fitzgerald," Mulcahey said solemnly.

"So you signed-up for Vietnam to get your ass shot off for the life-experience," Babineaux suggested.

"What do you want to write about?" Singleton asked cordially.

"Tell them!" Rosie chuckled, "Go ahead and tell them."

"Well, right now, I have about 600 pages done, but it's kind of off-beat, so I'd rather not."

"Go ahead," Rosie taunted, "It's not *that* off-beat. Let them hear about it."

Mulcahey drained his mug and Rosie re-filled it for him. "It takes place in heaven...well, not heaven exactly because there's no such place...."

"That's another thing," Levesque cut in, "Mad-dog's an atheist."

"...more like a huge ship that's going through an endless fog...and so, in this special place, everyone who ever lived throughout history can communicate in English...."

"They all have Yankee accents?" Hood asked.

".... regular, ordinary English, like in Chicago, and so these passengers meet in the dining hall or on the deck and have these incredible, dynamic conversations: Newton and Einstein tear into each other over gravity; Homer and Joyce argue about Odysseus; Shakespeare and Faulkner mix it up over the creative process...."

Rosenzweig's laughter grew audible above the bar noise and The Monkees' "I'm A Believer" at this point, which turned them all loose. Rosie threw his hands in the air and said, "Wait! I'm going to need lots more beer to hear the rest."

"You were right to join-up," Hood said. "A year in Vietnam will just make your book that much better."

"Thanks a lot, Rosie," Mulcahey grumbled. "You knew that was gonna happen."

Linda -- so beautiful, Mad-dog said, she could "fire the ardors of a dying hermit" -- dropped off two more pitchers and collected money from the pile of bills that was their centerpiece. Mulcahey, pie-eyed, turned to Singleton and slurred, "So you said 'black and white'. S'that mean t'so kay to call you 'black'?"

For some seconds Singleton paused and they watched to see if he was offended by the question or just considering it. Then with meticulous precision he said, "In his speech on The Mall, Dr. King used both terms, 'Negro' and 'black'. So I guess either one is currency now. I'm from New York City, and I don't believe I ever heard the term 'colored' before I arrived at basic training. For myself, I'd rather be called Rick or Singleton because that's who I am. And I'd rather you did *not* call me a scion of wealth from Harlem who was born with a silver spoon and sent to a very expensive private school so that I could move on to study dramatic arts at Yale... because that's also who I am but referring to me in that way could destroy my sterling reputation." He stopped and looked at them poker-faced, alert to whatever response they might have. None of them had known Singleton before today and they were clearly taken aback by the first young man of African-American descent they had ever encountered who was more urbane and at least as well educated as they were. Babineaux, Hood and Rosenzweig never had black classmates before; Mulcahey and Levesque had some with whom they had never spoken. So Rick Singleton was a new experience for them all, back then. His reputation, now presented, would only grow more sterling in the months to come.

At a nearby table sat a middle-aged man, alone, sipping beer and engrossed in a book, oblivious to anything else, it seemed. In the quiet moment following Singleton's commentary, he put down his book, slipped horn-rimmed glasses into the pocket of his plaid shirt and studied them. In an unfamiliar bar, at night, they all took notice of this sudden attention from the broad-shouldered stranger, except Mulcahey, who was lost in his beer mug, singing "Happy Together" along with The Turtles. The man stood, took the book and a fedora in hand and stepped up to their corner-booth. "Gentlemen, do you remember me?" he asked. Hood said, "Yessir. You were with the colonel today at orientation."

"That's right. I'm Major Alexander Cardenas, aide to Colonel Donahue. Would you men mind if I joined you for a moment?"

One of the tenets drummed into them to shape them into soldiers was enlisted never spoke to officers unless they were spoken to first. None of them had ever been spoken to by the lieutenants and captains they glimpsed only at a distance in basic training and none of them before they were snapped to attention at today's orientation had ever actually seen a major or colonel except on a reviewing stand, glaring down at passing troops. So a five-count of silence passed before Hood said, "Nosir. Pull up a chair."

Cardenas put his items down, lifted a chair into the open side of their booth and sat. "I won't take much of your time," he said cordially, "but it is important that you know and understand certain things. Introductions will not be necessary because I know a great deal about each of you already, as well as your twenty-four classmates in ES-3-1967. I had final say on who was selected for the group because this MOS, the ES series, is my project. I proposed it to Colonel Donohue initially, against fierce opposition from some who are hoping it will fail and I will fail with it. That's why I'm taking the risk of talking with you in this setting. When I was younger than you are, I shipped out for Korea, an enlisted man with an artillery unit. I wasn't drawn to the military; I enlisted to help my family, as the oldest son of dirt-poor farm workers who didn't speak English. What I gained from Korea was self-respect, respect for the military and a career that took me away from the poverty I knew growing up. What the Koreans gained was that 20 million of them don't live today under an inhuman, soul-crushing dictatorship. What I lost was eleven friends," he glanced into each of their faces, "like the friends you are becoming now.

"A year ago, as the war was ramping up in numbers, I realized that we were competing for top-flight candidates from OCS and West Point, and the quality of recruits we needed to do a complex job without direct supervision was slipping. I discovered a talent-pool for the asking in men like you. Draft deferments for students were on the slide and enlisted men were coming in who were capable of doing this work. You are the so-called cream of the crop. Each of the men in ES-3 has one college degree or more, graduated at the top of his class, has maxed-out on the battery of tests at enlistment, and one other qualification: Each of you was pulled aside at basic and offered a slot in OCS. You all declined it. That permitted me to argue for an enlisted track into a field reserved for officers. The kind of agent who can run a field station, work alone and unsupervised, usually under cover as an apparent civilian, developing rapport with both American and Vietnamese, military and civilians, gathering information that can save hundreds of American and Allied lives at great risk to his own person....well, that kind of recruit is rare. And in fact, the qualities you men were recruited for would make you lousy combat soldiers. You're arrogant, over-educated smart-asses who want to have everything your own way, think you know it all, and don't like to either follow or give orders.

"If you were serving in artillery, as I did, or infantry or armor, I guarantee I would not sit with you in a bar and fraternize with you. It's not done. But the Army can't get what it needs out of you by pulling rank. And it needs a lot out of you. From today on, if you stick with the program, measure up and make the cut, you'll live more like civilian contractors than like soldiers. You'll have the chance to save many lives and preserve a civil society for millions of Vietnamese. If you screw up, you'll wind up in a body-bag or a military stockade before you can blink.

"Bear with me a little, and then I'll go home and leave you in peace." He lifted his glass, took a sip, gave them a moment to process. They thought about this career man going to his home and family while they returned to a concrete barracks far from their own homes.

"Fort Greyhawk is your chance to do something vitally important and interesting. There is a lot riding on this for you and for me. If it doesn't work out for most of you, then you'll be the best educated infantry out there sloshing your way through rice paddies with those new M-16s and I will get busted back to captain for daring to have faith in you. Gentlemen!" Major Cardenas stood up, tucked his book under his arm, placed the fedora at an angle on his head, and said, "Thank you for your time. Feel free to convey what I have said to your classmates. In fact, I'm counting on you to do so. And if... over the grapevine that develops in the dormitory...you hear a rumor that I have laid my cards on the table with other ES-enlisted on the evening after other orientation sessions...well, of course, I never had those conversations. And we did not have this one. Good night."

As Cardenas dropped money on the bar and headed out the door, Babineaux laughed and said, "That guy has a funny definition of what a conversation is."

"What in chrissakes just happened?"

"There is no need for blasphemy, if you don't mind."

"Chrissakes is not swearing!"

"You badly need to re-read the Second Commandment, Mulcahey."

Rosie called Linda over and said, "We'd like to see some menus, please, before my friends start throwing things."

"I've got to get back to the mess hall. I can't afford to eat out."

"Me neither."

Singleton dropped three twenties on the pile of bills in the middle of the table and told them, "My father who art in New York, blessed be his name, has instructed me that I am never to eat alone but always in the company of friends. He is all-knowing, all-powerful and very rich and I always obey him. So order-up. As for Major Cardenas, I've got a creepy feeling he might be on our side."

Babineaux replied, "I've got a creepy feeling he may be a gigantic prick." Linda had returned with the menus, so Hood said, "You'll have to excuse my friend here, ma'am, he was never taught how to talk with a lady present."

"Oh yeah. Linda here works in a bar across the street from an Army base and that kind of talk is new to her, right?"

"You see what I mean, ma'am. I hear rumors he was brought up by wolves."

Linda dropped the menus and left, so Babineaux was free to say, "Fuck you, Hood, and the horse you rode in on. If you want to talk about my folks, you can just...."

Rosie the peace-maker chimed in, "How come there's no country music on that jukebox? You guys come visit me in Nashville, I'll take you out to the Grand Ole Opry and show you what music is like when it's sung by real folks, not by Monkees and Turtles and Beatles and Mamas and Pappas and such.'"

"Damn straight," Hood thundered, "Earl Scruggs, Merle Hagard and Buck Owens, Doc Watson, man! *I'm a lonesome fugitive!*"

"Visit me in New York," Singleton said. "We'll go Lincoln Center and feast on Beethoven and Mozart...that stuff will send shivers up your back."

"Hell! Real zydeco out in bayou country, nothin' better'n that."

"Side-echo? What's side-echo?" they wanted to know, while Strawberry Alarm Clock filled the air with strains of "Incense and Peppermint".

With the next pair of pitchers came burgers and fries for Mulcahey and Rosenzweig; a T-bone steak, rare, with mashed potatoes and gravy for Hood, shrimp and rice for Babineaux; a Reuben on rye with a dill pickle for Singleton, and finally, baked haddock with a glass of white wine for Levesque.

Singleton headed for the men's and came back by way of the jukebox where he punched up Lou Rawls' "Love is a Hurtin' Thing." As he crossed the room, someone at the bar called out, "Why don't you take that jungle music across the river to North Philly where it belongs?" Singleton neither turned his head nor changed his stride as the bar-tender moved to talk quietly to his customer. A moment later, three tough-looking locals, hair-styles decidedly civilian, tipped off their stools and started across to the booth. Babineaux came off the end of the seat, signaling "stay" to the group with an open hand. The others sat stock-still, hands on drinks, alert.

"Didn't you hear me?" the biggest of them said, glaring past Babineaux at Singleton.

Babineaux stepped between the speaker and the booth and moved much closer to him, smiling happily into his face from inches away, hands out, palms up, and drawled in a calm voice, "Tell ya' what. Everybody you see here is headed for Vietnam before too long...which means what? It means all of us will be gone out of your friendly neighborhood road-house, never to vex ya' again, and ya' won't even have to start something that will bust up a lot of glass and furniture...'cuz we ain't takin' this outside...and the bar-tender, the one who's already on the phone talking with the cops, won't have to tell ya' never to come in here, ever again, which of course won't bother us either way 'cuz we'll be 9,000 miles away."

The big one glanced back and saw the bar-tender glaring at him, phone to his ear.

"On the other hand," Babineaux said, leaning in confidentially, "if ya' really have to do this the hard way, ya' need to know that the guy with the hands like a bear back there is a wrestler who can pull joints apart in closed quarters like this, and that nervous-looking, wiry little fellah in the back goes in for biting the soft parts off faces, leavin' guys with a whole new look...so there is that to consider. As for me, I carry a knife. Okay? So why don't I go over and play Billie Joe McAllister three times on my own quarter and ya' can say ya' won this fight the smart way."

Their leader gave it a moment's thought and admitted, "Works for me." They turned and walked back to the bar.

"Give me three quarters and hold your ears," Babineaux told the group. "We'll have to listen to that sorry-assed Ode to Billy Joe a few times, but we won't get any more trouble from those dicks. They've taken their best shot."

"You crazy or just damn lucky, Babineaux?" Hood wanted to know. "You taunt a gang of guys who out-weigh you, you could get stomped before we could climb outta this corner."

"I spent a summer working oil rigs in the Gulf. The roughnecks taught me the best way to avoid a fight, act like you'd welcome one." Babineaux gathered some quarters and headed toward the jukebox, feeling he was established now as the point-man for this circle of six.

On this night, the little television set on the shelf above the bar-tender's head showed Walter Cronkite announcing that Surveyor 3 had landed on the moon and that 33 people had been killed and 500 injured by tornadoes in Illinois that struck without warning. The young men huddled in the corner booth chatted away, oblivious to these news items, only vaguely aware that a brief war had left Israel in control of Jerusalem and the Golan Heights -- that 10,000 war-protesters had taken to the streets of San Francisco -- that Martin Luther King, Jr. had come out against the war and Mohammed Ali was refusing to serve in the military. There were not then massive screens on every wall raining opinion and violent footage down on them in a 24/7 news cycle -- much less pocket devices that drew them away from each other. They were left to create their own reality in face-to-face exchanges. Back then, their family and home-town friends who seemed far away really were far away, present only as long-hand letters at mail-call, evoking the memory of a face. So judge them kindly. They were creatures of their time and place, blustering and posing to carve-out an identity, a respected niche in this new circle in which they found themselves. Each was accomplished in the classrooms where they had spent so much of their lives until now. They were trying to seem casual and impervious when in fact they were naive about much in the wider world and they knew it. The tone within this new clan was brash and unyielding because they were, each in his own way, scared to be where they found themselves -- and not without reason.

On this first day together, Babineaux, Hood, Levesque, Mulcahey, Rosenzweig, and Singleton had become, for each other, The Greyhawk Six.

2

6 July 1967

FOXES AND HOUNDS

Four of them blew into Greyhawk Inn in tight formation on a steamy summer afternoon and took up their usual places in the corner booth. Without being asked, Linda brought over two pitchers followed by frosty mugs and a glass of burgundy then asked, "Isn't Rene coming?" One of the group narratives developed over three intense months together related how their pretty waitress favored The Gaunt One, the quiet, wine-drinking gentleman who never came in sweaty from the griddle of the summertime sidewalks, who wasn't boisterous like other soldiers from the fort. He alone she referred to by name, and she took no notice of Mad-dog's absence today.

"He may be late," Babineaux said. They poured a round until she had gone, then leaned into a huddle over the table, talking low about field exercises that had followed weeks of lectures, written exams and mountains of simulated operational planning, simulated intelligence analysis, simulated reports of various kinds written and typed in classrooms that were, windows up or windows down, always ten degrees hotter than the brain-baking temperature outside. Finally, they were moving through the streets of Philadelphia practicing what they'd been taught, opposed by counter-intelligence trainees, under close supervision by Fort Greyhawk instructors.

A small white bus took them across the Delaware five days a week and dropped them on the north side of Philadelphia's enormous City Hall. They were the Foxes. A second white bus followed close behind then split off to drop Counter-Intelligence trainees, the Hounds, on the south side of City Hall. For the next six hours, they had to remain within The Playpen -- south of Vine Street and north of Walnut Street between the rivers. Foxes tried to execute a series of operations while Hounds tried to catch them in "suspicious behavior," which would give them the authority to make an arrest and haul them into the Interrogation Center. Fear of washing out of the program and being reassigned, perhaps to a combat unit, provided motivation enough for the Foxes at first -- until peer-pride and the thrill of making fools out of the Hounds became the greater incentive. End-of-the-day drinks served as a review and re-hydration session after each summer-scorched day, and as an antidote for the adrenaline overload of "Foxes and Hounds".

"Who's seen Mulcahey and Levesque?" Babineaux asked. Nobody had since drop-off.

Babineaux said, "Listen. I've got to tell you what this crazy bastard did today." He jabbed his thumb toward Braxton Hood, who laughed quietly into his beer mug. "We were scheduled to exchange a live-drop outside a supermarket at 2:00. C.I. was dying to catch it, drag us both in, sweat us about what we were doing together. I worked a waitress on Market Street over the weekend, told her I owed money to some bad guys and if I came in Monday afternoon, could she help me slip out through the storage room. She and I worked it out. Sweet girl. I'll go back next weekend and catch up with her. So OK, I go in at 1:00, sit at the bar, order a beer. Two buzz-cuts come in, take a table. I ask nice and loud for the men's room, put $5 beside my draught and walk past the men's, like she showed me, out through the back. So I'm clean and go post up across the street from the market and I see Hood, large as life, through the front windows. He's got this shopping cart stacked up full. For a long time, I watch him mosey up aisle one, read a bunch of labels, wander back to the cart, drop stuff in. Then he plods up aisle two, same thing, then aisle three and four and five and six. I make at least two Hounds keeping tabs on him, trying to keep their distance." Braxton Hood was chuckling loudly as he refilled his mug. "This drags on for 45 minutes while I'm watching. Our meeting is late, but by then his cart is piled high, at the end of aisle nine, both these goons are watching it, so Hood scoots up aisle nine, crosses the back to aisle one and slips out the entrance door. We exchange the token and split and can see those two dummies hypnotized by the grocery cart inside the store. They're probably still there."

When the laughter died down, Hood said, "I'll tell ya' what. The secret to life...and I really need to talk to that Yankee dumb-ass Mulcahey about this...is to play it dumb. Those same two gentlemen who tracked me today had me in last week, and they worked good-cop-bad-cop and were pretty darn good at it. They were sharp, smarter than most their classmates, and I came close to messin' up after a couple hours. They were barkin' at me, pickin' at my cover story, and they shoved a form at me to sign. I almost signed the wrong cover-name. But their problem was, they're from someplace way north of here and I was puttin' on my slowest, dumbest Southerner for 'em. So they came to that market today under the profound impression that I wasn't any too bright. That can be very disarmin'. Instead of showin' off how smart you are, let the other guy underestimate you and see if you're not 'bout half-way home."

"I enjoy messing with them," Singleton said. He rolled a cardboard beer coaster up and down the fingers of his left hand, speaking quietly to it, as though the others were eavesdropping on a monologue. "Not of my own volition I left Yale half-way through my masters in dramatic arts, being told I had some talent for acting. That career was interrupted until these field exercises gave me the chance to continue my dramatic training. That's why I don't try to avoid Hounds. They give me a chance to role-play. They sit me in a chair and ask me to improvise a *dramatis persona* to interact with their own. One time I did as Braxton said and went with Uncle Tom, an inoffensive simpleton

17

with a single-syllable vocabulary, *jes' a know-nuffin' dufus tryin' to git-by bes' way he knowd how.* Another time I channeled Harry Belafonte, all smiles and Caribbean charm and a modulated Jamaican accent borrowed from a maid we had at the Dalton School. This morning I had a jolly time with two light-weights. They got hostile with me, so I dropped my nice, benign cover and admitted I was a member of the Black Panthers, planning an ambush of the Philadelphia police which would, I told them most solemnly, *commence with a murderous crossfire from the subway stairwells at 14th and Chestnut and when they duck behind their squad cars, Claymore mines will explode behind the plate-glass windows of the department stores to their rear, so shards of glass will embed themselves in the pig's asses.* Those C.I. kids stood there all wide-eyed, completely horrified by this skit, but I could hear the instructor, that crusty old warrant officer you've seen around, chuckling over in the corner, scribbling on a clipboard, so I said, *'Hey! I jes' messin' wiff y'all, man. I come to town to git me a new suit for Sun'ay church.'* Now where else can you get live-theater experience like that? You have to sustain these roles for hours sometimes with an audience that's two feet away. At Yale, we knew we were acting...here, no one knows when you are and when you're not. And so long as you don't come out and admit you're spying on the Philadelphia People's Republic, you're still going to pass the field exercises and stay out of the rice paddies." He set the coaster down, put his beer mug on it and grinned into their faces as though waiting for applause but though none came, it seemed to his friends that Rick Singleton did possess a rare gift that might someday make him famous.

Babineaux said, "I've got a joke for you. A nun walks into a bar...." They waited for the rest then followed his gaze toward the door to see a nun drifting toward Linda at the wait-station.

A large, silver cross dangling from her waist bounced off her white scapular as she walked.

"... to collect money for the orphanage maybe? Or because it's her birthday and she's decided to tie-one-on for old time's sake?" Linda placing a hand on the arm of the habit and laughing before she walked back to their corner to ask, "Would you gentlemen have any objection..." mirth overwhelmed her and she put her hands over her mouth, "...if Sister Philomena joined you for...." and Sister Philomena was there, the bleached face of Levesque nestled in her wimple like a chicken egg with eyes. Hilarity overwhelmed the corner booth, with only Rene Levesque maintaining perfect composure, hands clasped at his cincture, glaring down upon them with Jack-Benny scorn.

"What in god's name are you supposed to be?" Rosie gasped.

"Blasphemy is uncalled for," Sister Philomena chirped in a falsetto voice that set off another round of hysterics.

They made room for Levesque, who was brought a glass of burgundy. Mugs and the wine glass clinked in a toast of congratulations. "There's a great costume shop on 3rd Street that measured me last weekend and had it ready. I scheduled a meeting with a prospective recruit for today because rain was forecast. I had to wait for that. I didn't want C.I. to mess up this agent-recruitment, like they did the last one, so I led two guys, there may have been more, into Peter and Paul's, the big cathedral at Race and 18th, prayed for a time up near the nave to settle them in between me and the doors, then walked up toward the altar, hooked a left at the transept, and disappeared." Levesque smiled and took a sip of wine, savoring the burgundy and this moment of triumph. "It so happens, gentlemen, that this mighty cathedral provides the best slip-knot in The Playpen. I can tell you this because you're all atheists who never go near a church, so you won't go use this and screw it up for me. You see, noon mass is well attended, but it's held next door, at The Chapel of Our Lady of the Most Blessed Sacrament, a separate sanctuary with its own double-door entrance from 18th Street. Or so it appears. But in fact, as you approach the communion rail in the Cathedral...that's the little fence in the front for you un-initiated....and look to your left, you'll see a swinging door at the end of the transept that opens into the Chapel of Our Lady. If you were to pull this maneuver at 11:58, exactly, which I did, you could stride briskly toward the 18th Street doors, out those double doors into the narthex -- you'd call it a lobby -- pop down a flight of stairs on your left to the restrooms, closing the door at the head of the stairs behind you, check the lady's room to make sure the coast is clear before choosing a stall where you will have the privacy you need to become Sister Philomena. Now, you've bought yourself some time. The Hounds who saw you disappear around the corner of the Cathedral transept will be baying woefully, as hound-dogs do. When they realize you're not in the cathedral anymore, they'll discover the connecting doors to the Lady Chapel about the time noon mass is beginning. They'll try to scan the congregation for you... which will be an embarrassing process for them, looking into the faces of praying strangers without drawing attention to themselves... and they will conclude you slipped out the main doors of the Lady Chapel and go scurrying off down the hot sidewalks. Meanwhile, I hang my McIntosh on the stall door, unfurl the habit, retrieve the wimple and veil from under my shirt and drop them over my head. And by the time the priest says "Thanks be to God," Sister Philomena is ready to waft out and be about her Father's business. She got to the park on time for the meeting, but she had to repeat the recognition signals three times before my agent was sure I was really his contact. However, gentlemen, the recruitment was successful, and I have added another agent to my network, so as long as some honest woman turns my rather expensive coat into the lost and found, I'd have to say today went very well indeed."

"And if they caught on and hauled you in, what was Plan B?" Hood wanted to know.

"Plan B was to speak to them in Philomena-voice and defy them to lay hands on me. Plan C was that I was a pervert and a cross-dresser and defy them to say they had never tried on their mother's underwear."

"So you planning to show the MP your military ID when we go back?" Babineaux asked. "Because I really want to be there to see his face."

"I was rather hoping to meet up with some friends here who'd go across and bring me some civvies out of my locker. Any volunteers?"

Babineaux said, "I'll go but not yet. I'm naturally curious about nuns. So Sister, let me ask, how's this lifetime of celibacy working out for you?"

Levesque sipped his wine but some color graced his pallor and Babineaux was quick to pounce, laughing and pointing: "I'll be damned ! You're cherry, ain't ya' !"

"Yeah, well so's Rosie."

"Am not!"

"You are too. You told me so on bivouac."

"Rosie may be hopeless, Levesque," Babineaux said, "but we can fix this for you."

He shouted across, "Linda ! You got a minute, darlin'?"

"Behave yourself," Hood warned. "You show her disrespect, I'll toss you out of here myself."

"You and whose army?" Babineaux grinned. "Linda, dear, I have an announcement. Everyone at this table has just made corporal. Now corporal is a command rank, which means we'll be official NCOs. We can issue orders to lowly privates and even to Spec-4s. Did you know that only Artillery and Intelligence still have corporals? Everybody else has Spec-4s and Spec-5s, but we'll be mighty corporals, on our way up to being buck sergeants someday. And what that means for you, my dear girl, is larger and more frequent tips from your friends here assembled, hoping for another couple of pitchers." When she had gone, he said to Braxton Hood, "How'd I do? Did I treat the floozy like a lady that time or what, you scumbag?"

When the waitress returned with two more pitchers and, without being asked, a glass of wine, Babineaux said to her, "Watch and learn how generous corporals will be, my dear. How much have we spent in here so far this afternoon?"

Linda pulled ten bucks from the disorderly pile of bills and placed three singles in change on the table while she thought. "Four pitchers and a wine, thirteen dollars, so far I guess."

"Allow me to show you pure genius at work," Babineaux said. "Corporal Hood, how much should we tip this fine girl? If we are to leave her 6% of this evening's tab, that would be what?"

Hood said, "Seventy-eight cents."

"And if we leave an unheard of amount of, say, twelve-and-a-half percent?"

Braxton Hood blinked a couple of times and said, "A dollar-sixty-three, rounding up."

"Isn't that just amazing, ma'am? He's big as a horse, slow as a slug, plods around flat-foot like a farm-hand on a hot day, but it comes to math, he's a machine. I offer this to you for free, but it cost me fourteen dollars of my hard-earned money to learn that secret last night when he talked me into a so-called 'friendly' game of five-card stud."

"I gave your money back."

"So you did, Corporal Hood, to stop me keepin' you awake cryin' into my pillow. But take a warnin', y'all. This clueless-lookin' clod-hopper has memorized the odds on every poker hand, wild cards or not, and he's got some sort of goddamn system that can empty your wallet in twenty minutes."

"That's because it's not about luck," Hood said quietly. "It's about mathematics."

Mad-dog burst through the front door at his usual manic pace and raced between tables to them, shouting, "I've got two headlines for ya' so hold the presses!" He pulled a chair to the open side of the table, dropped into it and barked, "Jesus! What happened to you, Levesque?"

Levesque put his palms together and rolled his eyes toward heaven as Babineaux said, "It's a long story...Rene robbed a nun. So what's the news?"

"Well first, ES-2 just got orders for...ready? Germany! That could mean the war-zone is all stocked up with spooks and we're gonna get sent somewhere good! England maybe!"

"Or Korea," Babineaux laughed, "with eight zillion North Koreans fixin' to come across the DMZ and stomp our asses."

"Ever the optimist," Mulcahey said. "But this is the first ES class in months that's not headed straight for 'Nam, so it opens the door, right?"

They all silently dared to hope it did.

"And the other thing I got is, I found us a piano! There's this little mom-and-pop bar on the west side, up a side street near Drexel, and in the back room is a sweet little upright with a great sound."

"So now what? You gonna tell us you can play piano?" Hood asked.

But play piano he did. And the next four Saturday afternoons straight, they spent in the cozy back room at Benny & Ian's Place, where Mad-dog Mulcahey attacked the keyboard with huge enthusiasm and some skill, pounding out those portions of the American Musical Theater Canon that he carried around in his oddly-wired brain. Missing notes all over the place, he hammered out songs by Rodgers and Hammerstein, Lorenz Hart and even some Cole Porter, but it turned out he had a fine, clear tenor that could lead them through the plains of Oklahoma and the islands of the South Pacific, to the Texas State Fair and a show-boat on the Mississippi, until they all knew some of the lyrics and could, with adequate quantities of beer and Chianti (Benny & Ian's did not aspire to French vintages), produce a fair rendition of their favorites. Each of these Saturdays bonded them together with lasting memories as they finished their field exercises and waited nervously for orders that might send them to war or spare them -- that might keep them together or break them apart. And each Saturday session ended with Mad-dog's solo performance of his signature piece, "Look For the Silver Lining". He played and sang this song beautifully and it ended each time with a long, embarrassed silence that none of them knew how to break without sounding sentimental, and sentimentality, they sensed, could only get a guy in trouble.

3

1 September 1967

A CIVIL WAR

One sweltering Friday afternoon, they were barked to attention by an aide to Major Alexander Cardenas. The major strode quickly down the middle aisle of their classroom to the dais, assumed the lectern and ordered them to be seated. Class-A Khaki uniforms gave them the appearance of military decorum but after four hours in the morning and four in the afternoon in this stifling lecture space, the smell of a locker room hung in the air. The major told them, "I have orders from the DoD as to your disposition from this training school. As I call your name, report to the captain to receive your orders, then read them over carefully."

Long anticipated and no surprise, the identical pages nonetheless delivered a jolt: three weeks' leave would be followed by transportation to San Francisco for deployment to MACV, the Military Assistance Command, Vietnam. Each defendant stood when called, approached the captain, and was handed, finally, after the long trial and despite rumors of hope, the verdict:

Vietnam. Each paper was a copy of the 29 others with a different name, one's own name, underlined in yellow crayon. The remote army gods had bestowed the reality of it. Newspaper headlines and images of war flickering on screens were not it. The splotch of color that appeared like a waxing crescent moon on that large map of

Indochina was not it. This paper that said your body will be put on a large commercial jet jammed with other uniformed soldiers and will be flown to Vietnam, there to disembark down a long set of steps onto a concrete slab searing in the tropical sun, this page was it in fact, no longer an abstraction.

When the officers departed, the lieutenant conducting their lecture dismissed the class and Babineaux, his short-sleeved khaki shirt soaked with sweat, stood in the center of the room, shoving his copy of the orders into their faces, jabbing the page with his finger and explaining, "Right here in black and white, you dumb shit. M for Madrid, A for Andalusia, C for Cordoba, and V for Valencia. We're going to Spain and you're too damned stupid to know it!"

"By way of San Francisco," Rosie said.

"They're *secret* orders, written in code to fool the commies, you cluck. Sending us to California is part of the ruse!"

Hood said sternly, "Knock if off, Babineaux."

Singleton said, "Let's go for a ride and cool off."

The six piled into the platinum blue Lincoln Continental that Singleton's father "had sent down" from New York and for the next hour, they cruised aimlessly around city streets with the air-conditioner turned up full-blast. The Greyhawk Inn was not air-conditioned, nor were any of the buildings on the fort they inhabited, but this two-and-a-half ton monster with low fins front-and-back was like a meat-locker on wheels on this humid, hundred-degree day. They rode in silence, thinking about how to wring out of a 21-day leave everything necessary to tie up loose ends, explain to family, childhood friends and themselves about the absence that may be for a year or for forever. This unusual silence was broken just once, when Singleton pulled into a Citgo station and told the attendant, "Fill it up."

"And don't forget the wing tanks," Babineaux called out.

"Knock it off, Babineaux," Hood warned then suggested, "Let's ditch the Class-As and go get smashed."

Sprawled nonchalantly around the corner booth in their civilian uniforms, black chinos and short-sleeved shirts, they reposed in still life as Linda set out pitchers, mugs, pretzels and a wine. "You're so quiet today," she observed.

Babineaux said softly, "Yes, ma'am. Tell ya' what. Could you leave all this right here and bring us a round of tequila shots, maybe a little salt on the rims?"

"Make that five tequilas and a double brandy, no salt," Levesque amended.

"What is it with you?" Babineaux said, his perpetual smile conspicuously absent. "Beer isn't good enough for ya' and now ya' gotta take exception to a round of shots with the rest of us?"

"I don't like tequila."

"Then you should chip-in extra for your fancy-assed wine and brandy."

Singleton said, "I'll pay for it, OK?"

Rosie said lightly: "Maybe Levesque just feels abandoned by you, Babineaux. When the British showed up in Quebec, your people fled all the way to New Orleans and left his folks to suffer under the yoke of British oppression."

Babineaux: "Fuck you, Rosenzweig."

Mulcahey: "Don't make me laugh, Rosie. Two hundred years of British tyranny? Try a thousand years, with Cromwell burning every home and barn, Orangemen hanging generations of patriots and the Blacks and Tans gunning down innocent men and women in the streets."

A stunned silence followed this outburst, during which Mulcahey drained an entire mug of beer. The tequilas and brandy came and Hood lifted his to propose a toast: "Here's to all freedom-loving people...in Quebec, New Orleans, Ireland, Vietnam and everywhere else."

They chanted, "Hear-hear," swigged-down five tequilas or sipped on brandy. Glasses clicked on the table and another round was called for.

Mulcahey proceeded, "In Vietnam, of course, freedom-loving people in the South are being invaded by violent oppressors from the North...ironically, the opposite of our Civil War."

Hood said: "You out to start somethin', Mulcahey, 'cuz I'm in the mood. Or you just flappin' your big mouth 'cuz you got nothin' better to do?"

Rosenzweig poked Hood's shoulder and said, "Well, Mad-dog, Vietnam is a mess. Kennedy should never have started it."

Mulcahey: "This is Lyndon Johnson's war! Jack Kennedy had nothing to do with it! Kennedy was our greatest president ever until they shot him to get a Texan in the White House."

Levesque: "Oswald was a Communist, not a Confederate."

Mulcahey: "Oswald was a Texan."

When the tequilas came Singleton suggested, "Let's drink to Peace on Earth this time and then get out of here and go someplace else."

Babineaux: "To world peace. Hear-hear."

Mulcahey: "And another thing. Where would colored Americans be without JFK?"

Singleton: "Same place we are. Kennedy was dragged into it by King. And LBJ nominated Thurgood Marshall, not Kennedy."

Mulcahey: "Who's Thurgood Marshall?"

Singleton: "Jesus!"

Hood: "What IS it with you, Mulcahey? You never know when to give it a rest!"

Levesque raised his brandy glass to Mulcahey: "Thus his moniker!"

Mulcahey: "Shut up, Rene!"

When Linda delivered another round of tequilas, Babineaux asked, "Did we order these?"

Linda: "I figured you would...they're on the house. Orders for Vietnam, right?"

Hood: "How'd ya' guess?"

Linda: "I've seen it before and I have some advice. Finish this round and go home."

Babineaux: "Anyone ever listen?"

Linda: "Nope. But I give it anyway because it's very good advice."

When she'd gone, Rosie lifted his glass and said, "My turn for a toast. Gentlemen, about twenty minutes south of my home is a big, open field that I visit often, just outside the quiet little town of Franklin. Once upon a time, a Confederate general lost his temper there. The Civil War was already decided, a few months before Appomattox, but out of frustration this general ordered 20,000 men to attack fortified positions across two miles of open ground. They all knew it was suicide, but they were brave, veteran soldiers and they followed the order. Seven-thousand of them were killed or wounded in an hour's time, regiment after regiment torn to pieces by close-range artillery and rifle fire. Union troops moved out that night and the Rebels the next morning, leaving the locals of that shattered little town to care for thousands of wounded and bury the dead, which they had so little manpower to do that bones floated to the surface of that field for decades afterward." He raised his tequila and said, "So here's to us, the men of ES-3-1967, that we may spend the coming year in offices, bars and restaurants in Saigon and never know real war."

"Hear-hear," they said very quietly. And Braxton Hood mumbled to Rosenzweig, "Thanks for skipping the general's name, Rosie. No relation."

Babineaux: "Another round? Or shall we head over to UPenn and find some sluts?"

Mulcahey: "Why you always have to be so vulgar all the time, Babineaux?"

Babineaux: "OK, then how's this, Corporal Mulcahey? Fuck Jack Kennedy, fuck you and the horse you rode in on."

Mulcahey lunged, grabbing Babineaux's shirt sleeve and spilling Hood's beer onto his lap.

Rosie and Hood forced Mad-dog back into the booth, but he kept his grip on the shirt and tore it apart at the shoulder seam.

Babineaux's crazy grin and wild eyes came alive as he slid out of his seat and stood up: "Oh, Man! You just tore my favorite shirt...left to me by my pappy on his death-bed!" He grabbed his shirt-front in both hands and pulled until a button popped off, then another and another, then grabbed his undamaged right sleeve and yanked it off the shirt. "Oh, Damn! Look! It's ruined and gone forever! I can never replace it!" He broke out in maniacal laughter while his friends struggled to hold back a raging Mad-dog and tavern patrons stared in wary disbelief.

Linda came over to tell them, "My boss thinks it's time for you guys to take it somewhere else. My advice would be..."

"...home to bed, we know," Babineaux finished it.

It was thought best if Singleton and Rosie drove the seething lava-flow of Mount Mulcahey over to Benny & Ian's, where he could take out his temper on the keyboard and sober up. The others went back to the dorm to get Babineaux a better-looking shirt and Hood some dry slacks. "See you down there in a while," they called out to each other, although only Mulcahey actually expected a reunion.

"There's this student-nurse at Drexel who's having a party to-night," Babineaux told Hood and Levesque. "She got the impression somehow that I was a rich kid attending Wharton, so she gave me the address and said to bring some friends."

"You guys go," Levesque said. "I've got to see a man about a dog."

"I didn't know Linda had a dog," Hood said.

"I didn't know she was a man," Babineaux added.

By the time Babineaux and Hood rode the bus and subway and found the address, the party was in full swing, a nice, lively mix of college kids dancing, drinking beer and happily accepting every fab-rication they were fed. Girls who were not already spoken-for wanted to know more about the big athlete who had played defensive end at Florida State and the wild-eyed New Orleans man with the Spanish name who's father had vineyards in Spain and Colombia. But by midnight, it was clear their interest was all too innocent and decent so there was no fun in it.

There was an exchange of phone numbers, some of them perhaps even genuine, and the two newcomers headed for the subway.

There was still a light on at the far end of the cavernous bay when they returned and under it sat three worried men: Mulcahey had not slowed down at Benny & Ian's, where a gaggle of college kids had taken over the piano, which convinced Mad-dog that the gods were determined he should go on drinking tequila shots with beer chasers. By the time they shoved him into the back seat of the car, he was into a full-on manic frenzy, holding animated dialogues in theatrical voices between a lusty sailor and a defenseless grandmother, with the rape of the elderly lady almost a certainty ("with only me doilies to shield me!" she shrieked, waving her frail arms wildly); between Pierre The Lumberjack with an eerily profound bass voice somehow emanating from the wiry Irishman and a whiny, sniveling ski-instructor named DeWayne, debating who best could hear the true Song of The Mountain (which ended in another violent struggle on the back seat of the Lincoln, the ski-instructor getting much the worse of it); and a long rendition of Mad-dog's Aunt Mary (who had the softest, most feminine voice in his wide repertoire), a widow-woman so endowed with patience that she could offer a cup of tea to an attentive nephew, make him wait on the couch while she gradually began to meander in the direction of the kitchen to boil the water that she planned someday to pour over the teabags to steep in the kettle for a day or two while the nephew's throat seized-up and he died of dehydration there on her knitted afghan, gasping and begging for tea. But by then they were checking in with the MP at the Greyhawk gate, who mistook the withered form on the back seat for a sane person, merely drunk.

They figured Mad-dog had played himself out and was down for the night, so they left him on his bunk and headed for the showers. But when Levesque climbed the stairs, he reported he'd seen Mulcahey hauling a duffle bag out the front gate as he was coming in. "Where you going at this hour?" he'd called after him and "Doing my laundry" came back.

Their decision, an hour ago, to turn in and let the crazy bastard fend for himself proved unsustainable. It was being hotly re-debated when Hood and Babineaux straggled in. Rosie was pulling on street clothes, but Singleton was rolled up in covers, muttering "I'm not driving anybody anywhere."

"Then loan me your car," Rosie pleaded.

"It's not my car...it's a rental and I'm not allowed to loan it out."

"C'mon, Rick. It's after 2:00. We'll all go find him together," Rosie argued, turning to the others. Hood and Babineaux sagged in place, plenty drunk and exhausted, saying nothing.

Singleton rolled over, rose up on one elbow and glared across at Rosie. "You don't get it, do you, Rosenzweig? You really don't. So let me explain some things to you, wise ass. If you bothered to read something besides the sports page, you'd know that three weeks ago, the cops up in Newark, eighty miles from here, saw a black taxi-driver double-parked in broad daylight. They pulled him out and beat the crap out of him and when other black folks objected, they opened fire and left 26 people dead. Dead! Last week in Detroit, the cops set off a riot in a black section and they ended up calling in tanks and troops and left 43 folks dead. Dead! I dragged his sorry butt back here three hours ago and if he's decided to go running the streets again, I can't help that."

No one had seen either Singleton or Rosie lose their tempers before, but now they did. "I understand all that," Rosie shouted, "but we're supposed to be friends, aren't we? So what does friendship mean to you?"

"*You* don't understand!"

"Yes I do! Friends are there for each other, man! We're in it together and we watch out for each other...like we did for you when you played Lou Rawls...or what the fuck is all this all about?" He swept an arm across the arc of the fort.

Hood and Babineaux looked at each other, gave things a long minute to cool down, then closed in on Singleton's bunk. Hood said quietly, "Listen, Rick. I'm a son of Dixie, so don't tell me I don't understand. To a New Jersey sheriff, you're just a skinny black kid driving a stolen car in the middle of the night. But Rosie's got a point too. We're dead-meat without each other. Five months training together, man, I feel like you're all family to me, like my brothers at home. Well, maybe not Mad-dog. He deserves to be gutted like a fish. But I should be the one to do it."

"So come on out with us," Babineaux said. "I promise, whatever happens to you, it'll happen to all of us together, whatever it is."

Just before 3:00, they were cruising by a mini-mall many blocks from the fort when an island of sound and light shattered the silent darkness. And there he was, laboring under rows of fluorescent tubes in a 24-hour Laundromat, striding between machines with arms full of soggy clothes, wading two feet deep in suds which cascaded from a dozen washers, stepping more or less in time to *The Flight of the Valkyries* pounding out of the black Sony tape-deck he'd brought along. For a time, they stared in silence, stunned by the incomprehensible energy of the maniac and all that light and music and activity in the middle of the still night, the city sleeping all around this singular spectacle.

From behind the wheel, Singleton asked, "Who knew he was into Wagner?"

"He truly is insane, isn't he." Hood said.

"That's why ya' gotta love the idiot," Babineaux sneered. "Let's go fetch him home."

The black-and-white squad car pulled up in the midst of their work, with most of the foam and water mopped into the drains, the clothes sifted by Braille out of the sud-drifts and wrung out enough to pile them into the massive trunk of the Continental, Mulcahey in the back seat, muttering "I've gotta get ready" over and over. Hood, at 6'3" and 250 pounds, was the natural choice to lean over the patrolmen and explain politely that one of their own had received orders for Vietnam hours ago, had far too much to drink and had used too much Tide -- way-way too much Tide.

"I'll say," one cop said, looking over the carpet of foam, now only a few inches deep.

"It's just bubbles, sir, and we're mopping it up now, leave it all good as new."

"And what about the Negro," the other said. "I suppose you're gonna tell me he owns that Lincoln."

"Oh, nosir. That's Richard. His people been workin' our land for seven generations. When my daddy rented me a car for up-North, he sent me a driver to take me around, case I want to go bar-hoppin'."

"That's what I figured," the patrolman said.

They kept clearing up until the cops left, then piled into the Continental and drove back to the gate. Mulcahey nestled into Babineaux's shoulder, repeating, "Gotta get ready," from time to time.

Babineaux answered, "We all do, Mad-dog. We all gotta get ready."

4

2 September 1967

THE PHAM BROTHERS

The Mekong river system levels and creates its vast alluvial delta by a cobweb of large and small arteries, distributaries, swamps, islands and man-made canals which present a geography too intricate to comprehend. "The Mekong Delta," like say, "the universe," may be spoken aloud but it defies understanding.

One speck upon this alluvial plain amidst a nebula of specks in 1967 was the Provincial Capital of Can Tho, etched on the east by a bend in the wide Song Ha. The town huddled against the river bank then dissolved out to the west where small farms and canals full of boats traded with each other through a scattering of market-points. On the western outskirts of Can Tho was one such market, a row of shops two blocks in length that lined one side of a straight dirt road with a canal running along the opposite side. There a spacious restaurant, enclosed on three sides but open to the road, offered its customers a random collection of wooden tables and chairs of every size and shape, spilling out beyond the wooden floor onto the edge of the road. This popular eatery provided a lively scene on this holiday, "National Day," commemorating the Declaration of Independence pronounced by Ho Chi Minh in 1945 to a nation free at last from French and Japanese domination. That moment of jubilation had not lasted long before fierce Internationalist patriots aligned with global communism and equally fierce Nationalist patriots supported by Western nations provided kindling for a proxy-war that led to a North-South partition. This one day, however, September 2, provided the people a chance to remember that once, for a blink, the promise of independence, unity and peace had appeared before them.

The extensive and prosperous Pham family was held together through all this travail by the iron will of Grandfather Thanh, descended from generations of prosperous farmers, civil servants and scholars in and around Hanoi. Grandfather Thanh had organized the removal of the family from Hanoi -- including the ornate central house, every timber and door, every tile and fixture, art-work and furnishing -- down 1800 kilometers of refugee-choked roadways during the Great Migration of 1954. He had chosen the new location, fertile land near a Buddhist temple in the Delta town of Tra Vinh, bought with gold hidden in the hems of family members' clothing. This legendary feat so enhanced the authority of the patriarch and so bound the extended family members that they held together through later years of political and philosophical turmoil. Whatever wedges were driven between individuals by the extended civil war, they were overcome by their bonds to the Pham clan and the legend of Grandfather Thanh's heroism.

And so the family was gathered here on National Day not at the homestead in Tra Vinh, where local authorities were on the look-out for certain family members suspected of having ties to the Viet Cong, but here on the outskirts of Can Tho, a town where they might have legitimate business to conduct but where they were strangers. They traveled here in an assortment of parties, under various names and in casual association with each other on this national holiday, but each one knew his or her exact and cherished place in the hierarchy of the extended family.

Though this roadside restaurant might appear to be crowded with a variety of customers, in fact nearly everyone here was a member of the Pham clan. While small children escaped the afternoon heat by splashing in the canal, their aunts and mothers scolding them about crossing the busy road without looking, and while older men chain-smoked around an array of tables, it appeared that the two young men in the far corner huddled over a chess board, sipping tea, might be the same person: The same size and build, neatly dressed in white short-sleeved shirts and black slacks, sandals, in their mid-twenties, their similarity was confirmed when their concentration on the game was broken and they looked toward a young woman who called out to them. They were indeed identical twins.

"The rain is coming, so I am taking the children back to the compound to rest before the party," she shouted.

Pham Viet called back "Good," while Pham Minh said nothing. But even Tan could not be certain which was her husband, which one had answered her, because the brothers often played tricks on people, even family members. Their skill at chess did not distinguish them either, and they had since childhood engaged in long, intense matches, which they both enjoyed, seeing who could be first to win four games or six.

The rain came and was very heavy for an hour. Then as the afternoon waned and the storm tapered off, the restaurant became quieter, the families going back to their lodgings to prepare for the party. At the same time, the muddy roadway got even busier with bicycles, motor scooters, pull-carts, boat-people and merchants wrapping things up at the market, headed for home. The brothers played on until interrupted by the sick-cow bellow of persistent horns made by a pair of strange-looking jeeps that might have been military vehicles if not for being painted -- one bright orange, the other robin's egg blue -- each with four occupants in civilian clothes. The brothers walked to the open side of the cafe to watch the spectacle of these Americans pushing aggressively through the crowded market-road, beeping continuously and barking in English, "Move it! Godammit! Move your gook-asses out of the road!" The swirling mass of human traffic made no eye-contact with the outsiders nor the slightest concession to them, even when jeep bumpers came within inches of them.

As they stood together beside the muddy track, Minh asked his brother, "What are they saying?"

"I think you know," Viet answered. "The old man in the orange jeep is a major. The one beside the driver in the blue jeep is a captain. They are all with our Headquarters Company for IV Corps, bilateral intelligence, headed home from a busy day at the office. When they pass, you'll see 'SIC' painted on the back: Service International Corporation."

"So you know these men?"

Viet laughed and draped an arm over his brother's shoulder. "I met with them last month in Saigon, but you don't have a thing to worry about, my dear brother! I've worked with the Americans since 1964 and if I have learned one thing, it's that they can't tell us apart! We are a nation of identical twins to them!" And even before the second jeep had safely passed, the Pham brothers burst into uproarious laughter, slapping each other on the back and gasping for air. When he'd recovered a little, Viet said, "If I walked up to them right now and said in English, "Isn't it a nice day?' they still wouldn't recognize me. All they see is so many canaries!"

As the jeeps pushed out of sight through the crowd, Minh said wistfully, "If I had a couple of grenades with me, I could have done some good just now."

"Very silly idea, brother. ARVN would come in here and shoot up the market as a show of force and by tomorrow noon, the Americans would replace those barking dogs with another set of barking dogs and all that would change is the color of the jeeps. So let's finish this game and get dressed for the party, comrade."

"Don't call me that, Viet. You may be my dear brother, but until you come over, you're not a comrade. You sit in your office in a white shirt and kowtow to our enemies. You cannot imagine the suffering we endure to fight for our freedom!"

Viet gave him a long, neutral stare before telling him, "I am not a traitor to our country, Minh, and I am nobody's lackey. I am a patriot too, but on a different path to freedom for our people. When this war is over, we will still be on the same side: Pham-nation. And our motto is the same...survival in the path of Grandfather, by iron will-power and discipline. So sit-down while I check-mate your king, which I am very close to doing." Later, he added quietly, "Besides, the Americans aren't so bad...the French would have run over every-one in the roadway and never looked back. And they pay very well too."

Minh returned him a hard look, a wordless reminder that only one of them was a soldier who had known deadly combat and would soon return to it.

A generator powered the party lights that were strung all over the inner courtyard of the compound the Pham family had rented for their National Day event. The wealth and prestige of the family was on full display in the renting of this compound and a half dozen oth-er nearby lodgings, an abundance of ice, the lavish food, drinks and entertainments. Grandfather Thanh held court from a comfortable chair near the door to the main house. Long tables with delicacies and drinks lined one garden wall, and the women, beautiful in flow-ing silk ao dais, gracefully served the men, who were seated around four large tables in an order established by their ages. Four Buddhist monks in saffron robes were there as honored guests, to bless the family festivities and enjoy themselves. After they finished a formal blessing complete with bells and incense, a dozen family servants who had prepared the feast, but who would not eat until after the party ended, made final preparations and then served the elderly, children and single men while wives served their husbands. Four Chinese mu-sicians well known to the family had come from Tra Vinh to play traditional instruments while the family dined. Around 10:00, chairs and benches were arranged for the performance of eight young danc-ers from Tra Vinh, four men and four women, in traditional Khmer costumes -- the women in billowing purple silks with gold trim, the men in silk slacks to mid-calf and white blouses, all barefoot. Three Khmer musicians accompanied a series of traditional folk-dances in which the row of young women, their hands fluttering like graceful birds, seemed not to notice the existence of the young men gliding around them. The Vietnamese family was very attentive, young and old, and showed delight in this colorful and delicate entertainment. There was a conscious financial and political courtship behind these entertainments, as the wealthy family from the Hanoi region, arrived just thirteen years earlier into the ancient town of Tra Vinh, was cementing bonds of friendship with the older Chinese and Khmer groups who had long been there. Tra Vinh, in fact, had the oldest and largest Khmer community in all of Vietnam -- so these entertainers were lauded, praised, paid and lavishly fed by the Pham family, as well as appreciated for their talents: Another lesson in survival from Grandfather Thanh to his family.

At 11:00, the dancers and musicians were applauded, paid and fed, then everyone returned to his place for the grand finale of this holiday. Grandfather Thanh prepared to read the Declaration of Independence, which he had heard read by Ho Chi Minh over loud speakers in Ba Dinh Square in Hanoi, September 2, 1945. He was witness to this thrilling moment when he was a young man, an ambitious and rising star with a promising future in the new government created by the Declaration -- until it became Communist and he refused to submit, choosing exile in the South -- so that his annual presentation never failed to stir him, emotions rippling the surface of his calm, even baritone.

"Friends, you must teach your neighbors," he began, and all eating, drinking and socializing came to a reverential halt. "Parents, you must teach your children. Our family has tilled the earth of our homeland for centuries, has provided generations of government officials, scholars and patriot soldiers, always with the goal of securing freedom, unity and peace for all the people of our nation, including every language and religious part. In my youth, French Imperialists handed our country over to the Japanese military without firing a shot in our defense. The Army of Japan stripped our farmers and fishermen, starving two million of our people to death, but our Viet Minh League forced them to abandon our country, with help from

American forces. In that shining moment, Ho Chi Minh pronounced us independent of all foreign nations. This is what he said as I listened to him in Ba Dinh Square:

" 'All men are created equal. They are endowed by their Creator with certain inalienable rights, among these are Life, Liberty and the pursuit of Happiness.' This immortal statement was made in the Declaration of Independence of the United States of America in 1776. In a broader sense, this means all the peoples on the earth are equal from birth, all the peoples have a right to live, to be happy and free.

"The Declaration of the French Revolution made in 1791 on the Rights of Man and the Citizen also states, 'All men are born free and with equal rights and must always remain free and have equal rights.' Those are undeniable truths."

Grandfather Thanh continued reading the short document, which catalogued the violence and injustices suffered under French and Japanese rule and ended by declaring the Democratic Republic of Vietnam "has the right to be a free and independent country and in fact it is so already. The entire Vietnamese people are determined to mobilize all their physical and mental strength, to sacrifice their lives and property in order to safeguard their independence and liberty." He read this last portion with an increasing effort to discipline his voice, barely in control of his emotions. He was offered and took a drink of water, and then closed by saying, "The Communist Party now controls the Hanoi government, while the Western powers control the Saigon government. But this will not endure forever because the people...we the people of Vietnam... will never stop fighting for our independence."

Grandfather Thanh sat down while the family gave him a resounding and sustained ovation and then they began to file out, each pausing to pay homage and give thanks to Thanh for his hospitality on this occasion. At the very end, as the servants gathered for their late-night meal across the courtyard, there remained only his twin sons, heads bent together in deep conversation, reluctant to say good-night lest they never see each other again.

Viet's job as a top translator for the Americans not only paid him well and sustained his young family, but through it he made useful connections in the government in Saigon and often ran across information vital to the family. He was in fact the first to advise that this celebration be held in Can Tho, that authorities in Tra Vinh were watching the house for any sign of his brother and several cousins suspected of associating with the Viet Cong. And Thanh already knew that whatever suspicions the authorities had, they fell far short of Minh's actual achievements as a respected military officer serving with the elite 271st Regiment under Colonel Vo Minh Triet, a friend since childhood of Grandfather Thanh's. The leave papers and ARVN ID card Minh used to travel here were supplied by Viet, sourced from U.S. Army Intelligence personnel who thought they were cutting the documents for Viet, since he is the one they photographed.

As they approached him to say good-night, Grandfather Thanh gently placed his fingers on the backs of their necks. His left hand detected the raised, jagged scar, the result of a childhood fight, that Minh bore, so he knew which was which. He felt great pride that his grandsons were serving Vietnam in the way each one thought was best -- civil servant and patriot soldier -- in the Pham tradition that went back centuries. And he trusted that so long as they both survived, they could and they would watch out for each other, no matter what path history might take.

5

26 September 1967

DEROS

T he conveyor belt that fed more than three million Americans into Vietnam over a decade's time was a cattle-car operation laced with acronym-filled paperwork, immunizations, orientation sessions that threw much darkness but little light, and a lecture about avoiding V.D. that seemed especially irrelevant, if not insulting, to those combat troops whose main concern would be avoiding V.C. Their worldly possessions reduced to one overloaded duffle bag and their home to a passenger seat, row after row of soldiers in neat Class-A Khakis were then loaded on a massive commercial jet, strapped into place, and flown without frills to The Republic of Vietnam.

For Mulcahey and Babineaux, the flights from Chicago and Lake Charles to San Francisco and the twenty-hour hop from there to Tan Son Nhut Airbase in Saigon were their first experience of air-travel and nothing about it recommended it to them. The Greyhawk men sat together in two rows for the interminable trans-Pacific journey, forbidden to unbuckle safety belts except for extreme lavatory emergencies, a rule enforced by a cadre of sharp-tempered stewardess-harpies. While most soldiers chatted and slept between meals to pass the hours, a study-hall broke out in the Greyhawk rows.

Mulcahey spent hours taking notes in a spiral notepad on Joyce's *Ulysses*. "I may not get to read it if I don't do it now" was his nervous concession to being on a war-bound Boeing 707 over the deep, endless waters of the Pacific. To keep from thinking about the miracle of heavier-than-air flight, he bore down on the problems of affable Leopold Bloom, wandering the streets of Dublin while his wife, Molly, awaits her lover. With the help of Gilbert's guidebook, he was working through the roiling chaos of a carriage ride to the cemetery, but spoken words and memories and images passing outside the carriage window were all jumbled together in Bloom's brain. With the help of the guide and his spiral notebook, Mulcahey might finally have been able to sort everything out, were it not for bits and snatches of conversation from the soldiers around him that set off flashes of words and memories and images passing by the window of his own memory. "...hands all over me" brought back the horror he felt at being touched by a doctor who told him to cough; "...letter from my mother" recalled his own mother's pleadings when he left the Church for good. Mulcahey failed, for the present, to perceive the irony in his finding Bloom's thoughts so scrambled by the same phenomena that scrambled his own thoughts.

Levesque was lost in *The King James Bible* and found fascinating the many passages that were not part of the Catholic lectionary and which, therefore, he had never heard. "I thought Catholics weren't allowed to read the Bible," Rosenzweig said. "Well then, sir, your eyes deceive you," Levesque told him. It was a glib response and it protected him from having to divulge how disturbed he was by his first reading of the Good Book. Why, he wondered, did Noah build an altar as soon as they struck dry land and sacrifice some of the animals he had just saved? What was the point of torturing that decent man, Job, over and over for so many years when he had done nothing wrong and then, at last, telling him "I did it because I can"? Levesque felt his faith at the core of his being and he considered "He works in mysterious ways" an inadequate response to what he was reading. So he closed the book and his eyes at intervals and escaped into the memories of his four dates with Linda, with her attentive kindness and decency and their "understanding" that if he came back from Vietnam in one piece and if she had not changed her mind, they might be able to take up where they had left off and explore being together.

Rosenzweig's tastes ran to history, rather than pre-law, the degree his father was willing to pay for, so he had two books by Bruce Catton, *Grant Takes Command* and *The Road to Appomattox*. His religious education and identity as a practicing Jew were always given comic treatment around goyim friends, but his lineage back through millennia of violent history, persecution and slaughter at every turn, disturbed him. He was therefore drawn to the study of conflict and mediation on the grand scale and the personal, which drew him to pugnacious souls like Mulcahey, a walking laboratory of war-like behavior. Young men slashed and bayoneted and blasted each other to pieces at Chickamauga and Chattanooga in 1863 and these same men drew together for fried chicken and handshakes in 1889, vowing to create the second-oldest National Park in the United States to commemorate their bravery and sacrifice and make hallowed the battleground they fought over. There was a weird physics to human nature, Rosie thought, that some historian-Einstein may find a simple formula for someday that would explain it all.

Singleton was underlining passages in a paperback edition of Allen Dulles' *The Craft of Intelligence*, while Babineaux advanced his learning on the subject by skimming the James Bond series, full of improbable gadgets and exciting women. Fleming's stories were frivolous entertainments, certainly, but Babineaux had been in a few punishing street fights in the parking lot behind his high school and he recognized that the Connery-Shaw fight on the train in *From Russia With Love* was the only time Hollywood got it right and he wondered if that was inspired by the book. He found the fight-scene was not nearly so good in the book, but he was surprised that James Bond was killed at the end of it, by a woman no less. That was a lesson he would have cause to remember. Meantime, Singleton was jotting notes on the

end-pages of Dulles' book, such as "Baby steps at Greyhawk. We are
the scullery maids of the business, while at the top, strategic thinking
is being formed and history written by Intelligence activities."

Braxton Hood was immersed in the second volume of Norbert
Weiner's autobiography, *I Am A Mathematician*, a gift to him from his
thesis advisor at Clemson. Hood was thrilled by Weiner's arguments
that math theory and principals should be applied to every aspect of
human activity, not merely architecture and engineering but sociol-
ogy and politics and philosophy. Weiner portrayed himself as a ro-
bust and broad-minded thinker and someone for whom mathematics
was never an escape but vitally important to every other aspect of life.
Braxton drew enormous encouragement from this work, knowing it
would be impossible to share his excitement with the others.

For an hour, the plane baked on the concrete of Honolulu
International Airport, refueling while hundreds of soldiers took
turns peering out windows in vain for a palm tree or a lush moun-
tainside, any sign that they really were in Hawaii. All they saw were
other planes.

When the endless, soul-numbing flight was over, one-by-one they
experienced the sauna-like heat of a tropical country, often described
in various ways by Greyhawk instructors, but for Hood and Babineaux,
raised in the American South, the striking feature of Vietnam was
not the heat but the quality of the light. The midday sun at latitude
twelve degrees appeared directly overhead, blinding as a welder's
torch and throwing almost no shadow. The monsoon season was
tailing off on this day, 26 September 1967, with just a few weeks of in-
termittent downpours before the start of the dry season. About May,
the monsoons would come again, the timeless weather-pattern that
defined the year as reliably as any printed calendar. But this date,
26 September, began another inexorable annual calendar, the exact
calculation of the term of service every military person arriving into
country that day must survive before he would be allowed to go back
home. DEROS: the Date of Eligibility for Return from Overseas. As
firmly as his birth-date, the soldier's DEROS was engraved upon his

heart as the date he would walk back up that stairway to the door of the plane that would take him home -- back to the arms, he hoped, of a grateful nation, to be held in reverence as someone who had answered the call, done his duty, served his country.   26 September 1968 would be graduation day for each man just arrived, but who could say how he will have been changed by this year?

The first hurdle was five or ten days as POWs at the Long Binh 90th Battalion Replacement Depot. The Greyhawk Six were hauled off to a sprawling camp near Bien Hoa, dressed in fatigues adorned with corporal stripes they had themselves haphazardly sewn-on in hopes of being on civilian status and never having to see them again. They had new "jungle boots" that raised blisters in the damp heat, NCOs barking orders for them to fall-in, fall-out, line-up, report for various make-work assignments that threatened to set-off Mulcahey's temper or Babineaux's madness or Singleton's mockery, which might jeopardize their receiving an assignment to a nice, soft, civilian office with an intelligence unit -- so they stuck together and kept eyes on each other -- the chemistry of the whole sustained by the quirks of each.

Rick Singleton was the first of them, though, to arrive in Vietnam. At the end of the second day in the Replo-Depot, he was ordered to take a turn at "Guard Duty," loaded onto a truck with a dozen others and driven along the service road beside the chain-link perimeter fence. The first soldier ordered out of the truck asked, "Don't I get a weapon, sarge?" and was told, "Weapons will be issued by your as-signed unit, after you leave here." The other soldiers in the rear of the truck watched this solitary figure disappear in a cloud of red dust and fading light until he was a speck on the flat, open landscape, then the truck stopped again on the perimeter dirt road and the ser-geant called back, "Next man!"

Singleton was posted at a corner of the fencing, empty-handed and alone. A quarter of a mile away, across the open fields, sat a small village, a piece of the town of Long Binh, a covey of thatched huts surrounded by gardens. Singleton heard the voices of children at play, with women occasionally calling out to them in lyrical passages that reminded him of dialogue from an opera, some piece of stage-business between arias. This was the first Vietnamese he had heard spoken and the musicality of it, compared to the monotone quality of English, amused and pleased him. The huts appeared make-shift, from what he could see, perhaps thrown together by refugees from the war-ravaged countryside who had come for protection to a government-controlled area.

The voices quieted as the evening grew dark until a pole-light snapped on directly over his head, putting Singleton in the spot-light, center-stage, but with no script and no props. He understood then the role of the sentry, to draw fire in case of an attack, the canary in the mine. His having an M-16 would make no difference anyway, since he stood under a glaring light on open ground and any assault would come from the darkness beyond. Since there was no guard "post" as such, he strolled down the fence-line toward the next pole-light, until he was half-way between them, which made him feel a little less paranoid. From there, he could make out small lights moving around the group of huts, kerosene lanterns carried about by the people, and he recognized one cluster of lamps as women doing dishes, squatting over a tub that clattered and splashed as they worked, while they chatted among themselves in lively sing-song. Singleton drew comfort from this domestic scene, a sign that life was normal in the dark beyond the perimeter lighting, that this would be a regular night, like many others in which no one shot at sentries in the American camp.

The book title *Black Like Me* popped into his head. He had skimmed through it a few years ago, when it was a best-seller, but it had left no strong impression on him. A white man posing as a black man to seek out the black experience struck him as a hypocritical stunt. Singleton had learned to move comfortably between the genteel Harlem of his father's large, prosperous church and the privileged elite who attended the Dalton School, where Jews, Episcopalians, mainstream Protestants, and non-believers blended seamlessly together because they were all, as he was, born to wealth and headed for selective universities. He could be thrilled equally when his father's booming sermon to an aroused congregation ended with the gospel choir rattling the building as when the New York Philharmonic delivered up Beethoven at the glittering new Lincoln Center. He was at home in his worlds.

But it occurred to him now that he would not be a young black man in Harlem nor a rich man's kid at Yale. He would be living and working among people who were neither white nor black, whose world this was -- the world of wash basin and lantern-light and a strange, sung language. As urbane and broad as Singleton's life experiences had been, he suddenly realized how little prepared he was for this mysterious realm he was about to enter.

"Vietnamese like me," he said out-loud.

6

2 October 1967

III CORPS HQ

Trim, fit, looking every inch the nisei warrior he was, Hideo Shimazu, Commanding Officer of SIC in III Corps, sat under the downdraft of a ceiling fan that required weights to hold down every paper on his desk. The heat in this small, windowless room was oppressive, but he preferred this interior office to the rooms with doors and large windows that opened onto the second-story roof deck. Major Shimazu planned to retire after this last tour of duty and if German professionals had failed to kill him on Hill 140 and at Castellina when he was young, he wasn't going to give some guerilla kid with a grenade the chance at this late date. A third of his Japanese-American 442nd Regimental Combat Team had been killed or wounded in Italy, but luck and skill had carried Shimazu through, and he proudly wore his sergeant's stripes, purple heart, bronze star and campaign ribbons when he helped his family resettle in the Little Tokyo neighborhood of Los Angeles after the war. They had lost everything while in the Manzanar Camp, and he re-enlisted and applied for Officer's Candidate School so he could aid them in rebuilding their lives. As a first lieutenant during the Korean conflict, he pulled a training assignment state-side, so now a DEROS of 3 April 1968 was his goal and this hitch with a headquarters company in Saigon gave him very good odds to return safely to his wife and daughter. His 26 years in the Army would be over and he looked forward eagerly to being back home during Shizuka's last two years at USC and to founding "Shimazu's Family Restaurant," his dream second-career. That is why, instead of reading the stack of Information Reports, his attention was on a list of ingredients for The Dinner tonight.

"Say, boys," he called out. Belmont sauntered in and said, "Sir?"

"Could someone go out to the market and buy for The Dinner?"

"Leffanta's gone to Long Binh to bring in the replacements, but I could go."

The practiced informality of this exchange was an endemic source of psychic pain for the major. As he counted out purple, blue and brown scrip from the cash box, he re-wrote this scene in the context of the Infantry: "Corporal!" Belmont would dash into his presence, his uniform starched, the creases straight, snap off a salute and say, "Yes, Sir!" "Procure this list of supplies." "Yes, Major!" And Belmont would salute again, spin an about-face and stride from the office like a man.

Instead, Corporal Belmont leaned on the doorjamb, solid and big-shouldered, one hand in the pocket of his wrinkled chinos, the other on his hip, a cigarette pack bulging from the pocket of a plaid shirt unbuttoned to his sternum, a Marlon Brando expression on his unshaven face. Belmont was part of the deal Shimazu had made as the Vietnam War expanded. He had opted to transfer from Combat Arms to the Intelligence Corps for the same reason these unkempt college kids had -- to get through it alive. As Belmont scooped up the money, the major told him, "Get everything on the list. Shrimp in my special sauce tonight."

"Sounds delicious," Belmont said and sauntered back out.

For the next hour, Shimazu read over the Information Reports and a dozen others brought in by Pham Viet, the chief transla-tor, known to the Americans as "Mr. Viet". Each one was stamped "CONFIDENTIAL / EYES ONLY" in red ink at the top and bottom of each page. As important as that made them sound, each one in this stack reported the location of certain elements of Viet Cong and NVA all over III Corps -- from south of Pleiku in the Central Highlands, technically in II Corps, to the An Long River -- as they had been spotted five days ago or seven or ten by agents who may be telling the truth or merely spinning a good yarn to collect their pay. Charlie was always on the move out there, never in one place for long if he wanted to survive, so knowing where elements of the 9th or the 271st were a week ago was a waste of paper. By the time these IRs got to SIC Central then passed through to MACV, were evaluated again, compiled with others, then targeting recommendations made to field units in artillery or infantry, the war could be over. For now, the major checked each report against a list of agents, added his own comments on the likely reliability of the source, and put it in the out-box. Shrimp steeped in Shimazu Sauce on angel-hair pasta, with a side of broccoli, a garden salad and a good white wine, followed by vanilla ice cream swimming in Grand Marnier seemed much more interesting to him.

After lunch, a sandwich and iced coffee at his desk, the major worked on financial reports while a battle raged in the front office suites. Corporal Belmont harbored some romantic notions about combat because he did not know the first damn thing about it, and he wanted out of Saigon and into the field, "where the action is". Major Shimazu had promised him a field assignment as soon as the replacements came in, but that promise was now six weeks old, so the restless young man had launched a campaign to make himself so disruptive in the office that they'd be forced to reassign him for their own sanity. Since he misfiled, misplaced, or simply tossed out every piece of paper he got near, he was assigned errands like the shopping list, which he would do gladly because it got him out of the office and into the lively and dangerous combat zone of Saigon traffic and because, although he ran his errands dependably, it took him much longer than was required and involved stopping for drinks with some pretty bar-girls. Had this been the infantry, Major Shimazu would have had him busted to E-1, but this was not the infantry. It was the nonchalant country club of the Intelligence Corps, infested with college kids who thought more like his college-age daughter, so a different, more parental style of command was called-for. The major had First Lieutenant Stephen Aaronson, his second-in-command, supervise Belmont in the typing of the monthly report of all "SECRET" and "TOP SECRET" documents in their files. From his desk in the other front office, the Lieutenant could oversee this miserable task, which required typing perfectly, letter-for-letter, the lengthy official titles of each of these two dozen documents, followed by their lengthy official serial numbers, the original plus three carbon copies, on a Smith Corona manual typewriter, without any mistakes or corrections. A skilled typist -- and Belmont was a skilled typist -- could do this task with patience and care in an afternoon. But Corporal Belmont had a different agenda, so that every hour or so, he would shift his fingers off the home-row of keys and touch-type a line of gibberish. He would dramatically rip the pages from the platen and announce to the office, "Oh damn! I've done it *again!!*" and he would make the rounds, showing Leffanta and the lieutenant his "error". This performance would ignite Aaronson like a roman candle. Such a torrent of obscenities, threats and abuse was unleashed by the lieutenant that he had actually become hoarse over the days of this routine and Belmont's passive expression would take on the hint of a smile, which then set off another explosion of epithets and dire warnings.

The truth of the matter is that Major Shimazu found these events highly amusing and potentially profitable. On the one hand, his lieutenant had much to learn about how to command subordinates that they didn't teach him at West Point. Speaking with him about it had done no good, so Shimazu was using the rebellious corporal as a blunt instrument to pound his by-the-book, top-down second-in-command into a more effective leader of men. Ninety-day-wonders had often run afoul of hardened combat veterans in Italy in the 1940's, to their detriment, and bellowing was certainly less effective, now, among these citizen-soldiers of 1967. Shimazu hoped that his lieutenant could learn how to gain the respect of and motivate

Corporal Belmont in comparative safety. If he dressed down infantry in the field in this manner, it might earn him a grenade in his tent.

Furthermore, the major quietly admired Belmont's determination to exchange a Saigon office for the experience of war. Shimazu had been a warrior at Belmont's age, had tested his courage and earned self-respect under fire. He remembered that impetuous urge and the curiosity behind it -- and he admired the cool discipline Belmont showed in the face of an infuriated officer. There was an icy calm in Belmont, as though he were practicing bravery in this warm-up drill for the real terror that might lie ahead.

A flight of Hueys passed low over the office on their approach to Tan Son Nhut and the building rattled under the pounding rotors for a full two minutes, which brought the skirmish in the outer offices to a halt. Shimazu waited a few minutes before calling out, "Belmont." The young man slouched in and casually said, "Sir?"

"As soon as the lieutenant is done with you, could you find the time to make a run out to the base for water?"

"Yessir."

"And could you be back in time for dinner at 1900 hours sharp?"

"Yessir."

"Shrimp on pasta tonight."

"I know. I bought the shrimp."

"So you did. Now get a move on."

"Yessir."

Major Shimazu hoped that Aaronson had overheard every word of this quiet exchange and was taking notes.

In mid-afternoon, Corporal Leffanta drove in with the replacements, greenhorns fresh from Greyhawk with all their worldly possessions in heavy duffle bags. They got to hear Lieutenant Aaronson explain the command structure of the unit -- that a civilian cover was to be maintained at all times for security reasons but that they were not to forget, even if they didn't refer to rank, that this was a military unit, that they were to report directly to him and he would make the determination as to whether the major needed to be consulted. He and Major Shimazu were quartered here, in a spacious suite in the other half of the second floor of this villa, while their Vietnamese counterparts occupied the first floor. Enlisted men were assigned bunks in a so-called "civilian" compound a mile closer to Tan Son Nhut. Then he escorted them into the presence of their Commanding Officer.

Shimazu placed James Michener's *Sayonara* face down to hold his page and looked up at the twitchy youngster saluting him, "Corporal John Francis Mulcahey reporting as ordered, Sir."

"Are you in uniform, Corporal?"

"Nosir."

"Never salute anyone...not even General Westmoreland...unless you are. And if you are in uniform, never come anywhere near here."

"Yessir. Nosir." Mulcahey softly dropped the salute.

The other replacement was relaxed and wore an amused expression across a broad, generous face that was somehow familiar to the major, but that he could have seen him before seemed very unlikely. The young man calmly introduced himself as "Corporal Zachary Rosenzweig, but everyone calls me 'Rosie'." As they spoke, Shimazu was even more convinced he knew him from somewhere -- but where?

"Leffanta will take you over to the enlisted compound and get you settled in, then you will return here for The Dinner, which will be served at exactly 1900 hours." Shimazu did not miss the look of disgust that crossed Aaronson's face at this announcement. Enlisted did not dine with officers -- those were supposed to be the rules. But not under Shimazu's command. The major loved to plan and execute superb meals and he had no intention of doing so for himself and one other officer, especially one who took no particular pleasure in them. Also, The Dinner was another opportunity to model for this narrow-minded but dedicated junior officer how to win the respect and obedience of the men.

On the way to the enlisted compound, Bitter Louie Leffanta got some pleasure out of showing the new guys all the many and various ways in which life in Saigon sucked. Nobody could be expected to drive through a swarm of bikes and scooters without running over some lousy slope who'd then demand twenty in scrip-money or having a convoy of deuce-and-a-half trucks come out of nowhere and flatten you like a beer can so the crushed body of this baby-blue jeep would be your casket that they would ship home to your mother and she'd have to pay the cemetery a fortune to bury it. But don't worry, he said, neither of these things will happen before oil-soaked clouds of blue smoke from all the cheap-assed cyclo-cabs and scooters give you lung cancer, then your mother won't even get a purple heart to show her friends.

"You can't find the enlisted compound by street signs because they all look exactly alike... Gookese. Turn here at the whorehouse shaped like a pagoda." He pulled into a narrow dirt alley with a walled compound on the right that featured mountains of huge boxes piled up: Sony, GE, Sanyo, and Panasonic appliances rose high above the ten-foot wall. "Filipinos," Bitter Louie announced. "They come here, never fire a shot, empty out the PX and take everything that's not bolted down back to Manila." He maneuvered around a tight S-curve and barked to the Vietnamese guard to raise the pole-gate and let them into the central courtyard of a spacious compound. "About eighty guys live here...some in uniform, some not. I don't know who they are or what they do and I don't give a shit."

Mad-dog and Rosie were issued bedding and mosquito nets and assigned to bunks in an eight-man room on the second floor of one of the buildings. They made their bed, loaded their gear into footlockers secured with their own padlocks, and washed-up, changing out of the sweaty, dust-covered clothes they'd worn all day. Soon they were set up with beers in the cafeteria across the quadrangle from their room, sitting where they could keep an eye on Leffanta's blue jeep, anxious to know what "The Dinner" would be like. At the moment, they felt thrilled to have arrived in this exceptional place, first promised to them by a recruitment officer almost a year ago. IF they got through basic training -- IF they could handle one of the longest and most exacting Military Occupational Schools available to enlisted, then eventually they might find themselves on civilian status in an office, far from mortar shells and rifle rounds, free from the grinding-stone of the uniformed military. It sounded altogether too good to be true, but here they were, the Replacement Depot behind them, drinking beer in civilian clothes.

The Dinner too was beautiful beyond any expectation. Atop the flat roof of the villa, a large plywood enclosure had been built, screened-in on all sides, offering cool breezes to relieve the daytime heat and a panoramic view of the neighborhood below. The buzz of scooters, trucks and voices arose from a busy street, forty yards away, at the end of their entrance-alley. Transformers converted Saigon's 220 voltage into 110 for the refrigerator, the freezer, electric skillets, woks, grills, blenders, mixers and other appliances for Shimazu's kitchen operation. The major's pride and happiness were apparent as he served each of his guests -- Belmont and Leffanta seated on one side, the new-comers on the other, and a pouting, bristling Aaronson at the end below the salt. The lieutenant had ceased pointing out that officers and enlisted were to dine separately, but he would not offer to lend a hand, and no offer would have been accepted that interfered with Major Shimazu's grand presentation anyway. The wine was a dry white, chilled and in great supply, shrimp from the South China Sea the size of tennis balls floated in a rich sauce of mushrooms, scallions and garlic, the salad was crisp and sprinkled with parmesan, the broccoli was soaked in lemon-butter, and everything was lavishly praised by the enlisted men to the obvious delight of the chef and to the anguish of his lieutenant.

The major was taciturn and the lieutenant sullen, so the conversation ran with the enlisted men getting to know each other.

Even slouched in his chair, Belmont was physically imposing, with big shoulders, powerful arms, a rugged face, not at all the stereotype of a Bostonian born to considerable wealth. "I hardly squeaked-through school because I was more interested in thumbing around Europe, got into Harvard as a legacy, bummed around the back-roads in Central and South America in the summers. I'll save you the

trouble of not asking about the scar on my face...some guy with a machete tried to rob me outside a bar in Panama. I got the broken nose
in Venezuela," he laughed, "because my Spanish was lousy. *'Bastante'*
means 'enough' but I said *'bastarde'* instead, so I had it coming."

Bitter Louie was supposed to be in medical school right now instead of in a war he never asked for in this god-forsaken rat's nest of a
bake-oven, but they wouldn't give him the deferment he deserved in
time to enroll at Pitt or Penn or any other school because admissions-
office jerks kept turning down his applications until the draft-board
vultures forced him to enlist in Intelligence, which is a medical-
school-killer dead-end. So his father will now die with a shovel in
his hands out at U.S. Steel and never see a doctor in the family. It
struck the new-comers that the officers gave no response to this tale
of woe -- as though they may have heard it before, a few times -- and
that Belmont chuckled, as though Leffanta's story were a sort of dark
comedy routine.

Over ice cream swimming in liqueur, Mad-dog and Rosie filled-in
the outlines of their young lives. Mulcahey didn't mention his novel
and Rosenzweig left the bone-filled fields of Franklin, Tennessee for
another time.

Then Zach Rosenzweig turned toward the major and, unbidden,
it came. The overhead fluorescents struck his wide blue eyes and
Hideo Shimazu recognized him. It was the same way that he turned
to face him on Hill 140 in 1944. The young man stepped out from
behind a boulder and flashed expressions of surprise then resigna-
tion, knowing it was over, that the M-1 in Shimazu's hands was about
to kill him. The long-ago moment that they faced each other was
just one image floating in an ever-present river of such images for
Major Shimazu and he had not been haunted by it, but neither had
it been erased, so that now the uncanny similarity Rosenzweig bore
to that German youth called it home. This revelation did not show
in Shimazu's demeanor. The hooded eyes remained calmly on the
young corporal's face but the sound of his words were lost, as the
sharp moment of recall deafened Shimazu to the living present. His

breathing soon returned to normal and he said, "The new men will do the clean up this week. Belmont, show them how it is done."

Propped up in bed under his reading light, Major Shimazu ended his day by using a book-mark given to him by his daughter to keep his place in *Sayonara,* and then he placed across his knees the bound journal given him by his wife "for your troubled times," as she said. Four-fifths of this journal was filled with carefully worded entries compiled over two decades in Shimazu's precise handwriting. Hideo flipped to a blank page and fell silent in thought for a long time before writing a haiku:

His eyes wide and blue,
He sees me there by the rock.
Their last sight is me.

7

6 - 7 October 1967

THE GOSPEL ACCORDING TO BELMONT

"Say, Belmont." Hideo Shimazu sat in the convection oven of his small interior office with papers on his desk-top fluttering like trapped birds covered by an odd assortment of paper-weights. Belmont sidled in, hands buried in the pockets of the dirty, beige chinos he'd worn all week, and asked "Sir?"

"Sit down, Belmont. I have orders for your field assignment, as I promised you, but I haven't signed off on them yet. Here's the deal." Shimazu's range of expressions was always narrow, with heavily hooded eyes covering the top third of his irises, a solemn demeanor and quiet, even voice. He was rarely known by the men who served under him to show either laughter or anger. He neither asked nor told about personal matters. He commanded the office in a way that invited no argument, he read widely and constantly, and he single-handedly cooked and served the elaborate Dinner every night, promptly at 1900 hours, to everyone of every rank in the office whether they were assigned there or merely visiting from a field station. Therefore, he seemed, to Belmont at least, to be a contented man, a state the younger man could only vaguely comprehend. Belmont was never contented. And so even though the two were soldiers in the same army, just one generation apart in age, they may as well have been from different planets. Following an impressive silence, Shimazu continued,

"You and Leffanta are broken-in here. The work we do flows, water and supplies are kept stocked and you are well trained on where and how to buy proper ingredients for The Dinner and how much to pay. I would like it if you will...." the major finally settled on "It would be a great help to the office if you brought the replacements up-to-speed on everything, so there would be no disruption when you're gone to the field. Understood?"

"Yessir." Belmont couldn't suppress a smile of joy at the prospect of escaping the headquarters at last. "May I ask where my assignment will be?"

"Khap Noi, on the An Long River, with Dodd at Field Station C. He's short so we need...."

Belmont interrupted with a fit of laughter but Shimazu, once he got the joke, merely raised his eyebrows and said, "I meant to say that his DEROS is in a few months and he is a 'short-timer' as the saying goes, so will need to be replaced."

"Yessir. Not that he's four-foot-ten in combat boots."

"And there's another reason too. As you're aware, he's almost stopped filing Information Reports in recent weeks. He used to run a very productive station. That's not acceptable and I know you'll do better. Anyway, you should like Khap Noi, Belmont. There will be plenty of mortar and rocket fire from across the river, just what you've been asking for. Now please send in the lieutenant." Calling his junior officer by rank was a career-long habit Shimazu couldn't break.

"We're due downstairs for the Friday meeting with our counter-parts," he told Aaronson. "I want to be sure we're fully prepared."

Bilateral operations upended military organization, confusing the order of things, and Major Shimazu found the whole arrange-ment unpleasant. Two chains-of-command in two separate armies were supposed to work in tandem from top to bottom, but hidden agendas often clashed with the common, official ones and personal-ity conflicts could not be resolved by rank. And all of it was made

worse by cultural and language barriers no translator could overcome. Still, Major Shimazu was glad to see Mr. Viet at the side of his
counterpart, Major Han, rather than one of the less fluent translators. He strode into the conference room and firmly shook hands
with the half dozen ARVN officers present, all wearing civvies while
Aaronson trailed after his commander, trying to juggle an armload
of files and a clipboard while he shook hands.

For the next hour of tense discussion, only Shimazu and Han
spoke through Mr. Viet.

All others present watched in respectful silence. Major Han began
by loudly opposing every suggestion Shimazu expressed regarding the
disposition of personnel and operational matters. But the American
commanded the resources that paid the hundreds of agents and dozens of handlers and for seven field office operations, so in the end
each decision was made as Major Shimazu had proposed. Pay was
terminated for a dozen unproductive or unreliable agents and two
handlers over the increasing objections of Major Han, with Shimazu
never altering his calm, tightly-controlled delivery. When the agenda
items had been exhausted, Shimazu requested a word alone with his
counterpart and everyone else but Viet cleared the room.

"Please ask Major Han where he thinks I was born," Shimazu said
quietly. Viet paused a moment before translating.

"Major Han says that he does not know."

"Tell the major that I speak two languages fluently. One is
English. Can he guess the other one?" Shimazu's steady gaze never
left his counterpart's face, like a poker player watching for a tell.

"Major Han says he does not know."

"Please inform Major Han that I was born and raised in
California, that I speak no other language than English, and that
I'm an American officer in the American Army who has worn my
country's uniform for twenty-six years." Shimazu waited while Viet
translated before he added, "And tell Major Han that if he harbors
any resentment toward the Japanese and what their military did to

this country, that has got *not one* goddamned thing to do with me."
When it became clear that Major Han would have no response to this
statement, Shimazu arose and left the room.

Upstairs, Belmont's enthusiasm was boundless in training the replacements toward the hour he could trade a Saigon office for the
battlefield. He guided Rosenzweig through the elaborate filing system and rotation of forms to be compiled and disseminated while
Mulcahey, who proved a whiz at touch-typing ("Try eighty-eight keys
sometime," he'd said) had the notorious "Inventory of Classified
Documents" done perfectly in an hour. They stuffed a valise with
files for SIC Central and piled into the blue jeep, leaving Leffanta to
man the phone and await a mass of paperwork that would come up
from the bilateral meeting. Belmont stuck a snub-nosed .38 revolver
into his belt as they left, pulling his shirt over it.

"So somebody grabs for the valise, you'd shoot them?" Rosie
asked.

"Oh hell no," Belmont said, "those reports aren't worth anything
to anybody. The agents' names are coded and the info is three weeks
old. The side-arm is for shopping."

Clouds of dust, oil-laden exhaust and an ocean of odors--cooking oil,
kerosene, fish, meat, incense and a host of unidentifiable ones--swirled
along the river of traffic in the supersaturated air. This miasma baked
under a heat-lamp sun that seemed at times to place survival itself in
question for a few minutes after leaving the office until blessed sweat
soaked through shirts and pants. Belmont told them that driving
in Saigon was his favorite part of the day, gunning the jeep through
masses of pedestrians, bicycles, scooters, mopeds, Peugeot taxis and
pedi-cabs, black Citroëns, and military vehicles of every size, the largest of which presumed the right-of-way and sped through the streets
with complete indifference to the lives of others. Traffic circles were
free-for-all dogfights, with Vietnamese military police -- QC printed

on their white helmets -- and municipal police acting not so much as traffic cops as referees who rushed in after the frequent mishaps to care for the injured and settle on who paid whom and how much. Belmont loved it all and prided himself on not having killed anyone despite many near-misses.

SIC Central shared a heavily-guarded compound, the entrance bracketed by sand-bagged machinegun emplacements, with several other support units of the US Army, so men in civilian garb mixed with uniformed personnel while green jeeps with white stars sat alongside others in pastel colors. Belmont parked and told them, "We wait for 11:05 precisely, each Friday, then drop this packet at the counter and get the hell out. When we go in, you'll see a bald, heavy-set guy sitting at his desk in the center of the office. He's a tough, old-school warrant officer named Greeley...*Mr.* Greeley, if you ever speak with him...and he'll be screaming at the top of his lungs because every Friday morning he tries to patch a call through MARS, a ham radio service, to his wife. The phones system works badly when it works at all and calling outside the country is only theoretically possible.   So about 11:20, he'll give up trying and start looking around for something to kill, which is only marginally better than his usual mood. You'll hear the clerk say, 'Mr. Greeley wants to see you,' and I'll say, 'Next time. Gotta run.' Maybe one of you guys will be lucky and walk-in when he's not on the phone...then you can write and tell me what he's wanted to see me about every Friday for the last two months."

The scene in SIC Central was even more dramatic than Belmont described: Greeley was not sitting at his desk but standing at it, stocky and powerful, imposing in both size and sound, bellowing profanities and threats into a hand-set like an aria from *Don Giovanni* in English.

A half-dozen clerks scooted around banks of file cabinets and desks, apparently deaf and mute. While Belmont delivered the files and waited for a receipt, Rosie poked Mad-dog and pointed to office doors with signs that read "Colonel George Owen Donahue" and "Major Alexander Cardenas". "New CO, just arrived from The States," Belmont said.

"Mr. Greeley needs to see you right away," the clerk said to Belmont.

"Can't stay. Tight schedule," Belmont told him.

Six miles of white-knuckle driving later they arrived at the main gate of Ton Son Nhut Airbase, where they crawled ahead with vehicles of every description toward the heavily guarded entrance. They handed their photo ID cards to a blue-eyed Olympian in a starched MP uniform with the name "Swanson" over his breast pocket. He held each card in his spotless white glove and asked them: "Mr. Mulcahey, what is your civilian rank?"

"GS-11."

"Mr. Rosenzweig, what is *your* civilian rank?"

"GS-11."

"Mr. Belmont....R-I-G-H-T. Good morning, sir." He returned the cards, snapped a crisp salute and waved them through the gate.

"What was that all about?" Rosie asked.

Belmont said, "He's having some fun with us. We're all GS-11, and that would be a civilian contractor roughly equivalent to a major. Look at you, Mulcahey. No offense, but you could pass for a high school senior. You flash that MP a card that says GS-11, he just wants to say he's not buying it."

The replacements were justifiably awe-struck by the PX at Tan Son Nhut. Two football fields in area under one roof holding neighborhoods piled high with appliances large and small, clothes, books and music, stereo equipment and cameras, furniture and, specific to their visit, food and liquor of every sort. It was a virtual city, bustling with shoppers from a dozen nations. There was nothing remotely like this anywhere in the civilian world back home.

Belmont led them straight to the food section and pulled out Shimazu's list for tonight's meal. While he loaded the shopping cart, he told them, "The typing, filing, courier drops to SIC Central...all that comes second if you want a happy CO. The top priority each and every day is to complete the shopping by 4:00 at the very latest...1600 hours if that's how you like it. Meat, canned goods, cooking oil, booze and some staples from here first, then you drive the jeep straight back to the office with someone sitting in the back to guard the food because if you don't, the street urchins will clean you out like a swarm of locust and you'll have to start over. Wave the .38 at them if you need to, to back them off. It's not loaded and they know it, so they'll just laugh at you and call you names, but it's nicer than a tire-iron. After the PX stuff is stored-away, you'll have to hit the local market for the fresh produce, rice and whatever seafood the major needs. There is a lot to learn before you get everything the way he wants and three-quarters of it has to do with food. But I warn you, never let him down. Never, not ever. Because you'll have five-star eating and drinking every night in the evening breezes of the pent-house...all paid for out of the major's discretionary budget...and don't ever ask about that either...so long as it all clicks-along. But Aaronson hates it, he hates your being there, he hates you personally, and it also happens he's got Army Reg's that back him up. Only in SIC and only under Shimazu could you get away with this, so you best think of it as fragile and temporary. If you goof this up, you'll be standing in line with a tray in your hands at the enlisted compound, paying out of your pocket for cafeteria food or out on the economy, taking your chances with local cuisine that could put you in an ambulance.

"Now pay attention while we go over the meat products, beginning with tonight's choices for chicken to go in white sauce...."

Mulcahey and Rosenzweig began to understand the next morning, Saturday, why Belmont was eager to leave such a plush, safe and privileged assignment for the dangers and privations of Khap Noi.

Friday's crash course in shopping had taken them from the PX back to the office to run everything up to the roof-top enclosure, then on a seven-mile drive through hellish afternoon heat, only slightly relieved by a blinding downpour, during which they had no choice but to don rain ponchos and slosh through the mud between stalls at Saigon's sprawling main food market for specific salad-makings and unfamiliar spices. The jeep had no ignition key, merely an ignition switch, so had to be secured by a heavy chain welded to the floor under the driver's seat, which was threaded through the steering wheel and padlocked. They were soon hauling bundles of newspaper-wrapped produce under their ponchos. They pushed their way like enormous, brown balloon-people through crowds of lean Vietnamese in soaked but light-weight clothes of cotton and silk.

Each place they stopped involved a lengthy negotiation in pidgin, which the replacements barely followed but which Belmont rattled off fluently. As he pointed out to them, it was very important to offer less than half of the initial asking price, then the merchant would come down but only a little, buyer up a little, and when a price was arrived at, the buyer must pull out a wad of piastres, the Vietnamese currency no merchant wanted. "You no pay me Dong!" the merchant would shout, "You pay me Dollah!" and the price would be re-negotiated lower now, this time for the Military Payment Certificates issued to all foreigners, which the merchants preferred because the inflation-rate of Piastres was astronomical. Since it was technically illegal for the Vietnamese merchant to possess MPC, Belmont had leverage.

"Jesus Christ!" Mulcahey hollered over the downpour drumming on the corrugated metal roofs of the stalls. "It took fifteen goddamned minutes to buy four heads of lettuce! Pay the son-of-a-bitch two extra dollars and we could be out of the rain and home by now!"

"Dangerous thinking!" Belmont yelled back. "These people have sonar like bats. They can sense weakness or impatience a block away, just by the way you walk. Then you'll pay five-times what everything is worth and it'll come out of your own pocket because the major knows exactly what everything should cost and gives you only what he knows you'll need. It's even written on the shopping list. You'll end up borrowing from Bitter Louie to get yourself through the end of the month...and he'll screw you over worse than the merchants."

Their final purchase, for ten kilos of rice, was especially trying on Mad-dog's nerves. After extensive bargaining in rapid-fire pidgin, well beyond the new-comers' ability to follow, Belmont turned and began walking back to the jeep without the rice. "You no go!" the rice-lady yelled at him. "I show you something." Belmont turned to see her holding the hands of two sick-looking children with rags for clothes and dark circles under lifeless eyes. "Need cash-money for bac si! My children sick! My children die, I blame you!"

Belmont shot back, "Dese no you children you! I see dese children at shrimp-man!"

"You lie you!"

"I no lie!"

"Pay her for chrissakes!" Mulcahey screamed -- and saw the rice-lady immediately break-out in a wide, gap-toothed smile of victory.

Belmont slammed the 22-pound bag of rice into Mulcahey's chest and said, "You owe me three bucks."

As they pushed the jeep back through heavy bicycle and pedestrian traffic around the market-place, Rosie, in the back-seat, was in charge of warding off quick little hands that flashed in around the canvas top. He waved the .38, but to no discernible effect, so he spread his body over the groceries as best he could. They barely made it back to the office for the 4:00 deadline, then ran the food up to the penthouse and, using all four of the office typewriters at once, they piled into the load of paperwork Leffanta was churning through from the bilateral meeting. The whole translation pool was staying late so these reports could be in the hands of the counterparts downstairs on the same day the meeting took place. If they failed to do so, Major Han would claim at the next meeting that the pride and morale of his staff had suffered by the Americans' callous disregard for them in making them wait for the reports.

They finished-up after 6:00, too late for a round-trip to the enlisted compound, but there was a beautifully tiled shower in this one-time luxury villa and they made use of it to clean up and shave for the high-point of this day, of every day -- day-after-day -- The Dinner at 7:00 sharp in the penthouse. Delicious and extensive as all the others, with more food than could be eaten, more wine than could be drunk, and a sweet liqueur with strawberries and ice cream for dessert, this Friday's meal was another one for the books. The four enlisted men, exhausted from the day's work, managed nevertheless to carry on a lively conversation under the quiet gaze of two officers -- one contented and taciturn; the other sullen and brooding. Thus it came to be almost 10:00 by the time Mulcahey and Rosenzweig packed up the leftovers for the translation pool, the gate guard and the maids, and began the clean up, following instructions from Belmont, their mentor and guide on how to do everything properly.

He it was -- this same Belmont -- who stood over them now, Saturday morning at 6:30, reaching under the mosquito netting to shake each one gently, singing to them with unconcealed mirth, "Rise and shine, troopers. Busy day ahead. It's time to play sous-chef to Major Shimazu."

Mulcahey rubbed both hands over his eyes and groaned, "You've got to be shitting me."

Belmont lit a cigarette, blew a great cloud of smoke toward the ceiling fan, and chuckled, "Now you douche bags know why I've got to get out of this place, if it's the last thing I ever do."

8

9 October 1967

A SACRED MISSION

T he driver from SIC Central Headquarters arrived at the Replacement Depot in Long Binh at mid-morning one week after Mulcahey and Rosenzweig left for SIC III Corps. He wore a white shirt, tan chinos, drove a jeep best described as puce in color, and carried orders for Levesque and Singleton. "Change in the latrine," he told them. "I'll pick you up over there."

The pair said good-bye and wished luck to Babineaux and Hood, who were beginning to worry that they had fallen through cracks in the re-assignment floor and might spend a year at the Replacement Depot.

Perhaps it was because he was annoyed about his morning's duty assignment, or he was ordered to be discreet, or he was unnerved by the drive down Route 1, through small villages in forested areas that felt unsafe then into the cacophony of Saigon traffic that felt even less safe. For whatever reason, the driver maintained an icy silence throughout the trip. Their orders assigned them to SIC Central, so they began to worry that they may be facing a year stuck in a national HQ, surrounded by tight-lipped toads like this guy. When they arrived at a vast fenced-in compound of mixed military and civilian activity, the driver pulled up to a single-story building and broke his silence to say, "Go in there and report to Mr. Greeley." A sign on the door said, "Authorized Personnel Only".

Inside, at the counter, Singleton had to raise his voice and repeat his question twice because there was a large, bald, older man yelling obscenities with hurricane force, slamming books, binders and the flat of one hand on his desk-top, holding a phone in the other. Apparently not at all distracted by this spectacle, the young man behind the counter said, "Mr. Greeley will be right with you." He stood very still, looking quietly at them for a full minute after the phone had been violently thrown into its cradle before he took their manila folders from them and handed them to Mr. Greeley. They couldn't hear what he said to the old man, but they had no trouble hearing Mr. Greeley say, "What the hell do you want?" and "Where are they?"

'"Go with Corporal Jenks," he barked at Singleton and Levesque, referring to a young man in civvies. They were escorted to another building where they had their fingerprints taken, posed for photos, and were measured in a wardrobe area where several men worked at cutting tables and sewing machines. Back in the main building, they waited on chairs opposite the counter and were told "Nope" when Singleton asked if there was someplace to get food. After an hour, Mr. Greeley emerged from a door across the way and announced, "The major will see you now." Singleton whispered "Old home week" when he saw a nameplate on the door: "Major Alexander Cardenas".

A massive air-conditioning unit made this inner office a polar region by contrast to the outside world and cold sweat-soaked shirts clung unpleasantly to their hot skin. Cardenas, in a tan, light-weight suit, greeted them with a smile and called them by name, using "Mister". He shouted to his orderly to bring them all coffee, a hot drink sure to be welcome in this meat-locker, and asked, "What do you take in yours?" Singleton stifled the urge to say "A ham and cheese on rye," saying "cream and sugar" instead. The major pulled his office chair around to the front of his desk and placed it opposite their folding chairs. Small talk about the Replo-Depot at Long Binh filled-in until the coffee was delivered and the door closed.

Then "Soldiers follow orders, gentlemen, as you know," he said solemnly. "And yet, here you are...here we both are...in a kind of limbo, military men pretending not to be what we are, soldiers. In every other setting, men are demoted or sent to the stockade for any infraction of rules or insubordination, anywhere at any time in history, but I've never known anyone in your specific MOS to be so much as given K.P. At worst, you may get reassigned to some clerk posting. To be frank, this situation was born of jealousy we developed over the latitude the CIA is given to operate. So we've tossed out the manuals and stepped over the line...all the lines...with SIC. There are so few of us, maybe fifty in-country, and so much is expected. And we have our enemies, influential brass at MACV who are asking...demanding...that we be shut-down." Cardenas stopped and ran his fingers over his buzz-cut hair.

"Gentlemen, as I told you back at Fort Greyhawk that evening in the tavern, I had a great deal to do with creating this elite sub-sub-category of Intelligence and to be perfectly honest, it's not working. It kills me to say it, but SIC is producing crap. Millions of dollars, a great amount of effort, talented human resources, and all we've got to show is a steady stream of crap ...too late for battlefield action, too unreliable to inspire confidence, too low-level to be of any interest in strategic planning. Our enemies at MACV might be right...and I'm running out of ammo and time to fend them off.

"What we need...what we've got to have and we'd better get...is a home-run, something substantial, you see." He looked each of them in the eye, leaning in close but apparently too distracted to notice the chattering of Singleton's teeth or that Levesque, despite his best efforts to control it, was shivering violently.

"I'm going to ask each of you, individually, to volunteer of your own free will for an assignment that even as an officer in your chain-of-command, I don't feel I can order you to do. And there's one other complication: You must tell absolutely no one what you're doing. Colonel Donahue would never approve of it and I will be in more trouble than you are if he discovers it.

I have more to lose than you, so I am literally putting my career in your hands here. But I've got myself out on a limb and something has to change the game here, or we'll all be back in uniform and our combat troops will go on taking losses because we don't know where Charlie is or what he's up to out there.

"I think I know how we can produce important, top-tier strategic intelligence and bring SIC up to its potential. SIC could finally, through you, have a real impact on the war. But we'll need to step over one more line, an end-run around the rules. If you agree, you'll report directly to me, as my immediate staff, operating mostly in III Corps but by-passing normal channels, so without the support or knowledge of III Corps HQ. It will take two weeks to prepare you for the specific mission, and you may request at any time to be relieved of it, no strings attached, and go back for normal reassignment. But if you are in, I'll need your full commitment to the mission. We will be a team of three, despite our difference in rank, working as one...a triad, a....

"A trinity," Levesque said through chattering teeth, "Father, S..s.. son, and Holy Spook."

Singleton shot him a stern look.

"Exactly, which brings me to my specific plan, which we'll all need to work on together.

I believe, Mr. Singleton, that you drove a luxury car at Greyhawk, supplied by your wealthy New York City family...."

"That's true, sir."

"You, Mr. Levesque, have a Catholic education and once passed yourself off as a nun."

"C...correct," Levesque stuttered through blue lips.

Late that evening, having been assigned a small room at SIC HQ with two desks and a bunk-bed, and given the keys to a jeep -- mauve in color -- Levesque and Singleton followed directions to a road-side eatery where the food was reportedly both good and non-lethal. They chained the jeep wheel and got themselves seated around a small, spindly table with peeling paint, before they recognized in the shadows behind them Mr. Greeley, alone, hunched over a bowl and a brown, quart-sized bottle. Their bid to pass unrecognized didn't last long, as the older man waved at them, drained the last of his bottle, and came their way, staggering noticeably.

"You're the newbies," he said. "Never had a Lave LaRue, I bet." He yanked a nearby chair into their table, rocking it precariously, and dropped down, placing the bottle for their inspection. The label did indeed say "Lave LaRue". "Street-wash is what it means in French, Lave LaRue," he told them.

"Lavage de la rue," Levesque corrected but was not heard.

"Fifteen or twenty cents a quart and deadly...deadly." Then he broke down in tears, sobbing quietly into his hands. He worked his way through it in a couple of seconds, wiping his eyes on the short sleeves of his shirt, mumbling, "Sorry...sorry."

Singleton said, "Well, does Lave LaRue always put a guy in such a bad mood?"

"I'm sorry...don't tell anybody you saw me like this. But what the hell you gonna do?"

"We all have bad days," Levesque offered.

When a young boy brought lanterns to their table, the light revealed a picture of sorrow and defeat on Mr. Greeley's face: Slack jowls under drunken, blood-shot eyes, deep fatigue. "You have to understand...you see. It's this," he choked. "She sold my car...my wife, Sally, sold my '65 Mustang convertible that I bought new." He paused to get himself under control again. "I begged her not to sell it, but when I left I put her name on it so in case I didn't come home...."

"That's lousy," Singleton agreed.

"Now she won't even take my calls. We used to try to link up every morning, whenever the fucking phones would work. But now she won't...."

Levesque commiserated, "Yeah, we saw you were pretty frustrated when we came in this morning."

A silence passed between them before Singleton said, "Can we stand you a round of street-wash?"

"Naw, thanks. I better get back." Mr. Greeley pushed back his flimsy chair and lifted himself unsteadily. "Sorry to unload on you guys. Please don't let this get back to the men I have to work with. I figured you guys are headed out for the field pretty soon, so I just...."

Singleton said, "Sure...don't worry. We can keep secrets. It's kind of what we do." "Our lips are sealed," Levesque assured him. "Just take care of yourself, eh?"

"Thanks," Greeley said, took a few steps toward the open side of the enclosure, then turned back and added, "I can get another car... another Mustang...if I want to."

"Sure, of course you can," Singleton answered.

"But not another Sally." Then he stumbled out into the blackening night.

9

10 October 1967

NO DAY AT THE BEACH

T uesday saw the first ES-3 class reunion at III Corps HQ when Leffanta came back from the Replo-Depot with Mark Babineaux. A round of hand-shakes and derogatory jokes about cats dragging things in was cut short by Aaronson, who called the newcomer into his office for his set piece about respecting rank and the chain of command while simultaneously maintaining civilian cover at all times. But the prospect of putting the Greyhawk Six back together in Saigon dimmed when instead of sending him over to the enlisted compound for bunk assignment, Aaronson led Babineaux in to see the major "for field assignment". Never one for military protocol, Babineaux leaned across the desk and offered his hand when Aaronson barked, "Major Shimazu, your Commanding Officer."

"Mark Babineaux," the younger man said, smiling broadly. "Glad to meet you," and they shook hands cordially. The lieutenant muttered something inaudible as the major dismissed him.

"You know Major Cardenas from your training school, I believe," Shimazu began. "I met with him yesterday morning and he suggested you for an assignment we've had in mind. We know we need someone with strong initiative, leadership skills, experience and maturity."

"Well, thank you, sir, but...."

"Major Cardenas told me that he had no one available who fit that description, but that you were someone who might grow into it over time."

Shimazu displayed no sign that he was joking, so Babineaux didn't know how to respond, but he did think to himself that he would not like to play poker with this man, with or without Hood's ability to calculate odds.

"So I'm giving you an assignment, tentatively, that most men would say is a dream-post, and because it is one, I suspect you won't be there very long." Shimazu turned his chair ninety degrees and used a letter-opener to touch a map of III Corps at a point where the land met the South China Sea, south-east of Saigon. "This peninsula is called Vung Tau and it is where soldiers are often sent for in-country R&R leave. There has never been combat there for an obvious reason." The major turned his hooded eyes toward Babineaux and waited.

"It's a peninsula."

"Correct...good. Eight miles long and one mile wide, we'd cut off their retreat at the neck and pound them to pieces from land, sea and air. So it is a beach-resort in the middle of a war zone and it is interesting to us because it is the kitchen in the party." Shimazu turned to face him again and waited.

"If you want to meet everybody at the party," Babineaux offered, "you park in the kitchen and they all come to you."

"Exactly. Vung Tau is the Switzerland of this war...troops from every ally, contractors, diplomats, the CIA all go there to relax, get loaded, meet girls and forget about the war. Even VC who've been wounded and can't fight may end up there. So it's a gold-mine, not for the kind of tactical intelligence we're getting already, unit locations and such, but the higher-level strategic, policy and propaganda materials that Major Cardenas has been putting pressure on us to gather." The major turned again to tap the map with his pointer. "So I am taking a gamble here, with a new Vung Tau office and with you, to meet the requirements of my superiors, Major Cardenas and Colonel Donahue, and I hope I'm not making a mistake."

Babineaux thought of offering reassurances -- that it was a viable idea, that he was up to the job -- but he had spent the past week in fatigues and had been, two hours ago, slapping white paint on rocks at the margins of a sidewalk at the Replacement Depot, so he figured that his opinions might not bear much weight.

"...going Hollywood," the major was saying. "Do you know that phrase? It refers to actors and athletes who are suddenly made into stars. They lose themselves drinking and doing drugs, staying out all night, imagining themselves invulnerable, and they waste all of their talent and money and end-up sick and broke, without home or family, and even the whores don't want them anymore. In assigning such a young man to Vung Tau, I'm afraid I'm setting you up for going Hollywood on me. If I had a man in his forties, a family man with children...but I don't."

"Nosir," Babineaux agreed, smiling his big, happy smile. "All you've got is a wild-assed Cajun kid."

Shimazu's eyes widened and his features relaxed slightly, but nothing hinted at mirth. "That's what Major Cardenas said, more or less," he admitted.

"So at least Vung Tau won't make me any worse."

Babineaux spent mid-morning to mid-afternoon in Lieutenant Aaronson's spacious office, taking notes that would prove entirely useless in coming months: How to requisition equipment and supplies; how to file Inventory Reports, Status Reports, Budget Reports and Information Reports; how to manage relations with Mr. Duong (his assigned translator) and CP-E, (the code-name given his assigned counterpart) -- most importantly to remember never to divulge to them that he was not really a GS-11-level contractor but, in truth, a lowly enlisted man, E-4 in rank. Babineaux made mental notes on Aaronson too, to the effect that he was the most rigidly humorless, insufferable and egocentric pain in the ass he had encountered since enlisting in the U.S. Army ten months ago.

Babineaux departed at 3:30 with his duffle bag, newly minted GS-11 card (which featured the photo that was taken in basic training), the outlines of an "office supply business" cover-story rattling around his head, two sets of keys for the padlock of a canary-yellow jeep, and Joseph Duong, his translator, whose English was non-idiomatic but whose knowledge of bilateral intelligence operations and of Vung Tau was in-depth.

Babineaux said so-long to his class-mates, now his HQ staff -- with Aaronson barking in the background, "Get going! It's a three-hour drive and you can't be caught in the dark!"

Mad-dog asked, "Where are they sending you?"

"Vung Tau."

"We don't have a station in Vung Tau," Rosie said.

"You do now," Babineaux answered, shouldering his duffle and waving over his shoulder.

An acute hallucinatory state can settle upon anyone when fate tugs at the psychological rug beneath his feet. Something like that was taking place in Babineaux's brain as he engaged the Saigon traffic, a bizarre tornado of vehicular activity with bikes and pedestrians cheating death on every side, clouds of dust and blue smoke billowing in steam-heated air. The crabby three-speed transmission of the jeep bore no relation to the silk-smooth four-on-the-floor cars Babineaux was used to, and it seemed to ignore commands from the clutch pedal and the long, dog-legged stick that was supposed to be a gear-shift. Mr. Duong's directions -- "Turn left HERE! NO, THERE!" -- always came too late to avoid cutting through the path of other traffic and Babineaux -- suddenly, somehow, inhabiting the body of a person in an Asian capital, in civvies, behind the wheel of the first jeep he'd ever driven, taking commands from the first Vietnamese man he'd ever met -- was struggling to make it all seem real. Inevitably perhaps, the yellow jeep sideswiped a bicycle, sending an ARVN soldier and his shopping bags rolling across the pavement.

Mr. Duong hopped from the jeep and yelled, "You stay here, Mr. Bahno!" He helped the middle-aged soldier to stand and gather his scattered belongings while they took turns hollering at each other, waving arms around dramatically, threatening and defending in a wild dance of debate. Finally Mr. Duong rushed back and said, "You pay twenty dollars scrip, then we go."

"I pay him twenty? Why should I pay him? He swerved into me!"

"He has no money. His bike is broke. You are an American. You have money."

The argument struck Babineaux, in his altered state, as strongly logical, so he studied the odd-looking scrip in his wallet, chose two blue and pink notes that said "10" with somebody's mother engraved on the front and a skinny Statue of Liberty on the back, Duong handed them to the soldier and the two shook hands very formally.

Within thirty minutes, they were able to pick up speed on roads less crowded, so Babineaux found a gear that seemed to work and stayed in it.

Two miles below the neck of Vung Tau peninsula, the South China Sea appeared on the left, a magnificent band of light blue under translucent skies, decorated with massive, well-defined cumuli. They drove beside a wide expanse of white sand beach that ran for miles, curving gracefully in a crescent that plowed abruptly into a steep mountain that punctuated the peninsula. Mr. Duong read Babineaux's thoughts -- that this was the most beautiful place he had ever seen -- and said with apparent pride, "Welcome to Vung Tau. My home-town!"

Duong directed him into the resort town, crowded with soldiers on leave and the merchants who served their R&R needs, through back streets to a small shop, painted tan, offering "Office Supplies" according to the English-language sign. Babineaux chained-up the yellow jeep behind the building and Duong handed him a set of keys. "This for door; this for file cabinet; this for desk drawer," he instructed, "I fix for you. I hope you like." They hauled the duffle bag and boxes of supplies into a bare-bones setting -- a desk with one manual type-writer for English, a field table with another for Vietnamese, a small book-shelf lined with three-ring binders, storage room in the rear with a cot under mosquito netting, a sink with faucet, a hole in the floor covered by a wooden lid, and an ankle-level drinking fountain Duong called a "bidet". "You want to bathe?" Mr. Duong told him, "You have Pacific Ocean."

"This is OK. This is good," Babineaux assured him. "Thank you for setting it up for me."

"Many places to eat, all around. Very friendly town. I go now, stay with my sister and brother-in-law. I be back tomorrow 9:00, OK Mr. Bahno?"

Babineaux slumped into a folding chair, dragging open desk drawers full of typing paper, reporting forms, and legal pads while Vietnamese voices came and went outside the door, and he tried to digest the strangeness of his situation. Called from rock-painting at the Replo-Depot, he'd scrubbed white latex off, changed from fa-tigues to civvies, loaded his duffle into the rear of a blue jeep but was told by an ill-tempered driver named Leffanta "put it between your knees and keep a hand on it or the gooks'll steal it." His new CO had laid this halter around his neck -- a new field station -- while doubt-ing he was up to the job, then two-and-a-half wretched hours being lectured to by a miserable lieutenant, followed by learning to drive a jeep in the moving hell of the worst traffic he'd ever seen (couldn't they find one lousy hour in 22 weeks of training at Greyhawk to give a jeep lesson?). Alone in the hollow room, he felt isolated, abandoned in an alien place.

"I'm in Vung Tau. I'm in Vung Tau, Vietnam," he repeated over and over out-loud, trying to place a handle on his environment, and eventually he began to feel another way about it all. It was freedom. For a year, he had functioned like an ant in a colony, living an in-tensely social life. Now he was suddenly free to make his own way, his own decisions, with all supervision and cohorts beyond the horizon.

"It could be worse," he muttered to himself. "I could be stuck in an office with Mad-dog Mulcahey and that miserable lieutenant." And as tempted as he was in the late afternoon heat of this long, long day to put his head on the desk-top and sleep, he instead dragged himself out the back door and locked it behind him.

The soldiers on the main street across from the beach, some in uniform, most not, all more-or-less drunk, buzzed with an intense energy born of needing too much too fast out of a three-day pass. Women, some in au dais and others in peasant dress, conical hats dangling on their backs from strings around their necks, flitted through the field of soldiers like bees bumping flower to flower. "Sex," the soldiers seemed to say; "Money," the women answered. Scattered over the strand were clusters of men in swim suits or carrying shoes with soaked pants or sprawled on towels. Babineaux chose one of the larger, more upscale restaurants he saw and found a bar-stool.

"Menu?" he asked, and the bar-tender pointed to a board on the wall at the end of the bar. "I'd like the fish and chips and a beer," he said.

"You wan' bah-me-bah, Awzee o' 'merican?" was a question Babineaux didn't understand so he played it safe with "American".

The bar-tender put a lukewarm can of Budweiser in front of him and scooted off toward the back. He sipped bitter foam off the top and turned to study the room: Knots of soldiers, men in civilian clothes who might not be military, a table of four young Asian men who were larger than the Vietnamese he had seen, girls interspersed throughout, and he recalled, "If you want to meet everybody at the party, hang out in the kitchen." Two muscular guys with buzz-cuts talked beside him in pronounced British accents. They wore matching uniforms, short-sleeved shirts darker green than the fatigues he'd worn that morning, sleeves rolled up tight, cigarettes in one hand, a half-dozen beer bottles spread out around their elbows. The bar-tender brought him a plate of deep-fried, breaded fish but had substituted fries for the chips he'd ordered. Babineaux was baffled by what his server was saying but assumed it was about scrip, which also baffled him, so he fanned out a rainbow display of weird bills and let the man count out what he wanted. This brief exchange caught the attention of his neighbors and the nearer one, a fellow red-head, said, "Oi, Yank. Non'a moi business, but you jes' paid too much for your fish."

"I'm new in town," Babineaux admitted. "Don't understand the money yet."

"Weal then, let us bid ya' welcome and stand ya' a ripper." He turned his bottle toward Babineaux to show "Tooheys" on the label.

"That's English?"

"Moind yourself, mate. We're from Melbourne." He reached out a hand and said, "Able Seaman Ely, call me Mike. This 'ere's me mate, Able Seaman Davis."

"Vic," the other man said, leaning across to shake hands.

"Mark Babineaux, office supply business," he told them, wondering what would happen if they said, "We need some file cabinets." But as it turned out -- much the worse for Babineaux in the night ahead -- they were members of a Clearance Diving Team in the Royal Australian Navy, experts both in detonating and defusing, as the situation might call for, under the water or on dry land. Spirited, vulgar, funny and virile, they could down beers with the best of the Louisiana roughnecks Babineaux had known, and proceeded over the next several hours to sell him on the virtues of Tooheys, Australian women and life Down Under. "You ought'a take your R&R in Sydney, Mark," Vic said, "Most dinkum city they is."

Drunk and exhausted, Babineaux nevertheless did his Greyhawk training proud by answering at once, "My company doesn't give me R&R. I'd have to pay my own way."

The three stood on the sand with Tooheys in hand and watched the setting sun paint the whole horizon yellow-pink then red then purple and Babineaux, with nowhere to go but a cot in a storage room, accepted their invitation to visit their base. "You won' believe i' 'less you see i'," Mike promised him. The two broad-shouldered seamen filled the cab of their dark green ute, leaving Babineaux to hold on for dear-life in the flat-bed as they bounced and swayed three miles up a steep, switch-backed road to the top of Vung Tau's southern-most mountain. They brought him into the mouth of a cave, loudly showing him off to a dozen of their mates like a prize fish.

"This 'ere's Mark...a Yank tradie and a good bloke!" Mike hollered over the din of the roiling bunch of sailors standing around, leaning on bunks and on each other in happy, drunken camaraderie. "G'day!" echoed all around.

The Clearance Diving Team quarters were indeed worth seeing: In the distance, a generator purred, powering strings of lights that ran down both sides of the deep cavern as well as three refrigerators, a stereo and RAN communications equipment. At the rear were crates and boxes, some marked "high explosives," and along the walls, rows of bunks. The men swaggered around with the noisy, rowdy invincibility of feral youth. They seemed physically comfortable in these tight quarters, jostling and shoving each other, a happy scrum of hard-drinking sailors.

Handing Babineaux a cold bottle of Tooheys and clinking it against his own, Vic said, "We work the coast with your Riverines, but mostly, righ' now, we're blowin' caves li' this one. All the 'ills around 'ere are papered with 'em and if i' come to a fight, the'd be natural forts. This 'ere big one makes a righ' base, cooler tha' a tent and cheaper tha' a hootch, so this'll be the last one we blow."

Over the five hours that followed, Babineaux lost himself in the energetic joy of the team, joining the circle, arms around necks, to learn Aussie pub songs filled with mirth and vulgarity, swaying together with the group while they sang about *Itchycoo Park* and *Sadie the Cleaning Lady*. And when the group broke up to head for their bunks, he spent an hour with their CO, an RAN captain of Irish descent, sipping Jameson and discussing the differences between U.S. and Australian military tactics that resulted in the latter having many fewer casualties per engagement. "Slow and methodical, like a chess match," the captain said, "not rushing in so they can set up an ambush against you...like your General Custer."

Babineaux congratulated himself, thinking *Half a day in town and I'm talking tactical intel with an officer in the RAN! I'm in "The Switzerland of this war"* -- but he said aloud, "Couldn't tell you about that sort of thing. I'm just a civilian."

The captain smiled, raised his Jameson in mock salute, and said, "Righ' " in a tone that said, *"Let's not take me for a fool."*

"Le's get you 'ome, Yank," Mike called from across the way, but as Babineaux shook hands and thanked the captain for the whiskey, he found that he couldn't raise himself off the crate he'd perched on. Mike had to pull him to his feet and steady him, taking the glass from his hand, guiding him down the narrow path between bunks. "S'been a long day," Babineaux muttered, in amazement at how drunk he suddenly felt.

He sat in the cab of the ute this time, trying not to be sick as Mike spun downhill through the switch-backs. Babineaux directed him where to take a left off the beach road, but that proved to be the wrong street. The next street wasn't right either nor the next and in 40 minutes, Babineaux used up all of Able Seaman Ely's patience. "Look 'ere, mate," he finally said, "Shops open in a couple 'ours, sun's up then and she'll be righ' for you. No worries."

Drunk and fatigued to semi-consciousness, embarrassed and without a better idea, Babineaux agreed and climbed out of the truck, expressing appreciation for the good time.

As the hum of the ute faded into silence, one of the signal differences between towns in Vietnam and towns back home presented itself. There were no lights here: no street lights, no porch lights, neon signs, billboards or lighted windows, points of reference any American took for granted in the middle of a town. Here night was night and this one was moonless. Babineaux stumbled a few steps through the pitch-black before stepping off an unseen curb and landing on all fours, which finished what little resolve he had left to find his office-home. He sat on the curb, arms wrapped around his knees and drifted off toward sleep with a distant sharp buzzing in his head, like bees in a swarm. The persistent bees grew angrier, more annoying, and he raised his head, searching the skies in vain for some pre-dawn glow. The singular sound moved from left to right parallel to the shore-line, a few blocks downhill, then paused, began again and grew louder. Two, and then three headlamps came up the street in his direction, small-bore motorbikes rising from the beach-road. As the area around him lit-up, he thought of hiding but saw no alley or entrance-niche nearby and, besides, this was Vung Tau, the peninsula of peace. He pulled himself to his feet nevertheless, to appear less defenseless than he felt. The bikes came to a stop, a semi-circle of blinding headlamps fanning out across the narrow street forty feet from him. Vietnamese voices, male, young, more than three, came from the moving shadows behind the wall of light. Their talk grew louder, more excited, and Babineaux tried to sober-up and grasp his options. To fight the paralysis of fear, he fantasized about clobbering one of them and grabbing the bike for a downhill run, but there were four or five of them and he'd never driven a motorcycle. So he settled for facing their way and sliding the wallet out of his pocket, behind his back, slipping the GS-11 card into his hip pocket, leaving just a billfold of money he might offer them with a "take it and go" gesture.

They were shouting at each other now over the whining of engines, and they inched forward, forming an arc ten feet away. And then they stopped -- stopped talking, stopped advancing. And Babineaux's heart stopped too with the crack of a pistol behind him. He spun to see that the sharp noise was made by a louvered door that was slammed shut violently by a woman in cotton pajamas, ancient in years and tiny in stature, with a machete in her hand.

She advanced on them with a decided swagger, barking in Vietnamese and waving the machete in a universal language that said, "Move off my street or else." They shouted back defiantly but in the end, swung their headlights around and sped off toward the beach.

"They bad cowboys," she told Babineaux, "make trouble," and she grasped his shirt-front and dragged him inside the door. "You no talk. Lie down," she ordered, pulling him onto the floor just inside the doorway. She tugged off his shoes as she would have a familiar grandson she was putting down for the night, slid them under his head, latched the door and disappeared into the dark.

Relieved, rescued, secure, and exhausted beyond all measure, he soon let go and passed out. Bright sun poured on him seconds later, it seemed, and he became aware that people were stepping over him, going in-and-out of the door, talking quietly. He sat up, massaging his forehead to fight-off the worst headache of his life. A young girl in white silk came into focus, kneeling beside him, holding out a cup of tea. He scooted out of the doorway, propped himself against the wall and took the cup, thanking her. She walked away without a word. He sipped the hot tea and pulled himself to his feet just as the tiny woman, his savior, came through the door.

"What you do in street?" she scolded him. "You make fight with cowboys?"

"I got lost...thank you for helping me," he managed.

"Where you go last night?"

He laughed and said, "I was going Hollywood last night."

"No howeewood in Vung Tau," she informed him. "Next time, you come see me, Itty Bitchy." She pulled herself up to her full height and smiled at him with blackened teeth.

10

11 October 1967

AMERICAN HERO

ES-3 class reunion, part two, conjoined on Wednesday morning when Leffanta brought in Braxton Hood. The growing sense that bilateral operations in Vietnam was indeed a tight little clique that crossed paths often was challenged when Hood was asked about Levesque and Singleton. "They got picked up on Monday," Hood said, "had orders for III Corps."

"We haven't seen them," Rosie said. "They didn't come through here."

Rosenzweig and Mulcahey put both typewriters to work and turned up Armed Forces Radio to drown out the sound of Lieutenant Aaronson's chest-thumping lecture to Hood, followed by the usual march across to the major's small office for presentation of the new replacement to his CO. Even with the lieutenant sent away, Braxton Hood could barely squeeze his large frame between the desk and the wall.

"Do you think of yourself as having courage, Mr. Hood?" Shimazu asked cordially.

"Oh hell no, sir. I been scared plenty of times," Hood said smiling, disconcerted by the blunt question.

The smile was not returned, as Shimazu's heavy eyes studied the young man's face for a lingering moment. Then he used a letter-opener to point to a map beside his desk: "I ask you that because we have a field station in Cu Chi, an area that is at the center of VC activity in III Corps, and in conversation with my immediate superior, Major Cardenas...known to you from your Greyhawk training, I believe...he suggested you would be a good choice for this assignment. It's the only field station we have that is known to be under surveillance by the enemy. They have a vital interest in protecting this area of their operations and have maintained hundreds of miles of tunnels, some within twenty miles of Saigon. For years the French tried to close-down this extensive network and now it's our turn. They are professionals at playing cat-and-mouse, moving troops and supplies into a new tunnel system, abandoning an older one, staying a jump ahead of our efforts by moving back into the older one when we attack the new one. Since the strategy coming out of MACV is to push up the official "body count" and since there is a very low ratio of enemy dead to American casualties in tunnel-warfare, there's a great disincentive for us to pour resources into the area. Yet we can't afford to let him cache troops and supplies within a few miles of Saigon.

"However our station chief in Cu Chi, Mr. Monroe, has been having remarkable success over the past months in building the kind of agent network that could turn the tide in our favor. He is a brave and intelligent man, not afraid to live in the midst of the enemy while posing an increasing threat to VC operations, without regard for his personal safety. His network of agents has tripled in size and his counterpart, a man we call CP-D for security reasons, has called Monroe the most courageous and impressive American he has ever worked with. In the seven months I've been here, I have urged Monroe to move onto the Cu Chi fire base for his own safety and to accept an aide to learn the techniques that have made him so successful, someone to inherit the Cu Chi station when he rotates home in three months. I wish our other field stations were as productive of good reporting as Cu Chi. But he has been very stubborn in resisting my advice. He tells me his success depends on freedom of movement and he does not want anyone else placed in the kind of danger he accepts for himself." Shimazu turned from the map to face Hood squarely. "In the end, however, Mr. Monroe is a staff sergeant and I am a major and I have made a decision to assign you to his office. Before I assign you to serve in Cu Chi, where a deadly enemy knows you are there and considers you a threat, I want to have your assurance that you can be effective in such a setting."

Shimazu waited quietly for Hood to consider the offer and was pleased when the young man answered with calm resolve: "Well, I don't know if I have courage or not, sir, but I've got some relations who fought in the Civil War, a grandpa who shipped out for France in 1917 and a dad who fought in Korea, so maybe it's just my turn to find out."

"Good then. Monroe is a career man who outranks you, an E-6, so he will be your immediate superior and remember that he has been adamant about not wanting anyone assigned to his field station. So don't expect a warm welcome, but be useful to him and get along with him. You're there to learn the ropes from him, and you will arrive with a direct order from me that it is my decision to assign you to him." The major extended his hand as Hood awkwardly pried himself out of the chair. "I'll have Leffanta drive you up. Good luck," Shimazu told him.

Once clear of big city traffic on the far side of Tan Son Nhut, Hood found the countryside pleasant, which was more than he could say for his driver, who refused to stop at any of the road-side mom-and-pops to eat. "They'd sooner poison an American than shoot him," he told Hood. "Saves 'em a bullet." Nor did Leffanta extend any courtesies thirty minutes later when he turned left, following a narrow dirt road to a small, mud-colored building with no markings or signs.

"This is it," he said and spun the jeep around as soon as Hood and his duffle were out.

"That man needs a good thrashing," Hood muttered as he stepped through the propped-open door, hoping Leffanta had dropped him at the right place. "Teach him some manners."

Two pretty Vietnamese girls sat at field tables, focused on their transcribing like students in a touch-typing class. They typed fast and paid no attention to him as he walked past them to approach the small office's only other inhabitant, a wiry little man in a starched white shirt and a black tie. Should he call CP-D by his coded name -- or was there another protocol, he wondered. Leaning over a stack of reports, reading one while writing on another, the man reached out his hand to receive whatever was coming his way from the back-lit shadow approaching his desk. After a moment's wait and a few sharp words in Vietnamese, he finally looked up and seemed startled by Hood's looming presence. "What you want?" he barked.

"I'm looking for Mr. Monroe," Hood said.

"He not here." The man returned to his work.

"Yessir, I can see that." Hood shifted his heavy duffle over to his left shoulder, in case he was about to need his right hand for other things. "Could you please tell me where to find him?"

"He at Cu Chi Fire Base, 25th Infantry." He kept writing without looking up, translating Vietnamese into English, Hood noticed.

"When do you expect him back?"

"Maybe tomorrow. He very busy at fire base."

"Doing what?"

The little fellow stayed right with his writing business and a long moment passed until the message to Hood was clear: *I'm done answering your questions. Go away.*

Braxton Hood thought about flipping the desk over on top of him but figured a warning shot might be owed to a Vietnamese counterpart who hadn't yet seen his temper, so he stepped forward until his thighs met the desk-top and shoved the piece of furniture back, ramming the office chair against the wall, pinning the occupant.

"Now I'm going to ask you once again, partner. Where can I find Mr. Monroe?"

He had the man's full attention now but got only the same answer, "At Cu Chi Fire Base."

"I know. You told me. Where exactly at Cu Chi Fire Base and how do I get there?"

The little man, apparently excited, shouted at him in Vietnamese but then said in English, "PSYOP Office at Cu Chi Fire Base. You walk back to main street and find a cyclo."

"What's a cyclo?"

"A motor-bike-taxi. Tell driver, Cu Chi Fire Base, 25th Infantry."

"Now that wasn't so hard, was it?" Hood stepped back, freeing the man to shove the desk off his chest. "It's been a pleasure meeting you," Hood said over his shoulder as he strode past the young ladies, who were staring doe-eyed, no longer typing.

It was a long, dusty walk back to the paved road but it gave Hood a chance to work off his anger. He considered himself a true gentleman in that distinctive Southern tradition of being by nature and upbringing courteous and polite, formal in manners and respectful of others, but in contrast to his Ivy League counterpart, he would brook only so much insolence before he would feel compelled to stomp someone's butt, as the saying went. His tradition of gentility was rooted in the knight's code of honor rather than in the refinements of the tea parlor. He waved down a cyclo and squeezed into the cushioned seat, his duffle between his knees. At the heavily fortified gate of the fire base, he paid the driver some pink and orange notes and showed his ID to MPs who directed him to the PSYOP Office.

Half an hour later and almost a mile from the gate, he solved one of his two problems. The staff sergeant he spoke with checked around the office for him, then confirmed that no one there had ever heard of anyone named Monroe or anyone who worked for a contactor called Service International Corporation. But he did offer to grab a couple of sandwiches and a soda from the mess hall where they had told Hood they didn't feed civilians. The sergeant also agreed, since he was driving to Saigon anyway, to drive him back to his company's office, four miles back down the main road.

The earth trembled and air exploded around the jeep when they passed a battery of 175 mm guns that were, the sergeant said, "Firing

H&I...Harassment and Interdiction. That's when they don't have a real target, which is most the time, so they shake the trees and hope Charlie falls out."

They were just in time when Hood directed him, half way up the narrow dirt road, to "block his way! Go nose-to-nose with him!" The PSYOP sergeant pulled astride a black Citroën driven by CP-D, the two typists in the back seat. Hood leapt out of the jeep before it stopped, yanked the driver's door open and hollered in his impressive baritone, "Get out here or I'll pull you out!" By way of demonstration, he grabbed the shoulder of the silk sport coat CP-D was wearing. He stood the man against the car like an arresting officer, tapped side-pockets and ribs to make sure he wouldn't be facing a pistol, then pulled the ignition key out of the Citroën's dashboard, retrieved his duffle bag from the jeep and told the sergeant, "Thanks for the lift. I've got it from here."

Hood kept an eye on CP-D while he walked around him, opened the trunk of the car and dropped-in his duffle bag. Then he jumped into the passenger seat, shoved the key back into the ignition and ordered, "Get in and drive me straight to Mr. Monroe. No tricks and no detours. You understand?"

Without a glance or a word, the man did as he was told but with great deliberation. He straightened his rumpled sport coat, buttoned it with formality, and with shoulders back, chin up, eyes forward, he drove the Citroën in silence back down the main highway toward Saigon, around the perimeter of Tan Son Nhut, battled heavy traffic with expertise, following a mesh of avenues into the heart of the city, then pulled up to a wide, wrought-iron gate and honked twice. Braxton Hood had no way of knowing who was in charge here. Was this disciplined performance by an experienced intelligence officer on his native turf going to wind up with Hood as a fly caught in a web? Or had his size and temper made enough of an impression to command obedience? The young women remained tensely silent in the backseat, offering no clue. But at least they had driven into the center of Saigon, not out into some rural area where armed men ruled the world.

The guard who opened the gate did carry a carbine but slung over one shoulder. The wide, two-story villa was hardly visible from the street behind a barbed-wire-topped wall and a set of tall palm trees. CP-D parked between another Citroën and a group of motor-cycles and scooters and led the way from the courtyard up a flight of tiled stairs while the two young women slipped away toward a first-story entrance. Three doors opened onto the second story landing. CP-D unlocked the center one and held it open for Hood. "Please," was the first word he had spoken since being abducted. "No, you go first. I insist." Hood told him.

The spacious room CP-D stepped into was a shocking contrast to anything Hood had seen since leaving The States. A half dozen table- and floor-lamps set aglow a beautifully decorated living room ap-pointed with polished lacquer chairs around a lush rug threaded with black, gold and red patterns. Shelves heavy with books lined the walls between paintings. Classical music softly played. Beyond this movie-set, a Caucasian man sat at one end of a dining table, white long-sleeved shirt, an attractive woman in purple ao dai over butter-yellow pants at the other end. A servant was collecting dishes from the table. CP-D crossed the room, speaking rapidly in French -- Hood caught only "Monsieur Monroe" and "americain". As Hood followed, he real-ized that this beautiful room was cold and dry -- air-conditioned.

The man stood and said in English, "Thank you, Diem. You did the right thing." He was Braxton Hood's height, six-three, but rangy, light-limbed, and his face was most striking: Close-set, pale blue eyes, hawk-nosed with dark hair banded grey around the ears. He crossed the room with grace and confidence, extended his hand and said, "I'm Frank Monroe. Can I help you?"

Aware of others in the room, Hood introduced himself by name and said only, "an SIC employee. They sent me to get my training in your office."

Monroe considered the words for a moment, holding his steady gaze and hand-shake, before saying, "Very well then. Have you eaten dinner?"

"Not really, no."

"Won't you join us then? I can offer you chicken and rice in wine sauce, but I'm afraid we've finished all the soup and salad. Do come in...."

The servant was already placing a chair at one side of the table and stood behind it, holding it for the guest. "Join us" apparently did not apply to Diem, who left after an exchange in French. As he closed the door behind him, Hood said, "Hold on. I've got to get my bag out of his car."

"Your bag will be brought to your room by the gate guard...it's already been arranged," Monroe said smoothly. "Let me introduce you to Co Bian. She is a trusted employee of SIC, very useful to our whole operation." She raised her hand to Hood, who took it gently and said, "Pleased to meet you, Miss Co Bian."

"*Enchantè, Monsieur*," she responded, while Monroe quietly corrected him.

"Co is Vietnamese for Miss. So either Miss Bian or Co Bian is the standard form. She has been helping me improve my French. *N'est pas, ma fleur?*"

The servant eased the chair under Hood, adding one more new experience to a day that was already moving from strange to surreal. While the servant placed a glass of water, a bowl of chicken and rice, chop sticks and a short-handled little spoon before him, Hood tried to get a grasp on this whole unexpected turn of events and how to respond to them. "The bravest and most successful station chief" Shimazu had was living in a luxury villa in downtown Saigon, and he, Braxton Hood, was being served over his left shoulder instead of huddling in some hootch in the boonies of Cu Chi, as he had expected to be.

"Look, I'm sorry I got off to a bad start with your counterpart today. I was ordered...told to report directly to you and I ended up all over Cu Chi, gettin' the run-around. So I lost my temper."

"Diem, you mean. Yes, he said you threatened him."

"That's right, I did. I owe him an apology. But I need to ask you about a few things, when we get some time alone." Hood nodded his head toward Co Bian, who was closely studying her folded hands.

"No apologies needed...may I call you Braxton? Call me Frank. And you may speak freely with Co Bian...or even with my chef present. Neither speaks English and both are completely trustworthy. So what do you want to know?"

Hood had given up on chop sticks and was using the small ladle to dish up his chicken-rice meal. "Well, I was sent to Cu Chi because that's where III Corps said you live and work."

"Oh yes, the villa here. Let me be completely honest with you, Braxton." He swirled whiskey around a short-stemmed wine glass, then took a deep breath of its vapors, sipped it and studied its color while he spoke. "I quickly learned in Cu Chi last year that I could either live on the fire base, where I would be inaccessible to my operatives, or I could live in one of the village centers under civilian cover and stick out like a sore thumb. Either way, VC counter-measures would neutralize my operation or endanger my life. I presented two detailed operational plans to the CO at III Corps...the one who proceeded Major Shimazu."

Hood winced at this breach of "civilian cover," drummed into him from Greyhawk to Aaronson, but Co Bian was still lost in the study of her own elegant fingers and the servant was clattering pots and pans in the kitchen.

"And I was told to forget it, to stick to the story that I was a business consultant. That was patently absurd in Cu Chi, farm villages laced through with VC activity, 300 miles of tunnels that we know of...and we haven't found most of them...and it violated the Monroe Doctrine, which states, Never get yourself killed by incompetence...not your own and certainly not someone else's. As my operation has grown in size and effectiveness, it became impossible to think of centering it anywhere but here, in the middle of a bustling city, where agents and counterparts can meet and mingle in the urban confusion and with our tentacles reaching out into Cu Chi and beyond, into the Iron Triangle and up the Saigon River. So I've arranged all this...through a friend." His arm drifted across the panorama of the lovely room.

"You, of course, were inevitable. Major Shimazu has pressed me to mentor a subordinate, if you'll pardon my referring to you as such...it's his term. Is there something wrong?"

Hood had taken a gulp of his ice-water and nearly spewed it back out. *Is Monroe having me poisoned?* flashed through his mind. "What did he put in my water?" he gasped.

"Oh....cognac, my friend. It's a French colonial thing. Cognac in water clears the pallet better than wine. Thomas!" Monroe turned toward the kitchen. "Bring Mr. Hood a brandy."

As a short wine glass like the one his host drank from was set before him -- brandy, not whiskey, as he'd thought -- he tried to process how Thomas, a servant who spoke no English, had understood the command and could be trusted to know III Corps was headed by a "major".

"...for six weeks, I've resisted their assigning anyone to assist me, for the obvious reason that, as you can see, I'm living a cover-within-a-cover. SIC Central HQ, where I worked for several months before being posted to Cu Chi, still thinks I'm living in a wretched hovel, where the VC would have had me shot months ago to neutralize my operation. Or I'd be huddled down on the fire base, where my agents couldn't reach me with timely information and where the out-going fire would have jarred my nerves to pieces, even if the in-coming mortar and rockets didn't do worse. Instead, Braxton, I receive accolades for my excellent work. My network is saving American and Vietnamese lives, and I am living a very comfortable life, as you can see."

He set his brandy glass down and crossed his arms, leaning on his elbows, speaking confidentially and locking Hood's attention with the blue-eyed stare of a malamute. "Now, you have a choice to make, Braxton. You can go running back to Shimazu and screw everything up for me and for this whole successful operation...set the astounding stupidity of the military mind loose to give me twenty reasons why I can't do what I'm doing. And if you do, you'll realize a month or two from now, when you understand things better, that it was the biggest mistake you've ever made. Or you can settle in as my partner here. You will have a comfortable bed, your own hot-water shower, a private balcony, and Thomas will cook for you. You will learn everything I know, as Major Shimazu sent you to do, so you'll be following your orders. And ignoring our differences in age and rank, I will treat you as my partner and my equal in every way, bringing you along not just in bilateral operations but in the way of the world." He sat back with a smile of satisfaction, as though his argument had convinced even himself. "I'll even have Miss Bian teach you French."

Bian stood up as soon as Monroe did. He slipped an arm around her waist and she leaned into him as they crossed the living room toward their bedroom door. "Sleep on it, Braxton, and we'll talk at breakfast," Monroe called back to him. "Good night."

Thomas busied himself clearing the kitchen for half an hour while Hood sipped the strong brandy, swirling and sniffing it as he'd seen Frank Monroe do. Quick at calculation, he didn't need long to reckon that his choice was no choice at all. "Heads" was Shimazu assigned him to serve under Monroe and learn from him how to emulate the excellent intelligence produced by his field station. On the flip-side was "heads" again, live in a posh villa in Central Saigon instead of a fire base where constant H&I fire would be almost as terrifying as in-coming rockets. Besides, the cognac...the brandy... French. This older, wiser Monroe might be one hell of a teacher.

Furthermore, what was not to like when Thomas led him into a big bedroom, ceiling fan billowing the mosquito netting over a double bed, tiled bathroom with an enormous shower, shelves loaded with fresh linens, door leading onto a balcony with two chairs and a small table, perfect for morning coffee or a night-cap, his duffle bag across the foot of the bed?

When Thomas had closed the door behind him, he said aloud, "I guess I'll just have to sleep on it, Frank."

11

15 October 1967

A SAFARI IN EDEN

Morning sun was turning the bedroom into a bake-oven despite louvered shutters, but it was cigarette smoke that finally brought Mulcahey and Rosenzweig out from under their mosquito nets. Belmont slouched in a folding chair, using a footlocker as a hassock, blowing clouds toward the ceiling fan, quietly reading a tattered pocketbook entitled *At Ease.* "It's after nine," he said when they stirred, "you're missing your day off."

"There's no Dinner tonight?" Mulcahey asked hopefully.

"Oh yeah, there's a Dinner. There's always a Dinner. But otherwise, Sunday is R&R day, Rest and Recuperation for exhausted fighting men. We don't even have to go in today because most of the counterparts are Roman Catholic, like the rest of the government of the Republic... considered more trustworthy than Buddhists, Animists and so forth. They take the day off, so all we have to do on the Sabbath is show up at 1900 hours, bright-eyed and bushy-tailed, for light fare leftovers from Saturday, and a briefing from Shimazu on the week ahead. So pull on your duds and bring all your money. The rest of today is party-time, and I'll show you how it's done."

They piled into the blue jeep and set out through traffic that was a fraction of its week-day volume. Everything seemed quieter, cleaner, and the sun seemed less punishing. Belmont pulled up at a road-side bakery and they paid the asking price for croissants and a pot of strong tea, served at a long table shared by the locals. Little boys came from the street to beg, but the shop-owner ran them off, shouting "Di di mau," which Belmont said was a very useful phrase. By the time they left, the breeze through the open jeep felt wonderful on their sweaty shirts. They were disappointed when Sergeant Swanson wasn't on-duty at the Tan Son Nhut gate and the MP there accepted their ID cards without comment. Belmont drove to the PX "for necessary equipment," he said.

At the camera counter, he advised them on the selection of Nikon 35mm SLRs with carrying cases, a supply of Kodachrome 400-speed film and photo notebooks. While he tutored them in the fundamentals of shutter speed and focus, he also justified the expense: "If you race around all week trying to meet your deadlines and duties, putting up with Aaronson and trying to keep Shimazu happy, you're going to end-up like Bitter Louie. Sundays, Leffanta lies in a sweaty rack with a stack of mysteries, Mickey Spillane at best, then he goes across to the compound cafe and gets drunk and ready for six more days of bitching about Vietnam when the truth is, he's never been to Vietnam. He drifts through an exotic Asian country and all he ever sees is an office and an Army compound. And don't try to talk to him...it's a waste of breath. So look, photograph everything you see, familiar and strange alike, then learn to see what you've photographed. Log it all in your notebook. And if you're lucky, like I'm about to be, you'll get out of this bizarre mad-house of a city and get to see the heart of the country."

Next they picked up aviator-style Ray-Bans, combination locks, towels and swim trunks. ("You've got to be kidding," Mulcahey challenged, remembering the polluted, boat-choked harbor near the market. "Just stay with the program," Belmont commanded.) And finally, at the pharmacy counter, Belmont sprung for condoms, a twelve-pack shared three ways. Belmont's students emerged from the PX grinning like kids at a county fair, loaded down with prizes, eager and a little overwhelmed, and Belmont was playing it coy and enjoying himself immensely.

He drove them into the bowels of the massive airbase, threading between buildings of every size for more than a mile before pulling into a parking slot, chaining up the steering wheel and leading them into a single-story complex signed as "Officers Gymnasium".   Inside the door, they checked-in with a staff sergeant, the polar opposite of the crisp MPs at the main gate, who chewed a donut while glancing at their IDs. Belmont led the way into a locker-room and said, "Pick a locker for your stuff and try on your new trunks."

They were soon under hot showers, Belmont's authoritative voice echoing off the tile walls. "You've been here two weeks now, right? So you've got some idea of how this works. You bust your tail for six days straight, six a.m. until the dishes are dried and stacked at the villa, and you drive back to the compound, brush your teeth, say your prayers, and it's coming up on midnight by the time you hit the rack, your basic 18-hour work-day. By Sunday, you're a mess. But goddam-mit, you get one day all to yourself and if you work it right, it can be a pretty good damn day. Start it like this, if you want. Sleep late, catch a croissant at the bakery, buy yourself something at the PX, come here for a work-out. There's a weight room, basketball court, top it off with a full-body massage and a swim like a senator in ancient Rome. They've got two million massage parlors out on the economy and every one of them is a whorehouse with ladies who are too old or too ugly to compete on the open market, so they throw-in a massage. MACV's answer to all that is this place. If you want a massage, that's what you'll get here, and it's professional and free-of-charge. No dirt floors or creaky ceiling fans that might fall on you and cut off some vital pieces. Before I found this place, I ended up with a masseuse who was pregnant who tried to give me a hand-job under a wobbly ceiling fan that was about to come down and all I got out of it was nightmares for a week. I came home and moved my bed out from under the fan."

They all opted for the massage, which began by standing under a scalding needle-shower -- a sharp contrast to the dribbling, lukewarm showers at the compound -- then onto tables behind curtains where

Vietnamese girls in white silk jackets who spoke excellent English proved they were well-trained physical therapists. Mad-dog embarrassed himself by hooting, groaning and laughing maniacally until the masseuse agreed not to touch his feet, his butt or his ribs.

Sixty minutes later, their muscles pounded, kneaded and stretched to the limit of human endurance, they stood under the showers one last time then stumbled on legs almost too rubbery to bear their weight through a side-door and collapsed on the deck of an Olympic-sized pool. They stretched-out under the tropical sun, catching rays with towels over their heads until, baked on both sides, they slipped into the tepid water without standing up, like seals. Mad-dog worked himself up to swimming a few laps, trying to start a race with two junior-officer types, while the other two lolled around the tiled edge under a flawless blue skies.

By noon, Belmont was chaining up the jeep outside the Officers Club. They stuffed wet trunks rolled in towels under the seats and carried the camera cases into the lobby. Their GS-11 ID cards got them into the main dining area, where Belmont pointed to a row of pin-ball machines in heavy use. "Most of the guys standing around over there are pilots, Hueys, Cobras, fighter jets. They're a strange bunch. This morning, they were landing troops in hot Drop Zones, taking wounded out under fire, strafing and bombing, then they come here, get loaded and play pin-ball for hours with fanatic dedication. The afternoon shift comes in about supper-time and you can come here at breakfast and find the night-fliers tilting those machines, a high-ball glass in one hand. I come in here whenever I get bored, just to feed on the testosterone in the air."

They enjoyed a leisurely lunch, not up to Shimazu standards but good, with two Bloody Marys each.

"Note the crowd," Belmont challenged. "Who's missing?"

"Senior officers," Rosie observed.

"Right. All junior-to-middle grade. I'd love to know where the generals eat."

"And women."

"Right again. There are women on the base who hold rank, but you never see them here."

"Maybe the testosterone in the air scares 'em off, " Mulcahey guessed. And keenly aware of the prophylactics in his pocket, he asked, "Where do we go next?"

A half hour of heavy traffic later they were in the center of town. Belmont chained the jeep on Tu Do Street and they set off hunting for photo shots between bar-stops. At first it was all girls in colorful, flowing ao dais and girls in peasant black-and-white, smiling under conical hats, and girls in mini-skirts and high heels standing in tavern doorways and girls on scooters or riding in motor-cabs, but as they became more agile at adjusting the focus and finding the best shutter-speed, targets broadened to include street urchins at play in the spray from a fire hydrant, a flower merchant, ARVN soldiers holding hands in friendship and, finally, an exhausted pedi-cab driver asleep in his passenger-seat. They faithfully entered the shots into their notebooks, sometimes taking two or three of the same subject with varying exposures.

The photo expedition continued onto the veranda of the Continental Hotel for a glass of wine amidst French ex-patriots, adventure tourists and American soldiers, then to the rooftop of the Caravelle, the tallest building in Saigon, for Michelob in fine glasses amidst journalists, diplomats and American soldiers, then to the rooftop of the Rex Hotel for Miller High Life in ordinary beer glasses amidst civilian contractors (real ones, presumably, not like they pretended to be) and (other) American soldiers. In rapid succession, they dropped into three more humble taverns where bar-girls batted mascara-laden eyes and asked, placing a gentle hand on an arm or shoulder, if they would be kind enough to spring for a Saigon tea. Mad-dog felt he was getting close to the point where the Trojans in his pocket may be called upon, but he followed Belmont's lead in turning them all down. The only new experience for him, it turned out, was trying out the flash attachment on his Nikon as he took Rosie's picture with a bar-girl on each arm.

As they returned to the jeep under threatening skies, Mulcahey insisted on sparking conversations with a one-legged beggar, a group of young ARVN paratroopers, their pants stuffed inside their combat boots, and two well-dressed Vietnamese businessmen -- none of whom spoke one word of English -- then with a pair of American MPs who did -- at which point Rosie said, "You take one elbow; I'll get the other. You may have noticed, he really can't hold his booze worth a damn." They crammed Mad-dog into the rear of the jeep where, from under the canvas, he tried to get pictures of sights Belmont drove them past: The Soldier's Monument and the French Opera House, the U.S. Embassy and the President's Palace, the Cathedral of Notre Dame and more, until his film was all used up.

By 5:00, the cameras were stored away in footlockers and Mulcahey was much improved by three cups of coffee at the compound cafe, where Bitter Louis lay sleeping across his folded arms. "It's time for graduation," Belmont announced as they drove toward Tan Son Nhut. "And I'll be your commencement speaker. Gentlemen, you have mastered all the knowledge and skills you will need to keep III Corps rolling smoothly along to Major Shimazu's satisfaction and you know what to do on Sundays to keep from going bonkers."

"THIS HAS BEEN THE GREATEST DAY OF MY LIFE!" Mad-dog announced to the world from the back seat.

"Don't interrupt!" Rosie commanded.

"After today, I am no longer your tutor. We are henceforth colleagues and in fact, I look forward to calling upon you for aid and support as I set off on my adventure in Khap Noi to test my mettle on the field of honor, as patriots have done since the dawn of time."

"YOU'RE THE GREATEST MAN I'VE EVER MET !"

"Shut the fuck up!"

"Your first visit to shantytown will celebrate and mark this occasion memorably, I hope. There are any number of establishments closer to the compound where an array of fine girls will bring you a Budweiser and chat with you until you choose one that you favor. But those places you can navigate on your own. Shantytown, however, has rules: Never go alone, stay out of there at night, keep an eye on your watch and wallet at all times and stay alert. But be prepared for a great experience. When you get back home, you won't be as warmly received by your family as you are in shantytown, where you are a gold mine and a godsend to 10,000 desperate refugees. A few of them will feed their families tonight because you graced them with your divine presence. So bargain your girl or her mama-san down to $5, as I taught you in the market, and when you kiss her goodbye, give her $10 Hell! Give her $20! It's only money to you...it's bread on the table and shanty-rent for her."

Belmont pulled off the road three blocks short of the Tan Son Nhut gate and before he could lock-up the jeep, swarms of children emerged from the make-shift shacks beside the road, reaching for their hands and squawking like a flock of parakeets. They were pulled by their fingers and arms and pushed from behind, herded into the warren of improvised huts that stretched out, it appeared, for miles before them.

"Stay within fifty yards of the jeep and if I don't see you back there in twenty minutes, I'll pay this mob to lead me to you," Belmont hollered over the mayhem. "Now go do as God has bid thee and love your neighbor as yourself."

Mad-dog was grinning like a maniac as a half-dozen small boys dragged him down a narrow pathway between shacks, yelling, "You come see my sistah ! She numbah-one beau-ful."

With the others out of sight, Rosie turned himself forcefully back toward the jeep against the waist-high human tide of shouting children. Objections to this whole scenario had been filling his mind. He had not gone all-the-way with either of his important girlfriends at Vanderbilt nor with the pretty Evangelical who was the only female in his pre-law class. He didn't want his first time with a woman to be like this, in this place, this mud-floor flesh market conducted by pre-teen pimps. This was Belmont's medium, adventure and risk-taking, and Mad-dog was the walking definition of unfiltered impulsiveness. But this was not for him. The dozen shouting salesmen-from-hell, few of whom came much above his belt-line, were determined, however, to land this big fish. They had gone to bed hungry too often to let him walk away. So that Rosie was losing the physical fight and was forced to hold his wallet high over his head and yell at them, "I give you dollah, you take me jeep...OK?" and he began putting paper scrip notes into grasping hands, 25-cent note here, 50-cent note there, then one dollar notes, repeating, ""Now *you* take me jeep! Now *you* take me jeep!! Here, *you* take me Jeep!!" Unfortunately but predictably, his tactic released some invisible pheromone and a flood-tide of frenzied beggars, not all of them children, descended on him from every direction. Feeling the panic of a great caterpillar under siege by an army of ants, he twisted his body left and right, trying to wrench his clothing free of small, grasping hands until in his struggle, he slammed smack into a good-sized adult. In his blind panic, he thought it was Mulcahey coming to his aid, Mulcahey in a simple straw hat with a bright blue silk ribbon, grabbing him by his shirt-front and pulling him through the mob and into the doorway of a shanty. He was shoved inside and the door was pushed shut against the rabble. Then she turned toward him the most strikingly exotic face he had ever seen, large, wide-set almond eyes above high cheeks, flawless olive skin, an abundance of softly-flowing dark-brown hair pouring over the shoulders of her white au dai. She was taller than any other native person he had seen -- she seemed Vietnamese but not Vietnamese. She stared into his face calmly, seriously, for a long moment that left an eidetic image burned permanently into his memory.

"If you give away money like that, they will eat you for lunch. What were you thinking?" she said in barely accented English.

He tried to find an answer but was thoroughly rattled by his narrow escape and completely awed by her appearance, her fluent English, the deliberate, confident way she had intervened and taken charge of him. "I don't know," he finally managed. "I wanted to go home."

She found his feeble response amusing and added a great, mirthful smile to her other qualities. "Well, you can stay here for awhile and they will go away out there. Then you can go home." She lifted the straw-weave hat, sending mounds of luxuriant brown hair cascading over her shoulders and breasts. Her ao dai floated around her as she crossed over to hang her hat on the rusted iron bedpost of the only piece of furniture in the shed. She placed herself on the edge of the bed and patted the mattress beside her. "Come sit down," she told him. "I won't bite you."

Rosie started across the room, trying to be graceful but feeling like the Tin Man from Oz. He perched a good two feet down-bed from her.

"I would offer you something but I don't have anything." She waved an open palm at the room, ten-by-ten of packed earth with only this ancient, creaking bed and a fifty-gallon drum for catching rainwater through a hole in the corrugated metal roof. There was nothing else. "This is not my house," she said, "It belong to...belongs to mama-san," she corrected herself. A slant of the setting sun came through the loose boards of the wall and fell across her face as she turned his way, and she raised her hand in a graceful gesture to shield her eyes.

Rosie was trying to focus on her conversation...on anything at all...trying to convince himself that this wasn't some rabbit-hole he had been shoved down, less than a minute ago, some weird illusion from being hit on the head or something. "Where is your house?" he asked, vaguely aware he sounded like an idiot.

"I have an apartment...I *had* an apartment near Cholon. You know Cholon, the Chinese part of Saigon?"

"No, sorry. I've only been in Saigon for a few days."

She seemed puzzled then guessed, "So you got lost and you were paying money to the children to find your house?"

Rosie laughed, "No...no, not exactly. A friend drove me over here to...." He didn't know how to end it.

"To find a girl."

"Well, OK, yes."

"Did you find one?"

"No...I changed my mind."

"But you did find one...you found me!"

"Yes, but I think you were the one who found me. So thank you for helping me. I felt like I was getting in trouble out there when you came."

"You *were* in trouble out there."

"I was, yes, I was. So thank you for helping me," he repeated and then ran out of anything else to say.

They sat silent for a long moment until she said, "If you want to make love to me you can...you could."

"I...I don't feel ready yet...for that."

He twisted himself toward her and looked full-on into her face, her folds of chestnut hair caressing the white au dai, and it occurred to him that he could be making a colossal mistake here, one that might haunt him into old age. He struggled to find some sort of substantial reason why he should or should not, but he got nothing for it but confusion. "So your apartment near Cholon," he tossed into the void, "you don't live there anymore?"

"I show you." She stood, turned, and knelt at his feet, placing a hand on his knee for balance. Rosie flinched defensively and she looked up at him and laughed. From under the bed, she slid a cardboard box, lifted the flaps and pulled out a stack of folded clothes, colorful silks and cottons, then laid the box beside these in the center of the mattress. She lifted out a large manila envelope and very deliberately sat snugly up next to him, laying herself into his body, knee to hip to ribs, as a familiar girlfriend would do. She pulled photographs out of the envelope and set them on her lap. "This is my house," she said, handing him a 4x6 glossy, "...was my house." The white interior of a modern apartment in the picture was flooded by light, art pieces adorned the wall above a red couch with matching black lacquer endtables. In the center of the sofa, elbows resting on his knees, hands interlaced, sat a man, a Caucasian in a blue shirt and dark blue slacks that matched a uniform jacket that rested across his lap. "This my friend, Captain Blake, who taught me English," she said.

She looked into Rosie's face, trying to read his expression and perhaps his thoughts. "We are friends for two years before he have to go home, back to Auzona."

Rosie stared blankly at the picture, hardly seeing it but acutely aware of the warmth and pressure against his thigh, his hip and ribs, and that he was being asked a not-yet-spoken question for which he had no answer. "You must be a good student," was how he styled his evasion. "Your English is excellent."

"This is me on Captain Blake's scooter. But I don't drive it. Only he can drive it."

"And this is me in Phoc Tho, where my mother and brother live."

"This is my brother Huy. He is a brave soldier in ARVN, in artillery."

The last photo she chose was a tattered, cracked black-and-white of a soldier, smiling from under his service cap, his arm draped over the shoulder of a pretty, young Vietnamese girl half his size. "This only pitchah I had of my father, together with my mother. He was French soldier, very brave. He is why I have light hair and am so taller as other girls. But he die fighting Viet Minh in war and they take him home to bury. So sad my mother cannot visit his grave...."

"Rosenzweig, you decent?" Belmont pounding on the shaky door startled them both and they stared wide-eyed at each other.

"Yeah, I'm here."

"Time to go, man. We've got to get what's left of Mulcahey back and hose him down before The Dinner."

"My friends," he said awkwardly as she pulled out from under an arm he didn't remember putting around her. "We need to...."

"You want to go home, I know," she said and smiled at it.

"Maybe I can come back sometime...to see you."

"Sure...OK. That would be OK."

He crossed to the door, lifted the latch and pulled it open, then turned to see her standing by the bed in her long, white ao dai, photos in one hand, envelope in the other, an expression of sadness, he thought but wasn't sure. He raised one hand in a parting gesture then slid the door shut. The ocean of urchins milled around but were fewer and quieter, escorting their guests off the premises, hoping for that rare tip they might get for "watch jeep".

"They swiped my Timex and my belt in there," Mad-dog was muttering, holding his chinos up with one hand.

"I told you to watch your stuff, didn't I?" Belmont said. "You still have your wallet and your GS-11 card?"

"Yeah, I got it."

"So how was your girl? She worth a Timex?"

The maniac's leer returned to Mad-dog's face. "Young and pretty."

"And you used a rubber?"

"I'm not an idiot," he protested, perhaps too much.

To Rosie, "How did it go with you?"

"I don't know. OK, I guess."

"She old and ugly or what?"

Rosie stopped beside the jeep. Mad-dog stuffed himself into the rear and Belmont unlocked the wheel and jumped in.

"That girl, she...." Rosie leaned heavily against the canvas top of the jeep and surprised himself and both of them by fighting back tears. "Everything she has in the world is in a little cardboard box under her bed...everything. And she wanted to show it all to me...her pictures...her whole life, to a total stranger."

Belmont started the jeep and Rosie dropped himself into the passenger seat. He used the sleeves of his short-sleeved shirt to wipe tears off his cheeks and muttered, "It isn't even her bed." He shook his head like a dog, sat up straight, sighed and told them, "OK...I'm OK now."

Belmont said, "Welcome to Vietnam, Rosenzweig. In fact, welcome to the world. I've met the same girl in Mexico, in Peru, in Venezuela." He switched off the jeep engine and they sat a minute without talking.

"Go ahead," Belmont said quietly. "Go back and set her up or you'll never shake it. It'll stick in your craw."

"How? What can I do about the world?"

"You can do what you can do. Give her forty bucks in scrip and tell her to find a place for you. Tell her you'll meet her right here at noon next Sunday."

"What if she takes the money and runs?"

"What if you change your mind and don't show up?"

Rosie stared straight ahead, down the busy street, as though looking for something to come along. He told Belmont, "Thanks to you, I only have 20 in scrip left." Belmont dug out his wallet and stuffed two 10 dollar scrip notes into Rosie's breast pocket. "I'll be right back," he shouted over his shoulder.

"See if she can get my watch back," Mulcahey called after him.

She opened the door the moment he tapped on it, as though she'd been waiting for him just inside. It was obvious to him that she'd been crying.

"OK, listen. Can you find a place for us, an apartment like you had in Cholon?" He held the blue and purple scrip notes out to her.

She grabbed the bills eagerly and held them against her chest. "I knew you are a good man. I know when you say you want to go home." Tears rolled from her beautiful, wide-set eyes. "You same-like me."

"I will come here next Sunday at noon...at 12:00, OK? Right to this same place. And you will find a place for us, OK?"

"Yes...yes. Sunday at 12:00."

"I've got to go," he said, but he lingered, gazing at this most exotic and yet familiar person that had come into his life and, somehow, he into hers, in a half-hour's time, and the word "fate" went through his mind. He was doing the right thing -- the only thing he could -- and he never felt more alive. She lifted up against him and kissed his cheek, leaving his face wet with her tears.

"OK, then, Sunday," he said.

He'd made ten quick steps down the narrow lane toward the jeep before turning around to run back. He shoved the door open without knocking and shouted, "What's your name?"

She turned from her box on the bed toward him and laughed. "Co Sang," she said.

"Hi! I'm Rosie." She looked puzzled, so he said, "Rosie, like the flower."

"Co Sang," he announced back at the jeep. "Her name is Co Sang and she's half-French, really tall, maybe five-eight, with amazing hair."

"Quite a bargain for 40 bucks," Belmont said and he drove the jeep in a U-turn through heavy traffic. Then he laughed merrily and said, "Good for you, Rosie ! We're proud of you, aren't we, Mulcahey?"

Mad-dog hollered again for all the world to hear, "THIS HAS BEEN THE GREATEST DAY OF MY LIFE!" He reached around the driver's seat to grasp Belmont's big shoulders and shook him with all his strength. The jeep lurched from left to right and Belmont yelled, "KNOCK IT OFF, MULCAHEY, YOU'LL GET US KILLED!"

Mad-dog let go but continued yelling, "AND YOU ARE THE GREATEST MAN ON THE FACE OF THE EARTH, ALMIGHTY BELMONT, KING OF SAIGON!"

When they pulled into the compound to get cleaned-up for The Dinner, Rosie walked around the front of the jeep and offered his hand to Belmont. "Thank you, man." He shook his hand firmly. "This has been the greatest day of my life too."

"I had a good time too, Rosie," Belmont smiled. "Good luck with your girl."

12

1 November 1967

PETIT BUDDHA

"Field Station C in Khap Noi is of very great concern," Shimazu was saying but Belmont, slumped down in a folding chair in a wrinkled and filthy shirt, didn't strike the major as his answer to the Khap Noi problem. "The enemy is very active across the river in IV Corps, and Dodd was able to gather good intel from his bilateral network as well as from Navy SEALs who raid up and down the An Long. Riverine patrol boats bring many prisoners into Khap Noi base. But this flow of information has dried up since August and Dodd's counterpart blames him entirely. CP-C tells his superiors Dodd stopped coordinating with the SEALs, no longer assigns tasks for field agents and now rarely comes into the office. I am forced to believe these reports because nothing is coming from a station that once was productive and because Dodd has not attended the last two budget meetings, claiming to be ill. CP-C is a highly decorated infantry officer who lost a leg, so while counterparts run the gamut, CP-C is the best, a hero, a true patriot. He is, I need not tell you, furious with Mr. Dodd."

Belmont did not appear to be taking the briefing well. His demeanor was slipping from passive to sleepy and Shimazu wondered whether he wasn't making a mistake by sending him. Perhaps being taken under fire was his only agenda, to "prove himself on the field of honor," his mantra. This would have been the point, during the major's days in Combat Arms, when Shimazu would have snapped the corporal to attention, gotten two inches from his face and dressed him down. But alas, those days were over, so he said in a grave tone, "Mr. Belmont, I need you to revitalize the Khap Noi operation...is that clear? If you cannot, I will bring you right back here as Lieutenant Aaronson's personal aide."

It was gratifying to see Belmont's eyes widen as he pulled himself up straight, stammering, "Oh! Nosir, yessir, that won't be necessary! I understand...revitalize the field station, yessir !"

"Very well," Shimazu told him, "please remember that when you get out there. Now have one of the boys take you out to SIC Central. They will trade-out your .38 revolver for a .45 and a carbine and issue a jeep for your use. Shimazu arose and extended his hand with the slightest hint of a smile. "Good luck, Belmont," he said. "Take care of yourself and come back for The Dinner anytime."

Belmont was amused and a little moved by this unexpected display of warmth from a man who had shown him only polite formality until now. He returned the handshake firmly and said, "It's been a pleasure to serve on your staff, sir."

Mad-dog Mulcahey behind the wheel of the blue jeep was a spectacle to shatter anyone's nerves, even a risk-seeker's like Belmont. Speeding past bicycles, motorcycles and trucks, weaving through them like a slalom skier, would have been scary enough if he'd been paying attention, but he was emitting a steady stream of tour-guide prattle, pointing left and right at every passing object. "You see that? That guy's selling *octopus*, man! [LURCH] Hot girls with parasols, three o'clock! [LUNGE] Holy cow! That movie house is showing *The Green Berets*! *Whoa!* [divingbetweentwo-and-a-half-tontrucks] Almost missed our turn!"

"Pull over, Mulcahey, you-jackass!" Belmont screamed. "I'm driving!"

"Cool it, man! I've got it. We're good," Mad-dog assured him while tailgating a massive truck hauling a bulldozer chained to the bed, looming over the hood of the blue jeep.

"You've got to see the Old Man." The same clerk that was always behind the counter at SIC Central, a spec-5 wearing "Hofstetter" over his breast pocket, raised his thumb over his shoulder toward Warrant Officer Greeley's desk.

"Day of reckoning, eh?" Mulcahey said cheerfully, "I'll just wait here." He pulled a paperback of *Walden Pond* out and dropped onto a folding chair.

Greeley was bent over typed pages, so Belmont said very quietly, "Specialist told me you wanted to see me, sir?"

Greeley raised his large, bald head, turned bloodshot eyes up to Belmont and said, "Corporal, civilian-status, headed for Khap Noi, right?"

"Yessir."

Greeley pulled a manila folder out of a rack and laid carbon-triplicate receipts on the desk. "Sign for an M1911 caliber .45 sidearm here, for an M1 carbine here, for a non-regulation Ford M151 here, two boxes of ammunition here. I keep the white copy, quartermaster gets the pink copy when he issues the equipment, you keep the yellow copy somewhere safe because its proof of official issue and because it identifies you as a corporal in the United States Army, so when the VC pull this paper out of your civilian pants pocket, they are authorized by the Geneva Accords to shoot you against the nearest tree." Greeley smiled a jolly smile.

After Belmont had signed everything where indicated, the warrant officer took all the forms in his hands and pressed them against his chest. "Now...I have a personal favor to ask before you get even one little thing. Specialist!"

Spec-5 Hofstetter came from the counter and said, "Sir".

"Corporal Belmont here has clearance and a need to know, so you are authorized to tell him. As of today, how many personnel are assigned to SIC Bilateral Operations in the Republic of Vietnam."

"As of today, 136 personnel of all ranks."

"Very good, specialist. And how many receive their pay in MPC through this command?"

"As of today, 135, sir."

"How do you account for this discrepancy, specialist?"

"Staff Sergeant E-6 Francis P. Monroe, assigned to III Corps, does not receive his pay voucher through this command."

"Then how is Sergeant Francis P. Monroe paid?"

"We don't know, sir."

"Thank you, specialist. That will be all." Greeley had held his gaze steady on Belmont's face throughout this exchange. He again broke into his jolly smile. "How would YOU explain this discrepancy, corporal?"

Belmont shrugged his shoulders and raised his eyebrows.

"Your commanding officer, Major Shimazu, has no explanation either...tells us that Sergeant Monroe is performing well and has presented no problems. And yet..." Greeley pulled another manila folder from the rack on his desk, "...yet Sergeant Monroe's service folder is *empty*. It holds just one piece of paper, assigning him to III Corps, authorized in March, 1967 by our then-CO, Colonel Rogers, shortly before his return to The States. So where is the rest of Sergeant Monroe's records? Orders assigning him here to SIC? His training and promotion records? His evaluation reports and health records? Why am I holding an empty folder that should be five inches thick? And where in the hell is he collecting his pay?" But Greeley could see from his blank expression that the attention of Corporal Belmont had drifted off and that these questions, which had become his growing obsession, were not going to be resolved by this III Corps staffer. So he tore the white copy from all four carbon-packs and threw them at the corporal, who sauntered away in a very un-military gait.

From the doorway of their quarters, Singleton called to Rene Levesque, "Hey! I see Mad-dog at the command building." But he had time to run only a few paces in that direction before the blue jeep spun-out, throwing a shower of gravel so that he had to turn his back in self-defense. The jeep flew through the gate, dove into heavy traffic and disappeared.

Weeks of plotting his escape, making himself worse-than-useless in the office and hounding the major for a field assignment, then a month of holding his breath while he trained his replacements to take over III Corps and a morning of insufferable blather from Shimazu and from Aaronson and from Greeley -- the whole stinking pile of headquarters horse-shit was now behind him and Belmont was having, at last, an exhilarating, defining day. This was the kind of day he'd signed up for in the recruiter's office when he enlisted. He had argued with the quartermaster for something better than the lime-green jeep with the cracked windshield, but the clerk shoved the receipt at him and said, "Rather walk?" With a loaded carbine wedged between the seats, a heavy .45 tucked into his belt, pointed at his groin ("Don't chamber no rounds 'less yer ready to put a hole in somebody," the clerk had said) and all his earthly belongings in a duffle bag in the rear, he was sailing happily down the highway toward the Mekong Delta through countryside that reminded him of places in Latin America where he got his kicks in his college years. All those youthful adventures seemed mere preparation for this greatest one ever! He was an armed combatant in a war zone but under no one's direct command. He could engage the enemy if he called on himself to do so, but he could not be ordered into mortal danger by some incompetent slob who would get him killed. The Best of All Worlds! He had two bottles of rice wine, three cartons of cig's, beloved dog-eared copies of *The Iliad, The Red Badge of Courage*, and *A Farewell to Arms* packed away in his duffle and, best of all, the prospect of eating whenever he wanted without having to amuse a sour-puss Leffanta, a taciturn Shimazu and a West-Pointer who needed to have his face shoved-in -- *Man!*

Belmont tipped his head back and sent a long series of rodeo yelps into the blue Asian sky.

"You remember me, Mr. Huu?" Belmont asked the translator for Field Station C, who was smoking a cigarette in the doorway of the concrete-block hootch on the Khap Noi Military Compound. "Belmont from III Corps."

The quick-moving young man reached out his hand. "We knew you were coming, but we did not know when," he said. "Let me help you with your things."

Since Belmont already carried the carbine and his duffle outweighed Mr. Huu, the offer to help served merely as a gesture of welcome. The translator led a cursory tour: Co Cam, a typist who was reading a colorful magazine (with no paperwork anywhere on her table), the field desk that Belmont would be using (as barren as the one assigned to Jerry Dodd), and a spare back room with a bed, plywood wardrobe, and footlocker for Belmont to secure his carbine, ammo and other gear. "We are very happy you are here to work with us," Huu said.

With the carbine, rice wine, his camera and cigarettes locked up, Belmont dropped his duffle on the bed and asked, "Where's Dodd?"

"I come with you, Mr. Belmont. We find him!" Huu said as though it were an adventure.

Belmont crept the jeep through the compound, crowded with troops in jungle fatigues who moved with energy and purpose. *Warriors*, he thought, and he felt a new surge of excitement. Huu directed him along the perimeter road just inside the fence to a recreation field: A spirited game of flag-football across the way was fully manned, eleven to a team. In the near corner, a concrete slab was large enough for two full-length basketball courts, side-by-side. Huu leapt from the jeep and ran toward the courts, talked with a group of men and ran back. "Not here now. Maybe went to river."

Outside the heavily fortified gate, Belmont pulled the jeep over and slid the magazine of ammunition into the grip of his .45, which the MP had ordered him to remove when he arrived.

"All weapons will remain cleared inside the compound," he'd been told, "unless we're overrun."

Huu pointed the way through a village of thatched houses where children pleading for a hand-out were barked away, both men telling them "di di mau". They drove through a thicket of trees, down a dirt trail to the edge of a broad, chocolate-brown river that reminded

Belmont of the Orinoco, as it looked and smelled when he had been in Ciudad Bolivar. The surface of the slow-moving water was almost as crowded as the Saigon harbor, small boats threading through medium-sized and larger craft. A shell edged into the shoreline and Belmont counted 23 men, women and children wedged tightly aboard the narrow boat. A young man in the stern skillfully guided the craft using a long pipe, threaded through an oarlock, with a lawn-mower engine on the top end and a jury-rigged propeller attached to the bottom end.

"What if that thing tips over?" Belmont asked.

"Everybody swim since they born," Huu said. Then he exchanged words with some boatmen near shore who pointed further up-river and he said, "Mr. Dodd beyond the trees."

Three village fishermen were mooring their small boat among the trees, handing bamboo poles, bait buckets, and three heavy strings of fat fish from the rocking craft to the fourth member of their party, who had waded ashore. As this fourth man bent to drop gear on the pebbled ground, his wide-brimmed bush hat fell off, ex-posing a shiny, bald head, and Belmont realized with a shock that it was Jerry Dodd. An excited group of small boys flocked around him shouting, "Petit Buddha!" They smiled, laughed and grasped at his hands, carrying his bait buckets and poles and fighting over who got to carry the fish.

"Mr. Dodd is like movie star in the village," Huu said. "They call him Petit Buddha because he bald and always happy and not big and loud like other Americans." Huu studied Belmont's face for any sign that the comparison was insulting, but all he saw there was a look of amazement.

The rambunctious throng of children and fishermen headed away from them, so they jogged to catch up. Belmont called "Jerry!" three times before he was heard over the rapid-fire chatter of Vietnamese, which Dodd exchanged fluidly with the others. Then he turned his round, sun-burned face and shouted "Belmont! I heard you were coming." Paunchy and short, the same height as the other adult men, and beaming with contentment, his nickname suited him perfectly. "How do you like your fish?" he asked as the gaggle of boys tugged him along.

They climbed the river embankment to a set of thatched, bamboo houses and there the whole group enjoyed a feast of vegetables, rice and fish with Petit Buddha in charge of blending various sauces -- beer-and-flour batter was used to bread some fish, others were smothered in peanut or soy sauce or local nuoc mam. Dodd moved through the scene with stately formality, officiating over meal preparation and clearly aware of his celebrity status. Belmont had never seen anyone else so completely happy. As he sat against the base of a tamarind tree, watching the flow of the passing river as it bore the people up and down as it had for countless generations, breathing the clean air of the countryside, enjoying simple food and his first Shimazu-Aaronson-free meal, Dodd's joy seemed to spread through him also. Huu translated for him, explaining the life of the village and Dodd's place in it. Given that Belmont was at least six inches taller than anyone else present, he felt that he was watching a sort of puppet play, with Dodd's deliberate, self-conscious manner reinforcing the effect. A folding chair was brought and placed near the fire for Petit Buddha and this throne was soon encircled by villagers who were more comfortable resting on their own haunches than on an artificial surface. The image of Dodd as a gentle Yul Brenner, King of Siam, struck Belmont as comical but also fitting. The people appeared to hold him in genuine affection, his ready laughter mingling with theirs and his command of their language easy and natural. But perhaps they were keeping the words simple for him, as one does with a foreigner -- and perhaps the bags and crates of supplies from the PX in evidence all around accounted for some of the adulation he received. In any case, the meal, the flowing river and the afternoon heat induced Belmont to doze-off against the Tamarind tree, and the reasons for Khap Noi station's lack of productivity became obvious to him even before he began, in his first brief hours here, to become part of the problem.

When he awoke, his dishes had been taken away, and Huu was standing with Dodd in the midst of a village returning to its routines. Belmont pulled himself to his feet, brushed off his chinos and strolled over toward Dodd. "May I approach the Mighty One, The Petit Buddha?" he chided and Dodd returned a low, rolling chuckle that was a mannerism that had boiled Aaronson's blood during his briefing.

"How did you have your fish?" Dodd asked.

"I went with the peanut sauce...excellent. My compliments. But we've only got an hour of sunlight and we don't want to get caught in the dark in this part of the world, right?"

"Yep. We own the day; they own the night, as the saying goes. But you can't tell that to the SEALs. They prefer the night because that's what they're trained for and since they're looking for Charlie, that's when they're likely to find him. But anyway...." Dodd kicked dirt around with his sandal. "I just feel safer out here than in the compound."

"You stay out here at night," Belmont asked, feeling a shiver up his spine, "by yourself?" "Well, not by myself. I have the village." Dodd gestured toward the river. "Listen, Belmont, mortar and rocket fire have come down inside the base and missed me by sheer chance. The VC stay on the other side of the river for the most part. They don't want to get caught on this side, where we have our forces. So they lob shots into the compound from across the river and if the VC do come across, my people here will get me out by boat. Besides..." Dodd kicked more dirt, as if dealing up a confession. "Besides, my girlfriend doesn't have clearance for the base, so she can't stay with me if I go back."

Tested on the field of honor were the words that crossed Belmont's mind. Engaging in combat was one thing -- our team versus their team. But the prospect of spending nights out here, a lone American among these vulnerable, unarmed villagers, was that incomprehensibly brave or utterly naive? "Will you be coming to the office tomorrow?" he asked.

"Sure. I could meet you there. Besides, I'm bringing my team, The Khap Noi Capitals, to play the Big Guns, the boys sponsored by the 501st Artillery." And Dodd's round face broke out in a happy smile. "We're gonna massacre 'em!" he promised.

13

2 November 1967

A MASSACRE

It was love at first sight.

Some stage or other of anxiety had been the default condition for Jerry Dodd ever since elementary school, as all his classmates grew taller and he realized he wasn't going to. Losing a series of playground fights demonstrated some courage and tenacity but didn't in the end, to use the obvious term, improve his standing among his peers. When as a freshman he reported that he was 5'3" and weighed 120 pounds, the basketball coach just smiled and said, "Really." But because Dodd worked incredibly hard and developed a better-than-average jump shot, he was not cut until the second round his junior year and actually made the team his senior year, scoring eight points in the two games he was subbed-into. The lessons drawn from his youth were that life was hard, he had to put-in extra effort to find acceptance, and being smarter than his friends was a problem for them and nothing to brag about. His Valparaiso University years were better in some ways -- academic merit was recognized and he became a popular mascot for the jocks he partied with. But the basketball team played well beyond his level and he never found the right girlfriend among the few co-eds short enough for him to consider dating.

So Dodd was completely unprepared for the sense of bliss that enveloped him the first time he glimpsed the An Long River. "Mr. Huu, can we stop here?" he'd asked.

"Khap Noi four miles ahead," Huu explained.

"Yes but please, can we drive over there to those trees and stop for a moment?"

Huu's mission for the day was to deliver the new man, just arrived from the United States, to Field Station C and orient him. But the loaded carbine bouncing this way and that across Jerry Dodd's lap had made him very nervous. So he said, "If you clear your carbine and put it with your bag, we can stop here, Mr. Dodd."

From the muddy bank, Dodd felt that the An Long was holding open wide arms of homecoming welcome to him. "I grew up on a river like this," he told Huu, "along the Wabash, in Indiana. My father and my uncles taught me to fish on it. Do you fish, Mr. Huu?"

"I did as a boy. No more. I buy fish now."

"The people here are using nets."

"Yes, to catch the fish."

"We used lines. Poles and rods and lines." Dodd's distracted gaze never left the boats working the steady currents of the river as he asked, "Do you think I could have a boat here, perhaps a small boat to go fishing on weekends?"

"River very dangerous," Huu warned. "River patrols make trouble for boat people. Helicopters shoot them too. VC very active, other side of river. Besides, this village are Khmer Krom people, Cambodians who don't like Vietnamese."

"Why not?"

"They were here first. An Long was Cambodian river many years ago."

They drove alongside the thatched huts on a trace of mud road that led back to the highway and what Jerry Dodd saw from the jeep confirmed his sensation that he had found his true home half way around the world from his birthplace: Every man he saw walking the roadway between river and village was no larger in stature than he was -- and all the women, young and old, were shorter.

As was their habit, the teenagers of the Khap Noi Capitals basketball team ate breakfast together, rice and vegetables with tea brought to them as they squatted in concentric circles, uniformed members in a tight inner loop with other youngsters crowded around. Then they formed a parade, uniforms in the lead, and walked in silence beyond the edge of the village to a hut that served as their temple. It was the only painted structure anywhere near -- red and green on the outside with a white Buddha portrayed on the back wall, under the image of a gilded wheel with eight spokes. Jerry Dodd was waiting for them there, greeting each team member by giving him a fragrant joss stick to light as a tribute. The team then knelt together while Dodd lit a new set of joss sticks and made an offering of MPC notes at the base of Buddha's image. For twenty minutes, their silence broken only by distant voices or an occasional rooster or dog, the Capitals meditated. Then the rumble of a deuce-and-a-half truck drew near and Coach Dodd led the ten members of his team from the temple. They clambered onto the high truck bed while friends and relatives cheered and Dodd, waving from the rear of the truck, put his hands together and made a little bow of farewell.

The day before, in the post-prandial serenity of this quiet village, Dodd had promised Belmont a massacre. On this morning, amidst the cacophony of a well-attended basketball game, he delivered one. The Khap Noi Capitals, in gold and white, sporting white neck scarves that marked them as Khmer Krom, carved up their opponents, Vietnamese boys in red uniforms with "Big Guns" stitched on their jerseys. Dodd sat in virtual silence at the end of his team's bench, quietly subbing reserves in-and-out, while across the way four coaches from the 501st Artillery competed, each trying to out-shout the others.

The Capitals' guards had perfected a dribble-pass weave pattern that left one or the other open at the top of the key for jump shots they rarely missed. When this tactic pulled defenders to the perimeter, the guards were quick to take advantage, lobbing into their big center, 5'4" Le Han, or bounce-passing to forwards for back-door lay-ups. The Capitals' defense was equally effective and coordinated, stealing passes and forcing turnovers all over the court. Dodd seemed not to care that he, Mr. Huu and Belmont were alone on one side of the court while sixty or so GIs across the way cheered-on a team of youngsters who were being, as Dodd had said, massacred.

It would have been difficult for a late-comer to choose which team had scored 58 points and which had scored 16 as the players lined-up to shake hands and mutter "good game" to each other -- so subdued were the expressions worn by everyone. Belmont alone appeared excited by the victory, which Dodd said to him quietly, "Is what it is."

"But aren't you happy you won?" Belmont asked. "Aren't the boys?"

"Of course," Dodd answered, "but they win because of Mindfulness. They have higher goals than winning or they wouldn't win at all."

Dodd boosted his players aboard the Army truck and spoke to them before they left for the ride home. He, Belmont and Huu then walked across the base to the office.

"How did you get fluent in Vietnamese?" Belmont wanted to know.

Dodd laughed his rolling, deep-throated chuckle and said, "I'm nowhere near fluent. I can talk about fishing...catchin' 'em and cookin' 'em...and about round-ball, not much else."

"You said your team wins because they have, what, higher goals?"

"That's hard to explain..." Dodd turned to him and stopped walking. He clasped his hands together as if in prayer and focused his attention on Belmont's face for a long moment. Then he seemed to give it up and began walking again. "It's complicated and a little difficult to explain. You ever play basketball on a team?"

"No."

"Ever fish, not with a bobber but straight-line?"

"No."

"You religious?"

"Raised Episcopalian."

"Then I don't know how to explain it. The concentration the team brings to the game is grounded outside the game. Look, ever been in a car wreck?"

"Yeah, once."

"That where you got the scar on your face?"

"No, got that scuba-diving in Veracruz. I tried to grab a sting-ray."

"How'd you feel when you wrecked your car?"

"I felt pretty bad. It was my dad's car. I got in a lot of trouble."

"And before it happened, just before. How were you feeling just before?"

"Fine. I was going on a date. I felt fine."

"No you didn't. Something was interfering with your concentration. Recall!"

"I don't remember. It was a first-date, I think. Yeah, it was. I was dating a new girl."

"And your former girlfriend? Where was she?" Dodd had been walking faster and faster as they talked until Belmont was jogging to keep-up and Huu was lagging behind. Now Dodd turned and stopped suddenly and Belmont ran right into him, almost knocking him flat. "You didn't have an accident," he said, "you lost concentration and ran your father's car into another car. Like you ran into me now because you were focused on something else. Your wreck happened because you practiced the wrong Resolve, the wrong Conduct and the wrong Effort to be a good driver." Dodd interlaced his fingers and studied them as he said, "What I've learned from living here is the only thing we can control is ourselves. Detachment from the things that disturb you is the only road to being a perfect driver...in theory, one who would never be involved in a so-called 'accident'. Fear, anger, guilt, even joy can cause you to lose your concentration and have accidents."

"What a load of crap," Belmont said pulling a cigarette pack from his breast pocket.

"Is it? Mr. Huu keeps our team records. Go ahead and ask him how we did today."

Without being asked, Huu reported, "25-for-30 from the field. 8-for-8 free-throws."

"And why was that, Mr. Huu?" Dodd asked.

"Right Resolve, right Conduct, right Effort from the boys today," Huu said.

❧

CP-C marched rather than walked into the office despite having a prosthesis below his left knee, and sat ramrod-straight in a folding chair, hands folded. He was polite and soft-spoken but coiled like a snake, giving the impression he might momentarily spring at the man he was staring at, who was Jerry Dodd.

"Your counterpart begs to know your objectives for the month of December," Huu translated in a whisper, staring at the floor between them.

"They will be the same as for the current month, tell him. To be always mindful of an ever-changing world," Dodd said quietly.

It was not clear that Huu translated these words exactly as spoken, given that CP-C's demeanor did not change. "The enemy all along the river continues to show determination and strength despite increased activity by our artillery and air-power and many more incursions into his strongholds. What, your counterpart wishes to know, do you make of this?"

"Please answer this question by reminding CP-C that my tour-of-duty ends soon and Mr. Belmont will be the station chief after that."

Though Belmont heard his name mentioned in the translation, CP-C took not the slightest notice of him.

"Your counterpart respectfully wishes to inquire whether you will again be meeting with SEALs and Riverine personnel who have been in contact with the enemy or with interrogators of recently captured VC."

This stubborn exchange between the warrior and Petit Buddha persisted for another fruitless half hour without ever departing from the softly-spoken words thinly veiling their animosity. The patriot fighting for his country's survival butted his head against the resolute indifference of the younger man, a foreigner who fancied himself a mystic, a tyro-Buddhist whose authority resided in being an American with access to funding and firepower unavailable to the warrior born on this soil. It occurred to Belmont as he witnessed this tense exchange that if Dodd were newly arrived in Khap Noi instead of close to leaving, his life could be in much greater jeopardy from his counterpart than from the communist enemy. Frankly, Belmont felt more empathy for the wounded hero than for his own countryman, despite CP-C's refusal to acknowledge his existence before, during or after this first meeting.

The meeting ended when CP-C crossed the office to shake hands with Dodd, his steps making uneven sounds as the prosthesis came down on the concrete at every-other pace. The handshake, like the half-whispered exchange of translations, portrayed no outward hostility between them nor any warmth as CP-C strode past Belmont toward his waiting jeep and driver.

Belmont struggled to find the right words as he dropped Huu at his family home and then drove Dodd to the village, where the latter hoped to get some fishing in before sunset. He wanted to understand Dodd's reluctance -- refusal, rather -- to do his job as station chief, as a US soldier assigned to bilateral operations in Khap Noi. But on this, his second night, he decided it was too early to start stirring this complicated pot. He would keep his eyes and ears open -- and to the extent he could, his mind -- until he'd get his turn at being chief of Field Station C.

In the meantime, maybe there was something to be gained from learning about right Resolve, right Conduct and right Effort that would serve him well when he engaged in deadly combat -- which is what he had come here to do.

14

15 November 1967

TWO RUBBER MEN, ONE JESUIT

Rick Singleton was not-at-all himself, in keeping with his professional training. He was instead Theodore Michaels, "Ted," ambitious up-and-comer in the Overseas Operations Division of the Goodyear Tire and Rubber Company of Akron, Ohio. He cut a handsome figure in a beige, tailor-made suit, silk tie and wing-tipped brogues as he waited for Monsieur Pierre Guignon, Managing Director of Xuan Song Plantation, to finish reading his letter of introduction. In impeccable French, the letter made clear that Mr. Michaels had been graduated summa cum laude by Yale University, was highly recruited and had accomplished much in his five years with the company -- and that he was authorized to establish a Memorandum of Understanding for the purchase of rubber latex in large quantities from Xuan Song at prices competitive to what was offered by Michelin.

Monsieur Guignon folded the page and returned it to the envelope, speaking in French to Margot, his fading beauty of a wife. She translated his response in barely accented American English for Michaels: "You have a misunderstanding, monsieur. Xuan Song Plantation does not sell latex to Michelin. It is owned by Michelin."

"And yet I've been informed that the Guignon family have been its proprietors for over a century, is that not so?"

"Yes, well...proprietors but not owners, monsieur."

"But things have a way of changing, do they not," Michaels said agreeably, smiling. "May I suggest for Monsieur Guignon's discreet consideration, at his leisure, that the American military has a presence here. In fact, madame, without *Operation Junction City* earlier this year and *Operation Diamond Head*, being conducted right now all around us, Xuan Song would be in the hands of the communists and neither Michelin nor Monsieur Guignon could enjoy a claim of ownership. Nor would we be having this pleasant conversation."

Monsieur Guignon did not respond at all well to Margot's translation of this argument. His jowls quivered as he pounded his desktop with his fists during a response she interpreted, without emotion, as "My husband wishes you to know that these military tactics have destroyed 800 rubber trees on our land, worth half a million US Dollars, for which he has applied for compensation without receiving even one *sou* of the money promised him by the Americans...you Americans...and something else I don't remember." They exchanged words in French and she continued, "...Oh yes, and the communists are still out there running freely through the forest."

"Please allow me to point out," Michaels said quietly "that I can help with this problem of compensation. My company is not without influence and I have contacts in the Embassy and at MACV that might prove useful." Margot's translation of this went some small way toward calming the gentleman, so Michaels added, "I will retire for now, madam, but please convey my pleasure in meeting you both and that I intend to remain in Binh Duong Province, where my company plans to open a major production facility as soon as American fire-power has resolved the current conflict. I may be reached at the phone and address on my card and would be glad to accept a summons to speak with Monsieur Guignon about changing conditions here in the Republic that could assure this plantation for the future of his sons. I am given to understand that they attend school: Paul in Switzerland and Jean-Claude in Paris, is that not right?"

"You are very well informed, Monsieur Michaels," Margot told him. Monsieur Guignon begrudged Michaels a cursory handshake without standing up while Margot Guignon gave him a warmer one, and each received a little bow of the head in return.

Duke held the rear door of the black Citroën for Singleton then briskly jumped behind the wheel and adjusted his service cap. "How'd it go, boss?" he asked, slipping the car into gear.

"About what we expected for round one. You were right, he endured about twenty seconds of my high school French before he called her in, and her English is perfect."

"Four years at Bryn Mawr will do that for you," Duke said. "So he didn't have his thugs throw you out. That's good...that's as good as it gets from a fat old colonial who thinks Michelin is France, France is the world, and *civilization Francais* is god's gift to the natives."

"So what now? We wait by the phone?"

"No...we keep our eye on the ball. Monsieur Gallic Pride will never change. He's fourth generation colonial master-race. He builds schools and swimming pools for the workers, pays them nothing and has trouble-makers flogged. The result is...you know what they say of Jamaica? That it's 100% Catholic and 90% Voodoo. That's Guignon's work-force. It's 100% capitalist and 90% commie sympathizer. MACV can't even find the VC here, much less neutralize them. But if we get access, we could set up a network that sorts-out the active players from the ones who just want to get along and don't care who's in charge. And we'll pull out a shit-load of useful info, pardon my French, on NVA and VC infrastructure and modus operandi. So next I'll meet and cultivate the supervisor, a guy named Ngoc Nguyen. He lives in that bungalow beside the villa. When I worked for The Company, we had a file that said he played lackey to Guignon but talked treason behind his back. We better get him before the commies do, if it isn't too late for that. And on Sunday, Margot will attend 10 o'clock mass at Me Duc Tin by herself, so your job will be to grab the pew behind hers and breathe down her neck 'til she breaks out in goose-bumps."

"I got the distinct impression she didn't like me."

"Of course she did! There's no such thing as a middle-aged, married white woman who doesn't dream about a young black cat."

"Make you a deal, Duke." Singleton paused to consider, then said, "I don't call you a gook or a slope and you don't call me a black cat or a black anything else. Now just drive the car."

An hour later, they disturbed the quiet of the second-story apartment in the city of Tay Ninh that was their "safe house," where Rene Levesque was immersed in his French-language copy of the 1962 Roman Missal. Notes from it lay scattered on the field table, along with details about Me Duc Tin Cathedral and its chief priest, Nguyen Tuc, known to his large flock as "Père Martin".

Duke poured whiskey into three water glasses, chattering excitedly as he pulled off his chauffeur's livery and hung it in the wardrobe. They'd done it. They were in. Ted Michaels had done a brilliant job and they'd soon have a network carving up the Xuan Song infrastructure into piles of living allies and dead commies, those who didn't surrender under the Chieu Hoi program.

Singleton put his tailored suit on hangers in silence. After weeks of preparation, he had performed well, perhaps, but he didn't feel they had accomplished anything much, and he'd had enough of Duke's ebullience and hyperbole for one day. He set a whiskey on the study table, but Levesque just said "Not for me, thanks" without looking up.

"I found out why the CIA fired Le Duc," he announced. "The gook is a hard-core racist."

"They did not fire me," Duke protested, buttoning up a red, yellow and green Aloha shirt. "I was terminated *without prejudice*...note the *without* part...because despite the fact I spent half my life in California and earned two degrees from USC, it turned out that...unbeknownst to me... relations on both sides of my family and most my childhood friends who live here are commies. All I knew growing up in 'Nam was that they were aunts, uncles and playmates. It was guilt by association, gentlemen, a vile injustice which I protested but to deaf ears." He took a gulp of whiskey and added, "And incidentally, I am NOT a racist."

"Tell Rene what you said about me and Madame Guignon."

"I meant that as a compliment, a tribute to your charm and *savoir faire*."

"So how did you end up in the Army?"

"I'm not. You guys are in the Army, pretending to be civilians. I'm a civilian contractor for MACV, working for the Army. The pay stinks compared to the CIA, but it's way more exciting than selling real estate back in L.A. Running stunts like today's gets in your blood, man. And besides, I've got lots more latitude than I did with Langley. MACV doesn't care if contractors go bar-hopping, get smashed and jump the girls." He slipped into a pair of sandals and went to the door. "You guys gonna sit around here or come with me? I could translate for you."

Singleton looked toward Levesque, who was ignoring both Duke and the whiskey, and said, "We may come along later."

"You know where to find me." Duke opened the door, then turned and waved a string of condoms at them. "Nothing but Trojans for a Trojan alum," he said. "I wonder if Xuan Song supplies the rubber for these."

When he'd gone, Singleton asked, "Aren't you going to celebrate my spying debut?"

Levesque's expression mixed sorrow and anxiety into his usual sober demeanor. "You're a trained actor, Rick. Of course you did well. I'm not, and I feel like I'm going in way over my head tomorrow. You're trying to penetrate a business from the outside...I'm getting shoved into a deep-cover role Greyhawk never trained me for. I think Le Duc sold Cardenas a bill of goods and I'm stuck with it. Cardenas thinks Catholics are interchangeable parts, like soldiers. You move them around from one unit to another and they fit right in. But six years as an altar boy doesn't make you a priest. Canon law, church protocol, liturgy, I feel like I'm walking into a minefield. Vatican II is rolling out changes in the church nobody can keep up with." Now he took a sip of the warm whiskey. "I'm scared to death about trying this, Rick, to be honest."

Singleton had looked over the notes strewn across the field table while he listened but only knew enough French to pick out random words. He tried to find the right thing to say to console his friend, but the best he had was, "Remember, Cardenas admitted it was a long-shot, but that The Church was such a treasure-trove of information it was worth a try. Worst-case scenario, you walk over to the bus stop, board the next jitney to Saigon and tell Cardenas it was a no-go. If Guignon sees through me, he'll have his goons break my legs. All Father Martin will do is send you away. Besides, Goodyear never heard of me, so I'm a forgery going in. You've got an actual letter signed by the archbishop in Saigon."

"Yeah, based on a forgery from a bishop in Quebec, so we're both on borrowed time."

Singleton suddenly broke out in laughter. "Oh hell, Rene! How fucking crazy is all this anyway? All you wanted was to stay out of combat and type reports in a nice, clean office and all I wanted was rehearsal experience in the real world...and what we've got is a run-down apartment in a god-forsaken town we share with a lunatic, Amer-Asian, CIA-reject, and we're assigned a couple of fantasy-land missions. It's all too weird, man. You couldn't make this shit up!"

This riff cheered Levesque a little and he laughed too.

"Let's go get something to eat, somewhere Duke isn't," Singleton suggested.

Rene finished his drink and stood up, pushing his notes into a pile. "But off the record, I've got another problem with this whole thing," he said. "I'm Catholic."

"That's why Cardenas chose you, isn't it?"

"What I mean is, I almost left for Canada...actually it was on the same day I met Braxton, Mark and you. But I felt I owed something to my country, to serve I guess. Even if the war is wrong, even if I never asked to be a spy and my recruiter lied, still I have an obligation as an American. But acting as a priest is not the same thing as dressing up like a nun for some foolish field exercise. I've never been gung-ho. If I could think of any way out of this, I wouldn't do it."

A long period of silence passed between them, Levesque staring down at the materials on the table, Singleton with his arms folded, watching. Then he said, "Hey, I live in two worlds too, man. Always have. So I think I know how you feel. In my neighborhood, around my father's church, I can be myself, a black kid who belongs to a tight-knit family and community in Harlem. When I go downtown to private school or off to Yale, somewhere with mostly white friends, I can be myself there too, a guy who loves theater and wants to be a part of that world someday. I have to change the way I speak, my clothes, even the way I walk in-between the two. But I'm at home in both worlds. I belong to both. So what I'm saying is, when you cross the threshold into that church, just be there. Be the Catholic you are. Feel at home because you will be."

Rene picked up the apartment keys and his wallet, put them in his pockets, and held the door for Singleton. "Thank you, Rick," he said. "I hope it's going to be that simple."

"Oh no," Singleton laughed, "I never said it was simple."

Before dawn the next morning, Rene Levesque gave up trying to sleep, kicked the sweaty sheet to the foot of his cot and rolled out quietly, trying not to awaken the others. He washed himself as best he could over a pewter basin then dressed in the black suit and clerical collar of Father Jean Andre, S.J. He touched the inside pocket of his jacket for whatever assurance the archbishop's letter assigning him to the Cathedral Church of Me Duc Tin might offer. Still feeling sick-at-heart and utterly alone, he left his note of thanks where Singleton would find it and carried his small suitcase to the door. He stared back to where they slept for some minutes without being able to sense their presence in the dark room, then with more reluctance than he had ever felt about any previous thing in his life, he slipped out.

Tay Ninh was already stirring, in a land where bake-oven afternoons encouraged early starts. Rene passed several food stalls but decided a cup of tea was not worth the price of being an apparition in their midst, a solitary priest, impossibly tall and pale, looming out of the dark. He seemed to himself not just a foreigner in these streets but a different species from the people breaking their fasts in the glow of kerosene lamps or the occasional fluorescent tube. He waited at the jitney stop for nearly an hour before a three-wheeled Lambretta came with Me Duc Tin painted on the side. He offered the driver a handful of piastres from which the man, without making eye-contact, counted out some, leaving the rest. Rene wedged himself into the little passenger compartment -- suitable enough for six small people, three to each bench, but a human cigarette pack by the time the driver shoe-horned eight aboard, given that one was a six-foot man with a suitcase. As they bounced down twelve miles of rutted road toward Me Duc Tin, the rising sun slowly turned the jitney into a convection oven on wheels. Each frequent stop brought the promise of relief as passengers dismounted, directing the driver to untie their cargo from the roof, but these were immediately replaced by the same number as before who wrangled with the driver about how to tie up their cargo. So it was mid-morning before Father Jean Andre unfolded himself from the fetal position and lumbered onto his feet, sweat-soaked and aching from his ordeal.

The jitney unloaded everyone at the foot of the Cathedral steps, five of them that ran across the entire length of the portico like widespread arms of welcome. Father Andre slowly straightened his aching back, rose up to his full height for the first time in hours, and let his eyes drift up the whole facade from steps to cross. "Cathedral" in his mind assumed the granite-and- rose-window European model copied in Quebec and New England. But Me Duc Tin was instead a cut-to-human-size stucco edifice, freshly painted in pink, orange and white, tones that under the intensity of the tropical sun dazzled his eye and lifted his heart. Niches half-way up the twin towers bore alabaster figures of The Blessed Virgin and Christ bearing a lamb on his shoulders.

On the portico steps, he paused to brush the dust from his pants and shoes, then stepped across the threshold into the cool, softly lit interior. Singleton's words returned to him and he felt a great contentment, a serenity he had not known since coming to Vietnam. He felt at home. He placed his small suitcase on a pew half-way up the aisle, genuflected, and fell into prayer.

During the two hours that he knelt there, the timeless concentration of rote prayer bathed him clean of the dialectic that had obsessed him -- ever-present as background music since his first days at Fort Greyhawk, when he was forced to choose between patriotism and idealism. This dialogue had placed his obligation to his country and its laws, along with friendship and peer-pressure, on one side of him against a moral purity he had always defined himself by and thought of, simply, as his soul. This struggle had never ceased wrestling inside him since the hour he knew he had been deceived during his military recruitment. Now, in this quiet sanctuary, these voices ceased their tortured debate and the serenity that had always been his natural state returned to him.

When he was ready, he arose from prayer, crossed himself and walked to the foyer where he asked for "Père Martin". Vietnamese parishioners pointed toward a red-roofed house on the church grounds. Simple gestures by staff in the outer office bid him wait for a few minutes before he was led in to meet Nguyen Tuc, Père Martin. He was relieved to find that, as reported, the old priest spoke fluent French, without the flat Quebecois accent of Père Andre. Père Martin looked up with a beaming face after his cursory reading of the archbishop's letter, which spoke of a Jesuit from Quebec called to serve the needs of the poor in a country shattered by war -- to assist under the direction of Père Martin in any capacity desired. He held both of young Andre's hands in his own to make clear how welcome he was, what an unexpected blessing.

"So much suffering, so many funerals," Père Martin said with deep emotion. "This Cathedral has had no bishop for more than a year, so great have been our losses. I have served as head priest until a bishop can be found to replace the one who died."

Père Andre was happy when Martin suggested they begin his ministry with a prayer of thanksgiving in the sanctuary. Parishioners petitioned Père Martin as he made his way with the help of his cane across to the church and they gazed with curiosity at the giant stranger in clerical collar at his side, but they left the two in peace when they knelt together.

After some minutes, Martin arose and Andre asked, "Would you extend your pastoral care to me and hear my confession?" They took up places in the confessional booth and Père Andre began with the formula, "Pardonnez-moi, mon père, car j'ai péché...." and ended with "pas un prêtre ordonne, mais un officier du intelligence Américain."

"A spy?"

"Yes, Father."

A long silence passed before Père Martin asked a series of technical questions:

"Were you baptized and confirmed in The Church?"

"Yes, Father."

"Have you been raised a good Catholic?"

"Yes, Father. Twelve years of Catholic schooling and four at Catholic university."

"Was your last confession four months ago, as you said? Where was that?"

"Yes, Father, at Sts. Peter and Paul's Cathedral in Philadelphia, in the United States."

"Can you say The Apostle's Creed by heart?"

"Yes, Father. I believe in one God, the Father Almighty, Creator of heaven and earth...."

When Andre had gotten to the end, Père Martin said, "This is a very grave matter. I will have to think about what to do, but in light of the fact that you did not try to deceive me.... We will place you in a guest room for tonight and tomorrow, we will make a decision."

"Yes, Father."

"Perhaps God has sent you to us for some reason...His wonders to perform."

"Yes, Father."

At the close of this remarkable day, a sleepy Rene Levesque crouched over a page of stationery by the light of a kerosene lamp in his little bedroom and wrote:

> *Dear Linda,*
> *I'm sorry it took me so long to write you, but I have been thinking of you and of our very brief time together every day. Things here were very confused and unsettled until today, but I finally have been assigned to my post and things are working out for the best....*

15

16 October - 16 November 1967

THE CLERK'S MAFIA

As promised, Frank Monroe had come to breakfast ready to talk on Braxton Hood's first morning at the Saigon villa. First, a series of questions: Did Braxton find his room to his liking? Was there anything he needed? Would he prefer eggs or pancakes, sausage or bacon, what kind of juice? Didn't it seem smart, in the cold light of dawn, to base the operation in Saigon, hidden from the VC, rather than in Cu Chi? Didn't it make sense, so long as Major Shimazu was happy with results, to keep the Saigon villa a secret from him so he wouldn't have to defend the whole operation to his superiors at SIC Central? Diem and "the girls" went to Cu Chi six days a week anyway, so the on-site presence was well established. Had they lit-up the H&I fire when he was on the base? Could he picture himself sleeping through that every night? How were his eggs?

Hood agreed down-the-line. He was Monroe's aide, after all, sent to learn from the master and besides, Monroe's enthusiasm and engaging charm could sell ice boxes to Eskimos, so selling Hood on the safety and comfort of this Saigon mansion presented no great challenge. The last question of the morning was "You know how to ride a motorcycle?"

After breakfast, Hood was given keys for the living quarters and for a sweet, clean Honda 350, red and white with lots of chrome.

Frank coached his learning session, how to change gears and apply brakes, up and down the alleyway. Then they spent two hours riding matching Hondas through Saigon traffic, making two round-trips from the villa to Tan Son Nhut and the Rex Hotel.

"The gate guards take care of the cars and bikes, keep them gassed-up. There's four or five guards, all related and all named Nguyen, I think," Frank said when they got back. "These two doors lead to Diem's and the girls' quarters. This one leads to Control."

He unlocked an iron security grate, then an inner door to a vast space below the living room, kitchen and dining area upstairs. One small, barred window looked out over the second Citroën, the one Diem hadn't taken to Cu Chi. Fluorescents flickered to life revealing walls lined with maps and charts, a cork-board heavy with bits of paper that fluttered under ceiling fans, file cabinets, a large desk and a solid plywood-covered table in the center of the room smothered in binders, folders and wire baskets full of papers. In the far corner, an open cabinet was stocked with weapons of all kinds. "This is where the magic happens, Braxton," Frank announced with a grand gesture. "This is where the Cu Chi operation lives and breathes and this..." he strode over to the cork-board, five feet square, covered with 3x5 note cards scotch-taped in a haphazard arrangement, "This is the network! Seventy-two agents, six handlers, Counterpart D above them, me at the top, Diem and the typists to my right, III Corps to my left, and it all hums along like clockwork. When an agent fails to produce or proves unreliable, he's terminated, fired, paid-off, killed-off, whatever and replaced by a better source. I keep control of everything as the funding source, but the key to it all is Diem, the little man you pushed around yesterday. No need to apologize...he understands you were under orders to report directly to me and he's OK with you. We spoke this morning before you were up. He's a brilliant operative and I couldn't do this without him. He gathers info from Cu Chi, translates everything into English, manages the flow of reporting, and all I have to do is check it out for accuracy and wait for feedback from above, MACV down to SIC down to me, grading our performance."

Frank spun toward Hood, tossed his head like a show-horse, held out his hands, palms up, and asked, "Is this cool or what?"

Hood had counted, as he always did, and found the six handlers above twelve agents each, for a nice, even seventy-eight of them, a symmetrical table of eighty, counting Diem and CP-D.

It was a result too perfect to have arisen from the cob-web pandemonium of this Jackson-Pollock quilt-work, cards scattered here and there in clusters with names scrawled across them, crossed out, written over and under. All Hood said for now was, "Really cool."

"Take a look back here." Frank strode to the gun cabinet. "If we're lucky, Braxton, we will never have to drive into the boonies. But if we do, I'll set you up with an M-16, standard issue, or we'll get serious..." He pulled down a stocky, fat-barreled rifle and handed it to him. "An M79 Grenade Launcher, packs one hell of a wallop. In fact, here's a .45 for you to keep in the footlocker in your room. Here, a holster, couple boxes of ammo...here. You'll feel better having something even if you're not likely to ever need it in the city."

"Well thank you, Frank," Hood said, juggling the gear in his hands, trying to hand back the M79. "But don't I need to sign for these?"

"Oh hell no, Braxton. Nobody ever asks a civilian where he got a weapon and none of these are registered anywhere. They're all so-called black-market, which is another word for free trade. So let's go up to lunch and I'll show you how to work your new side-arm."

As he locked up the iron gate, Frank said with the glee of a child, "Every day is Christmas around here, my friend. You've got great quarters, a sleek Honda bike, and a sidearm." He turned his blue eyes into Hood's face and added, "And you haven't been here a whole day yet."

Lunch was fish soup with some sort of pastry floating in it, which Frank insisted needed a dry Chablis to fully complement. Co Bian, he explained, had family in Saigon who kept her occupied in the daytime. Thomas, the chef who supposedly spoke no English, busied himself around the table as Frank lectured on "The Clerk's Mafia".

"Never heard of it," Hood said, "sounds sinister."

"It is, my friend, the very opposite of sinister. Older than the Roman legions, it has been the lowest-ranking soldier's union, insurance company and family. The factotums who grind-out an army's records, payroll, requisitions, and all that sort of thankless, mundane but oh-so-vital work are the invisible hands behind the war machine. They do not win accolades, they do not march under clouds of confetti nor past the cheering throngs as returning victors do, they receive no medals. So their only solace or reward comes from the loyalty and service they render to their peers and are rendered unto in kind. For many years, I served in those lowly ranks...as you can see, those days are behind me for now. But my connection to the great corps of clerks and my devotion to their intimate society remains. In fact, my former colleagues believe me to be still among their ranks, with one or two exceptions. Clerks forever!" Frank held his wineglass on high in salute and ordered Thomas to bring another bottle of Chablis to the table. "Before the first spy in the history of mankind came the first scrivener, creating the narrative of history in any way he saw fit, judging the pharos, rigging the books, profiting from the Pyramids. My friend...." Frank leaned in confidentially as Thomas re-filled the stemmed glasses. "Braxton, my friend, fortune smiles upon the lowly clerk with the same intensity as upon the five-star general, but without the fanfare." Frank's speech showed the effect of his fourth wine. He seemed lost in reverie for a long, silent moment then he smiled and said, "Braxton, I'm really glad you're here. I like doing things my own way. I told Shimazu I didn't want him to appoint any helper... but it got to be...things got to be pretty...solitary. Solitary. With nobody around all day and just Diem and Co Bian coming in after work. Diem is all business and I have to learn French to talk with Bian."

He pushed back from the table and stood up, perking up from his dreamy monologue.

He polished off his wine and said, "Anyway, riding the bikes this morning was more fun than I've had in awhile. I enjoyed it and I know we're going to make a great team. It'll be terrific fun!"

He set the glass down and headed for the door, calling back, "Now I have to get to work and earn my keep around here. Thomas will get you anything you need."

"Want me to come with you?" Hood offered.

"It's complicated and I need to concentrate on it. You just got here...settle in for a couple days then I'll bring you up to speed." He turned in the doorway and added brightly, "And to be clear, the bike and the .45 are yours to keep, gifts to you from the Clerk's Mafia. When you leave the country, sell them, give them away, whatever you want." And the door closed.

Hood enjoyed a busy, profitable afternoon. He wrote letters assuring family and friends of his safety and giving them the simple APO address that would bring their responses to III Corps HQ without using any of those designations. He became more confident in controlling "his" Honda as he snaked the main arteries of Saigon until he found his way back to Tan Son Nhut, where he mailed his letters, bought some personal items at the gigantic PX there, and found that his GS-11 ID gained him entrance to the Enlisted Men's Club, where he sipped a gin and tonic and watched a report on TV that explained how the "Summer Of Love" movement had devolved into drug-fueled anti-war demonstrations that were increasing in violence.

All these activities engaged one part of Braxton Hood's conscious mind. Another part, that facet where complicated mathematical problems were wrestled with, was analyzing the data gathered over his first 24 hours as Frank Monroe's aide. "How did the successful Cu Chi operation work?" progressed into something more like "Where was the Cu Chi operation?" By the time he had managed to find his way back to the villa, Hood had tentatively concluded that the key missing piece of the puzzle was Counterpart-D. The strange space Monroe called "Control" was the funding source, and that wily, tough little Diem and his typing duo generated the flow of Information Reports, but where was the ARVN officer who was supposed to be in charge of this so-called "bilateral" network? He also concluded that the less curiosity he showed, the more uninterested he seemed, the sooner he'd learn what Shimazu had sent him to learn.

For three weeks, Hood projected the clueless good-ole-boy -- easy-going and friendly. Apparently he liked to read in the air-conditioned comfort of the living room and write letters home while Thomas cooked. He often rode out on his motorcycle, not a thought in his head. Monroe continued to mentor him along in everything that didn't matter: hopping hotel bars, refining his tastes in art and antiques -- about which Frank Monroe knew a great deal -- and showing Hood that his GS-11 card got him into officer's facilities of all sorts, on and off the air base. Braxton came to be called "Buddy," and they developed an easy, genuine friendship outside the business of the Cu Chi network, the exclusive domain of Frank Monroe. Hood came to understand the covenant between them, but that only made him increasingly curious.

On their fourth Friday together, Hood was invited into Control again. "Time to put you to work, Buddy," Monroe said. He handed him a beat-up leather valise with faded gold lettering that advertised "*The Eagle-Tribune*, Lawrence, Massachusetts". He also gave him a card featuring Hood's military photograph and identifying him as "Buddy Foster," a member of the press corps.

"The Clerk's Mafia?" Hood guessed.

"Through which all things are possible, Buddy. Here's what I need you to do starting Monday. Get yourself over to the roof-bar at the Rex Hotel. Pull up a seat in the very back row for The Five O'clock Follies. That's what you working journalists call the daily briefing MACV gives for the press. I think you'll enjoy it. The press gives the brass a hard time and the spokesmen pretend to ignore the cynicism. If anyone asks, you're not staff with any paper...they could check that. You're just a humble stringer looking to score some free-lance bread. Keep a low profile, they won't bring it up anyway. There's a pecking order and you're not in it. Take down everything they say on III Corps action north of Saigon. We'll check it against info we're getting from agents and see what doesn't ring true. And dress down, man. You look too good. Stringers are notorious slobs, drunks and whore-mongers. Any questions?"

Braxton had lots of questions, starting with "Are you kidding me?" But he kept his response to "Nope."

His first experience at the Rex Hotel briefing did, however, fill four pages of his notepad: An ambush at Ong Thanh, north of Cu Chi, had claimed the lives of 64 members of the 2nd Battalion, 28th Infantry, including their CO, a lieutenant colonel. It was believed they faced the veteran 271st VC Regiment under Colonel Vo Minh Triet. The enemy had suffered heavy losses and was being pursued into the area around Tay Ninh and the Xuan Song Michelin Plantation.

Frank Monroe was thrilled to have this report and he met with Diem in Control for several hours over Hood's notes, delaying Thomas' duck with dumplings special, which precipitated a shouting match between the chef and Co Bian. Hood waited in vain for Monroe to call him down to Control. At dinner all was well again, as Monroe lifted his glass several times in tribute to the delicious entree, which he elaborately praised in English, and to Buddy's fine work.

Three days later, a drop-in lunch-guest took Mad-dog and Rosie by surprise. Hood had waited in a ramshackle diner a half block from III Corps, wading through several pots of tea and a couple chapters of *Heart of Darkness*, until he saw the blue jeep go by, Rosie at the wheel. He left money under the teapot, jump-started his Honda, and dropped in on their six o'clock. When they pulled up outside an officer's mess outside Tan Son Nhut's main gate, Hood dropped his kickstand beside them, pulled off his Ray-bans and said, "Remember me?"

They enjoyed a spirited chat full of gossip about Babineaux and some very impressive fellow named Belmont, the curious cases of Levesque and Singleton, still missing, and the III Corps office.

"Come back with us," Mulcahey said. "Have one of Shimazu's great meals and stay over at our compound."

"No can do," Hood said, leaning in confidentially. "But I need your help with something. And not a word to anybody, not even the major, got it?" They nodded. "Cu Chi is one strange set-up. I'm not sure what I'm looking at and I'm not getting much access from Monroe. So I've figured out I need two things, for now at least, maybe more later. First I need you to type me a copy of all the IRs that came in about that battle up in Ong Thanh. Just the text, clean copy on typing paper, no forms. Stick it under your shirt and bring it to me over at Dong An, the little food place down the block from you, red and white sign, you know it?"

"We can find it."

"Noon tomorrow. OK? Now when does Cu Chi have its next budget meeting with Shimazu?"

"Sometime early November. Each station gets a day during the first week of the month," Rosie said.

"Remember the photo class at Greyhawk? Telephoto lens, natural light, cloak the camera, all that? Here's what. Arrange the jeeps so when Cu Chi comes in for that meeting, they've got to park out by the wall. Then set up to get some shots of Counterpart-D from the office window. Don't let Monroe catch you at it, or anybody else. Can you do that?"

"Can do easy, GI!" Mad-dog told him, craning his neck and grinning like a horse.

16

11 October to 14 December 1967

THE WORM IN THE APPLE

Each day was virtually the same for Mark Babineaux, but each three weeks was different.

The rising sun cut the sea breeze at dawn and the heat settled over his face as the air stopped moving. He sat up and struggled to his feet, stacking the two foam pads and folding the mosquito netting. By then the girl would return with his tea and pastries on a small tray and he would joke, "How did you slip away without waking me up?" This amused him for two reasons: The girl never did awaken him when she slipped away before dawn, and no matter how many mornings he repeated the question, the girl would laugh.

After he gave her six dollars in MPC scrip and she had gone, he set his breakfast on the hood of the yellow jeep outside the rear door of his office/home and ate standing up. Then he shaved and washed up, brushed his teeth, ran a brush through his unruly red mop to no effect and dressed for the day in a shirt and pants laundered by the girl.

His first class met at 9:00, so he had to gather his materials and start up the hill by 8:45. He had the timing down so that when he arrived at Itty Bitchy's sprawling compound, a dozen young women and a few children of various ages would greet him with "Good morning, teacher!" To his surprise, beginning English proved to be much harder work than the advanced class. There was next to nothing to build on and everything had to be based on concrete nouns: "This is my shirt," he'd say, grabbing his collars. They repeated it. "These are my sandals." An hour of this left him, and them, exhausted. "Advanced" English wasn't all that advanced, but at least there were enough abstract words to weave a story-line together and the hour went by faster. Ngon Bich, the founder of the school and dozens of small businesses -- the diminutive old lady the Australians had named "Itty Bitchy" -- sometimes sat in on his class when she had the time.

Over lunch at a beach-side cafe, Babineaux marked up the papers from each of his 25 or so students. Some qualified as writing samples, others were barely legible efforts to copy block letters by peasant women who were illiterate.

At 1:00 he met Duong in the office and they made out lists for his weekend runs to Saigon, where Duong visited family while Babineaux hit the Tan Son Nhut PX to keep the office supply business going and to keep Ngoc Bich's young women stocked up for their dozens of enterprises, which ran the gamut from retail merchandising to personal services, without exclusion. A tarp in the rear of the yellow jeep secured the mountain of supplies as they drove back through Saigon streets.

The "Office Supply" cover was problematic from the start. Apparently someone back in III Corps thought that a beach resort would have no use for this business. They would lie on the beach tanning, supposedly, while an intelligence network operated out of a shop that may as well have advertised "Lion Taming". But from the first days, the civilian businesses of Vung Tau took full advantage of the new outlet. Hotels, restaurants and retail businesses all came to Babineaux to save them a trip to Saigon. So from 1:00 to 5:00, five days a week, he and Duong had to sandwich intelligence work between customers who bought items or put in orders for product-in-quantity. Babineaux objected to the whole thing until the first month turned a net profit of $550, much more than his corporal's pay. Still, it was a time-consuming distraction.

The network grew steadily despite Babineaux's resistance. Shimazu's mandate had been to acquire "strategic and political" information rather than merely "tactical". Vung Tau was unique in being far from the fighting and close to where liquor was served to a variety of knowledgeable sources on-holiday. So when Duong urged him to include yet another soft-drinks distributor or another nuoc mam salesman or fisherman, Babineaux resisted, demanding to know how this agent would further their mission.

"He is highly qualified!" Duong would argue.

"Qualified to sell nuoc mam. What else can he give us?"

"He is highly mobile!"

"I don't care if he's bolted to the ground. Who are his sources?"

"He is highly recommended by CP-E!"

Babineaux was never certain that the last "highly" was any more valid than the others, since CP-E never came near the office and when they met in Saigon, he was sullen, unfriendly and spoke no English. Duong might have said, "CP-E highly wants you to date his daughter" without Babineaux knowing if that was true of not. In the end, he suspected most the network were relatives or friends of Duong or the Counterpart or both, and he based this conclusion on the evidence that not one of these agents -- ever -- produced one shred of useful information. They were all, however, paid on time for as long as it took Babineaux to get them fired at the monthly budget meetings and then replaced by another who was equally useless and/or, as far as he knew, actually the same man using a different name.

At 5:00, he and Duong closed the office and Babineaux met his girl for drinks and dinner at some favorite place. They walked along the beach, watching splendid sunsets over the South China Sea, then went home, spread the two pads under mosquito netting and made love before falling asleep.

Each day was unwavering in its simple pleasures and familiar routines. Each day was like all the others, week after week.

Yet each three weeks introduced stark and unsettling differences because of the girl.

On his very first morning in Vung Tau, reeling and sick from his all-night party with the Royal Australian Navy, he leaned against the wall at the main entrance to Itty Bitchy's sprawling compound. Dozens of women, her tribe, various children and clients, passed in-and-out of the main doorway, the scene of his rescue hours before from the "cowboys". Rubbing his forehead, squeezing the nape of his stiff neck, sipping hot tea, fighting off the vicious headache that was his just reward for drinking with the Australians in their cave, he squinted into the morning sun to see Itty Bitchy leaning up against him, looking up at him from just under his sternum.

"This Hang. She nice girl. Boocoo pretty. Clean you house, do laundry," she explained to him, presenting Hang as she might have any other piece of merchandise. Hang's excited, smiling face was a great selling-point. She was indeed beaucoup pretty and Babineaux did feel, at this moment, both deeply grateful to Bich for saving his hide on the dark street and, actually, in need of much care. "She take you home now, off-supply."

"Yes, office supply, thank you," Babineaux answered, relieved to hear it but bewildered at how Bich knew he was the new proprietor of a business he had visited for one hour and had not mentioned to her. *News travels fast in small towns,* he figured.

Bich reached out her hand, which he offered to shake until she said, "You give me tea cup. You pay Hang six dollah."

Hang walked fast, trying to guide him along without touching him or walking in front of him, a sign of disrespect, like a friendly sheep dog in the guise of a pretty, smiling young girl.

Twisting through the narrow streets, she somehow led him right to the office supply shop. The moment Babineaux unlocked the door, Hang flew to work, handing him a towel, nudging him to the wash basin, hanging clothes from his duffle bag, dusting, sweeping, arranging and smiling to herself the whole time as though this place was the home she had always dreamed of.

As soon as Duong showed up, Babineaux had him explain to her that they had to go somewhere and had to lock the office. She could not stay. Duong said to give her six dollars.

Once paid, Hang smiled happily and went her own way. But that afternoon, she was back, hauling two foam pads and two tote bags of her belongings for the storage room, where she settled in for good and all.

And on the morning of the second day in Vung Tau, Babineaux awoke in the stillness of first light, the sea breeze having ceased its gentle flow. Hang had gone, slipped out without disturbing him. He struggled to his feet, stacked the two sleeping pads and folded the netting, by which time she had returned, smiling happily, with a small pot of tea, just one cup, and pastries on a small tray. Babineaux said, "Thank you, but how did you slip away without waking me up?"

She looked at him quizzically but laughed, despite not understanding what he'd said. Then she held out her hand, as though to shake, and said, "Six dollah."

The pattern of Babineaux's days was set and Hang's role in them was very sweet to him. She was a happy, tireless girl, excellent housekeeper and laundress, a pretty companion for sunset walks on the beach and a gentle, delightful lover, inexperienced at first but affectionate and always willing -- an all-around beautiful girl -- young woman. *Young,* he thought, *how young exactly? What IS the age of consent in Vietnam?* He tried not to think about it.

And so it came as an unpleasant shock to him when, on November 2, after three weeks in Vung Tau, Itty Bitchy took Babineaux aside after his advanced class and said. "Hang have machine now. She make shirt."

"A sewing machine?" Babineaux guessed. "Well, that's good."

"She make shirt now, for Bich."

"She's going to make shirts for you?"

"No, Mr. Bahno, you wallaby. For Bich!" She dragged him by the sleeve into the narrow street and pointed toward the South China Sea.

"Oh, OK. For the beach, for R&R GIs."

"Yes, *for beach*! So now, Ly come you house, make you happy." She presented an older woman, perhaps already in her 30's, who had been standing nearby, scowling. "She take care you. Same-same, six dollah."

"Oh no, wait! But I like Hang," Babineaux pleaded, trying not to sound like the whiny, jilted adolescent he felt like. "I want Hang to stay with me, OK?" But Bich had spoken. Ly followed him back to the office supply like a lost puppy, somber, silent, lagging back. Ly lacked Hang's cheerful nature, youth and striking beauty -- completely -- but she had gifts of her own to offer Babineaux.

"Whose great idea was this anyway!?" he demanded to know one afternoon while waiting on a dozen customers who wanted carbon paper, ink blotters, receipt books and to place special orders. Duong and he had gotten almost no time to work together for several days due to the stream of Vietnamese customers who actually needed -- and expected -- office supplies. "This has become a nightmare!" he yelled at Duong. But Ly came along a day later and proved a shop-keeper's dream. Somewhere, she had acquired all the skills needed to run a retail store and she quickly took over running the cover operation top-to-bottom, so that his weekend run to Saigon with the list she had made up and Duong had translated was the only trouble the office supply business caused him. All this and his breakfast tray for just six dollars a day.

Babineaux, meantime, had acquired an extensive wardrobe of beach wear, finding an excuse most days to stop by Hang's crowded clothing store, hoping to have a moment between other customers to bathe in her lovely smile, drink-in her ebullience, an antidote to the dour companion he now had. He tried to make clear during these stolen moments that he wanted her to come back, that he missed her, but if she understood, she only smiled in response on her way to her next customer. He was not pining away, exactly, without Hang's company. He was merely hoping to have his cake and eat it too, which is where matters stood on November 21, when Itty Bitchy took him aside after his advanced class and informed him, "Ly want office supply shop. Make you good offer."

"She *WHAT*!?" Babineaux barked. "Tell her she can't have it! It's mine! It's not hers!"

"She do everything. You and Duong do nothing. Six dollah day. No good. You numbah ten, Mr. Bahno," Bich scolded. "She want you out today."

"*OUT!?*" Babineaux wasn't certain he had understood correctly. "Where would I go?" he stammered. "It's my home!"

"You stay Qui. She have good house. Make you happy."

Babineaux then realized that this was a three-way conversation between himself, Bich and an extraordinarily beautiful woman who was by far the best student in his advanced class, a delightful young lady on whom he already had something of a crush.

Why am I arguing? he thought. *Bich is offering to trade a sour-puss for a beauty, get the office supply business off my back, and move me from a stuffy storage closet into a house.*

Unlike the other two, Qui walked from the start with her arm through his, close to his side like a familiar lover. Babineaux was surprised but should not have been, knowing Itty Bitchy as he did, to see that the office supply sign had already been replaced by one in Vietnamese that ended "Co Ly". Qui was as strong as she was beautiful, he noticed when she lifted one handle of his heavy footlocker in her right hand, bundling his beach wear collection in her left, so that together they made the two-block move to her adorable little bungalow in one trip. Further proof that he had made a clever bargain came that afternoon when Qui appeared stunningly beautiful in a powder-blue two-piece swimsuit, showing off, besides her tight body and long legs, the English he had been teaching her: "Last one in, rotten egg," she said.

Her language ability allowed Babineaux to learn much more about this girl than he had about Hang or Ly. Qui was born and raised on a boat on the Mekong River -- which explained why she could swim farther and faster than he could. When an American helicopter shot the boat to pieces for no reason at all, she said, her father lost his living and the family their home. Qui came to live with

an aunt in Vung Tau, but they fought and she was thrown out. "So I am like you in October, left in street with no home. A nice man, old like my father, take me home, teach me English for one year, went back to his home in Melbourne, leave me with Co Bich."

Babineaux didn't know how to respond to this story -- whether to congratulate her on her survival skills, apologize for the chopper attack on her family, or take her into his arms and cry. But for her part, she seemed to be....was it resigned? or recovered? or just tougher than hell?

"C'mon, you wombat! Let's go swim!" she said, snatching up towels and bouncing out the door.

On land, a gazelle; in the water, a dolphin: Qui was the best athlete of either gender Babineaux had ever been around. He met with Duong at various restaurants, where they poured over whatever paperwork was brought to him from the boxes and files the translator had moved to his sister's house when Ly ordered them out of her shop. Babineaux ate a light lunch, drinking tea or water. He had to cut alcohol and heavy food out of his diet because Qui was already embarrassing him on land and in the water and his only hope was to go into training mode.

A few weeks into this regimen, with Qui as an inspiration, Babineaux was in the best shape of his life. He now outran Qui whenever he made her laugh at the spectacle of his enormous effort, grunting and pumping his arms in the final yards of a quarter-mile sprint, gasping, "I've...got...you...this...time...." Qui would pull up, howling with laughter, and he would win. In the water he still had no chance, but his strength as a swimmer was coming along, as even Qui admitted.

Her athleticism extended to the bedroom of her little house as well and, combined with her youth and enthusiasm, Qui ended each and every day by turning an already exhausted Mark Babineaux into a complete basket-case -- a man pleading in the night that he had a "big day" tomorrow, a headache or an upset stomach, he needed to get some rest or else...or else...then he would feign sleep for self-preservation. In the morning, he awoke with Qui standing over him, tea tray in hand, and he would say "How did you slip out without waking me?" Qui understood the joke perfectly and said "Magic" or "I'm not telling" and held out her hand for six dollars.

By mid-December, Babineaux was barely hanging on. He lay in bed long after Qui took her money and left, a Pharaoh's mummy of pain-racked immobility, until he must move to make his classes. He downed four aspirin with his tea, tried to stretch-out without scream-ing, and stumbled off to class with all the grace of Boris Karloff's Frankenstein. He hoped to recover enough during the day to survive another decathlon training session with the Amazon-from-hell, beau-tiful though she was, which ended only when he could plead his way out of it, sometime after midnight. He stretched his weekend trip into Saigon to two days so he could crash with Rosie and Mad-dog and spend a day reading in bed, convalescing.

Therefore when he saw Itty Bitchy hanging around the rear of his class as he taught his Buddhist and Animist students about Christmas in America, he felt a secret surge of relief. Never one to let him down easy, she announced, "Qui go work in new Awzee hospital. She boocoo sexy girl. Speak numbah one English. Meet Awzee doctor. Go live Melbourne."

Babineaux pictured himself dozing on the sand with a book in one hand, beer in the other, a towel draped over his head, no longer being lashed by a sadistic drill sergeant who knew how to play on his male ego. But he wasn't going to roll over without a fight this time. Here was his chance to bargain. "I love Qui too much. Maybe I'll take her to United States with me, better than Melbourne."

Bich stepped back and peered up at him, taking his measure. Then she said, "You lie, GI. I know you. You six dollah day cheap-charlie."

"Maybe Qui wants me to stay in her house with her."

"Not her house. My house. OK, you stay my house but Qui stay with me. Go live Melbourne with Awzee doctor."

"OK," Babineaux relented, glad that he had at least stood up for himself and kept his home. "I'll stay in your house. I'll pay you six dollars a day."

"You stay my house," Bich said, pulling him roughly through the door by his shirt-front, "Twel' dollah." She broke out a black-toothed grin and waved her hand, presenting to him a set of identical twins, young and very petite, dressed in matching ao dais.

"Jesus Christ" was all he could manage to say.

17

23 November 1967

TURKEY DAY

Braxton Hood had made a conscious decision to let it go for now. Told in advance that Frank Monroe was brilliant, personally impressive and courageous, he had spent every day in his company from mid-October to mid-November and had to admit, Monroe was all that and more. He commanded every situation, moving and speaking with such confidence that one could not resist being pulled along in the wake of his boundless enthusiasm and curiosity. Sometimes he attended press briefings with "Buddy Foster," Hood's journalist-cover, under an assumed identity of his own, to enjoy peppering the MACV spokesman with witty, sharp-edged questions designed to elicit some embarrassing admission. Every antique and art dealer in town knew him as a reliable client who drove a hard bargain and knew his stuff. Hood was often sent off to Tan Son Nhut to see that these treasures were shipped to an address in Lawrence, Massachusetts. They frequented high-end bars and restaurants all over Saigon, enjoying long, boozy conversations that ranged widely over the terrain of Monroe's interests. Braxton was charmed and intrigued by Monroe, whom he saw as a mentor and man-of-the-world. That was exactly the impression Monroe worked hard to earn.

But Braxton Hood fully understood that this charismatic man was a charlatan. In a shoe-box kept in trust in Rosenzweig's footlocker were photographs of Monroe arriving at III Corps for a budget meeting in the company of Counterpart-D who, even behind sun-glasses, bore a strong resemblance to one of the villa's gate guards, all of whom were called "Nguyen". And even though Hood now worked alongside Monroe in "Control," sifting through Diem's reports from Cu Chi, discussing them, comparing them with MACV reports and making decisions about which agents to keep and which to dismiss, there were Monroe-imposed limits: Hood was not given keys to Control nor to the locked file cabinets where agent files were kept.

Yet harboring these suspicions had gained Hood nothing because the reputation of the Cu Chi station was rock solid. Hood met discreetly with Rosie and Mad-dog at the Dong An eatery where they poured over evaluations of IRs, feedback from SIC Central and MACV, and Cu Chi was judged to be among the best bilateral operations in Vietnam.

So what if CP-D doubled as a gate guard or was a figment of Monroe's imagination?

So what if that haphazard, constantly evolving chart of the network was always and ever mathematically symmetrical -- six handlers, twelve agents each, a perfect pyramid in a chaotic world, a house of cards that never faltered?

So what if the so-called network actually had only eight bilateral employees instead of seventy-eight: Diem, two typists, Thomas and four gate guards? So what if the other slots on the chart were empty place-holders? So what if the $3,500 monthly budget was Frank Monroe's bonus for producing good intelligence that was saving US and ARVN lives in the deadly tunnel complexes of Cu Chi and the Iron Triangle?

In the end, so what? There was so much more to Frank Monroe than met the eye.

Their first pool "match" -- so-called -- had come about on a Friday, November 10, the first time Hood had been invited to work in Control. Hood was still trying at that time to gather information about Monroe, playing the guileless Southern yokel to Monroe's sophisticate, waiting for him to make a slip. At 5:00, Monroe pushed a bell-button that signaled Thomas to bring down cold gin and tonic, lime slices and ice, then he asked for help in clearing the large central table, very much surprising Hood with the fact that they'd been working all afternoon on top of a pool table -- cues, balls, chalk and rack hidden under the plywood.

"My favorite hobby," Monroe said, sucking gin and tonic over ice cubes. "I've been playing since I was ten and I admit, it has provided a source of income now and then."

"Paid your college tuition?" Hood fished for biography.

"Would have if I'd ever gone to college, but I preferred the university of the streets."

Hood smiled benignly.

"Always play for money," Monroe said, placing ten $10 MPC notes on the rail.

"Too rich for my blood," Hood said.

"Of course. You put up one dollar to my hundred, if you allow me to break first. Three games of eight-ball for the pot, OK?"

Monroe did all the talking for the next twenty minutes, reminiscing merrily about the days of his youth, when he would ride into some small town, lose a few games and win a few in pool halls that were a common feature of the town square back then, teasing up the betting against the best players. He would beat them all every time, then head for the bar or the men's room, being sure to leave his beautiful, two-part cue stick lying across the table, jump his motorcycle and roar away, leaving the locals to fight over who got the cue stick. "Lost hundreds of dollars worth of really nice cue sticks, but I got to keep thousands of their hard-earned bucks and my teeth," he concluded, having run the table three consecutive times without missing a shot while Hood leaned on his stick in complete awe. Monroe picked up the $101 in MPC and asked, "Hungry?"

That was one of many events that, taken together, had tugged Braxton Hood little by little into Monroe's gravitational field. The man was utterly fascinating in so many ways that the idea of throwing a monkey wrench into the machinery of his elaborate schemes seemed to Hood a betrayal, mean-spirited and ungrateful. It would be like throwing paint over an extraordinary art work for no good reason. And Hood was coming to genuinely like the man, con artist or not.

Hood later said he could pin-point the moment when he ceased plotting against Monroe and came up with the universal mantra "So What?"

Five straight work-days ended with Monroe bringing Hood's pool game along. With infinite patience and cheer, he spent hours coaching Hood's shots, teaching him to put English on the cue ball and plan ahead. Until one day Hood stopped, laid his cue stick across the green velvet and admitted, "I'm never gonna be any good at this, Frank. It's just not my game."

"What is your game, Buddy?" Monroe teased.

"Poker, actually," Hood said and at once felt the clod-hopping Southern mask slip away.

For the next week, Hood became the teacher and Monroe the hungry, eager student who wanted to know everything. One corner of the unused pool table's cover became their classroom for hours on end. Hood wrote out the odds for every possible hand of five-card and seven-card stud, with and without wild cards, which Monroe struggled mightily to memorize. Then he coached Monroe on the more difficult and crucial part, figuring the betting ceiling and floor on each of these hands, as a percentage of one's holdings, with four players or six or eight.

By Thanksgiving, Braxton Hood and Frank Monroe had forged bonds of genuine affection based on mutual admiration: Hood would never be in Monroe's league at a pool table and Monroe could never hope to juggle calculations in his head that would give him Hood's advantage at a poker table. Their relationship was also based on mutual distrust. Braxton knew that Frank was an accomplished con-artist who lived for the thrill of the game -- and Frank knew that Braxton knew it. "So what?" They had a great time together, living the good life.

The partnership that was established over intelligence work, pool and poker, in bars and restaurants and antique shops all over Saigon, was consecrated at the Thanksgiving feast, that most American of traditions. Thomas rolled out a masterpiece of Euro-Asian cuisine: seaweed-wrapped hors d'oeuvres then soup then fish then duck then salad, all topped-off by cheese then sweet lychee nuts in syrup. Cognac and wine flowed freely across a noisy table and even the dour Diem was caught up in the spirit as he tried to translate into English the cause for the tipsy typist-girls' giggle-fits until he himself was lost in hilarity and couldn't go on. All four indistinguishable gate guards came in for plates of food that they carried back to the courtyard to eat. And taciturn Co Bian was more animated than ever, leaving the table often to switch-out selections on the tape-deck, blending European and Vietnamese music. She chatted happily in French, which Diem and Monroe translated for Hood.

This long night of celebration was concluded with Monroe entrusting to his Buddy the keys to the kingdom -- but not yet the scepter and crown.

The typists had tottered off to bed at 2:00, giggling all the way, and Thomas was banging around in the kitchen, quite drunk. Diem, Bian and the Americans carried their brandy cordials into the living room area and nestled into the plush furniture.

"Six weeks from now, all this will be yours, Buddy," Frank announced with a sweeping gesture, "to do with as you please."

"That, sir, is a terrifying thought," Hood said.

"Any guy who counts cards in his head like you do can handle it, I'm sure."

"I don't count cards, Frank, I calculate odds."

"Remember your first day at the Five O'clock Follies? There was an ambush at Ong Thanh. A bunch of GIs got killed."

"Sixty-four of them."

"Oh, yes! Ever the numbers-man." He raised his glass in salute. "Well, that may all have been our fault, you see. Those guys tripped over a major supply base and troop concentration."

"That's what they're supposed to do, isn't it?"

"Yes, of course. But if they'd received better intelligence, they might have found some supplies somewhere else -- a small reserve cache perhaps -- and captured a few stragglers and everyone would have been better off." Frank sniffed his cordial and sipped. "Mr. Diem and his network got into a lot of trouble over that one."

While Hood fought to clear the fog of inebriation from his mind, Monroe spoke to Bian in French and she rose to leave. Ever the gentleman, Hood arose and wished her "Bon soir."

Frank moved into a lacquer chair next to Hood and said, "She'll be right back, and when she comes, she'll bring what you're going to need to keep the operation going after my DEROS, which is January 11th. So it is time for you to grab a handful of reins, my friend, and begin to guide the wagon."

Hood studied the folders Bian brought him but with limited success. They were full of forms in French and all he could tell was they were dated from *janvier* through *mars* of 1953.

"Co Bian keeps tons of these with her family. They report underground caches, quarters and transverses in and around Cu Chi found by the French over a seven-year period. Many are now abandoned; others are still used. I run them against MACV's operations and eliminate those they've already discovered. Then Diem runs the others by his sources in Cu Chi...well, actually his one source in Cu Chi. This man is in a position to know where the NVA and VC have vital interests. In point of fact, Charlie is starved of supplies. As a result of all the bombing we've done, the NVA is stretched too thin to lavish much of anything on their South Vietnamese brothers. Anyway, the point of the exercise is to save lives...ours and theirs...everybody's. As a numbers-man, you won't have missed that in the two months of your attendance at MACV's 5:00 briefings. American losses have been growing. This is becoming a war of attrition, if it wasn't already. So I figure... Diem and Bian and I figure...avoiding casualties is how America can win this war. Keeping our troops exploring places the NVA won't fight to the death over reduces US casualties. Everyone wins."

Hood did not respond immediately to Monroe's pre-dawn lecture. The mechanics of the operation as well as the level of deception were equally breath-taking. It all seemed perfectly reasonable, even laudable, to hear Monroe tell it, combining older French intel with refined in-put from an NVA source to keep forces from engaging in major battles. But the great unanswered question was this: If Hood said, "You're bilking the military out of $3,500 a month and I'm not going along," would his friend Frank Monroe have the gate guards bury him in a Cu Chi rice paddy? In seven more weeks, he'd be in charge and could shut it all down if he wanted -- or not.

For now, he chose naivety. "So the agent chart in Control is...."

"Bogus, that's right. But Buddy, I thought you'd already figured that out on your own. Otherwise, I would not be letting you in on everything, like I'm doing now."

"I guess I had my doubts about it."

"You're the numbers-man. You know that enlisted guys like us don't live in villas, Buddy, with gate guards and a chef and a couple of Citroëns." Monroe squinted his blue eyes and studied Hood's face before asking, "So...what's your thoughts here?"

"I'm thinking," Hood told him, "I'll need a lot of help if I'm going to take over this whole thing in January."

18

Christmas to New Years Eve, 1967

EVERY STRING PLAYS OUT

Besides "Always play for money" and "It's never really *about* the money," there was this oft-repeated tenet of the Frank Monroe Doctrine: "Sooner or later every string plays out."

With Christmas approaching and just three weeks left before he would be placed in sole possession of the Cu Chi shell game, Hood was worried that the house of cards would fall on his head -- about the time Monroe's plane was touching down in California. He began to think that Plan A might be to kick it all down the day Monroe leaves, confessing to Shimazu that he had discovered -- was *shocked* to discover -- that Frank Monroe had been running a scam, that there was no network in Cu Chi but only a paper-chase.

Plan B did not run a close second in his mind: Keeping Co Bian, Diem and even Thomas and their luxury villa bank-rolled might be possible, but it wouldn't be easy and it sure wouldn't be much fun without Monroe, the pied piper of Saigon.

"Ready to go?" Monroe tapped at his bedroom door. "Big night, Buddy!"

Two gate guards rode in the back seat of the Citroën, carbines across their laps, as Monroe drove to the Caravelle, the finest hotel in Saigon and the tallest. "How you feeling, champ?" he asked in a tone that betrayed more excitement than Hood wanted to hear.

"I'm fine," Hood answered calmly. "How are you holding up?"

"I admit, I'm pumped. I'll be OK once we get to work and everybody shows. I'll be good."

"It's all just math, Frank," Hood said to settle him down, "some luck but mostly math."

Two blocks from the hotel, Hood stepped out of the car, slipped into his tailor-made suit coat and walked the rest of the way. He took a table at the rooftop restaurant, ordered a salad and a bottle of wine and began thumbing through a copy of *Newsweek* he'd brought along. When his meal came, the waiter poured a tasting for him, Hood sipped and approved, and his wine glass was filled. As soon as the waiter had gone, Hood poured all the wine from the bottle and half from the glass into a potted plant next to his chair and proceeded to read about Eugene McCarthy, who promised to end the war and who was running to replace Lyndon Johnson.

Twenty minutes later Frank Monroe approached his table with two other men. "Mr. Slidell, I thought you were going to come down and join us tonight," Monroe said.

Hood tried to fill his empty glass with his empty bottle as he answered heavily, "All y'all 'bout wiped me out last week...figured I'd hang on to what's left of my money if I could."

"This might be your lucky night, my friend...law of averages. And these gentlemen really enjoyed your company last Friday, right?"

"Sure did, Mr. Slidell. We felt bad for you last time. We'd like to give you a chance to win it back tonight," one said.

"We love your stories about growing up in Georgia...wouldn't be as much fun without you," the other said.

"How's about five hands, Mr. Slidell," Frank pleaded. "If you're not ahead after five hands, we'll agree Lady Luck has it in for you and we'll chip-in and buy you a girl to take home."

"Oh, I reckon five hands won't hurt nuthin'. I'm just feeling sore 'bout last week."

The game in Mr. Given's room -- the name Frank had established with his marks for three Friday nights before Mr. Slidell had arrived in Saigon and proved to be such a lousy poker player -- lasted until past noon the next day. Six men besides Monroe and Hood came and went and came back again in the course of that eighteen-hour period. These six businessmen worked in various fields of the private sector -- just as Slidell was in the cotton trade, which is how he met Givens, the textile manufacturer from Lawrence, Massachusetts. But these six had one other thing in common. They all drew their pay-checks from the CIA and Frank Monroe knew it. He had found it out somehow. He never said how.

Mr. Slidell did not have a perfect night, but he had a better night than the week before, when he had bad luck that cost him several thousand dollars in US currency.

In fact, in the course of the long, boozy night and morning, Mr. Slidell actually lost most of the time. But he hung in there bravely, leaving the table only during breaks in the game to use the bath-room. The steady flow of gin-and-tonics Mr. Givens kept pouring for him seemed not to take much of a toll, though the others did become much the worse for wear over time. And as luck would have it, each time betting grew heavy and there was a real show-down between strong hands, Mr. Slidell seemed to win most of those hands. In fact, when the CIA men looked back on it, he had won all of them.

The pain that would usually be felt by men who had put very considerable amounts of money on a card table and left broke was very much mitigated in this peculiar instance by the fact that only a little of it came out of their own pockets. The nature of their work -- their actual work, not their cover-story work -- required that funds be readily available for any possible exigency. Discretionary funds at the field level were limited and supervised, but the source of those funds   -- what Frank Monroe referred to as "the mother lode for Southeast Asia" -- resided by necessity in Saigon Station, the same office where these gentlemen all had their desks. And from their office safe, in a panic to recover their losses, they brought wondrous gifts.

"What're these?" Mr. Slidell wanted to know.

"Lira...actually Turkish lira," he'd be told or "rubles" or "I'm not sure...I think they're Chinese yuan renimbi. How about I put up 20,000 in this stuff to cover your last $200?"

"How 'bout you put in 50,000, just to be sure," Mr. Slidell suggested.

Even for an experienced, natural-born huckster like Frank Monroe, this had been one hell of a night. *"Chrissakes! Look! At! This!"* he screamed when they were together again in Control. Scattered across the plywood cover lay colorful mountains of MPC, US dollars, dong, rubles, yen, francs, riel, kip, baht and other even less common notes. "You see those suckers!? You'd break one, he'd make a trip for 'cigarettes' and before he got back, another would be gone to 'check the telex back in the office,' like some sort of bucket-brigade, hauling in piles of dough to lay before the Divine Mathematician! Man! Buddy!" He laid hands on Braxton's shoulders, laughing maniacally, "You were fucking amazing! This has been the most fun I've ever had in my whole life...I mean, thank you, man!"

Hood chuckled appreciatively. "Most fun I've had too, Frank. But if I never drink another tonic on ice, it'll be too soon." Then the adrenaline rush of it all began to fail him and he dropped his big body into an office chair. "How much you suppose is here?"

"That will take awhile," Monroe said. "I'll lock up the MPC and dollars here, take the whole rest of this rainbow pile to some antique dealers. For a cut, they'll convert anything, turn it to greenbacks on the black market."

"Then what?" Hood said, fading away.

"Then we buy this house, so we don't have to pay rent," Frank laughed. "I don't know... something will come up, it always does. Besides, you know...."

"Yeah, it's never about the money." Before Frank finished laughing, Hood was asleep.

What to get the man who has everything? Days before Christmas, Braxton really did want to give Monroe something, a token of their time together. In three weeks, he'd be in Lawrence, Massachusetts sorting out his art and antique treasurers and finding ways to import his half of the estimated $62,000. in poker money he'd agreed to split with Hood -- plus whatever else he'd been skimming from the Cu Chi operation and a year of Army pay. Hood did the math and whistled. Still, Monroe had shown him a great time and was as good a friend to him, probably, as it was in Frank's nature to be to anyone.

But Monroe was adamant when asked about a gift. "Look," he said, "I dread boredom like death, Braxton. You pulled me out of the doldrums by showing up here. You've already given me the greatest gift of all...your friendship. So let's you and I present Diem with a Seiko watch, Co Bian with a couple bolts of nice silk, and Thomas wants a good blender and a fat bonus. These will be from both of us, so they'll remember me and welcome you as the new chief in January."

So on Christmas Eve, a festive and delicious dinner, equal to Thanksgiving's, was enjoyed and gifts given out, along with generous cash awards to the gate guards and the giddy typists. But there was always more to Frank Monroe than met the eye. Always.

When champagne had washed everyone away to bed except the two Americans, Frank said quietly, "I have a surprise gift for you, my friend." He handed Braxton a crisp, new $20 MPC note, leather brown on one side, pale green on the other, pretty ladies featured in oval frames.

"Where have you seen this before?" he asked.

"Haven't."

'That's right, Buddy. MPCs come in denominations under $10 for another week. But The Republic of Vietnam is going to wake up on Tuesday, January 2, to explosive news from every radio and newspaper. MACV will announce 'Conversion Day,' which will mean that every MPC note stuffed in the mattresses of every merchant and government official is and has been worthless, retroactively to 1:00 a.m. that morning. All military and contractors will then be paid in new currency...in this new $20 denomination and completely redesigned MPC notes for all the lower denominations. MACV can't print MPCs faster than the Vietnamese can hoard them, so they have to do a C-Day now and then to discourage that."

"How do you know about this?" Hood asked.

"How did I know about CIA's Saigon Station and all those cocky young agents?"

"Clerk's Mafia," Hood guessed.

"Buddy," Frank lifted his champagne flute. "A toast to pandemonium! Merchants large and small and corrupt government officials and black marketers, will all be in a panic. They will turn to GIs and American contractors for help because we can convert old-to-new in limited amounts for a limited time. But the magic wand for us is a vital contact I have in Army Payroll who has agreed, for a cut-of-the-action of course, to a one-time exchange up to $300,000, old-for-new. This will be...for him and for us...a New Year's Bonanza! Just the thing I need to fund my retirement and the crowning achievement of my splendid year in Vietnam, the smart-man's paradise! In two boxes down in Control, I have ten thousand of the new notes, which comes to..."

"$200,000," Hood said.

"That right, minus the $20 you're holding."

"Hold on, Frank, I don't know," Hood sat up straighter. "This isn't a poker game...."

"Hear me out, Buddy. This money has not been stolen or even loaned. It's been purchased at fair exchange. In fact, we paid a premium for it, so we actually have $220,000 invested in it. We own these notes, fair and square."

"We..."

"Yes, well...the poker money provided some of the investment. I forked over the rest."

"I don't recall voting my shares."

"I had to move fast, Buddy. Timing is everything on this one. Here's the plan: Beginning tomorrow, Christmas Day for

6% of Vietnam that's Christian but not for the rest, we'll make stops at a half-dozen of our favorite high-end art and antique dealers. Because we like them, and to turn a profit, of course, we will give them a heads-up that next Tuesday will be a Conversion Day. They'll beg us to convert a wad of their MPC holdings, which we tell them we can do from our company's vault and, in fact, we'll graciously agree to return the next day and help them out, for a cut, with some of the new notes advanced to our company by MACV. We'll offer $4,000 of the new $20's in trade for $5,000 of the old currency, take it or leave it, no haggling. After C-Day, we'll tell them, the mark-ups will be much higher, if they find anyone who can help them at all.

"So tomorrow, Monday, a nice, easy go-around on the Hondas, three shops before lunch, three after. Tuesday, Wednesday and Thursday will be a big challenge for us but loads of fun. We'll come back with the Citroën, Diem and a couple guards. Every stop we make will have the shop owner with ten or fifteen grand on hand, absolutely desperate, trying to grab more than the $5,000 we offer. A group of his relatives and other customers will be there too, trying to piggy-back as the grape-vine kicks in and panic spreads. Diem will translate for me, you'll do the math for us, and we'll put the squeeze on them. The merchant gets 4-for-5, as promised, but the other folks, we made them no promises. The exchange rate will slide in our favor as the amounts get bargained up and, the way I figure it, we can trade out the whole $200,000 by Thursday, or I'll eat my hat. We'll have more fun than we had at poker and take away $280 grand or more to split between us, 50-50, as always. The night of C-Day, January 2, we meet my pay-master clerk, give him ten grand more... he already has twenty from the first premium I paid on the notes... and he will trade-out the rest, old MPC for new, even money. Like you, he's a trusted friend of mine and he's guaranteed $30,000, a pretty good bonus for an E-6. Then all we do is hand Diem and the guards a fat wad of cash, and you and I will settle up for poker and this gig. You're the math-man so you already got it. If you don't start the new year with $80,000, I'll make up the difference myself. Not bad for three days' work, right?"

The figures did indeed add up in Hood's estimation -- another beautifully detailed sleight-of-hand from the ever-surprising mind of Frank Monroe. This time, however, was a great deal more dangerous -- running around Saigon with a trunk-full of money that wasn't even supposed to be in circulation yet, trying to jack-up very savvy merchants who weren't born yesterday and who hadn't been drinking for eighteen hours. But the pay-off quadrupled their poker winnings.

This is a war-zone, he thought, *plenty of E-4s who are putting their lives on the line every day for three grand a year would be more than happy to swap places with me for an $80,000 pay-day. And my poker money is already tied up in the deal.*

Monroe was still jabbering on, anxious about Hood's obvious hesitancy. "I know I should have talked with you about this first. I invested your money without asking...but we still haven't gotten all those foreign notes converted. There are limits on who wants to take rubles and lira and I'm trying not to get screwed on that stuff. So look, Buddy...on January 4, III Corps holds the budget meeting for Cu Chi. I want you to present our funding request to Shimazu. I'll take a back seat as your advisor. If you do well...if the network budget we agree on going in gets approved as amended by III Corps, we'll drive straight to a bank and I'll cut you a cashier's check for every penny you've earned." The malamute-blue eyes studied him closely and Monroe asked, "OK?"

"Sounds fair enough to me," Hood lied. Monroe had taught him that each shot on a pool table had two objectives: To sink the target ball and to position the cue for the next successful shot. *Nobody does this better than Monroe,* he thought. *By the time he climbs on that plane, I'll be the new face of the Cu Chi scam, or if I refuse, I'll be out 50 grand, a villa, and $3,000 a month steady income after expenses. Oh, and we'll both be living in the Long Binh stockade.*

Hood too raised his glass in salute. "OK," he said.

The week sped by in a blur of frantic action that was by turns terrifying, exhilarating, and exhausting. Diem told all the shop-owners, "Don't tell anybody...we tell you this in secret..." and "We won't come back with the new money if word gets out." These warnings had the desired, opposite effect.

On Tuesday, the first four shops chewed up the whole day. They never got to the other two. High-ranking government officials sent their henchmen to issue threats and demands if $20,000 weren't traded out, right now, on already very generous terms for Monroe. Competitive bidding soon shifted the odds even further in their favor. Rich relatives and high-end clients of the shop-owners were ready to undercut the more influential and dangerous types, with further leverage coming to the Americans from the two ominous guards with shouldered carbines that followed them. Premiums of 33% and higher were agreed to and Hood was kept busy juggling exchange amounts in a swirling, screaming trading-pit of foreign-language anxiety.

"What's 40% of 9,000?" Monroe would shout.

"Thirty-six hundred."

"Ask him for twelve-thousand-six-hundred in trade for nine-thousand," Monroe told Diem.

Trading slowed down and got even uglier on Wednesday, in the final two shops, as they had only a few thousand new $20 notes left and competitive bidding sent premiums soaring.

"What did he call me?" Monroe asked Diem. "He just called me something, didn't he!"

"No, sir. He just said you are very smart, so you must have good parents."

By dinner-time on Wednesday, one full day ahead of Monroe's estimate, four heavy boxes jammed with $10 and $5 soon-to-be-obsolete notes, were taped shut, sitting in a corner of Control and five soon-to-be-valid $20 notes were given to each guard and fifty to Diem. "To our New Year's Bonanza!" Monroe said, standing at the head of the table and raising a wine glass. "On Tuesday night, January second,

Braxton and I will go out under armed escort and it will *really* be an out-with-the-old-and-in-with-the-new to remember! We'll hold our budget meeting on the fourth and I'll have just one week to get my affairs in order and get ready to...." The last word stuck in his throat and all present were somewhat shocked to see his blue eyes glisten with tears. Beautiful Co Bian rose, walked around the table and put her arms around him. Monroe draped an arm over her, swallowed hard and said, "You've all become my family...."

In the wee hours of Friday morning, Hood's bedroom door opened and he awoke. He remembered his .45 was in the bedside table just as he heard Monroe whisper, "Buddy, wake up."

"What's up, Frank?"

"There's been a slight hitch. Nothing we can't handle," Monroe whispered in the dark. "Diem overheard the guards and he thinks they're planning something. They know we're sitting on a mountain of money that's still good for two days. They could buy a lot of stuff this weekend before C-Day takes everybody by surprise. Diem's gone to get the white mice and when he gets back, we need to skedaddle. So pack light, we'll throw the MPC into the Citroëns and convoy down to the beach for the weekend, drive back on Monday night for the money-exchange. Don't turn on any lights."

For the first time, Hood laced his belt through his holster, chambered a round, checked the safety and slid his .45 onto his hip. He hauled his duffle out to the dark living room then put on his shoes. Frank arrived just as voices arose outside. Under the courtyard light, Diem was barking sharply in Vietnamese and a guard swung the gate open for four QCs in a jeep. Monroe unlocked Control and they loaded the four big boxes of money into the Citroëns, two filling each trunk, so they had to put their baggage on the back seats. Bian took a place in the passenger seat of Monroe's car, so Hood slid in beside

Diem and they pulled out into the quiet city street, leaving the cops and the guards wrangling loudly behind them.

On the southern edge of town, the two-car convoy pulled to the curb and Monroe came back to say, "Let's make a stop here, wait for sun-up." Diem was sound asleep in moments, slumped against the wheel, but Hood sat awake for two hours, nervous as a cat, .45 in his lap, checking the mirrors and windows for whatever threat the night might hold. When the sky lightened to pale blue, Monroe honked twice and started his engine. Hood shook Diem awake and they drove south through awakening rice farms and villages.

Three hours later, they were enjoying coffee, tea and pastries at an outdoor table across from the most spectacular beach Hood had ever seen. Caucasian men and Vietnamese of both sexes sun-bathed, swam and walked together as if there had never been a war. "Safest place in the country, Buddy," Monroe said, "Eden before The Fall."

They checked into a sea-front hotel where they watched hotel staff struggle up the stairs with the heavy boxes. Then for two days, they lived like royalty, buying clothes, food and drink, boxes of cigars for the men, jewelry for Bian, tipping lavishly with money that would turn to rags at midnight on Monday like Cinderella's dress. Diem vanished Sunday morning with only an aside from Monroe, "He had to go back to Saigon to take care of the operation."

Braxton spent the weekend on the beach, recovering from the exhausting week, observing Monroe and Bian together, and calculating. Decision-time had arrived, slipped up on him, and he was nowhere near sure how to handle it. Frank and Bian were lovers about to part, and away from all the work and madness of the villa, they seemed to draw closer. Would she vanish after his DEROS on January 11th? Would he take Frank's place with her? Or would she keep her room, leaving him to his, and continue her work for the network? What *was* she paid? She had not appeared on the budget Rosie had shown him at the compound. And Diem? "About average pay for a translator," Rosie said. But surely he was paid more, as capstone of the Cu Chi scam.

As he watched Monroe and Bian wade through low waves together, he shirtless and in shorts, she holding her ao dai in her arms, Hood resolved that Monday, New Year's Day, on this beautiful beach, he would confront Monroe for a birds-and-bees talk. "Either tell me how this thing all works, or don't expect me to run it when you're gone. I can't fly the plane, Frank, if all I've been is a passenger," he planned to say.

But Sunday night was unlike anything three and a half months as Frank Monroe's aide and partner-in-crime could have led him to expect. The lovers descended from an afternoon in their room looking resplendent -- Frank in an off-white silk suit with a festive tie and Co Bian in a new ao dai, a striking heliotrope over white slacks, jewelry sparkling around her pretty face -- and neither of them were themselves. In the role of Bian was a glowingly happy, vivacious girl leading a conversation in French with her adoring lover. And Frank Monroe played the part of a carefree, modest fellow, much more interested in other people than in himself.

"It's wonderful that we got this holiday together, sharing a beautiful night with you," he said. "So Braxton, what's your family like? What does your dad do? I bet you played football...."

And not once in the course of an evening of food and wine and walking along the moonlit beach did he use the name Buddy. Mr. Intensity had morphed into Mr. Serenity and at the evening's end, Co Bian stood on her toes to give Braxton a kiss on each cheek. Frank Monroe clasped his big paw in both hands and said, "Sleep well, my friend. Tomorrow starts a brand-new year!"

19

THE CONVERSION

Monroe and Bian were not at the hotel cafe where they agreed to meet when Braxton Hood came down from his room. They'd all stayed up drinking and talking into the wee hours of the morning, so he took a table with a view of the beach, ordered coffee and waited. At 9:00, he ordered eggs, ham and toast while the sea-side came fully to life across the way. By 10:30, he had waded through both *The Saigon Daily News* and *The Saigon Post*, two English-language papers that would shout "Conversion Day" in tomorrow's headlines, announcing what Frank had called a "*fait accompli*". He paid his bill, leaving a $10 note for the waiter, then reconsidered and placed another $10 note on top of that. Then he went up to knock on their door but found a maid changing the sheets. He tried gestures and pidgin without success, then frightened her by advancing into the room and was not completely shocked to find the closets and bureau empty. *Tomorrow starts a brand-new year,* Frank had told him. "But the same old Frank Monroe," he said aloud. He raced down to his room, expecting to find his two boxes of scrip either gone or filled with newspapers, but they were still in his closet. He peeled the tape to be sure and saw the stacks of $10 and $5 notes there. But they would soon be worthless without Monroe's Payroll clerk to switch them out. *So you decided to steal away with your half and stick me with eighty pounds of scrap paper,* he thought, *but why?*

Feeling like a sucker for doing so, he nevertheless went to the hotel desk to ask if there were any messages for him. There was one. The clerk handed him a small box bearing his name neatly written in Bian's French schoolgirl hand. He dropped into a chair in the far corner of the lobby and tore it open. Inside was a book, *The Great Imposter* by Robert Crichton, which told the story of Ferdinand Waldo Demara, a con-artist and master chameleon who passed himself off as a military surgeon, a prison warden, a philosophy professor and a Trappist monk, living each of these roles for some length of time before moving on. On the title page Monroe had inscribed, "For my brilliant friend Braxton Hood, my Bible. I will always treasure the memory of our time together and the thrills we shared. Take care of yourself and remember: It's never about the money, Jim. PS. Don't ever return to the villa."

Two slips of paper marked pages in the book: The passage that described the town of Lawrence, Massachusetts, where Demara was brought up, was book-marked by a Vietnamese document that apparently registered "Braxton Hood" as the owner of a "1957, six-cylinder Citroën Avant". Another passage, describing successful operations performed by Demara when he posed as a Navy surgeon, was marked by a cashier's check made out to Hood for his share of the marathon poker game, $31,272.

Hood remained in the lobby chair for a long time, wrestling with the double equation of Frank Monroe, "Jim" somebody, and trying to resolve the emotional turmoil of this abandonment or reward or betrayal or settling of accounts or final farewell -- or whatever this was. As adept as he was at resolving equations, Braxton Hood could not solve for either "x" or "y". At length, he stuffed the check and auto registration into his pants pocket and crossed the lobby to yet another surprise. His hotel bill had been "paid in full by your friend."

Hood packed up and cleared out, tossing the heavy boxes of MPC notes on the rear seat of the Citroën, half-hoping they'd be stolen, since they were evidence that he had taken part in Frank Monroe's latest scheme. Tomorrow, he would convert as much of it as was legally permitted into the new currency.

Diem had driven the old Citroën with ease, but Hood found changing gears using the dog-leg stick that protruded from the dashboard unwieldy to say the least. It was a tribute to French engineering that nothing he did actually dropped the transmission onto the roadway as he lost his way, found it, and lost it again before recognizing a familiar boulevard in Saigon. His arrival at the enlisted compound drew a small crowd of men off-work for the holiday, who had nothing better to do than ask him where he got it and how it drove.

Much in need of company, friends he could trust to be who and what they said they were, he was disappointed to find Rosie and Mulcahey had gone out. He sprawled across Rosenzweig's bunk to think about how much he should tell his friends. For a month, his Greyhawk classmates had secretly helped him investigate Frank Monroe, bringing classified budgets and reports to him from the III Corps office at some risk to their own security clearances. As far as they knew, he was on the side of the angels, trying to get the goods on that shady character, Monroe. Did he have to tell them now that he helped that charlatan shaft CIA officials out of sixty grand? Or that he took advantage of knowing Conversion Day was coming to help Monroe cheat the locals out of thousands more? Did he EVER have to tell them or anybody else? "Jim" had covered his tracks -- why should Braxton Hood have to be the fall-guy?

What I'll do, he concluded, *is come clean with Shimazu on the Cu Chi network -- lay it all out straight with Diem's role and Bian's role and my own. But the schemes we ran, I'm gonna sweep under the rug. That's no skin off Shimazu's nose and it was all crooked and I could end up in the Long Binh stockade and might anyway, just for the network scam. Tomorrow, I'll sign the poker check over to some Vietnamese orphanage, convert as much scrip as they'll allow, then toss the boxes of old scrip into a trash barrel down on Tu Do Street and leave the keys in the Citroën for the first thief who comes along.*

"It's shark goddamn it!" he heard Rosie shout in the stairway.

"It's red snapper, Rosie. I know shark from red snapper," Mad-dog shouted back.

"I come at a bad time?" Hood greeted them. "You sound like an ole married couple."

"Hey Braxton, where you been?" Rosie asked.

"Been busy. What's all this shark-talk?"

"Major sent us for red snapper for tonight's New Year's Day Dinner, but the fish we put in the fridge over at III Corps doesn't smell right. I think we were screwed at the market."

"You'd be the first GI ever cheated down there," Hood said.

Mad-dog stuck to his guns. "It's red snapper," he insisted.

Hood said, "Listen. Cu Chi's budget is scheduled for Thursday. Could the major move it up to tomorrow?"

"Nope. Can't," Rosie said. "There's a pow-wow of top brass at MACV tomorrow. Mark Babineaux put together some big report and everybody's going…Shimazu and the lieutenant. Major Cardenas helped Mark prep for it."

Mad-dog broke out in gleeful laughter. "They're gonna shoot him against a wall, watch and see! It's Babineaux, man! The crazy Cajun we all know-and-love! He'll stand up and say, 'Good morning, gentlemen. I've called you all together to tell you to go take a flying leap on a rollin' donut, you pompous wind-bags!' and he'll smile his big, wild-assed smile and that's when they'll shoot him against a wall!"

"Knock it off, will ya'?" Rosie told him. "We helped him gather data and maps and stuff for it, and it's a pretty impressive piece of work. Even Shimazu thinks so."

"The report's OK," Mulcahey said, "but the presenter-in-question is a crazy-ass and MACV doesn't go for comedy routines."

"I think Vung Tau changed him a lot," Rosie said. "At the budget meeting, he was dead-serious and all business. We couldn't get a laugh out of him, could we? He's not the same guy."

"He had a bad day," Mad-dog said. "But trust me, he hasn't changed a bit inside."

"Don't count on it!" Hood said forcefully. They both turned to look at him. "Being out in the field can change any man. Believe me!"

Braxton declined their pleas that he come to Shimazu's New Year's Day Dinner, which was his loss because the onion-garlic-cilantro-oregano-pepper-and-black-olive, cream-of-shark-with-potato stew was outstand-ing, as Rosie and Mad-dog repeatedly assured the chef.

When they left early Tuesday morning to help Shimazu and Aaronson prepare for Babineaux's presentation at MACV, they speculated about what sort of dignitary had left a black Citroën four-door sedan in the parking area. "It musht be dee Geshtapo!" Mad-dog opined and made another educated guess about the cardboard boxes resting on the back seat: "Untershirts und Untershorts for dee Untermenschen, ya voll!"

"It's a French car, you idiot," Zach Rosenzweig scolded him, "and I am probably *not* the guy you want to amuse with Nazi jokes."

When they'd gone, Hood showered in the cold water that was the lot of those who didn't live in a villa, dressed, then pointed the Citroën toward Tan Son Nhut. An MP named Swanson carefully studied his ID card and said, "Did you trade your red-and-white Honda for this, sir?"

"No Sergeant," Hood said, feeling unsettled that he'd been recog-nized, "I drove this ole car because I figured it might rain."

Swanson glanced up at a blue sky that hadn't hosted a cloud since October, smiled and said, "Yessir."

Step one of Hood's plan was to convert as much scrip as the law allowed before dealing with the rest and the car. He stood in a long line at the counter where contractors were paid -- his Army pay was deposited directly into the Military Payroll Office across the way. Two young men in front of him in line hotly debated the merits of some song lyrics that had only two words, apparently: "hello" and "goodbye".

"What the hell's the world coming to, Perry? We're in the middle of a war here, people are dying, and they're walkin' around singing hello-goodbye-hello-goodbye, Jesus Christ!"

"It's a breakthrough, I tell you, a classic. It's minimalist and absurdist. It's brilliant. Be around fifty, a hundred years from now, I promise you."

This went on until they got to the counter and one of them pushed a pay voucher and his ID card at the clerk. "What ever happened to narrative?" he muttered as the clerk had him sign the voucher and began counting out $10 MPC notes, chocolate brown, with the profile of somebody's sister in the center, one-by-one, each of them identical to the four hundred $10 notes in Braxton's pocket. Without warning, a huge paw landed on the shoulders of both men and they were swung open like a set of gates. The large man who did this to them wore a savage, bug-eyed expression.

"Hey!" and "What do you think you're...." were ignored as he shouted at the clerk, "Turn those bills over!" When the startled clerk did so, beckoning an MP guard with his free hand, the face of a skinny Statue of Liberty appeared on the notes' reverse sides, pink trimmed in brown. They were the same design as the MPC everyone had been using all year. The MP approached with his .45 drawn, held low but ready. He barked at the big man who seemed to be causing the trouble but was ignored.

"Have you seen one of these yet?" Hood demanded of the clerk. He shoved a $20 note across the counter, pale green and brown.

"Yessir, I have. That's counterfeit, been showing up here all week."

"Step back from the counter and come with me, sir. Do it now," the MP told Hood.

Noticing him for the first time, Hood said "OK" and to the others, "Sorry for the trouble."

Outside the door, Hood explained he'd been upset to realize someone had stuck him with a counterfeit $20 and got a little excited.

His civilian status got him off with a warning, but during the whole conversation, his attention was focused on a Citroën parked a hundred yards away, unlocked, with well over one-hundred-thousand dollars in perfectly valid MPC notes sitting on the back seat.

"It's not about the money," he told the MP. "It was just, I was so surprised."

Neither *The Saigon Daily News* nor the *Saigon Post* made any mention of a Conversion Day when Hood flipped through them at the PX, after locking two forty-pound boxes of MPC in the trunk of his locked Citroën.

20

15 December 1967 to 2 January 1968

CASSANDRA, YET AGAIN

Mark Babineaux was young and strong so he recovered quickly, both emotionally and in body, from the exhaustion of his six-week competition with the beautiful tyrant Qui, with whom he could never keep up in water or on land, though he nearly killed himself trying. Phuong and Long, the petite identical twins who came to stay with him in the bungalow owned by Bich, were very nurturing and attentive to him, more solicitous than any of the other girls to his needs and moods despite their knowing not a word of English. They fluttered around him like dainty, lively birds, chirping in Vietnamese and flapping their thin arms in oversized ao dais.

Babineaux's revival after what he called "The InQUIsition" came none too soon. At the December budget meeting, Major Shimazu had demanded to know how the field station had spent almost $2,000 in November while producing just six Information Reports, all judged by MACV to be "Incomplete" or "Unreliable". "Much is expected from Vung Tau Station," Shimazu warned Babineaux, CP-E and Duong. "My superior officers are demanding to know what has gone wrong and I don't have answers for them, gentlemen. Do you?" But all Babineaux could think about during that December meeting were his calf muscles, throbbing with acute pain from a vicious, double charley horse that had struck both legs simultaneously at 2:00

that morning. He had bolted out of the mosquito netting, howling in agony. He rolled around the floor crying, while Qui straddled him, kneading each cramp in turn with her strong hands. Her efforts made the pain even more intolerable, but when he screamed at her to stop, would she stop? No! She continued pulling on the knots in his legs, calling him a big baby while she ripped his flesh apart with her powerful fingers. As Shimazu spoke, Babineaux could feel his right calf beginning to tighten dangerously and he feared he might leap up at any moment and limp around the conference table in pain. "One more month like this," Shimazu was saying, "could be the end of the Vung Tau field station."

One more month with Qui, Babineaux reflected, *and I won't be here to see it.*

But then came the twins, Phuong and Long, who soon worked such magic that Babineaux began to turn his energies toward saving his safe, privileged life in a resort town. He drove the yellow jeep up the mountain road to the cave of the Clearance Diving Team and -- completely sober this time -- held a lengthy discussion with the Royal Australian Navy captain of Irish descent about the military tactics that won battles with reduced casualties. The RAN captain put him in touch with infantry officers who fought the Long Tan battle in August of 1966, which resulted in hundreds of VC killed with the loss of just eighteen Australian KIA. "You hold 'eem in place and you creep 'round 'eem, see, and you neever follow a line of pursuit 'lest you steep into a trap, see," was the gist of what they taught him. Command of the skies and a monopoly on heavy artillery didn't hurt either, but Babineaux was more interested in creating a viable narrative than in getting it right. Saving Vung Tau station seemed much more urgent to him now that Qui had moved on. If he lost it, he would lose the bungalow. He would lose the beach. The twins would go live with some guy who would treat them badly. And he would be transferred away from this serene setting to a place where people shot at each other. Qui was off his back now. This was a different ball-game.

Each afternoon, he and Duong worked furiously to underpin his strategic narrative with evidence from field agents. The dozen or so currently employed reported only that soft drink and nuoc mam sales were brisk and fishing was good -- so they had no choice but to generate an entirely new branch of their network, made up of young prostitutes who had wiled their ways into the bedrooms of high-level sources. No such agents yet existed, but that was a detail they could work out later, when they had more time. First, they had to save the Vung Tau station.

Babineaux titled his report "White Paper on the Near-Term Course of The War" and once he got going, it flowed out seamlessly, based on a series of perfectly sensible questions.

"Was it true that Australian infantry units engaged the enemy as vigorously as American units with many fewer casualties and more favorable kill-ratios?" Babineaux asked. Nobody had any idea, so it would seem reasonable to assume it. It became a settled fact, grounded in two beautifully crafted IRs from the new field agent named Hang.

"If there were a high-level NVA source familiar with current thinking in Hanoi who came to Vung Tau to mend his battle fatigue and to forget two years of personal trauma caused by near-death experiences and the loss of many friends, would human nature not find him getting drunk and pouring his heart out to a pretty girl, who happened to be agent Co Ly of Vung Tau station's newest network?" A man is a man, whatever his politics. Two more Information Reports.

"Could a popular uprising bring down the government of Nguyen Van Thieu under the weight of its alleged corruption and well-documented suppression of the Buddhist majority by the ruling Catholic minority?" Perhaps, but of course that had not happened and the large American presence made it unlikely, so would war planners in Hanoi grow tired of waiting? Of course they would! They would seek the advice of an experienced commander, who would then return to the South and the advice he gave to them, he would carelessly repeat to a pretty prostitute named Qui. It was just the way of the world and it was good for three more Information Reports.

All of these things took on a life of their own as Babineaux typed-on. He read himself to sleep with his dog-eared copies of James Bond paperbacks, checking his amateur efforts against professional practice. He edited and re-wrote his White Paper and the Information Reports streaming from the all-female branch of the Vung Tau network, code named "Big Fish". These newly recruited agent-whores, code-named Hang, Ly and Qui, were at last realizing the full potential of this unique resort-based station, generating a "treasure trove of strategic and policy intelligence," as SIC Central had been demanding. Duong was completely on-board with the White Paper. He too wanted to remain safe and happy, living in his sister's house in Vung Tau, so he translated everything Babineaux wrote, pre-dating his work so it would appear the Vietnamese versions came first. And when CP-E asked to meet with these alluring agents, it proved impossible to contact them, working girls being the sort of wandering, rootless types who followed wherever opportunity led, day-to-day. CP-E was consoled with bottles of American whiskey with which to drown his disappointment.

At the end of each day's intelligence work, the much more serious business took place that would turn Phuong and Long into spectacular bar-tenders, employing their natural grace and seamless coordination into a drink-mixing phenomenon of beauty, teamwork and expertise, irresistible to men on leave. Such men would someday pack "Babineaux's Seaside Lounge" to watch the dainty duo fill their orders and fulfill their fantasies. This project began when Babineaux found the twins flipping through his copy of *Old Mr. Boston's De Luxe Official Bartender's Guide* one afternoon. He talked his Aussie friends into a trip to Saigon and loaded their Ute with booze, mixes, glasses, tumblers, and so forth from the PX. Sweating from the effort but also from the risk, he was spending every dollar he had on this gamble, but he felt he had no choice. The twelve bucks he gave the twins each morning was roughly equivalent to his Army pay, and Ly had almost finished paying him off for the office-supply shop, so even if the White Paper saved the station, he was fast going broke. By February, he figured, he'd either be famous at SIC and solvent in Vung Tau or neither. And he might finally get the better of Itty Bitchy. When she came along to steal-away his girls, she would be unable to force the twins to leave their profitable new careers, their employer and teacher and lover, and their happy home. Bich would fail and he, Mark Babineaux, would have gained the upper hand at last!

And from his point-of-view, he had found the perfect relationship: The twins delighted in everything he did for them, every moment they spent together. Even the language barrier was a source of continuous amusement as they used faces and hands, touches and gestures and onomatopoeia, while they learned the lingo for every cocktail ever made and all the ingredients and tools of the trade. Babineaux's Lounge would be no dive-bar but a classy place -- not the kind of "treasure trove" Shimazu wanted but one that would provide a solid income for him and his delightful twins. He had to admit to himself that those days when he climbed under the mosquito netting with just one girl, having drunk only beer, deserved to be a fading memory. He was grimly determined to keep what he had. "Not this time, Itty Bitchy," he promised as the little fingers squeezed lime juice into a tumbler and pierced a maraschino cherry with a plastic sword, "Not this time!"

But all these dreams fell apart if the White Paper failed to save the field station. So it was a great relief when the first draft was well received at III Corps. Major Shimazu's suggestions for implementing and improving it were all incorporated in the final draft forwarded to SIC Central. Colonel George Owen Donohue himself ordered Babineaux to report for a debriefing on what the colonel called "A report with the most profound implications for strategic planning yet produced in-country." A presentation to high-level commanders was called for January 2nd at MACV.

Foregoing a night of holiday celebration with his twin mixologists, Babineaux reported to SIC Central mid-morning of New Year's Day. Major Cardenas took charge of preparing him for his performance, beginning with a haircut and being measured for a tailor-made suit.

Graphs illustrating the increase in U.S. casualties throughout 1967 were prepared to support the central thesis of his paper: That war planners in Hanoi had made the decision to turn away from the fall of the Saigon government as their central war aim in favor of inflicting high numbers of allied casualties to fuel war-weariness in the U.S. and force Washington into peace talks. Furthermore, by adapting infantry tactics developed by the Australians, Hanoi's objectives could be thwarted by reducing American casualties while still vigorously prosecuting an offensive war against the enemy. Donohue and Cardenas were very tough on him during final rehearsals, peppering him with cynical questions and working on his pronunciation so he would sound not-quite-so-Cajun. In the late evening, he was fed, given a final fitting for his suit, handed a GS-16 photo ID to replace his GS-11 and sent to bed.

"Who's gonna believe I'm a GS-16?" he'd asked Cardenas.

"Everybody in the room knows we are the Army bilateral intelligence outfit. They don't know your rank so we introduce you as someone they need to listen to." Then Cardenas went out, gently closed the door behind him and, like the family man he was, murmured, "Sleep well, Lad."

Sleep well he did not. He'd spun the White Paper narrative out of whole cloth, along with the Information Reports and, for that matter, the agent-whores and their sources. The only factual part was rising US casualty figures. But the beauty of the Vung Tau site was, it was a transient resort-town where 70% of the population turned over every week. If asked to produce an agent or her source, he could plausibly say, "Can't find her. She's moved on." He had Vung Tau to lose -- this magnificent stretch of sand and sea, his safety, his brace of beautiful twins, his dream of a fancy bar and lots of money -- set off against being sent-off to a war-zone. It was worth a gamble.

By every account, Babineaux performed brilliantly at the top-secret briefing. High level MACV brass listened attentively as he lapsed only twice into a bayou accent while presenting them with a compelling and reasoned case for making tactical adjustments in order to lower allied casualties -- thus frustrating Hanoi's strategic aims. The most pressing questions he was asked, as predicted, examined his claim that Hanoi war-planners had actually made the decision to drive America into peace negotiations by manipulating State-side anti-war sentiments. Babineaux told them he had high confidence in his sources. "It is a strategy," he added, "that certainly would have worked in 1863, if Pickett had broken the center of the Union line and sent Meade fleeing back to Washington." He saw Colonel Donahue wagging a "no-no" finger at him, for some reason, from the back of the room.

Babineaux was elaborately thanked in the briefing room of the MACV Annex that day, his hand shaken by a number of officers old enough to be his father and who out-ranked him by orders of magnitude, then he was sent on his way. When he had gone, the highest-ranking officer present said, "What are we supposed to do? Re-train the infantry to fight like Australians in the middle of a war?" Everyone agreed with him, and all copies of the White Paper were collected by staff for filing way deep down in the file system.

But were Babineaux's conjectures about Hanoi's intentions -- reasonable as they were, even if based on fiction -- correct? Did he guess right?

As it turned out, logical as they sounded, they were not correct on the day that Babineaux spoke. The military leadership in Hanoi was deeply divided, but the faction that predicted a popular uprising and the collapse of the government of Nguyen Van Thieu was in the driver's seat. The faction that argued for a war of attrition and the driving up of American casualties for political effect was not calling the shots on New Year's Day, 1968.

And that is how it would stay for four more weeks.

That's how it would stay until Tet.

Then the faction that had hoped for a collapse of the Saigon government lost influence, following catastrophic losses suffered during the offensive and the failure of any sign of popular uprising. And the faction that backed a war of attrition ascended.

In the aftermath of the Tet Offensive, Babineaux's White Paper, by then filed-away and forgotten, would have become accurate and insightful, a potential game-changer -- despite its being entirely a figment of his fevered brain, a child of his desperation.

21

8 - 10 January 1968

A WIZARD EMERGES

"**P**lease ask Mr. Viet to come to my office," Shimazu ordered his second-in-command, Lieutenant Aaronson, "immediately."

"What's up, major?"

"When I find out, I'll tell you," Shimazu told him curtly.

"Yessir," Aaronson made a mental note not to call his CO by rank in the setting of this "civilian contractor's" office -- the Service International Corporation's sign clearly identified this large villa to everyone who passed by -- but as with all previous times, he would relapse into Regular Army mode within the hour.

"You wish to see me, sir?" asked Pham Viet, known to the Americans only by his given name. He was asked to take a seat, a folding chair wedged into a corner of the sweltering, windowless closet, shoulder-to-shoulder with a very large American he had never seen before.

"Mr. Viet is Chief of Translation Services for III Corps," Shimazu said from behind his desk. "This is Mr. Hood from the Cu Chi Field Station and I want him to tell you what he's just told me."

The American wrapped his huge hand around Viet's and said, "Glad to meet you, sir." Then in an accented English that Viet struggled to understand, Mr. Hood explained what he had reported to his superior: He had discovered a week ago, on New Year's Day, as he had long suspected, that the Cu Chi station chief had been misrepresenting the size of his network and had been filing false Information Reports and inflated budget requests. In fact, Mr. Hood suspected most reports he filed with III Corps had been based on false information fed to him by his translator, Mr. Diem, who had derived them some unknown source.

"You hired and supervised Mr. Diem," Shimazu said quietly. "What do you know of him?"

"He came to us very highly recommended from the University of Saigon, an excellent student fluent in English and French, and his security clearance is renewed each year, as with all translators. Mr. Monroe never complained about him to me."

"Mr. Monroe, it appears, was his business partner," Shimazu said. "The two of them collected thousands of dollars each month for an operation that claimed over seventy field agents but had how many, Mr. Hood?"

"None that I know of. Six or seven people were employed by Frank...Mr. Monroe...but I never met or saw any field operatives."

Viet was as shocked by Hood's report as Shimazu had been, apparently. "But I don't understand...the information was good from Cu Chi Station...so many tunnels and bunkers and supplies discovered! Good evaluations from MACV."

"Perhaps last summer," Shimazu interrupted, "but there's a disturbing pattern: Those tunnels were often abandoned before they were reported and the last major battle in the area...in November, when the 28th Infantry tripped over that major supply depot defended by the 271st VC Regiment...Cu Chi never mentioned the 271st in the area until two days after the engagement. More recently, reports of heavy infiltration by NVA Regulars and reinforced VC units have been flowing in from II Corps and I Corps, while Cu Chi did nothing but turn-over more obsolete tunnels. I intended to press Mr. Monroe on these matters at the January budget meeting, but Mr. Hood believes he has gone AWOL."

"These are very serious charges...deception on a very great scale... treason perhaps!" Viet muttered, then asked, "What must be done?"

"We will find Mr. Monroe and seize the files at the Cu Chi office. If Mr. Hood's claims prove to be true, Monroe will be arrested and charged under the US Uniform Code of Military Justice. Mr. Diem's case must be decided by our counterpart, according to the laws of the Republic. In the meantime, you must act swiftly and with discretion. When Mr. Diem and CP-D arrive this afternoon for the budget meeting, they must be detained, by force if necessary, and we will announce the suspension of the Cu Chi operation jointly with our counterpart until we can investigate this matter thoroughly."

After Viet had struggled free of the jammed confines of the office and gone, Hood told his CO, "I'm sorry I didn't catch on sooner to what was goin' on. I feel like I let you down."

"It appears Mr. Monroe has fooled everyone here. He is, if you're right about all this, a very skillful liar."

And I hope I've learned to be one too, Hood thought, *or when they catch up with Diem and Monroe, I'll be going to jail with them.*

Forty minutes later, Aaronson and Hood pulled up to the cinderblock building that had once housed the Cu Chi Field Station, allegedly. They leapt from the jeep with loaded carbines, ready to hog-tie and drag back to Saigon anyone they could find, along with every last scrap of paper on the premises. But it all went down exactly as Braxton Hood secretly prayed it would. Aaronson waved his weapon at the empty room, throwing open the lavatory and storage closet doors with dramatic violence, yanking out empty file drawers and rifling through desks containing only office supplies, lacing the air around him with curses and threats while Hood made as many grunts of disappointment as his inner joy allowed him to. Images of The Center at the villa in Saigon, with its pool table, messy bulletin board and loaded file cabinets, danced through his mind and he appealed to all the gods of his soul that Monroe's secret mansion would never, ever be discovered.

"We have a situation in III Corps, colonel," Major Alex Cardenas announced to the CO of the 581st Military Intelligence Company (known all over Vietnam as SIC) Colonel George Owen Donahue. At Cardenas' side was Hideo Shimazu, CO of III Corps. "One of their station chiefs has been padding his budget requests."

Donahue raised his enormous head and pointed his aquiline nose at them like a weapon. He had a reputation for decisiveness and he showed it now. "Then cut his budget," he snapped.

"Yessir. Major Shimazu immediately closed the station down but the man responsible for the overstated...."

"Oh come now, major," Donahue interrupted. "Let us allow cooler heads to prevail here. You don't close-down a bilateral operation over a padded budget. That's throwing the baby out with the bathwater. Simply reprimand the miscreant, strip him of his rank and replace him." When the two officers remained before him in silence, he narrowed his eyes and demanded, "Did I not make myself clear, major?"

"Yessir. But there is more to it in this case...." Cardenas hesitated, but no way to soften the blow came to him. "The bilateral operation in Cu Chi doesn't exist...may never have existed in fact...and the station chief may be on the lam."

The change in George Donahue's color was wondrous to behold and the white stubble of his buzz-cut seemed to bristle to attention. "What in the hell are you talking about, major? A network of agents doesn't just vanish! And a soldier can't hide in a war zone! Just send MPs into the brothels and bars until you *find* the son-of-a-bitch!"

Cardenas crept forward like he was feeding a mouse to a cobra and gently placed a folder on the edge of the desk, at full arm's length. "We have some suspicions, sir, that in this particular case, Sergeant E-6 Francis Monroe may be a cover-identity."

Donahue shook his noble head once, sharply, as though he'd been slapped, and his eyes narrowed to mere slits. "*Godammit, major!*" he bellowed, "Soldiers and units cannot be allowed to disappear!

Find the bastard! *Replace* the bastard! *Court martial* the bastard! And put the goddamned field station back together, *up-and-running*! Understood?"

"Yessir." Cardenas had closed the Colonel's door and his own office door but through both, they clearly heard Donahue holler for Warrant Officer Greeley. They pictured the Colonel waving a single piece of paper over his head, signed by his successor, Colonel Rogers, ordering Sergeant Monroe to report to III Corps for further assign-ment, as he bellowed, "Where is this man's file?" Greeley's muttered response elicited, "What does payroll have to do with it?" and "It's your JOB to know, goddammit!"

When Greeley was heard in the hallway, Cardenas slipped his door open and pulled him into the office. The warrant officer seemed to be on the brink of crying.

"You're sure there's no other files?" Cardenas whispered. "Have you phoned MACV Personnel?"

"Phoned? No, I haven't phoned MACV. I've *driven* to MACV! I've TELEXed Pacific Command and the DoD, for Chrissakes!" Greeley's fists opened and closed at his sides like they were squeezing the words out. "I'm the one who's been yelling about this for five months...and now I catch all the blame...It's all *my* fault!" Tears did well into his eyes now, adding embarrassment to his rage.

"Monroe must have stolen his own files, back when he worked here."

"Oh no," Greeley waved an index finger at Cardenas, "Monroe couldn't have pulled this off without help. This is an inside job... somebody here helped him out...maybe others too, outside the 581st."

"He had help in Cu Chi too," Shimazu said. "His translator, his counterpart, office staff that he hired and paid were all in on it."

"Hired and paid?" Greeley looked stunned. "What was he, a rich man?"

"Don't tell Donahue this," Cardenas muttered, "but he was claim-ing to have seventy agents on the payroll that didn't exist. That gave him a chunk of money to pay and bribe people with."

"I don't understand..." Greeley said, "how he could, I mean...the paperwork alone, all the IRs we got from Cu Chi!"

"It was a very elaborate scheme, very complex," Shimazu told him, "and Monroe might have pulled it off all the way to his DEROS. But an honest young man in my command figured it out and blew the lid off it."

"OK, look, we need to do damage-control here," Cardenas said. "This gets out, bilateral loses all credibility at the worse possible time. We're getting a flood of warnings from all four Corps that keep me awake at night. Revived VC outfits that MACV wrote-off months ago are cropping up, reinforced and better-armed and supplied. Large-scale NVA units are moving from Laos and Cambodia into The Republic. And MACV isn't buying any of this. They're closing the books on the VC, based on their bogus, so-called 'body-counts'. The Vung Tau White Paper got laughed out of the room last week. Our word isn't worth the paper it's printed on at the moment. If we open an investigation into an empty-box network, where our own guy played us for suckers, they'd order all of us to wrap things up and report for further assignment. So here's what's got to happen. We open a totally new Field Station D in III Corps, report to Donahue that everything has been repaired, moved to a better location, and in the meantime, we need to bend every effort toward *not* finding Monroe...*not now...not ever!*"

"That shouldn't be a problem," Greeley said. "Given his contacts, he's out at Tan Son Nhut right now, waving a photo ID at the Pan Am counter, claiming to be GS-16 George Donahue."

It was a nice apartment, small but with a second-story balcony overlooking busy Tu Do Street. Cozy and inviting, the walls lined with shelves half-filled with books and half with polished, lacquered vases that featured golden birds and fish painted on the sides, gifts from one of them to the other. Despite the noise and bustle of the street, a domestic calm usually pervaded the little studio apartment with its decorative pillows stacked along the daybed and dishes drying on the counter of the kitchenette. "Usually," but not at this moment.

In their fourteen weeks together, they had never before had a fight -- not a real one -- not until Rosenzweig tried to put his foot down here in his own house, which *he* paid for, along with Sang's tuition and books and food and...well, not clothes because she made her own at the sewing shop where she worked. But he had, after all, found her in shanty-town with nothing to her name but a cardboard box of clothes and old photos. And he'd lifted her up into a pretty good deal here. She was a student with a future, had her own home and an American contractor who was deeply in love with her. She owed everything she had to him, and she was now going to listen to him or else.

He stood on the little balcony, gazing down on the traffic but seeing nothing, hands buried in his pockets, until the lump in his throat began to dissolve. Then he turned back into the room and said, "Sang...."

"She is my mother!" Sang barked without raising her eyes from the text or her pen from the spiral notebook. She jotted some notes to demonstrate she was too busy for further discussion.

"We *know* things!" he exploded. "People in my company are very well connected and they are telling me heavy fighting is coming! Bring your mother here! Phoc Tho will be a very dangerous place! And even when you lived there, they didn't want you around because you were half-French...so why would you *ever* go back?"

Her eyes remained on her textbook while she said, "We do this every year at Tet, Zachary. It is never a problem. Everywhere in Vietnam, even in the North, we all go home to family at Tet every year...always...before you ever came here. There is a truce and, for one week, peace and joy of family together...."

"Not this year, Sang! I'm telling you the NVA is moving down from Cambodia and the VC...."

"Why this not on TV? Why Ho Chi Minh himself is announce truce for Tet? You people don't know Vietnamese people...."

"We'll talk about this later," he cut her off, "after you calm down."

"*I* calm down?!" She slammed her book shut. "*You* the one who go *dinky dau*! I go see my mother every year! Captain Blake never tell me no-can-do!" Sang had never once mentioned her previous lover, the Air Force officer who taught her English, since the first day they had met. The name, shouted now in anger, hit Rosie like a punch in the gut. He didn't trust himself to answer but even now, enraged as he was with her, she seemed to him the most courageous and beautiful human being he had ever known. She was going to visit her mother no matter what he said, and it was precisely *because* she owed everything to him and would risk it all, even her life itself for her mother that he... So without another word, he walked to the shelf by the door, picked up his wallet and keys and went out. Behind him, as he locked the closed door, she shouted, "*Every night*, you go to dinner with your boss! *Every! Night!* But I cannot see my mother in Phoc Tho *one time*?!"

He unchained the scooter with hands that were still shaking. Was it breaking apart, this perfect love-affair -- the deep intertwining of their lives that had overcome all their differences? He could remember so vividly their time together: That Sunday he had driven through a downpour with the canvas lid of his jeep dripping on his lap, his heart pounding in his chest, to find her as she had promised, waiting for him on the roadside at shanty-town, her ao dai and cardboard box of possessions soaked through, long strands of wet hair hanging from under her straw hat with the blue ribbon, their shared joy as she slid into the jeep and said, "You remembered!" Finding their apartment and setting up house, nest-building with a lover for the first time in his life, hauling furniture with help from Mad-dog. He patiently, gently corrected her English as she patiently, gently refined his amateur love-making, a mutual exchange of expertise that hit a speed-bump on their third Saturday together when he took her to lunch at the Caravelle in celebration of her birthday. He proposed a toast with expensive champagne, "To Nguyen Sang, the most beautiful girl in the world, on her...which is it?" "Sixteenth," she said, smiling brightly, and his glass stayed there, suspended in mid-air, while he absorbed the unexpected news that he was sleeping with a...a child! Her exotic, Euro-Asian face had tricked him into guessing her to be, like him, in her 20's. He smiled and sipped from his glass and got through the meal but was subdued for several days afterwards while he worked-through the implications: For starters, the Army would jail him in a heartbeat for statutory rape if the arrangement came to light. Second, he had not yet considered where this affair was going, but now it was not going toward a happy homecoming, bearing a war-bride back to Nashville. Even if he extended his tour-of-duty in Vietnam, he'd be discharged from the Army before she was 18. And the third thing, he called the Blake Dichotomy. If he felt that it was immoral and criminal for Captain Blake to take a 13-year-old refugee into his bed, then what made it the most wonderful thing that had ever happened in his own life that he did the same thing when she was just 15?

Eventually, the depth of his feelings for her overwhelmed all other concerns. And thus it was that -- after some days of doubt, suffering and moral struggle -- Zachary Rosenzweig came to be "all-in" with Nguyen Sang and could not imagine life without her.

Talk at The Dinner (well-marbled steaks, mashed potatoes and gravy with peas and little white onions) was all about the Cu Chi problem and how Aaronson and Hood had found the field office stripped and deserted. Major Shimazu impressed on them the importance of treating the situation with absolute confidentiality while it was under investigation, especially since the role played by counterparts and translators was unclear. "Don't say anything to anyone. Let me handle it," Shimazu ordered, adding, "If it were not for Mr. Hood, Sergeant Monroe might have gotten away with this deception. But we will track him down now and press charges." Then he raised his glass of claret and toasted, "Good work, Mr. Hood. You did well."

For Braxton Hood's part, he could not detect any hint of irony in Major Shimazu's voice, but the heavily hooded eyes of the disciplined old warrior seemed to stare right through him over the wine glass.

Did the major really believe it had taken four months working with Monroe in the Cu Chi office to discover the truth? Or was Shimazu playing him along, as Monroe had, until investigators had evidence on him too? How long would it take them to confirm that neither he nor Monroe had quarters on the firebase at Cu Chi? Even if Monroe had disappeared for good, what would Diem say when they caught up with him? But all Hood could do for now was raise his glass and respond, "Thank you, sir. I did my best."

For Stephen Aaronson's part, he refused to raise his glass, say "hear! hear!" or in any other way credit Hood. He smelled a rat in this Cu Chi matter and saw in it a pattern of systematic deception by all of the enlisted men in III Corps, who collectively played for a sucker the nice old man who spent each afternoon working as their chef and waiter -- and who would well deserve whatever reprimand, demotion or court-martial proceedings the investigation into this scandalous unit would inevitably produce. The lieutenant couldn't wait until they asked for his testimony. He would expose them all, Corporal Hood up through that sap, Major Shimazu.

John Francis Mulcahey, for his part, was very happy to raise his glass and give a cheer in tribute to his friend -- and his roommate for the past week, since Hood took up residence on New Year's Day in the bunk assigned to but long-ago abandoned by Rosenzweig. Mad-dog had covered for Rosie with the enlisted compound administration, changing-out unused sheets and towels each week, taking phone messages for him from III Corp, saying he had just left and would be back soon. But sharing a six-man room with Bitter Louie Leffanta, rotating strangers and an empty cot had been no picnic for the garrulous Chicagoan, especially since his visits to the Tu Do Street apartment drew such a stark contrast with his own Spartan arrangement. Hood would give Mulcahey someone to bar-hop with, company at breakfast and lunch and at the officer's gym and pool at Tan Son Nhut, perhaps to the shanty-town back-alleys if Hood had the courage for that.

Rosie was only vaguely aware of Shimazu's toast to Hood or anything else that transpired, engrossed as he was in rehearsing scripts in his mind that would persuade Sang to remain in Saigon during Tet. Twenty-three of SIC's twenty-six field stations across Vietnam (exceptions being Vung Tau, Khap Noi, and of course Cu Chi) had been waving red flags for weeks, citing troop movements, VC units thought to be extinct reappearing with improved weaponry, NVA battalions once based north of the DMZ cropping up in II and III Corps -- everything was pointing to a major offensive sometime after Tet -- everything but the stubborn teenager Rosenzweig was in love with. She was determined to walk right into the middle of it and get herself killed and he had failed to find anything he could say that would stop her.

Lastly, working around the table, Bitter Louie Leffanta was on his fourth glass of wine and heard in the major's tribute to Hood an opportunity to express his resentment at being left-out by Rosenzweig, Mulcahey and now the new-comer, all of whom went off and left him behind with nothing to do but drink himself to sleep in the compound cafeteria. "To Braxton Hood," he joined in with raised glass, "someone to finally sleep in Rosenzweig's empty bed!"

Aaronson pounced at once. "Where does Corporal Rosenzweig sleep then?"

"Damn-fino," Leffanta slurred. "Out with the gooks somewhere." Never before had he let slip any of his rich vocabulary of racist terms in Shimazu's presence, but he was angry and drunk and had reverted to habit.

"A different room...downstairs...temporary arrangement...." Mulcahey jumped in, too late.

"Exactly where DO you sleep, corporal?" Aaronson demanded.

Rosie blinked, startled, as someone waking from a sound sleep. "I have my own place... a rental. I can't sleep in the compound... too noisy."

"If I find out you've been shacking up with some Vietnamese slut, I'll have you up on...." Aaronson didn't finish the threat before he was on his back, sprawled on the floor with his shirt-front gripped in Rosie's left fist, trying to shield his face from the right fist. The efforts of both Hood and Mulcahey were required to drag Rosenzweig off his prey and pull him back, while the lieutenant picked himself up, sputtering promises to file assault charges, have the corporal thrown in the stockade, dishonorably discharged.

"Lieutenant!" Shimazu's voice instantly commanded attention, "I want you to go over to our quarters and attend to yourself at once." The flow of blood from Aaronson's nose and mouth had already covered his shirt-front and filled his cloth napkin, so he did as he was told. "Corporal Rosenzweig, you are restricted to your quarters, which as of now are limited to the map room and the bathroom across the hall from it, nowhere else. Right now!" Hood let go of Rosenzweig's collar and he walked away without comment. "Corporal Leffanta, you have KP: I want this area ready for my inspection in one hour. You two, follow me."

Hood and Mulcahey trailed Shimazu down the stairs from the roof-top enclosure to his tiny office. As the overhead fluorescents flickered to life, the major settled into his office chair and the other two adjusted folding chairs in the narrow confines until Shimazu said, "You do not have permission to sit down." This brought the two not exactly to attention, eyes front, but something like it. For two minutes, they stood in silence, fixated on the wall over Shimazu's head, not daring to look at him. They heard him moving objects around on the desktop, as though arranging pieces on a game-board. Then he said, "The lieutenant thinks I am a fool. Do you agree with him?"

They sputtered "No! Nosir! No!" as they stood in the narrow space.

"The Dinner, every night, my insistence on it, no exceptions...the care I take. Don't you find it a little odd?"

"Nosir, really! We appreciate it," Mad-dog insisted.

"No you don't, corporal. Permission to speak freely is granted. It's a pain-in-the-ass to you, isn't it. You would stop doing it tomorrow if you could."

"Maybe four nights a week would be enough, to speak freely, sir," Mulcahey conceded.

"And Corporal Hood, do you remember what I asked you when I assigned you to Cu Chi?"

"You asked me if I was brave enough, sir."

"And were you brave enough?"

"Nosir. I wasn't."

"...or you would have reported Monroe's double-dealing weeks ago...months ago."

"Yessir, I should have."

"Why didn't you?"

"I was afraid of him, sir. He could be intimidating."

"There was something about Sergeant Monroe I didn't like from the start," Shimazu said, "I learned in Italy, when I was your age, how to judge other men. I had to, to survive. Monroe was a manipulator. I know because I can be one to, when I need to be. I saw that in him. He was a wolf. I sent Aaronson out to Cu Chi three or four times and each time, Monroe had just left, just gone to the fire base, was meeting with his counterpart somewhere, and so on. His translator lied to us and his counterpart was a mute who never said a word at budget meetings. So I had no other means but to throw you into the lair, corporal. And the wolf ate you up." Shimazu put his palms together for a moment, then said, "You may be seated."

When they had squeezed into folding chairs, he said, "So why do I insist on having Dinners, Mr. Mulcahey?"

"Beats me, sir. I don't know. So our lives can have some central purpose, I guess."

"To make us a team," Hood said with assurance, "unit cohesion."

"Precisely, Mr. Hood. I cannot command twenty-five men scattered all over III Corps unless I know them well. I need time to study them, watch them interact with each other."

"Didn't work too well tonight," Mad-dog said, still speaking freely.

The major actually smiled at this, a rare occurrence. "If you hope to judge the character of a man, there is no better time than in a crisis," he said. "I learned nothing new about Leffanta or the lieutenant, but my suspicions about Mr. Rosenzweig, his moral character and his situation, were confirmed. The third week he was here, he began riding a scooter to work, arriving alone. I assumed he had found someone else to live with, someone he was committed to. But here is what must be done now." He leaned over the desktop and they instinctively followed suit, forming a huddle.

"First in importance, we must deal with Cu Chi. By telling Mr. Viet that we wanted to have Diem and CP-D arrested, I think it is safe to say we will never see either one of them again. Mr. Viet will do our work for us there. We must hope Mr. Monroe can make good his escape, aided by his wide circle of contacts and given that we will make no attempt to find him."

"But you said..." Mulcahey broke in, "the investigation...." Hood glared at him.

"And that leaves only the cache of files that disappeared from the office. If either Monroe or Diem barrel-burned them, so much the better. If not, I will ask you, Mr. Hood, to do whatever you can to see they are disposed of and say nothing to anyone, ever, not even to me.

"Second, Cu Chi Station has a reputation with MACV so Colonel Donahue has ordered it to continue operations. Therefore, we will re-establish it immediately with a new counterpart, new translator, new station chief, at new location."

"But then it won't be the Cu Chi Station," Mulcahey observed. Hood glared at him.

"It will be housed at the 25th Infantry base in Tay Ninh, with quarters and an office in that compound and limited to a maximum of five field agents.

"Third, I will have to resolve the matter between Mr. Rosenzweig and the lieutenant. Assaulting an officer is a serious matter. Something will have to be done about it.

"And fourth, first thing tomorrow morning, you two will sign-out a quarter-ton from SIC Central motor pool and deliver three cots with mosquito-netting, footlockers and necessary linens to the map room. Starting tomorrow, III Corps will be a unit, living and working under the same roof. Now go get some sleep while I deal with the lieutenant."

From the doorway, Braxton Hood turned to ask, "You wanted three beds set-up, sir? There are four of us."

"Leffanta will sleep in Tay Ninh tomorrow, with the 25th Infantry," came the answer.

As he passed down the open-air passageway between the two wings of the villa, Shimazu paused in silence outside the map room door until he heard stirring within, assuring him that Rosenzweig had followed orders. It would be a miserable night for the young man, Shimazu understood, with only office furniture, maps and re-gret for company.

Aaronson's first words when he entered the officers' suite were, "I'm pressing charges."

Shimazu pulled a chair up to Aaronson's and sat down facing him. "Let me see," he said quietly. Aaronson raised his head for inspection. "Not so bad...no permanent damage," Shimazu assured him. "Even your wife won't notice any change, once you've healed up."

"I'm not married, major, as you know."

"That's right...your fiancé, then."

"I don't have a fiancé."

"No, lieutenant, you don't," Shimazu confirmed. "But I believe you told me both your parents were still living."

"Yes," Aaronson said tentatively, feeling cross-examined.

"Then your mother will see no change in your face when you get back home." Shimazu continued to study his face from inches away.

"What's your point, major?"

"My point, lieutenant, is that you will have a wife or a fiancé some-day and you will punch-out any man who calls her a 'Vietnamese slut'."

"That's not what I said..." Aaronson stammered, "...not what I meant! He physically attacked me without...."

"That is *precisely* what you said, lieutenant. I was right there and... look me in the eye, Lieutenant Aaronson! I was right there and I heard distinctly what you said."

"Major, I have every right...."

"Assaulting an officer will not be tolerated, lieutenant, but I want you to allow me to handle it. This is my outfit, I'm the CO, and if you press charges, you make me look bad at a time when Colonel Donahue is unhappy with me about Cu Chi. Listen to me! I would be in more trouble than the corporal. And I have a hell of a lot more to lose than he does, a twenty-four year career, one year from retirement!"

"But, major, he was completely...."

"Why don't you think about what would satisfy you and tell me in the morning. I'll bring him up on Article 15 and strip his rank, confine him to quarters, assign him extra duty...whatever you think is right. But we will keep this matter in-house, Lieutenant Aaronson!"

Without conceding the argument or promising anything, Aaronson arose from his chair, said, "Good night, sir," and retired to his room.

At ten o'clock the next morning Aaronson was trying to wrestle the right words into place on his report, "Incident of Assault on a Superior Officer by Enlisted Personnel, 9 January 1968". Without admitting either that he had provoked the attack or that he had been mauled in a one-sided fight, he was finding it hard to be specific. The voices and clattering from the hallway eventually broke his concentration and made it impossible to work. "What's all the racket out here?" he demanded of Corporals Mulcahey and Hood.

"Sorry, sir," Hood replied. "We'll try to hold it down."

Aaronson's eyes widened when he saw they were wedging a foot-locker through the doorway of the map room. "What the hell are you doing?" was answered by "Major's orders." Aaronson launched himself toward the major's small office, then thought better of it -- given that they had eaten breakfast together without a word spoken between them -- and paced instead back into his office. He rifled through volumes of US Army Regulations, taking notes, so that by the time he tapped on Shimazu's door, he had become a calm man, steely in resolve and well armed with facts.

"The first two citations are those you will find most relevant, major," he pointed out as Shimazu read the pages of typed notes, "The other two are supplementary but supportive. Clearly, sir, enlisted personnel and officers must not share quarters except in extreme... that is to say combat conditions. Furthermore, how can Corporal Rosenzweig be punished for his conduct if he is moved from a six-man room in a compound into a room of his own in a villa?"

Shimazu chose the "civilian contractor" title by saying, "Your points are well stated, Mr. Aaronson. But SIC by its nature does not conform to military standards and as a practical matter, how can I confine Rosenzweig to quarters if he's over in that compound?"

"But sir, if we...."

"And he is not getting a room of his own. I'm moving them all over here."

"Them all? All who?"

"All III Corps personnel assigned to Saigon will reside here for security reasons and better unit cohesion."

"But we can't just...It's not permitted!"

"I do not take your commitment to military order lightly, Mr. Aaronson. I'm Regular Army like you, a career officer. We disagree only in our means to the end of command-and-control. So if there is nothing further."

From down the hallway, Mad-dog's whiny tenor rang clear and distinct: "Damn it, Braxton! What have you got in your footlocker? *Bricks*?!"

Saturday was usually a light-duty day in III Corps, but this one was full-tilt, full-time. After the move-in, Hood and Mulcahey returned the quarter-ton truck to SIC Central motor pool (explaining that the fender Mad-dog had scraped along the compound wall was "Absolutely that way when we got it."), then they helped Bitter Louie Leffanta find cardboard boxes and pack up his belongings for the drive out to Tay Ninh. Then far behind schedule, they faced a very long and complicated shopping list for The Dinner, requiring stops from Tan Son Nhut to the harbor-front. But first, they had a more personal errand. Nguyen Sang was at home when they called at the apartment on Tu Do Street. She tore open the sealed envelope and read Rosie's note with her head down, her lips moving silently:

> *Dear Sang, My company has sent me on an important assignment to Thailand for a week or two. Enclosed is money for you to visit your mother. I am sorry we had a fight about it. I just want you to be safe. I love you very, very much. Zachary*

She folded the scrip notes into the letter, tucked it back inside the envelope and said, "Thank you, Mr. Mad-dog. Tell Zachary I will miss him very much." Her voice was shaking and she took no notice of the big stranger standing behind Mulcahey.

Back in the jeep, Mulcahey made an observation: "Rosie can pick 'em, eh? Man! Is she beautiful or what?"

And Hood made another: "But did you see her face? She thinks she's being dumped. She got a dear-jane letter with a wad of cash delivered by a third party."

"Hey! That gives me an idea!" Mad-dog said brightly.

"No it doesn't, Mulcahey. Just drive!"

After they'd picked-up scallops and vegetables at the market, they drove to Tan Son Nhut, where a blue-eyed MP named Swanson asked them earnestly, "There any job openings at SIC, sir?" "Not at the moment," Mad-dog told him, and they were saluted crisply and waved through.

On the way back to III Corps, Hood asked Mulcahey to stop by the enlisted compound.

"Why? We didn't leave anything there but rolled-up mattresses and empty lockers," he objected, so he was astonished to watch

Braxton walk over to the mystery-car, the Citroën that had them baffled all week, unlock the door and start the engine.

And so it was almost midnight,10 January 1968, when there came a tapping on the map room door. That small noise and Braxton Hood's wrestling himself out from under the mosquito netting that hung over his creaky cot awakened his roommates. Major Shimazu stood in the doorway in bathrobe and slippers, a spectral figure in the dim light, bearing a tray with cookies and three glasses of milk. "I thought you boys might be hungry," he said.

22

OUT WITH THE GOAT

Every morning was a beautiful morning this time of year. The pale yellow sun rising into a flawless sky was not yet the inescapable heat-lamp it would be by noon. From the balcony of Diem's family house in Sa Dec, they could watch an occasional big freighter majestically plough upstream or float down in the deep mid-river on this major branch of the Mekong. The Pham brothers shared a large pot of tea, the ideal accompaniment for shrimp banh cakes, while they questioned their cousin Diem's preference for coffee.

"It carries the aroma of a goat shed," Minh opined.

"Bian's husband taught me to like it when I was young," Diem said, referring to Jean Reynard, his first employer, killed in action against the Viet Minh shortly after marrying the young Euro-Asian beauty, the daughter of wealthy plantation owners.

"Americans drink it by the gallon, usually with milk and sugar," Viet mused, "then they switch to beer and liquor at 5:00, so then they carry the aroma of a drunken goat."

Their eyes rested on a large ship grinding its way against the heavy current and they shared a rare moment of tranquility and security, a respite from lives filled with feverish activity and danger.

Diem's sisters hurried in and served them more food and hot beverages, then left.

"How much does the American know?" Minh broke the silence to ask.

"Don't worry. Nothing that matters." Diem assured him. "Monroe has no real information about weapons caches or plans for Tet. So even if they catch him...."

"When they catch him," Viet said.

"When and if they catch him, he knows only that his information on the tunnel system was...let's call it 'obsolete,' based on Reynard's files from fifteen years ago. And he'll be seen as a criminal anyway for lying about the agent network and for counterfeiting MPC notes. So nothing he says will be believed. As for Bian, she can take care of herself. She'll put it all on Monroe and cry big tears of innocence."

"But the other American...." Minh said.

"Young Mr. Hood? He knows less than Monroe."

"I met with him last Thursday," Viet told them. "He is already borrowing his words from Co Bian: Monroe ran a scam with the network and he didn't know anything about it until last week. Not a word about counterfeit scrip or the villa in Saigon. They are launching an investigation, so I think what we need to do is...."

"It's being taken care of, even as we speak," Diem said, pouring a fresh cup from the carafe. "I have ordered the guards to turn every piece of paper to ashes, which makes me very sad because I did all that work for Reynard years ago, and for III Corps the last four years, and my sisters typed up every page of it in French and English and Vietnamese, and now it will all be burned and gone by the time we return the keys to the landlord. Nothing left of all those years of work."

"I'm going to see to it you are made a hero of the People's Republic for all you have done, Cousin Diem," Minh announced firmly. "There must be a statue to you in Hanoi after the war."

"For pigeons to roost on," Viet quipped, drawing a stare of reprimand from his twin.

"You have protected the supply bunkers at Cu Chi and four regiments of reserve forces on the plantations, you have destabilized the currency of the doomed puppet regime in Saigon, and you are personally responsible for keeping the Americans in the dark about Tet."

"The Americans aren't in the dark as much as you think," Viet cut-in.

Diem thanked Minh for the tribute but smiled and said, "Misleading Americans is not an act of heroism, Cousin Minh. Monroe is a clever man but deeply immoral so Bian and I hardly had to convince him to play our game. It gave him a villa, a beautiful lover and made him rich...."

"Himself, Bian and you," Viet said.

"Yes, Bian and I got rich. Monroe already had loads of money from previous scams when we recruited him. But we did protect our soldiers from...."

"Our soldiers and theirs too," Viet cut-in.

"Very well, both sides from needless fighting. And when you had the idea to undermine faith in the MPC currency, Cousin Minh...."

"Wasn't my idea," Minh said. "It came down from high command. They supplied the counterfeit bills."

"Well, in any case, Monroe took that idea and ran with it. All I had to do was supply him with the currency you gave me. As for the young man, Hood, he is not the scoundrel Monroe is, but he has watched too many movies about American cowboys, I think." Diem broke out in a fit of laughter at a happy memory: "The first day I met him, he became angry with me. I was very busy in the office and I told him to go out to the 25th Infantry Base by taxi to look for Monroe just to get him out of my way. He took offense at being dismissed and got all sweaty with me. He pushed my desk against the wall with me squashed in between and began yelling insults and threats at me and I look behind him...." Diem bent over in laughter which spread to the brothers as well. "...and both my sisters have their revolvers pointed at his back and I'm scared to death! Scared to death! They can't shoot worth a damn! They're going to open fire and kill us both!" The threesome melted into helpless laughter while Diem gasped enough air to go on. "I was shouting in English, 'OK. I will tell you where to find Monroe' and in Vietnamese I was yelling, 'Put those things away, goddammit! Hold your fire!' " Diem wiped tears from his eyes. "All the way back to Saigon, my sister Lan had her .38 pointed at Mr. Hood's seatback and I'm thinking, 'How do I explain to Mr. Monroe about the dead American in my Citroën?' "

When they had calmed down, Minh said solemnly, "You should go with Diem."

"Not again," Viet objected. "We've been over this already."

"The Capital City will not be spared, Viet. You will not be safe there."

"And what will that look like to the Americans? I don't show up for work the week a big attack is made. They trust me and I want them to go on trusting me. Besides...."

"That won't matter, Viet! They will be gone in a week, as fast as they can pull out, once the corrupt puppet-regime has collapsed and the people have risen-up to claim their rightful..."

"I respect you, my brother, but listen to me. The people in Saigon cannot overthrow the regime now, as long as the Americans and their allies are here, and they aren't going anywhere."

"They will blow away like smoke, Viet! What can a few thousand do against...."

"Five-hundred-thousand, with tanks and artillery and planes...."

"Five-hundred-thousand cannot stand against millions of patriotic Vietnamese led by our fighters and Regular troops from the NVA, ready to die for their country! We will flood the streets with weapons from Cu Chi! Ho Chi Minh will call for the people to rise up on every TV and radio, and the puppet regime will collapse under the weight of its corruption. Thieu and his lackeys will be shot and the Americans will have no basis for remaining another day! Even in America, the people are rising up against this Colonial occupation, with rioting in the streets! Colonel Vo and I heard this from an American businessman we met at Xuan Song Plantation. You must take Tan and your daughters and hide-out with Diem until the fighting is over."

"I could give you the same advice, Minh, but you won't take it. You'll return to your unit and put yourself in the middle of a hopeless fight against overwhelming fire-power, no matter what I say. The Americans, I tell you, are determined to stay the course! Just look at the plan to disrupt the economy with counterfeit money! The American floodtide of wealth washed it away without even taking notice! I am afraid this attack at Tet will meet the same fate and I fear for your life, my brother!"

"I make you a solemn promise!" Minh shouted. "When Grandfather rises to speak on National Day in September, he will stand upon the ground of a free and united Vietnam!"

"I must go!" Diem's announcement, as he intended, broke up this argument that had sputtered off-and-on for two days between his cousins, marring their time together. "If you need me, Grandfather will know where to find me."

Viet helped Diem carry a large cardboard box and two suitcases to the Citroën while Minh had gone to his room to pack and change into the ARVN uniform he wore to travel, showing the photo ID Viet had given him whenever he was questioned. In this moment between them, Diem said to Viet in English, "I must admit, I will miss working with the Americans. They're incredibly naive, simple-minded and ignorant of the world...the opposite of the French...but there is a kindness in them. They are always eager to be everyone's friend, not so?"

"We work in offices, cousin. I'm sure on the battlefield, they are not so kind-hearted."

"In warfare, Viet, everyone is a soldier, all alike. But I have worked for the French and I find the Americans are much friendlier, not easily offended, even the schemers like Monroe."

"What are you-two talking about?" Minh asked in Vietnamese.

"We were discussing whether, when the war ends, we will be friends with the Americans."

"There is no friendship between nations," Minh said with authority, "only a change in weaponry. And we are ready for that too, after the Spring Offensive wins our independence. Colonel Vo and I are laying the groundwork for the future People's Republic of Vietnam and believe me, the Pham family will again have a place of importance at the table of our nation."

He studied their faces quietly for a moment, then asked, "Have you ever considered operating a rubber plantation?"

23

SHIMAZU DUBS A KNIGHT

igarette in one hand, coffee mug in the other, Belmont sweated in the mid-morning sun as they talked on the rooftop balcony outside III Corps' offices. "Dodd is not dysfunctional," Belmont explained. "He's doing what they sent him to do...winning the hearts and minds of the people...establishing rapport with the Vietnamese."

"Not the way the major sees it," Mulcahey said. "If he never files IRs or comes in for budget meetings, what good is rapport? The IRs from Khap Noi are all filed by you."

"I report on useless crap, where VC units were last week, lies told by prisoners. SEALs bring these kids in blind-folded. If they're hard-core, they'd die before telling us anything and if they're civilians, they'll make stuff up. If you want to know what's happening on the An Long, you ask Dodd. Last two weeks, he says weapons and troops are flooding down from Cambodia, new VC units with support from the NVA. He thinks they're building up for an attack after the Tet truce, maybe on Saigon itself. But how can I write that up? 'Here you go, MACV: Saigon's about to be overrun. Jerry Dodd heard it on the grapevine'. Even our counterpart doesn't buy it."

"Major says he's gone native, but he could be right about the build-up. We're getting swamped with red-flag IRs about it, but MACV keeps fobbing us off."

"Well 'going native' is why they tell him stuff. He sits out in his little village, surrounded by his Khmer Krom fishing buddies, and they talk around the fire...."

"I haven't seen a cloud in four months...not one," Rosenzweig interjected, his face tilted toward the pure, pale blue of the Dry Season sky.

The non sequitur caught his friends by surprise. "You OK?" Belmont asked.

"He's very far from OK," Mad-dog announced. "PFC Rosie is under house arrest!"

"Shut up, Mulcahey."

"Greater love hath no man than to give up his stripes for another."

Rosenzweig tossed the coffee out of his cup and came at him, but Mad-dog stood his ground and said in baby-voice, "Ooo! You gonna smash my face in like you did the lieutenant's?"

"I'm thinking about shoving this coffee cup where the sun don't shine."

Belmont stepped between them: "Did you really punch-out Aaronson?"

Mad-dog cackled like a witch: "Rosie pummeled his ass, didn't you, private?"

"I swear to Christ, someday I'll...." Rosie raised the cup as if to throw it, but by then they were laughing it off.

"And it was all your fault, Belmont," Mulcahey said, "you were the one who set him up with a regular girlfriend back in October. If he joined the whore-of-the-week club, like me, he wouldn't be in this mess."

"Talk to me," Belmont told Rosie. "Tell me what happened." And Rosenzweig did: The apartment, his getting "all mixed up," as he said, with the girl he met in shanty-town, his blowing up at Aaronson and losing his rank, being confined to quarters for thirty days, and worst of all, having to submit a formal letter of apology and read it aloud to Lieutenant Aaronson. "It's why we all sleep in the map room now," he concluded, "so I can serve out my time under supervision."

"You really did punch-out ole Aaronson?" Belmont smiled at him.

"Afraid so."

Belmont placed two hands on Rosenzweig's shoulders. "My man!" he called him.

The budget meeting for Khap Noi Station was tense but productive. CP-C demanded Jerry Dodd's dismissal as station chief for the fifth time in five months. Major Shimazu promised to consider it but kept the focus on Mr. Belmont, whom CP-C grudgingly admitted was doing "satisfactory work" and might be "sufficient" as Dodd's replacement. Two field agents who had been unproductive were dropped from the payroll "with prejudice" while two new names were submitted for vetting as replacements.

"Follow me," Shimazu said quietly to Belmont as the meeting ended. Instead of going back upstairs, Shimazu led him to a jeep, handed him keys to the chained-up wheel and slid into the passenger's seat. Shimazu then directed him to Saigon Harbor, where their IDs got them admitted to a club principally occupied by US Naval Officers. Belmont expected to spend this lunch-time making excuses for Jerry Dodd, which had become like a second career to him, but as they studied menus, Shimazu asked him, "Have you proved your courage yet?"

Belmont was surprised by the question, in part because it seemed so personal, even friendly, coming from his rigidly formal commanding officer. "Nosir," he admitted. "Rockets come onto the base now and then but that's all. I've tried every which way to talk myself onto a Riverine patrol, but it's no-go."

"Fighting is done in teams, Mr. Belmont. You're not on a SEAL team or patrol boat crew so they can't use you. Besides..." Shimazu read the menu for some time. "...fighting in war will not be what you think it will be."

"What will it be then?" Belmont ventured to ask.

"It will not be what you read in Homer or Stephen Crane or Hemingway."

Belmont was impressed that his CO had remembered which books he had carried around the office months before. In his own defense he said, "Well that's why I want to be there, sir, so I can write my own war book."

Shimazu studied him with what might have been an affectionate expression and said, "It may be a stretch for you to imagine, Mr. Belmont, but you remind me of myself when I was young like you and anxious to prove myself in combat. You have less to prove than I did... your countrymen don't look at your face and question your loyalty... although they may question how you received the scar across your cheek."

"Bar fight when I was at Harvard, sir. The townies came after us college kids."

Shimazu silently filed-away the discrepancy between this account and the one Belmont had given in September. "Well," he said aloud, "had you attended military school in Germany a century ago, you could claim it was from dueling and that would have proven your courage." Then Shimazu looked over Belmont's shoulder and said, "Mike! Thank you for coming." Belmont rose from his chair to be introduced to Commander Mike Hopkins, USN, as "the young man I was telling you about. Mike and I taught in the Platoon Leadership Program at Quanitco years ago."

"Friends ever since," Commander Hopkins added, taking a seat. "So you're in Khap Noi and want to go swimming with the SEALs, is that it?"

"Yessir."

"Hideo asked me...Major Shimazu asked if I could get you a ring-side seat on a Riverine. I can but under strict conditions: First, you'll be Cinderella. You'll have four weeks exactly to dance with the prince, then you turn-in your gown, carriage and both slippers and you're done. Second, you'll operate under my authority and direction and do as I tell you to the letter. Third, if I call the game over at any time, it's over then and there. You able to live with that, Belmont?"

"Yessir, but what...."

"The 'what' is this: You'll get a crash course in The Navy Way for three days and learn a whole bunch of special lingo, you'll get a haircut, give up your cigarettes and learn how to bear yourself like a military man. Then we'll supply you with camo uniforms, jungle boots and a big, shiny badge that you will under no circumstances lose, on pain of death. When you return to Khap Noi, you'll be able to board any patrol boat on the An Long. You won't be welcomed but you'll have the authority. Then you can go where they go, see what they see, as long as you stay the hell out of their way. But at least you'll get your shot at combat."

"I don't understand, sir. How can I be...."

"I thought you said he was a highly trained intelligence agent," Hopkins said to Shimazu.

"He has potential," Shimazu assured him.

"You're being invited to temporary duty as a Special Agent with my command."

"Then I'll be...a sort of...."

"A cop," Hopkins told him. "Welcome to The Naval Investigative Service, Office of Naval Intelligence, Mr. Belmont."

24

WITNESS TO WAR

Belmont didn't like the Navy any more than he did the Army -- maybe less. He had to salute the Khap Noi base commander, a Naval Lieutenant who kept him waiting over an hour. He passed the time reading the book Major Shimazu had recommended as "a primer in warfare," *Le Morte d'Arthur* by Thomas Malory, which turned out to be a long, boring catalog, page after page of Sir Lancelot slaying other knights by the dozens in a businesslike fashion, going to work the next day and doing it again.

"You're here to investigate what, exactly?" the lieutenant wanted to know.

"I'm not at liberty to discuss it, sir. You'll have to ask my CO, Commander Hopkins."

"And I'm supposed to give you free run of my base?"

"Nosir. As Commander Hopkins' letter states, all I need is to accompany any Riverine going on a night mission."

The base commander raised hell. He objected. He needed more information. He didn't see any possible point. But in the end, he acceded to the wishes of a senior officer in Saigon and wrote an order giving Belmont what he claimed to need.

Hopkins instructed Belmont to carry no weapons, just a logbook for a detailed report of everything Belmont observed -- to be typed in duplicate for Shimazu and himself. He was not to interfere in operations in any way, not even by offering opinions or engaging in conversation at all that was not absolutely necessary to his central mission, which was to stay out of everyone's way. And he was to disembark only when the boat was safely docked at Khap Noi or sunk under the water. He was forbidden to follow the SEALs ashore. Belmont had wanted to experience combat and two professionals were making it possible, at some risk to their own careers, so he could best express his appreciation by being a silent and mysterious presence, an observer, not a participant. Belmont was asked repeatedly during his four days of training if this was clear. He said it was. But in his defense it should be pointed out that he was suffering from addiction-withdrawal in the extreme at the time he made these vows, not having had a cigarette in days. Perhaps he hadn't understood the full implications of the promise he was making.

He left the lieutenant's office and reported to LTJG Fred Stevenson, who was no older than Belmont but who was nevertheless Officer-In-Charge of a Riverine boat assigned to insert a SEAL platoon up the An Long that night. Stevenson studied his base commander's orders and Belmont's ID and shiny badge and repeated the lieutenant's question: "What's this about?"

"It's an ongoing investigation, so I'm not at liberty to talk about it," Belmont parroted.

"Not talking is a good start," Stevenson said without humor, "How good are you at staying silent and the hell out of the way?"

"Exactly what I intend to do," Belmont assured him.

"I don't like this...and I don't get it. You been out before at night?"

"Nosir."

"Then you may want to re-think this. It's pitch black out there, we're running engines the VC can hear two miles off, trying to find the correct spot for the SEALs, then we're sitting ducks while we wait for extraction, and if we don't get lit-up at some point by AK47 and RPG fire, it's a pretty rare night. My bet is, you're gonna wish you weren't out there with us."

"I have my orders," Belmont said.

"Your funeral," Stevenson said, "Be here at 2300 hours sharp with a weapon and plenty of your own ammo."

"I'm not allowed to carry arms during an investigation."

Stevenson's eyebrows shot up. "OK, fine, then be here at 2300 hours with a first-aid kit and plenty of your own gauze."

The dock was alive with activity when Belmont arrived back at 2230 hours, the crew of five crawling over the 30-foot Riverine like ants on a beetle. His clean, new camouflage fatigues made him stand out amidst the SEALs, a motley bunch of warriors with bandanas rolled around their heads and grease-smeared faces, faded fatigues bulging with ammo, grenades, knives and good-luck charms. Three of the SEALs descended on him for their own amusement, which Belmont accepted as an initiation for a newcomer. They helped him into a ten-pound flak jacket and a five-pound armored girdle that strapped on between his legs, making sure it was drawn up tight enough to make him wince.

"How come you-guys aren't wearing these?" Belmont asked.

"Because they don't stop an AK47 round at close range," they said.

Then one of the three smeared his face with black camouflage grease -- not dabs of it like they wore but three full tubes of it, layer upon layer, until he looked like Al Jolson.

"Where'd ya' get the fuckin' scar," his make-up artist asked.

"Knife fight in a cantina in Mexico," Belmont said as impressively as he could manage.

At 2300 hours, the SEALs embarked, the twin diesels rumbled to life and the Navy men cast off from the dimly-lit floating dock into the blackness of the river. Armored like a floating tank and bristling with mounted .50 caliber and M-60 machine guns, a grenade launcher and many M-16s, the Riverine lumbered up-stream against a swift current. Stevenson guided his boat toward the darker port-side river bank, away from the occasional lantern and fire-light of the heavily populated starboard bank. On their left, only the interruption of starlight marked the jungle horizon. Belmont nestled on the stool assigned him in the armor-plated corner near the wheel-well, where Stevenson could keep an eye on him. And so for two hours did it go, feeling their way along the port bank, whispering over a map, searching for the insertion point.

When they found it, a smaller craft called an MSSC was waiting for them with a Mobile Support Team that had scouted the area all day. The SEALs transferred to the MSSC, which sat lower in the water and ran quieter than the Riverine, and they slipped away into the dark. There was nothing to see over the edge of the gunwale, so Belmont watched the phosphorescent glow of Stevenson's watch ticking off the minutes -- six, seven, eight -- that they were "sitting ducks, waiting for extraction." The steady, soothing gurgle of the diesels, holding their position steady in mid-river, was broken by a staccato drum-roll of AK47 fire, immediately answered by thud-thud-thud from the MSSC's .50 caliber and a pop-corn chorus of M-16 fire. As Belmont peeked over the gunwale to see muzzle-flashes all along the port-side bank, Stevenson ordered, "Light 'em up" and a crew member sent a flare arcing across the black sky. The star flare, drifting down on its little chute, bathed the jungle scene in that eerie, ice-blue glow particular to white phosphorus. The MSSC was shown nosed onto a flat, muddy shore, pouring fire into the tree-line fifty yards off her bow and to her left. Muzzle sparks from the AK47s twinkled through the tangled jungle.

"Hold fire," Stevenson ordered, "They're too close-in." The hiss, and boom of an RPG rocket exploding set Stevenson to muttering, "Get out of there...get out of there" just as two men slipped over the gunwales of the small craft, sunk into muck to their mid-thighs and put their shoulders into the hull of the craft. "They've run aground. Let's go!" Stevenson said. He shoved the throttle full-forward and spun the wheel, racing toward the shoreline on the port-side of the MSSC. When they were 200 yards closer and at a better angle, the Riverine crew opened up with the twin .50 caliber in the bow and both M-60s at the rails, showering Belmont in a hailstorm of shell-casings too hot to touch. He heard AK47 rounds smack against the armored gunwale inches from his head, so as badly as he wanted to see the fighting, he thought it better to crouch down into his corner of the hull. A crewman fired two more flares out over the jungle, while another threw a rescue-line in the direction of the MSSC, but the coil splashed into the water between them. "Get closer-in!" he shouted at Stevenson over the chorus of gunfire. "Too shallow!" Stevenson yelled back. "We'll both get grounded!" The crewman tried twice more to fling the coil of wet line, side-arming with all his strength and exposing himself to fire, but the line fell slightly short of the stranded boat.

MY CHANCE! was all he remembered thinking. Nothing more. Belmont took two mighty bounds across the deck and jumped overboard. He would swim the rope over, rescue the men, prove himself in combat. The five feet of water he figured to leap into, however, proved to be only eighteen inches of water flowing over bottomless tidal mush into which he spiked himself like a dart in a cork-board. He was in water from shoulder to waist and in mud below that, unable to do anything but splash around, fighting the current, trying not to tip over and drown. He twisted his body back toward the hull of the Riverine but could see no one there. A cacophony of firing continued from machine guns, punctuated now and then by the thump of the 40mm grenade launcher, all of it underscored by the bass roar of the twin diesels.

A ripple of fear coursed through his brain as it occurred to him that perhaps no one had seen him jump -- or even if they had, his life might not be a priority for them during a fire-fight. When he twisted back toward the MSSC, he saw them succeed in freeing their craft from the mud-flats and begin backing-out. Belmont began to scream just as the Riverine throttled up, spun around and knocked him flat with a tsunami from its twin water-jet propulsion tubes. The tidal wave that swept over him was nine-parts mud to one-part water, so when he splashed his way back toward a more or less vertical position, a thick mass of muck adorned his head and shoulders. It may have been this camouflage that saved his life after the Navy boats had receded into far-distant buzzing sounds and the VC took possession of the battlefield, chatting excitedly and scouring the muddy shore for any booty left behind. Belmont, terrified beyond his wildest dreams, crouched as low in the water as he could, given that he couldn't bend his knees. He watched scores of the enemy, carrying AK47s and RPG tubes, inspecting the open flats where the MSSC had nosed-in. He was close enough to see their individual faces before one, and then both the remaining flares dropped into the trees and the coal-black of a Mekong Delta night swallowed up both them and him.

Their voices faded away, mixed with laughter, perhaps of relief at having survived the battle or of victory, that they had run the Americans off their side of the An Song. But the surge of gratitude Belmont felt at being, against all odds, neither dead nor a POW quickly gave way to another round of creeping fear as he fought to stay above water against the steady, heavy drag of the current. Every effort to twist himself free merely served to dig his legs in deeper, as he recalled from Cape Cod summers when he stood at the water's edge feeling the waves dig his feet down into the sand. He stripped off the flak jacket but couldn't free himself from the heavy girdle-belt. The muscles in his arms and back began to quiver from the exertion of fighting against the boundless energy of the current as an hour passed, then two, with no sign the Navy would return to rescue him. He tried to float, lying back and relaxing, but his anchored legs pulled him under water unless he fought to stay erect. He was sinking or the river was rising or both -- he had no way of knowing -- but the water was creeping higher up his chest. The only sure thing was that he was losing this fight for his life. Bubbles popped in his ears as he went under, fought his way back to the surface, then went down again, each round giving him less time to grab air before being submerged and less of his face above water. His determination waned and a half-moon rose above the tree-line during the hours that he wrestled against a tireless foe. He listened in vain through the better medium of the water for the sound of diesel engines, the

Navy returning for him when they realized he was missing, provided they would care if he was or not. "Combat is fought in teams," Shimazu had warned him, "and you are not a member of any team." Choppy waves splashed continuously over his face now, turning his eye-sockets into pools, and his muscles involuntarily started to relax into his fate, his death by drowning. He began to choke as he took in more water than air with each gasp, spewing air and water toward the pale moon above.

It was this strange, unnatural sound that caught the attention of Lanh's teenage daughter, Chi. They were on the dangerous river at night because they were stealing fish from their neighbor's traps. When Lanh lost his sons -- one to ARVN, one to the VC, one in an ambush on his way to school -- he fell into a very dark place and he slept all day, every day, and all night, every night, for many months, unable to rise from his bed to work. Chi and her mother tried argument and medicine and praying, but nothing moved Lanh from this dark place until Chi told him she was going out to face the dangers of the An Long by herself at night, to steal fish from the traps of others. The river, a free-fire zone for both sides at night, was dangerous enough, without considering what the victims of her thievery would do to her if she were caught. It was this desperate act that had dragged Lanh reluctantly from his bed. He spoke not a word but he did stumble into the boat to go with her.

"What is that noise?" Chi whispered into her father's ear. "It sounds like a gas engine that sputters but won't start when you pull the cord." Lanh skillfully managed pole and stern paddle to guide their little boat toward the sound until they found the source -- a large, black face, the same color as the water, bobbing in the moonlight on the surface of the river like a dinner-plate upon a table, sucking in river-water and spewing it back out again. This was a sight unlike anything they had ever seen before. Perhaps it was a very short person standing on top of the muddy bottom or a tall one who had grown up out of the riverbed like a reed or -- much more likely than either -- one of the River Gods emerging up from the deep as was cited in many of the stories told by the elders. "We must help him, father! He is drowning!" Chi whispered.

"It is a River God, daughter. We must not disturb it." Lanh ordered.

"But he is choking, father!" Chi pleaded, "I believe he is a man like you!"

"Hear me, daughter!" Lanh spoke loudly, shattering the silence on the dangerous river, "If he is human, it is bad luck for our family and our village if we tamper with his fate. And if it is a River God, then this is its realm and it does not need our help!"

The question became moot for, as he spoke, the oval face glimmering in the pale light of the moon disappeared beneath the surface and only bubbles carried by the current remained. Without another word of argument -- for her father was the head of the family and the central authority of her life, so argument with him was futile -- Chi overcame her fear, slipped into the river and dove down, searching for the struggling creature she had seen. When she re-surfaced, she had a grip on a piece of cloth. She clung to the side of the boat, struggling against the current while Lanh sunk the pole deep into the mud on the down-river side and used it as a fulcrum to balance the hull in place. With enormous effort, the old man used feet and hands to hold the boat positioned against the axis of the pole while his daughter. hanging from the gunwale, wrestled to pull the cloth toward the surface. This acrobatic performance held momentarily while Chi pleaded her case: "If the River Gods fated him to drown, father, why did they bring us to him?"

Lanh was so furious at his daughter's disobedience that he considered pulling up the pole and leaving the River Gods to decide her fate too. But he also felt panic at the thought of losing her to her foolishness after already losing his sons. So he fought with pole and steering oar to hold the bucking boat against the current, to stay with her, while he cursed her savagely for her impudence. And then she was gone.

The remnants of Belmont's consciousness led him to a vague awareness that the tugging on his shirt collar was a human fist -- a rescuing hand from above -- and he grabbed Chi's right arm with all his strength and pulled her under. She lost hold of the gunwale with her left hand but managed somehow to find the shaft of her father's pole, anchored in the mud, just as the current pushed her past it. She wrapped her legs and free hand around the axis and pulled until Belmont's arm bounced against the stout shaft of the pole and he transferred his death-grip from her thin arm to the solid post. With a strength born of desperation, Belmont gripped the base of the pole with both hands and pulled with all his might, bucking hips, then knees, then boots out from the mud as he climbed the pole hand-over-hand up toward air. His first violent gasps gave him, oddly enough, a blinding headache. Someone above him was screaming orders at him but in Vietnamese and he feared that, whoever it was, they were about to open fire on him. He looked up at a man who, like him, had both hands gripped around the post as he shouted words full of fury. He had one narrow chance to escape alive and he took it, pushing off toward the tree-line silhouetted against the moonlit sky. He'd made his way only a few yards, stroking through the shallow water, before exhaustion overcame him and the weight of his clothes, girdle and boots began dragging him down. He half-crawled, half-waddled, pushing against the muddy bottom, leapfrog-ging toward shore until he could hold his head above water on hands and knees. To his surprise, the screaming man didn't shoot at him.

Chi meantime lifted herself back into the little boat without looking up at her father, who was spewing into the night air all the violent rage that had been bottled-up inside him during the paralysis of his depres-sion. Chi is a worthless snake, a traitor, an ungrateful wretch who never listens to her father's warnings! She is a living symbol that the gods cursed all their family and their whole village from the exact moment of her birth down through the ages for generations to come! She is an insult to the memory of their honorable ancestors...and much more.

"Yes, father," she mumbled, looking down, "I know, father, you are right...." And she cried tears of overwhelming joy. Her father had come back to her.

When his venom had spent itself, Lanh worked the long pole free from the mud and set their boat adrift on the current. Father and daughter watched in awe as the strange creature they had encountered emerged from the river and wobbled to its feet on the moonlit mud-flats. It had lost its head, for the moon reflected nothing where its face should have been, were it human. Outlined against the shoreline, it frantically flapped its long, black arms in an effort to fly while squawking-out monotone calls, unintelligible and nothing like human speech.

Safely downriver from it, Lanh told his recalcitrant daughter firmly, "Now you see why you must always obey your father! I told you, bad luck to interfere with River Gods!"

"Yes, father," Chi said obediently, "I promise it will never happen again." And she happily counted six fat fish in her grass basket as her father steered them toward home.

25

28 - 30 January 1968

SCRAM

Since settling into his position at Me Duc Tin, Rene Levesque had become indispensable to the overworked and elderly rector, Père Martin. Privately, between them, Levesque -- known only as Andre to the priest -- was considered as having been called to a vocation and entered into Formation to the Deaconate. As such he had no authority to consecrate the Host or to grant Final Absolution, among other things, but he assisted Père Martin in numerous ways, making it possible for the rector to bear the burden of the parish and its war-ravaged congregation. Parishioners, for the most part, accepted the tall man they called "Frère Andre" without regard to the subtleties of doctrine. With help from the church's sexton, an older man who learned French during Colonial times, Andre proved his devotion to the people at all hours of the day and night, praying with the sick and the dying, consoling the bereaved, and assisting at mass. Andre suggested that he could relieve Père Martin of the chore of saying Morning Prayer if permitted to do so in the Latin tradition, and the familiar old litany soon became so popular among older members of the parish that attendance doubled at this daily service. Many years of difficult progress in accepting Vatican II guidelines were thus erased, but each day in the hour before dawn, when Andre's clear tenor reached Père Martin's ears, the old priest rolled his gray head over on his pillow and thanked God and Andre for one more hour's sleep. And this devoted but bone-weary servant of The Lord did not see how he could have survived the crushing demands of that Christmas season, with increased death and war all around them, without the energetic assistance of the young man who had miraculously appeared at Me Duc Tin.

After the morning service each Monday, Frère Andre boarded the first jitney to Tay Ninh. He did so with the rector's knowledge and understanding that two masters were being served.

At the safe house, Levesque typed a two-page memo to Colonel Cardenas reporting "further steady progress in establishing liaison within the hierarchy of the organization to which I've been assigned." By pre-arrangement, Levesque's memo did not take the form of a traditional intelligence report, nor did it mention such terms as "priest" or "church". But he nevertheless finished it by stamping "CONFIDENTIAL" and "EYES ONLY NEED TO KNOW" in red ink at the top and bottom of each page and on the envelope addressed to "Mr. Alexander Cardenas, SIC Central Office". Each week, he wondered how much invention, prevarication and excuse-making he would need to get away with filing thirty-five more such vacuous reports. Perhaps if Cardenas had other, larger fish to fry, he would let this "long-shot" just play-out until Rene's 26 September 1968 DEROS.

To Le Duc, who delivered these reports to SIC Central by hand, he also hinted at progress, but with Rick Singleton he was honest. Every Monday, over a leisurely meal, they commiserated about their very different but equally absurd and daunting assignments. When Rene admitted to blowing his own cover on his first interview with Père Martin, Rick said he envied him.

"You know, I thought you might do that. When you said 'I'm a Catholic,' I could see where that was going. So you think Martin is going to tell his bishop?"

"I don't think so," Rene said. "He said I told him as a Confession, so it's privileged."

"Does the Catholic church use 'Need To Know' too?"

"We Catholics invented 'Need to Know'. Besides, he really needs my help. He's been carrying that big parish by himself for over a year, and anyway..." Levesque studied the label of the acrid red vinegar the cafe owner had called "merlot". "It's really what I want to do... maybe what I'd be doing if I was home in The States."

"Me too," Rick said, giving a mock salute with his glass of rice wine on ice. "If I were back in New York, I'd probably be selling tires for Goodyear."

Over the course of ten such luncheons, Levesque found he had less to say and Singleton found he had more. As Rene's role at Me Duc Tin settled into a round of rituals and pastoral duties, Rick's at Xuan Song Plantation became increasingly intricate and uncertain. Duke's prediction came true: Madame Guignon developed a keen interest in the young American businessman Ted Michaels and invited him to dinner or cocktails at the mansion more and more often. She reminisced with him about her college years at Bryn Mawr, where she majored in classical archaeology and, to make her academic life easier, minored in French. It seemed that he too had spent some time in Philadelphia, on business, and was very familiar with the city's rich art and music scene and its many museums. Monsieur Guignon fostered no such friendly feelings toward Michaels and treated him as though he were some unpleasant servant his wife had hired -- but that was how he treated most other people too.

Among the guests who attended the social life of the plantation were a pair of businessmen important to Monsieur Guignon because they supplied workers to him at a time when war had placed labor in critical shortage. The older man, Gia Trang, was able to get by in French while the younger man, an assistant he called Minh, spoke no French. Singleton immediately found the two of interest: How did they supply hundreds of workers to the rubber plantation for, as Monsieur boasted, a very modest commission, and why should they have shown, through Madame, an avid and friendly curiosity about him from the start? Each invitation to Xuan Song ended-up with the four of them off in a corner or out on a balcony discussing the war, world events, life in America, or the international trade in rubber in a mixture of French, Vietnamese and English. These two were strikingly well informed and intent on pumping Singleton for information, so he was soon seeking Cardenas' advice on how to proceed with them. Should he try to establish contact outside of Xuan Song? On what pretext? For what purpose?

"Something's up with them," he told Levesque during their lunch on January 8. "They do a quick social curtsey to Guignon, their bread-and-butter contract, then walk through a room of influential guests so they can corner me and ask about Eugene McCarthy, do I think he will beat LBJ, how do Americans feel about the Vietnam War and protests, will black Americans rise up against the government, do I think somebody shot down Otis Redding's plane...."

"Who's Otis Redding?"

"See? They know more than you do, these two so-called businessmen. I'm scared this is some sort of a recruitment riff, man. Too many questions about how I *feel* about the war and race relations. I'm being set-up here and Cardenas is no help. 'Let things develop,' he tells me. When you're young like this Minh-guy is, maybe you're curious about foreigners or maybe you just want to get to know a black guy, but Gia Trang is a heavy-weight, like Cardenas. He's been around a long time and he's got an agenda here. I'm getting in over my head."

"You think they're VC?"

"If they are, be afraid, man! They've got the whole plantation loaded up with their hand-picked workers, five or six hundred of them. Guignon could wake up tomorrow morning and look out his big windows at three companies of VC infantry where his workers used to be."

On January 28th, Mr. Michaels' chauffeur, Le Duc, brought a written note to the Tay Ninh safe house from Madame Guignon. It invited Ted to visit Xuan Song on Tuesday evening, January 30th, for an after-dinner drink, if convenient. He arrived in the foyer of the mansion in his second-best suit, expecting a casual hour of small talk and hoping not to see Gia Trang. But the four people seated around the second-floor library were not having a casual conversation. Madame was wiping her eyes with a handkerchief while Monsieur perched on the edge of his red-velvet wing chair, waving his arms and barking at his guests in French. By the time Singleton caught the mood, he was halfway into the room, so he froze and waited until Madame Guignon noticed him and waved him over to her. She muttered something to her husband, then rose and offered her hand. "You will forgive us, Mr. Michaels. You have found us in one of those little dramas families go through." She dabbed at her tears, sighed, and composed herself before introducing him to a couple, he white and she Vietnamese, both looking embarrassed.

"Mr. Michaels, this is our daughter, Bian Guignon, and her fiancé, Mr. Bradley. May I present our good friend, Ted Michaels, a business executive from America."

Singleton bowed, raised the hand of the beautiful Vietnamese woman in the heliotrope ao dai toward his lips, and said "Enchanté". The gentleman arose, a tall man with piercing blue eyes, gave Singleton's hand a firm grasp and said in English, "Jim Bradley. Glad to meet you."

"When Bian told us we would finally get to meet her fiancé," Madame said, "I thought it would be nice to offer him the company of a fellow ex-patriot, but we seem to have been...."

Monsieur could contain himself no longer. He exploded into a rage that needed no translation as he directed angry words at his wife and daughter while his accusing finger jabbed repeatedly toward Mr. Bradley. Monsieur Guignon clearly disapproved of his daughter's choice and made not the slightest attempt to hide it. As the arguments developed between them, Singleton found a moment to whisper into madame's ear, "Perhaps at a better time."

"Of course," she whispered back, offering her hand, "and I apologize for...."

"No need, madame," he said, raising his eyes to hers. Then he descended the stairway to the foyer where the servant held the door for him. He crossed the paving stones toward the black Citroën where Le Duc would be awaiting his report. As always, Duke played his role well, holding open the rear door of the car in his black livery, but as Singleton's eyes adjusted to the dark, he realized too late someone was standing behind him.

"He has a gun," Duke said matter-of-factly, "so please just get in."

Doors closed behind Singleton and then behind Le Duc, who whispered as the other man walked around to the passenger side, "Do you know who this guy is?" The dome light briefly lit up the face of Gia Trang's aide, Minh, easily identifiable by a distinctive scar on the back of his neck. Then the door slammed and they were wrapped in darkness. Minh spoke so quickly that Le Duc had trouble keeping up the translation: "He says you must know...that you need to be aware of Gia Trang's true importance...significance." Le Duc exchanged a few words with Minh in Vietnamese. "He says Gia Trang holds you in sincere regard...true friendship. So that after the war-time, when the Americans are gone from here...are not in charge...Gia Trang wishes to see you again, here at Xuan Song...you and others of your company. Rubber industry will be important... with other industry...to rebuild the state when the war is over...for a strong socialist economy of a free republic, democratic people's republic...." They again lapsed into Vietnamese. "The gist of it goes," Duke went on, "sooner than we think, the war will end and when it does, the new nation will be ready to do business with Goodyear. Now I'm supposed to drive."

Singleton heard the jangle of keys being dropped into Duke's lap, the engine rumbled to life and the headlights backlit the two men in the front seat. They chatted quietly as Le Duc drove out through the gates and some way down the road, while Singleton sat silent, making a mental note to store a weapon somewhere he could reach it next time, if there was ever to be a next time. The Citroën slowed, then pulled over and stopped. Minh got out, spoke to Le Duc for a moment, and they drove away.

"That was Minh No-Last-Name, the Gia Trang side-kick I've been writing about in my reports," Singleton said. "And in answer to all our previous questions about the two of them, yes, they are Commies."

The ordeal over, an adrenaline wave swept over Duke, who had seemed calm throughout, and he had to pull the car off the road and stop. "Man! Shit!" he yelled, "*Man! God! I'm shaking so hard I can't drive! Look at my hands!*" Singleton couldn't see his hands but his voice was like someone else's. "Jesus! I thought he was gonna blow me away back there! Before you came out, he wouldn't say a word... just took my keys and stuck a gun in my back!"

"Need me to drive?"

"No, I'll be OK. Just give me a minute here," Duke stammered, his breaths coming short, fast and audible in the dark confines of the car. "One more thing he said, when he got out. He said if you and Gia Trang were to conduct business in the future, you would need to leave here now -- tomorrow, tonight maybe -- for Saigon. Stay in the Caravelle, he said, where Gia Trang can find you. Or you'll end-up like the Guignons, he said."

"Jesus, Duke! What's that supposed to mean?"

"It means 'Scram'." Duke put the car into gear and pulled back onto the dark roadway.

Early the next morning, Ted Michaels arrived unannounced to find Madame having breakfast alone on the veranda. "I'm glad you're here, Ted" she smiled, "I wanted to explain...." Singleton had been rehearsing scripts in his head all morning, while he argued with Duke that this visit was necessary, that he was going to stop-by Xuan Song with or without his chauffeur, but he was still far from certain what he would say. So he was grateful for the delay while she ordered tea brought for Mr. Michaels and prattled on about the domestic squall between her daughter -- who was demanding a dowry or inheritance or something, which Monsieur Guignon was not about to grant -- so she could run off with this American she has been living with in Saigon. "My husband can be very stubborn, as I'm sure you know. He ordered my daughter out of our house and told Mr. Bradley, who seemed perfectly charming, that if a man claiming to own an art and antique gallery in Boston can't afford a wife, then he has no right to one. But this is Bian's one chance to escape the war and she's had such a hard life. Pierre never accepted her as his daughter and her first husband was killed by the Viet Minh weeks after they were married...."

Confused, distracted with his own thoughts, Singleton responded thoughtlessly: "You say 'my daughter,' madame? I had assumed she was adopted."

A moment of embarrassed silence passed before she told him, "Of course because she is Vietnamese, anyone might make that assumption. But when I was new to this country, our marriage endured some hard times. I learned to love Vietnam by loving Bian's father." She smiled at her confidant and chided, "Why...did you imagine that I have never been young? That I never had a heart to give away?"

"No, of course not," he lied, "I understand." He stalled a little longer, refilling his tea and tearing at a croissant. Then he asked, "Has Bian returned to Saigon, then?"

"Yes, early this morning."

"Then I have a bold suggestion to make to you. I have some money put aside. Why don't we pool what we have and make up an impromptu dowry...a wedding gift? I'll have my driver take us to Saigon, you can properly introduce me to Bian and her fiancé over lunch and I can have you back here before dinner. It will be an adventure!"

It appeared to work. She laughed warmly and looked at him over her raised teacup. But she said, "You are a wonderful friend, Ted, but also a very foolish one. I no longer do things behind my husband's back. If Bian is to have a dowry, it must come from both Pierre and me."

Two sharp blasts from a car horn caught the attention of both the woman, who could not imagine a mere chauffeur expressing impatience, and the young man who knew he was. "Margot, you must listen to me." Singleton's use of her given name for the first time raised her brows in surprise. "My superiors in the company are very well connected and you must believe me that I have it on the very best authority that Xuan Song is not safe for you or monsieur at this moment. I urge you to come with me, to harbor in Saigon temporarily until...for a time. You must believe what I am telling you...."

She held up both hands and scolded, "Please stop. That is impossible. Xuan Song has never been a safe place to be, not ever. Pierre will not leave, not even if he is in peril as you say, and I could never leave him here. So even if you are right...."

"*I am!*" he yelled, surprising both of them.

Two blasts of the Citroën horn caused Singleton to push his chair back and stand up, most involuntarily. "Will you not reconsider?" sounded trite and useless, but she answered, "Of course I will... every ten minutes for the rest of my life." She rose and offered her hand, which he took firmly in both of his and kissed, then turned and moved toward the car.

Something was in the air at Me Duc Tin. Latin Matins had three times the usual number in attendance and as Frère Andre ended the service with "et spiritus Sancti," they bolted from the pews and fled down the aisles. By the time he kissed the surplice and placed it on its hanger, he was the only person left in the building. As he crossed the grounds toward his quarters, the normal dawn hustle of the nearby streets resembled something closer to pandemonium, with excited shouts as people ran and two-wheeled traffic moved in a blur.

Père Martin sat in his office, waiting to call to him, "In here, Frère Andre. Please close the door." Then he stood and said, "Something is happening. Many in Me Duc Tin have relatives on both sides and there is much talk of green men coming from the North."

"Green men?"

"Regular soldiers. The Army of North Vietnam. Time now for you to go."

"Yes, father. I see you are busy."

"No! Listen! Time for you to leave Me Duc Tin! Now!"

"My place is with you and the church," Andre said, faithful to his divine calling. But as soon as the words were spoken, Levesque felt a chill run up his spine.

Martin looked him in the eye and sighed. "Andre, my young friend," he said, dropping the honorific title. "We do not have time to pray over this. As I am your superior in Holy Orders, I am commanding you to leave for Saigon on the next bus or jitney."

"But I feel strongly that I must...."

"Enough! There is no time! You are two meters tall, an obvious foreigner, and your presence here places me and the whole congregation in jeopardy! You must leave...that is all!"

Martin rose and offered his hand. "The faithful of Me Duc Tin will miss you...and I most of all. May God bless you and keep you, my dear friend."

Ten minutes later, Rene Levesque stood holding his small suitcase outside the church, where buses, jitneys and taxis were being mobbed by hoards of people as desperate to leave as he was. His heart sank as he assessed his options: Thumbing a ride, buying or stealing a bicycle or walking eighteen miles to the safe house in Tay Ninh. "God is telling me to stay," he muttered to himself.

"Hey, Father, you need a ride?" were the first words in English he had ever heard spoken in Me Duc Tin. He turned to find Rick Singleton leaning against a black Citroën, his uniformed chauffeur at his side.

26

31 January 1968

SOMEONE YOU KNOW

For two days and two nights, Belmont lived within the quandary his few seconds of impulsive action had created. No means of escape presented itself to get him from his hiding place, the thicket at the water's edge, to Khap Noi. He was on the enemy-infested side of the An Long, so the Vietnamese he heard using the trails behind him at night were VC or civilians sympathetic to them, and by day, he heard no one. This was a free-fire zone for any passing helicopter or riverboat but crossing the river seemed impossible: Belmont's near-death experience left him terrified to go back into a river that was a half-mile wide with currents so violent that large freighters could be seen churning full-power just to inch upriver. Hours turned into days with plenty to drink but no food, evenings and early mornings when clouds of mosquitoes descended on him. He felt less and less sure he could find a way back. So he hunkered down in hiding, buying one day of life at a time by staying-put, waiting for some act of fate to rescue him.

Lanh's daughter, Chi, had past these mud-flats several times in these two days: Once with her father, while setting out their own fish traps again, now that he was better, and once with two cousins on a trip to Khap Noi to buy food and gifts for the celebration of Tet. Each time she strained to see any sign of the man she had saved from drowning (for she had felt his death-grip where her forearm was still bruised and she did not really believe he was one of the River Gods), but they were not very close to shore and she saw nothing.

On the morning of January 31, with preparations for Tet in full swing, her curiosity and rebellious temperament got the better of her, and she enticed her cousins, two boys slightly older than she, into a secret adventure, a trip to the place where she claimed to have seen a River God. The three teenagers slipped away from the village on some pretext and had soon worked their way upriver in a motorized skiff, following Chi's guidance. They pulled the small boat onto the muddy shore and, walking in a flat-footed manner borrowed centuries ago from ducks, they easily crossed a span of mushy silt that any jungle-booted GI would have sunk into knee-deep. They exchanged giggles and whispers as they approached the tree-line, following Chi to the very spot where the mythical creature was last seen. On higher ground, they looked for tracks, broken branches and other clues and were rewarded by finding mounds of shiny shell-casings, a sign of recent combat on this spot, along with many fresh prints in the mud made by Vietnamese sandals.

Chi froze, covered her mouth and waved the others over. The boys crept forward toward the strange sight she had found: A sleeping giant with a face as black as charcoal but arms and bare feet as white as a fish belly, splotched with patches of red welts. Was this hideous creature the one Chi had seen? Was it dead or alive?

When they tip-toed closer, its eyes popped open, it stirred and sat up! It saw them and immediately leapt to its feet, rising to a terrible height, twice their stature, and worse, it thrust both its enormous arms straight up toward the sky and bellowed at them in its mythical language!

They fled like deer toward the boat. The monster gave pursuit but sank deep into the mush that they flew across at top speed. They pushed the skiff into deeper water and piled in, one of the boys yanking on the pull cord of the engine. In his panic, he flooded it and the coughing gurgle of it reminded Chi of the strange noise that had led her to this spot three nights ago. As they drifted along with the shore current, they looked back to see the giant kneeling in the mud, his palms together in a universal sign of supplication, speaking now the universal language of grief, pleading with them between wails and sobs.

"I believe he is a man like my father," Chi announced, "a very large man, though, perhaps an American who has become lost on the river."

"But Americans I see are either black or white, not both like this thing," one cousin argued, while the other struggled to start the engine.

"Still, he has been here on this spot since I saw him on Sunday night, so I don't think he is able to leave here."

"Well, cousin Chi, I for one am not going back."

"Me neither."

Then they heard him singing as he knelt, a strange, repetitive sound that might have passed for "Khap Noi". He sang this many times until, with the engine purring again, they surged closer against the current and asked him in Vietnamese if he wanted to go to Khap Noi. He struggled to get to his feet but sunk deeper into the silt with each attempt and, flopping around like a wounded bird, wailed "Khap Noi" and shook his enormous black head up and down. Soon the youngsters were laughing at this slap-stick spectacle, as he shouted now about "Petit Buddha" and "Khmer Krom," references they also knew well. He even mimed a bulging belly and a bald head when he shouted "Petit Buddha".

"See? He knows the American fisherman who lives in the village of the Khmer Krom," Chi said. "That is closer than Khap Noi and we could take him there on the way home."

Eventually Chi's pleadings won-out, that it would be cruel to leave him here, where he had obviously been stranded for days, an American doomed on this side of the An Long. They inched closer to shore, barking orders to him he seemed to understand by raising his hands, palms out, moving slowly into the water, but he almost capsized them by the awkward way he clambered aboard. The words they knew in common were repeated by them all -- Petit Buddha, Khmer Krom, Khap Noi -- as the cousin using the long pole to push them into deeper water watched alertly, ready to use it as a weapon if need be. Belmont watched the skillful use of this staff attentively, remembering that one just like it had saved his life. He wished he could tell his story, in gratitude to these wonderful kids, but he knew they would not understand him.

He crouched in the bow and turned his attention toward the water, away from these young people, children almost, to ease their apprehension of him. They chattered excitedly among themselves for twenty minutes while the current helped the motor speed them downriver. Khap Noi was nowhere in sight when they veered toward port, angling into the shore controlled by ARVN and US forces. Belmont hadn't eaten in three days, his clothes were mud-caked and his arms and face were raw from bug bites and his scratching, but he was alive and headed for safety, as Dodd's village emerged from the trees above the bank.

Chi was first to spot them and she raised the alarm, pointing to the thatched houses of the Khmer Krom on the ridge above the shore, to the mass of dark figures running through the shadows under the trees. Too numerous to be villagers, all running left to right, they had to be soldiers. For civilians who wanted to stay alive, all soldiers of every kind were to be avoided. They banked the skiff into a sharp turn and ran back toward the center of the river. Chi argued they should take the American to Khap Noi, but her cousins refused. It was too far, they would be gone too long and in trouble with worried parents, "especially your father," they told her.

Behind them, big engines whined and then roared closer. They all twisted back to see an OV-10 Bronco, distinguished by its twin fuselage, diving down toward the river at a steep angle, then leveling off to lay rockets and machinegun fire into the village of the Khmer Krom. It pulled off and was replaced by a second Bronco that pumped more rockets and machinegun fire into the mass of troops in the village. First white and then black smoke rose above the trees as Belmont prayed aloud: "Oh, God! Oh, God! Oh, God!"

The skiff headed into the port-side shore a half-mile below the village where, without prompting, Belmont jumped out and waded toward the embankment. When he turned to thank them, they were sitting still in the water, watching him leave in an awed silence.

"I don't know why you saved me," he said, "a complete stranger you'd never seen before, but I thank you with all my heart." He placed both his palms flat against his chest in a gesture of gratitude and when he did, he heard the clank of his dog-tags. He pulled the bead-chain from under his shirt, squeezed the tiny union-link and slipped one of the two tags off ("Bring one tag back to the man's unit. Leave the other with the body," he'd been trained). He waded back to them and offered the metal tag as the only gift he had to give. The young girl received it into her hands and studied it closely, trying to decipher this talisman given to her by the man whose life she had saved.

"Now you will know who I am," Belmont told Chi. As the current began to drift them apart, they waved the palms of their hands in a universal sign of farewell.

Belmont followed a footpath inland that led him to a point on the main road he knew, about three miles from Khap Noi Base. It was an hour before he arrived at the main gate for he had to rest frequently, physically too weak to keep a steady pace, and he walked much of it backward, hoping to flag down a public conveyance of some sort or a jeep. Military traffic was heavy but in a hurry and all jitneys were completely full. Through everything, he'd managed to hang onto his wallet and Navy badge, but his ID was mud-caked and had to be rubbed against his pants-leg to make it legible. The MPs took not the slightest notice of his disheveled condition as they passed him through. He stumbled past the mess, where the smell of cooking only made him feel nauseous, and on to the side-street where his office/bedroom sat, front door ajar.

Inside, Huu was typing away until Belmont's shadow in the door-way caught his attention. He leapt up and shouted, "Mr. Belmont!

You alive! You here! I so happy see you!" Belmont allowed his hand to be shaken vigorously but without much strength to respond. Arrived back home against all odds, instead of elation, he felt only utter exhaustion. "Have you seen Mr. Dodd?" he asked in a monotone.

"Oh, yessir. This morning at Base Headquarters."

A flicker of joy arose in Belmont, more than he felt at his own survival. "How long ago, exactly?" he asked.

"We go find Mr. Dodd, like the first day we meet!" Huu led the way to the lime-green jeep and unchained the steering wheel. They twisted through the maze of buildings toward the floating docks and pulled up outside Base HQ, Huu driving while Belmont tried to stay awake. Standing beside the building entrance was a Buddhist monk in saffron robes, head shining in the sun, wearing a homemade cardboard sign around his neck that read: "FIND BELMONT".

"Mr. Dodd stand here three days, three nights, on hunger strike," Huu said. "They move him away, he come right back. Navy say you MIA."

Belmont approached the little monk, who neither blinked nor looked up at him but maintained a focused stare, straight into the center of Belmont's mud-covered shirt. As still as a statue, he was lost in meditation, his vision locked into an unseen world, his open eyes no longer registering the external. Belmont said "Jerry" softly, a half dozen times, as if waking a sleep-walker. Then Dodd blinked rapidly, came back from within and raised his eyes to Belmont's face.

"Oh Belmont, there you are," he croaked. "I had a dream that you were drowned."

He wrapped his huge arms around the little monk. "I did drown," he said, tears filling his eyes. "But a fisherman saved me with his boat staff and some kids brought me across the river." He lifted the cardboard sign from Dodd's neck and slipped an arm around his shoulder as they walked back to the jeep. "You never gave up on me, did you...a hunger strike, really?"

He settled Dodd into the passenger seat and stepped back to study this strange image: An American from Indiana recast as a saffron-robed monk, an enlisted GI reborn as a pacifist priest.

"You really are one-of-a-kind, my friend," he told him.

"Everyone is," Petit Buddha replied. "Every soul is unique, a gift to be treasured."

Belmont climbed into the rear of the jeep, knowing they both needed to break their fasts before he was ready to tell the sad news about the village of the Khmer Krom or Dodd was ready to hear it. The overwhelming fear and sorrow Belmont felt when he thought he knew someone who had died would be so much greater for Dodd, who knew everybody in that place.

27

31 January 1968. The Night of Tet

FAULTY INTELLIGENCE

The distinguished gentleman in the nicely tailored beige suit might have passed for a civilian were it not for his black leather shoes, polished to a mirror-like perfection. The first thing Stan Morgan (not his real name), real estate developer (a cover) from California (not really) noticed were the shoes, and that would have given George Owen Donahue away as a military man if Morgan hadn't already known it. Morgan was amused by this flaw in an otherwise formidable-looking man who, as he rose in greeting, bore a strong resemblance in face, voice and bearing to Charlton Heston in his Marc Antony role. The handshake was warm and firm as he said, "Thank you for taking the time, Stan."

"No bother at all, George," Morgan assured him.

Colonel Donahue knew Morgan only casually, from a few brief conversations at MACV, and he wanted to make a good impression. He had arrived early but deferred ordering a drink, so he was relieved to hear Morgan say, "Double martini, dry, two olives," and he echoed, "Me too." They made light conversation while the drinks arrived and began to warm them. Donahue had chosen a remote corner of the Caravelle's rooftop restaurant, away from the cacophony of the Tet celebration below, in anticipation that the talk would get serious between the CO of the 581st Military Intelligence Company and the Chief of CIA's Saigon Station. When their steaks had been ordered and the waiter retreated, they got down to business over a second round of cold gin.

Donahue shaved his baritone down to a whisper, slid a black and white photo across the table and asked, "What do you make of this? That banner is stretched right across An Vuong Duong Street in Cholon and it says in Chinese and Vietnamese, 'Spring Offensive weapons will be available here to all comers'. This some form of psych-warfare, trying to scare the hell out of us? Or is it really a public service announcement with weapons to follow?"

Morgan had seen photos of this banner before and he answered, "We think they can deliver. We put the number of VC militia embedded in Saigon at roughly 8,000. But will other young men from the general population line up for AK47s? We don't see that happening. There's too much American money flowing through the economy and too much firepower visible all around, so where's the incentive for anyone who's not one of the 8,000 guys already signed-up?" Morgan took a draw from his drink and added, "Do we think a storm is brewing? You bet. But if the VC expect a rising of the masses, they've been reading too much of their own propaganda."

"Our shop isn't authorized to do those kinds of assessments," Donahue admitted, "but I can tell you there's been a crescendo of tactical activity over recent months, units, whole regiments, moving in force that MACV designates as 'No Longer Effective'."

It may have been the gin or his sheer fatigue from weeks of butting heads with ignorant men with large egos -- whatever the reason, Morgan felt a genuine affection for this earnest, uncomplicated soldier. Donohue worked at a lower level of the profession, bean-counting military units, but he was honest enough to admit the simple, inevitable truth that an attack was coming. So Stan Morgan slipped his leash.

"George, do you know how many of the enemy there are in-country right now, counting NVA, VC, irregulars, political cadres, everything? There are 299,999 exactly. Not one man more or less, and that number hasn't changed in two years."

"How can you know that?" Donahue played along, sipping his martini.

"Because that is the number the Pentagon wants to hear, the number Congress wants to hear, the number the American public will accept from now until after the November elections. Now if you sit here and tell me there will be a Spring Offensive, I can tell you that 299,999 demoralized fighters scattered around the country in decimated units are incapable of mounting a serious attack against overwhelming firepower. Isn't that comforting to hear? Aren't you relieved? Won't you sleep better tonight?"

Annoyed at being toyed with, Colonel Donahue bristled, "So is that what you think?"

"No, George. No, it's not what I think. Our guys put the number at 500-to-600,000 VC who are heavily reinforced by NVA regulars, plus spirited, well-organized militias recently equipped with AK50s and lots of RPGs. Furthermore MACV refuses to talk about two or three million civilians under VC control who are drawn-on as needed for support. Instead they compare their current estimate of 220,000 combat effectives against 500,000 GIs, ignoring the fact that 90% of our men are support-troops, not front-line combat soldiers. So what I think, to answer your fair question, is we're going to get knocked on our asses just as soon as the Tet truce ends. Superior firepower only takes you so far down the road...but then, I've been reminded a number of times lately that we are a civilian outfit and I'm a civilian who should not go around impugning the judgment of the professional military." By the end of this speech, Morgan realized that it had become a rant, an exhale of emotions that had been building up through months of haggling with MACV over evidence they refused to accept. Now, across a small table from a sympathetic colleague, he was letting it all out.

"And you know how it's all going to end up, George? When *Time* and *Newsweek* and *The New York Times* all share the same headline: 'A

Failure of Intelligence'? That will be the final irony of it. Everybody back in D.C. demands to be told the war is winding down, victory is at hand, and if the generals want to keep their jobs, that's what they'd better say. So they ignore a barn-load of evidence to the contrary, parrot the political line, and when it blows up in their faces, the DoD, Congress and LBJ will call it an Intelligence failure and you and I will get the axe for not speaking up!" Morgan drained his stemmed glass and signaled the waiter for another round.

Clearly taken aback by this tirade and concerned that the volume of Morgan's voice had risen, Donahue leaned in closer and said very quietly, "Well, I would assume that Langley could persuade the political people to listen...."

Morgan's outburst of laughter struck the Colonel as extremely rude, as it was, and the Saigon Station Chief immediately apologized. "I'm sorry, George, forgive me. I've been hoeing a tough row lately and the strain is showing. I can see why you'd think so, but all power in D.C. emanates from the ballot box and the electorate must be appeased, like a child in church, told whatever is necessary to keep it from shrieking during the sermon and, as you know, that child has been getting worked up lately over this Asian-war thing."

"I don't think LBJ loses much sleep over a bunch of hippies and spoiled college kids," Donahue offered.

"Maybe so, but the draft is starting to cut deeper into the student body, sons of the middle class, and Eugene McCarthy's gaining traction with the Primaries coming up, so some major set-back here could make it a horse-race. Anyway, truth is LBJ and Congress don't want any advice from Langley. What they want is political support, which means Saigon Station had better toe the line that MACV's right, the VC are melting away, victory is nigh, at least through November when the elections are over and the child can shriek his head off out in the church parking lot."

The waiter came, then left, so Morgan continued. "This morning, MACV returned our latest assessment for what they called 'revision'. I stormed over there and demanded to know what was wrong with it. They said it was 'inadmissible'! 'Like evidence in a court-case?' I asked. They told me that certain journalists could draw conclusions from it that might be 'gloomy'. *Gloomy!* God forbid the news that half a million Commies are planning to attack every base and city in the Republic should cause gloom! Now *that*, George, is what an intelligence failure looks like, up close and personal!"

The steaks came with numerous side dishes that were carefully arrayed on the small table. As the two men began cutting into dinner, Morgan apologized again, this time for being such lousy company, and he suggested they talk about something else, anything else. Donahue took the opening and ran with it. Would Morgan support him in seeking a position with The Company, perhaps putting him in touch with some helpful contacts at The Farm?

Morgan was amused by the coded language but asked straight-out, "You want to work for my outfit after everything I just said?"

"I retire next year and this line of work is all I've been doing for a long time," he said.

"Well if you take my advice, you'll go into real estate or insurance. But if you're serious about it, let me see what I can do," Morgan said. "We can talk again after the Spring Offensive either blows over or blows up. Meantime, you may want to do what we're doing: I've ordered every field operative in the country to gather all their sensitive material and shelter on a large military base or in a city. I've got a lot of our guys in Saigon hotels and I'll keep them here until things sort themselves out militarily."

Donahue said, "But if there is an attack after Tet, the Caravelle could be a target."

"What I'm betting on is the dozens of big-time journalists who stay here. They'll be as well defended as anyone in Vietnam...otherwise, they could develop a gloomy picture of how the war is going."

"We're not like you," Donahue said. "We can't afford to put our guys up in fancy hotels."

"We can't either. Sixty grand went missing from our discretionary funds last month and nobody will admit knowing a thing about it. Doesn't turn up," Morgan said gloomily, "I may be coming to you for a job."

It was the grandest pool-party MACV had ever thrown: Stephen Aaronson -- resplendent in red trunks with yellow palm-trees print-ed on them and, like many others, sporting an oak-brown tan that stopped above his elbows at the edge of cod-white skin -- sat on the pool's deck, sipping gin and tonic from a paper cup. Actors played the roles of an old man with a goat's head and a baby monkey in diapers. Vietnamese men and women mingled with Americans, shar-ing food and drink, pop music that ranged all the way from Frank Sinatra to Dean Martin and a stock of penny firecrackers, all free to the guests. Young officers took turns cannon-balling off the one-meter board, splashing lukewarm water over by-standers as best they could.

When Aaronson finished his drink, he looked around for some-one to talk with, perhaps someone he knew, and it saddened him to realize that he didn't know anyone in Vietnam outside the III Corps office. He hated that office and everyone in it, but he almost never left it except to run paperwork over to SIC Central. He knew he had to change this situation before it drove him insane, and he resolved to start by getting the damned enlisted men out of the map room, three of them now with Hood's cot wedged between Mulcahey's and the violent monster Rosenzweig's. They all sat at dinner even now, plotting against him -- even Shimazu, who had declined to come with him tonight.

He dropped his cup in a trash barrel and strolled to the table where fireworks of various kinds were laid-out for the pleasure of guests. He chose a short string of lady fingers, picked up a match-book and carried them over to the spacious lawn where young men were lighting fuses and tossing the harmless explosives out over the grass. If he lit the string, he knew they'd be gone in seconds, so he twisted them off one-by-one, making a game of seeing how high he could throw them into the night-sky. The sharp report, blinding flash and bits of paper floating down afforded him pleasure, the first he'd felt in months. Half-way through the string, one of the tiny red cylinders exploded between his thumb and index finger, burning him painfully. He licked and blew on his fingers, hoping no one had noticed his mishap. He walked as casually as he could to the pool-side and inspected the damage under the light of a Japanese lantern. His thumb was OK, but his first finger was scorched and throbbing with pain. Something cracked sharply as he examined his damaged hand. He raised his head and looked around but couldn't see any source for the odd sound, which had been caused by a tiny bit of lead breaking the sound barrier a few inches from his right ear. Another puff of sound drew his attention overhead to the paper lantern that had just burst open, spewing scraps of scarlet paper that drifted down on him. Then came the angry-bee buzz of a ricochet, which solved the mystery of these odd occurrences for Lieutenant Aaronson, and he threw himself headlong into the pool.

Dinner in the roof enclosure of III Corps was in high spirits. Aaronson's absence removed the usual undercurrent of tension between him and the enlisted men, especially Rosie. And the city resounded with fireworks bursting on the ground and in the air all around, a strange way to celebrate the suspension of war. Comparisons with the Fourth of July led to shared reminiscences of holidays at home: Christmas and Hanukkah, Easter and Thanksgiving as practiced in Nashville and Chicago and Clemson and among the Japanese-American fami-lies imprisoned at Manzanar Camp during World War II.

Without warning, the fluorescent lights went out, which alerted no one but Hideo Shimazu to danger, since power failures were common-place. But Shimazu had seen a man open the screen door and reach for the light switch. So as the three young men talked about where to find candles and flashlights, Shimazu's hand found his steak knife and he silently rose to his feet, circling the right side of the table toward the shadowy figure faintly outlined against the soft glow of the Asian city. His plan was to kill the intruder and explain later if it turned out to be Aaronson playing a prank, returning drunk from the MACV party. As he closed in, holding the knife underhand for a thrust into the man's throat, a cigarette lighter flickered in the face of Papa-san, the ancient, pot-smoking gate guard who had never before been seen in the American quarters of the villa. Shimazu continued forward, prepared to kill to defend his unit, when the old man turned away, went back through the doorway and with the small flame of his lighter, beckoned him to follow. This spectacle had silenced the men still seated at the table until Mad-dog asked, "What the hell WAS that?"

Shimazu's low baritone came from the direction of the doorway, not from the end of the table where they all assumed he still sat: "Be silent. Come here."

As quietly as they could, bumping into chairs and each other in the dark, they stumbled forward, reaching out hands like blind men. As they stepped out onto the open roof where there was more ambient light, their eyes adjusted enough to make out two dark figures crouched down behind the three-foot-high wall that bordered the roof. They crept forward, bending low, forming a line along the wall.

The city below was alive with people enjoying the Tet holiday, these few days of peace in a place that had suffered war off-and-on for thirty years. An undertone of smaller fireworks far and near was punctuated by bursts of sky-rockets and the explosions of larger devices. The dimly-lit streets at the end of their alleyway were teeming with happy people shouting and laughing, but in the ten minutes that they hunched against the wall, a subtler drama unfolded itself. They each came to recognize that the dark figure to Shimazu's left was the old man who served as a gate-guard in the parking area, his wrinkled face under the bill of his fatigue cap lit by an occasional rocket flash, using the barrel of his carbine to prop himself up against the low wall.

As still as a pointer-dog, his attention never strayed from the alley below where, after some minutes, they began to see in the flickering lights what he was seeing: Patches of movement outside the compound gate, two or perhaps three figures milling around, not speaking loud enough to be heard. More minutes of stillness went by before Papa-san saw what he had been expecting. He snapped the safety off, rested his carbine across the wall and fired twice. As he ducked back down, a grenade exploded like a thunder clap amidst the jeeps and bicycles of the parking area. Then the old man raised up and fired four more aimed rounds into the alleyway before lowering his weapon and crawling along the wall to a new firing position fifteen feet to his right. From there, he peeked over the edge, assessing the field. Apparently satisfied, he snapped the safety of his carbine and continued to steal glances over the top.

Shimazu spoke in a low, calm voice to Mulcahey: "Bring a chair, a soda and plate of food out here for Papa-san and don't turn on any lights." To Hood and Rosenzweig, he said, "I'm going for M-16s for you. Set up on the corners there and there, keep low and show the old man anything you think is suspicious but don't fire at anything until he does. Mulcahey will relieve you at 0600 then we'll set up a rotation."

Papa-san, who spoke not a word of English, received a hand on his shoulder and a bow of thanks from the major. The old man returned a wide, nearly toothless smile as he settled himself into a squatting position on the surface of the folding chair Mad-dog set up for him, a perfect height to maintain his vigilance on the alleyway. Before Shimazu returned with the weapons and a dozen loaded clips, flashes of light followed seconds later by thunderous booms came from the direction of Tan Son Nhut and they knew for sure that the wide-spread attack they had expected after the Tet truce had arrived, for real and well ahead of schedule. During that long night, sneaking peeks over the wall, the young men of III Corps got their second taste of what it might be like to be a soldier, recalling Basic Training. Rosie's thoughts were all with Co Sang, his defenseless civilian lover, visiting her mother eighty miles north of Saigon, and Hood's thoughts, oddly, wandered to Monroe and Bian and where they might be tonight.

When Mad-dog came up at dawn, bearing some sort of Swedish rifle no one had ever seen before, they shared the remnants of their dinner with Papa-san and stared in awe at the still, black-clad form of the man he had killed. Small-arms fire could be heard on every side, with large explosions from the direction of the air base. Each of the Americans caught a four-hour shift while the major worked the overloaded phone system to reach his field units and SIC Central.

Papa-san remained on the roof throughout the day, napping inside the screened enclosure from time to time, using his rubber sandals as a pillow. He was a newly-revised entity for them all. This grandfather or, more likely great grandfather, had been a familiar figure to them, pulling the steel gates open for their jeeps when they left or arrived, shuffling stiffly in sandals made of discarded motorbike tires, his carbine slung over his frail shoulder, his face a map of many decades spent outdoors under a tropical sun. They had admonished him, using gestures and shouted English (better understood by those who speak none than softly spoken English) for converting a pesticide can into a water pipe, but they never had gone so far as to buy him a replacement. When Viet occasionally translated a shopping list into English for him, they brought him those few simple items from the PX -- bars of soap, lighter fluid, a fatigue cap -- and accepted a wad of piastres from his brown, weathered hand in return, never counting it. But they had been united in the certainty that, as a guardian of their lives and property, he was useless. In his 80's or 90's -- who knew? -- maybe 130 pounds, with a dinky carbine on an improvised strap, what good would he be in a fight?

But now he stood revealed before them as the professional combat soldier he was. He had killed before. He had seen a man flip a grenade over a wall before. And he had immediately understood the vulnerability of the brightly lit roof enclosure full of Americans sitting at dinner when shadows advanced toward him down the alleyway.

The experience, courage and decisiveness of this veteran had saved their lives.

Everything had changed on those portions of Saigon's streets they could see from the roof. Trucks sped past with ARVN troops hanging out the sides, American MPs and Vietnamese white mice raced this way and that through streets that were almost completely deserted otherwise. Civilians were hunkered down inside, sheltering in place.

Soon after Mulcahey's four-hour shift on the roof, Hood and Papa-san had a ring-side seat for an air strike. Huey helicopters were as common as pigeons in the skies over III Corps, but these two hovered in place, so low the pounding of their rotors shook the whole villa then, in response to some request from ground spotters, they fired two rockets each from almost directly overhead. The detonations were heard a mile or two away, out of sight, but the distinctive whoosh of the launch was a sound Hood would never forget, and anything like it caused his abdomen to coil like a rattle-snake for decades after. This awesome demonstration of firepower was followed, as soon as the Hueys sped off, by the familiar clank of their steel gate. Hood and Papa-san raced to the wall and cautiously peeked over, weapons ready, but it was only Mad-dog Mulcahey closing the gates behind the blue jeep, idling behind him in the alley.

"Where in the hell do you think you're going?!" Hood yelled down.

Mad-dog waved a paper like a flag as he turned back toward the jeep and jumped in.

Hood bellowed curses and threats in his thunderous baritone while Papa-san echoed in a torrent of Vietnamese, but Mad-dog paid them no-nevermind and gunned the jeep down the alley, giving wide berth to the dead man, and spun tires into the street.

Shimazu raced up the stairs, M-16 in hand, to discover what the excitement was about.

"It's Mad-dog, sir," Hood said. "He's taken a jeep and gone shopping."

Shimazu's face conveyed the depth of his confusion. "Who ordered him...told him he could...gone shopping *for food*?"

"Yessir."

"Is he *crazy*?!"

Hood wasn't sure how to answer that question with regard to Mad-dog Mulcahey. "Well, sir," he drawled, "If you mean does he have the judgment of a two-year-old and the impulse-control of a squirrel, then by that definition, yessir, he is crazy." Hood had never seen Shimazu, the iron major, so close to losing control of himself. For some moments, he was silent, clenching and unclenching his free hand, then he said, "Tell him I wish to see him...if he ever comes back."

It was a long, nerve-wracking wait for all of them. Mad-dog pulled out before 11:00 and didn't return until almost 7:00, much the worse for wear. He came wobbling up the alley, past the corpse, on a bi-cycle, twenty pounds of shrimp on melting ice, rice and vegetables swinging from the handlebars, both knees torn and bloody, lacera-tions across his face and scraped, bleeding hands. Papa-san opened one side of the gate for him and helped haul his bags up the stairs.

"*God Damn!*" he sang in the stairwell, "It was a *son-of-a-bitch* out there today!"

He staggered to the roof enclosure with Papa-san's help and be-gan the familiar routine of storing the groceries.

Rosie, standing sentry, did not seem at all happy to see him. "Are you fucking nuts, or what, Mulcahey?" he snarled. "Or just born too damned stupid to live?"

Mulcahey's response sounded disturbingly sane: "Hey...some-body had to do the shopping or there'd be nothing to eat. Hood had sentry duty and you were asleep."

Hood pulled open the screen door and announced, "Major wants to see you."

"I didn't ask anybody else to go, did I?" Mad-dog continued in an aggrieved tone, "because it's kind of risky out there right now and there was no sense in...."

"Major wants to see you *now!*" Hood barked.

"Who me?"

"Who else, Mulcahey?"

"Well..." Mad-dog pushed past Hood in the narrow doorway, "I know he's gonna be pissed about the jeep, but that wasn't my fault."

During the long hours of waiting and worry, Shimazu had gained control of his temper and even spent time trying to see things from the young man's point-of-view. He hadn't disobeyed orders, Shimazu told himself, nor had he deserted in the face of the enemy -- far from it. He'd shown courage. He'd taken initiative. He had completed his mission and gotten back safe with the groceries. So why was it, Shimazu quizzed himself, that he felt an overwhelming urge to thrash the son-of-a-bitch with a belt?

"The shopping list and money were on my desk, in the usual place," Mad-dog explained, occasionally dabbing bloody cuts on his face with the torn sleeves of his shirt. "And the guys need to eat, sir, especially doing sentry-duty all night."

"So you're sure it was the MPs at Tan Son Nhut?" Shimazu asked as calmly as he could.

"Oh yessir. There was a pair of tanks sitting across the gate, so I stopped a long ways away and got out of the jeep. I shouted to them, 'You know me! I'm an American! I shop here every damned day!' One of the tanks swiveled his cannon at me, sir! Then for no reason at all, they started shooting hell out of the jeep with me standing there, right beside it, unarmed, fifty, sixty yards away, not even moving! They didn't aim for me, I think, just the jeep, but I got cut by all the flying glass, so I high-tailed it out of there."

"So then you stole a bicycle?" Shimazu asked.

"Oh, nosir. I bought it fair-and-square, bargaining like Belmont taught us. I got the owner down to seventy bucks, which was more than I had of my own money, so I owe petty cash thirty dollars."

"So then you went to the market on the bike, did you?"

"It was a bitch, sir, pardon my French. Every stall in the whole place was closed, which is why it took so long to get back. I had to knock on doors, security gates, windows, go house to house down there to find everything on the list. Everybody is really nervous right now because of the fighting going on, so only a few of them would open up and the prices were outrageous. I had to do a lot of bargaining. I understand their problem, sir. ARVN is shooting up their whole neighborhood so bad, I had to crawl between streets, dragging my bike, tore my pants and they were brand-new."

Able to stand no more for now -- and still uncertain whether this was some bizarre form of theater or (what was it Hood said about a two-year-old and a squirrel?) -- Shimazu said, "OK, Mr. Mulcahey. Why don't you go get cleaned up and I'll see what I can do about cooking."

"Yessir."

"And Mulcahey, don't leave the villa again without my permission."

"Am I under house arrest, sir, like Rosie? I really am sorry about the jeep, sir."

"You displayed a lack of sound judgment," Shimazu euphemized, "that almost got you killed. Are you aware of that or not?"

"Yessir, I am." The color suddenly drained from the young man's face. He sagged in the folding chair, looking exhausted and depressed. "And the shrimp aren't even very good."

"I must ask you, Corporal, why you did it? What were you thinking when you drove out into a combat situation to shop for food?"

"I don't know, sir." Mad-dog said, looking to be on the point of tears. "Everybody tells me I'm fickle."

"Fickle?" Shimazu repeated, trying to absorb the meaning of the word.

"Yessir, that's what Rosie calls me."

Mad-dog rose slowly from the chair like an old man and squeezed out the door through the narrow space. He turned back to Major Shimazu and said, "I guess I've been this way since they shot President Kennedy." He turned away and muttered, "Jack Kennedy was my president."

28

5 - 18 February 1968

THE YEAR OF THE MONKEY

Early on the fifth day after Tet, an ARVN truck backed into the alley and unceremoniously tossed in the foul-smelling victim of Papa-san's marksmanship. Everyone in the III Corps office suite was exhausted from nightly guard-duty and working so furiously they failed to notice it. Distant sounds of small arms and machinegun fire caused them to pause occasionally, raising their heads briefly before returning to work, masking it behind the clatter of manual typewriters. Hood sat with Major Shimazu, aiding with the preparation of a report for MACV, while Rosenzweig and Mulcahey hammered away on materials for the February budget meetings and the backlog of IRs pouring in from the Translation Pool. Lieutenant Aaronson had been escorted home by MPs the previous afternoon from a MACV pool-party that ended with sniper fire and the theft of his jeep. He had snarled at feeble attempts the enlisted men made to welcome him back, had skipped breakfast this morning and gone straight to work in his office with the door shut. The fighting had ended their sumptuous dinner routine. The hard-won supplies Mad-dog fought so valiantly to secure had been donated to Mr. Viet's translators and typists, who had to navigate dangerous streets between home and work, and the young women who did the typing were now supplying restaurant food to the Americans in exchange for payment in scrip. Just scraping through day-to-day was bringing home to them a realization of how luxurious, secure and taken-for-granted their lives had been under Shimazu's benevolent rule before Tet changed everything.

Before noon, Hood gathered the finished report into Shimazu's leather valise and carried it, following his commanding officer to the last remaining jeep. Hood gave wide berth to the patch of blood-stained earth as he chauffeured the major toward MACV. Lieutenant Aaronson stood on the roof-deck watching them leave, then he returned to his office, gathered his own papers together in a briefcase and strode rapidly into the space between Rosie's and Mulcahey's desks.

"Atten'HUT!" he shouted, "*On Your Feet, gentlemen!*"

Their incredulous looks gave him great pleasure, as did the way they gradually arose, leaning on the office furniture in postures no one would have mistaken for "Attention".

"This farce is coming to an end here-and-now, gentlemen!" he barked. "As second-in-command and in the absence of the commanding officer, I am placing you both under arrest! You are to consider yourselves my prisoners."

They paid no particular interest to Aaronson's ranting until he lifted his .45 out of its shoulder holster and chambered a round. Then they looked at each other in alarm and stood straighter, arms at their sides.

"Corporal Mulcahey, you are hereby charged with the theft of an Ak 5 assault rifle of Swedish manufacture. There is no such weapon registered with our company or authorized for use and it has *prima facie* been stolen from its rightful...."

"I found it in the map room!"

"You can explain that to the Adjutant General at your court-martial, corporal!" Aaronson turned on his nemesis, narrowed his eyes, dropped his voice and hissed, "And you, private, have put the security of this whole operation in jeopardy by cohabitating with a Vietnamese..." a slur crossed his mind, but he recalled the violent outcome of a previous remark and chose instead, "...woman of unknown loyalties, perhaps a Communist agent. I have documented all these charges in detail," he waved the briefcase at them with one hand, the semi-automatic with the other, "and God as my witness, you'll spend tonight in the Long Binh jail, awaiting trial!" He waved the .45 at the door in a herding gesture. "The AG is expecting us, so get moving!"

"I'm waiting for the major to get back," Rosenzweig said firmly.

"I pray that you will resist arrest, private, because then I will gut-shoot you and watch you bleed out right here on this floor and, believe me," Aaronson sneered, "nothing would give me greater pleasure." He snapped the safety off and pulled the hammer back into firing position. The madness in his eyes did not tempt Rosenzweig to gamble he wouldn't do it.

"Were gonna have to walk," Mulcahey announced flippantly. "Hood took the major in the last jeep we had."

"I'm ahead of you there too." Aaronson tossed a ring of keys onto Mad-dog's desk. "Corporal Hood is being charged with the theft of that big, fancy car, obviously procured with government funds embezzled by the Cu Chi Station Chief. I'm turning all this over to the AG in Long Binh right now, today...the car, the stolen rifle and you two...and Major Shimazu will be faced with a *fait accompli* when he returns and have no choice but to support these charges."

Aaronson marched them downstairs at gun-point, seizing the Swedish rifle on his way past the map room. He sat in the rear seat of the Citroën, keeping the .45 pointed their way and prepared to direct them to the AG's Office at Long Binh, 25 miles northeast of Saigon. His suspicion that Mulcahey was stalling was false. Mad-dog had never been inside this car and had no idea how to start it or how to shift. He found a key-hole that worked and played around with the rod protruding from the dash, got it started, ground the transmission loudly until the car leapt forward, knocking over a half dozen bicycles, while Aaronson issued a series of threats from behind him.

But once he shuffled the car around in the narrow confines of the courtyard and slipped through the gates held by Papa-san, he quickly got the hang of it. He made his way down the alley and to the main road, where his heart rejoiced at the massive horsepower of this machine, a wild stallion compared to the donkey-ride of the M151 jeep. His adrenaline surged as he got the feel of the gears and the quick, responsive accelerator and was not only back in his element -- war-time Saigon traffic perfectly wired to his nervous system -- he felt he was flying above it. Even Rosie, a veteran of many trips with Mad-dog, clutched the door handle and dashboard in fear for his life.

The great disadvantage for the lieutenant was that his distaste for the enlisted men meant he had never before been a passenger in a Mad-dog-driven vehicle so had not developed that faith in the immortality of Mulcahey that others, over time, had come to concede. Warnings, threats and shrieks emanated from the rear seat whenever Aaronson wasn't collapsed into one corner or the other by forces centrifugal and centripetal following each other in rapid succession, but they went unheeded by the driver until -- despite his perfect four-month record of never actually colliding with anything -- Mad-dog misjudged the width of the big car and sideswiped a Red Cross ambulance speeding in the opposite direction. Not the sort of cad who would hit-and-run, he did the morally right thing and smashed the brake-pedal into the floor, producing a smoke-cloud from all four locked wheels. The body of Lieutenant Aaronson, already airborne, made a violent impact with the seat-back, face-first, stunning him like a fish that had been oar-smacked. Without intending to, he squeezed-off a round that entered the top of his right foot an inch below the ankle, exiting through the sole of his shoe at mid-arch.

The .45 was designed to stop drug-crazed Filipino guerilla fighters in their tracks, and so its slug is immediately consequential to anyone on the receiving end of one. Mad-dog barely had time to utter "Did someone shoot at us?" before Aaronson released a primal scream that sent chills up the spines of both the men in the car as well as dozens of drivers, cyclists, dogs and pedestrians within a respectable radius.

Fortunately for Aaronson, the Red Cross ambulance team was right there at the scene and experienced at dealing with traumatic injury, even close-range gunshot wounds. They stopped the bleeding, wrapped the wound, and sedated the patient in minutes, loading him alongside others they were transporting to the base hospital at Tan Son Nhut.

As soon as the ambulance was gone, Mad-dog pulled the car off the side of the roadway and they exploded into a childlike laughing jag, reignited by "Think we should take him flowers?" and "They'll think he did it on purpose to get out of the war!"

When they calmed down, Mad-dog said, "Hood's not going to like I bashed-in his door."

"Hey, he was about to lose the whole car, plus whatever's in those boxes in the trunk," Rosie pointed out, "and face charges too. He's not going to mind some body-damage. Now let's get back to the office and burn every last scrap of the lieutenant's reports on us before the major gets back from MACV."

When Shimazu and Hood returned, they found Papa-san stirring a fire in the burn-barrel they used to destroy classified documents and the men still hard at work at their typewriters. "While you were at MACV," Mulcahey reported, "there was an accident: Lieutenant Aaronson..." his cheeks puffed out and he fought back tears -- or some other strong emotion. He looked at Rosenzweig, who had his face buried in both hands. "Lieutenant Aaronson..." Mulcahey finally managed to get out between surges of strong emotion, "he shot himself in the foot!"

"Really?" Shimazu asked, probing to see if it was a metaphor. "How bad is he hurt?"

"The medics said he'd be OK. They took him to the hospital at the air base."

Two weeks later, they were told by SIC Central to pack-up the lieutenant's belongings for shipment back to The States and they felt sorry -- a little bit sorry -- that no one, not even the major, had found the time to visit him while he was in the hospital.

267

On February 20, a diminutive captain with wire-rimmed glasses, Bill Kearney, was assigned as Shimazu's second-in-command. He proved to be as affable as his predecessor was irascible and also a genius at procurement. Happily, his arrival coincided with Major Shimazu's Mexican and Middle Eastern cuisine phases. Now that fighting in Saigon was limited to Cholon and the Phu Tho racetrack, Dinners were renewed, so the Captain disappeared for hours on special assignment, returning with taco shells, avocadoes and blue-corn flour or lamb, couscous and grape leaves. There descended an unprecedented harmony over III Corps, the unit cohesion Shimazu had always sought, and the young men quartered in the map room were favored almost every night with a visit from their CO, bearing a pitcher of milk and a tray of baklava or sopapillas with honey. They heard on Armed Forced Radio about heavy fighting in Hue and elsewhere, but for the men who enjoyed enchiladas, guacamole with chips, and pitchers of sangria to wash it down, life was good. Easy camaraderie was the order of the day and the work of the office ran smoothly along -- until the third Sunday in February, when Mad-dog got horny.

Braxton Hood lay propped-up on a plastic chaise lounge beside the Officer's Pool at Tan Son Nhut, unable to concentrate on *The Confessions of Nat Turner* for three reasons: First, he'd been watching his quiet, even-tempered friend Rosie slip into a deep depression since Tet -- distracted and silent at Dinners, taking long naps, moping around the office, declining to come out to the pool today, for instance. Hood was considering a confrontation over it, anything to pull him out of the doldrums. Second, whoever was in charge of the P.A. system had played "Hey Jude" three consecutive times already and was starting it again. And third, Mad-dog was a fidgety mess, even more than usual. Flies were biting him, his soda was flat, there were no open lanes to swim in. Finally, Hood put down his book and snapped, "What in hell you want me to do about it?"

"About what?"

"About the two dozen thorns under your saddle?"

"You could come with me to shanty-town."

"I don't do shanty-town. It's not my thing," Hood said. "And if you say 'faggot,' I'm gonna punch you in the face and throw you in the pool."

Hood hated giving up his quiet afternoon of relaxation, but when the idiot gave "Hey Jude" another spin, he picked up his towel and started toward the showers, muttering to himself.

Beside the road at shanty-town, Hood relieved Mulcahey of his wallet, watch, sunglasses and belt. "Your belt holds up your pants, so you won't be needing it," Hood explained, "and they stole it from you last time."

When the gaggle of barking children dragged him into the warren of shacks, Mad-dog was seen gripping his chinos with one hand and holding $10 in scrip high over his head with the other. "If I'm not back in twenty minutes, come find me," he shouted over his shoulder.

"You're on your own, pal!" Hood answered, not meaning it.

Hood worked the jeep through the traffic to cross the busy street, finding a shady spot on the other side away from the army of children, accomplished salesmen all, with more needs than anyone could meet. He dallied with his book but kept a watch through the moving curtain of the roadway in case Mad-dog needed to be rescued. The swirling street was the same dirt-blown, exhaust-choked convection oven it always was, but Hood had grown used to it and now, in the midst of the dry-season, the heat wasn't as soul-permeating as during monsoon time. He decided that when he got back to III Corps, he would declare by the authority vested in him by his superior physical size and strength that Rosie was going out bar-hopping with him along Tu Do Street, end of discussion. *No More Moping*! he would command. And it may have been merely because of this confluence of thoughts -- of Rosie and Tu Do Street and the ever-horny Mad-dog -- that when a jitney pulled out of the traffic-line twenty feet to his right, he thought he saw someone he knew among the passengers alighting from it. He had seen her only once, briefly, accepting Rosie's letter from Mad-dog and -- sure all Vietnamese look alike to Americans -- but this girl was unusually tall and strikingly beautiful, and Rosie had said he met her at shanty-town.

He leapt from the jeep and hollered, "Lady! Hey, ma'am! Miss!" But she gathered up her shopping bundles, paid the driver, and began crossing the busy street. Hood started toward her but realized he couldn't abandon the jeep without chaining it up and she was moving away fast. So he jumped back in and drove straight across her path. She was startled by this sudden obstacle in her way, but she nimbly danced around the rear bumper while the stranger shouted at her, "Ma'am! Wait a second! Lady! Come back!"

She picked her way through the maze of fast-moving vehicles, thinking to herself in her own language, escaping the annoying man who was yelling at her, who nearly ran her down, the fourth or fifth American today who had said something to her, trying to pick her up. This kind of unwanted attention was a condition of her daily life and surfing through it was something she had gotten used....then she heard "Zach Rosenzweig" and she stopped at the roadside and turned back, switching her mind to English. The large, powerfully-built stranger was standing beside his jeep while taxi and motorbike horns beeped at him like barking dogs. She had never seen him before, this man. She was sure of it. But he was shouting over the orchestra of annoyed drivers, "You're that girl, right? Aren't you that friend of Rosie's?"

Sang stepped further back, out of the traffic, and nodded her head as Americans do, and her little straw hat with the bright blue ribbon bobbed up and down.

29

6 - 23 March 1968

REMIX

The young man wedged into the folding chair was dressed neck to sandals in a spotless white robe. He was clean-shaven above and below his white head-band. He smelled of perfume and spoke sleepily, with a studied tranquility. "They risked their lives to save mine," he told Major Shimazu. "I was too drunk to walk, so they hauled me like a duffle bag out the back door. Minutes later, the VC tossed a satchel charge through my bedroom window that blew the building apart. That would have been me in there, wasn't for my friends. I owe them my life."

"I understand," Shimazu said, "but that is not an excuse for the fact that not one IR has been received from Tay Ninh for a whole month...since Tet!"

"I have been working incredibly hard, sir," this transformed rendition of Louie Leffanta said, "learning the ways of Cao Dai. God has founded our new religion to combine the teachings of Taoism, Confucianism, Buddhism, Islam and Christianity. Do you think that's something you can wrap up in a month?" The beaming smile that lit Leffanta's face was unlike anything the angry racist who'd been assigned to Tay Ninh could have achieved. Shimazu had seen war bring about all kinds of profound changes in men, but never anything like this, and he found it both disturbing and fascinating.

"There are 36 levels of Heaven and 72 planets with intelligent life aligned between Heaven and Hell," Leffanta went on earnestly, "Earth is number 68...."

"Mr. Leffanta," Shimazu interrupted, "Cao Dai may be wonderful, as you say...."

"They saved my life, sir."

"Yes, I know...."

"The translator, Mr. Nhat, is my teacher and my friend. I wouldn't even be alive weren't for him, much less a disciple of Cao Dai. There are three million of us in the Republic, did you know that?" Laughter like a series of hiccups erupted, a sound no American in Vietnam had ever heard from Bitter Louie Leffanta.

"Fine, but I need you to meet with Mr. Nhat, your counterpart, CP-D and find a way to...."

"I can't call him CP-D, sir," Leffanta cut in. "He is The Honorable Nguyen Khan, a bishop in Cao Dai, very high up at the Holy See."

That decided it for Major Shimazu: He attended the budget meeting for Field Station D, Tay Ninh, formerly the train-wreck known as Cu Chi Field Station -- without including Leffanta or Nhat or The Honorable Nguyen Khan -- and announced to his counterpart, Major Han, that there was no longer a need for an operation in Tay Ninh and therefore no need to discuss a budget for it. Colonel Donahue was not going to like it, but Shimazu's DEROS was April 3, one month away, so SIC Central could take the matter up with his successor. He ordered Leffanta to pack up his gear and the office files and report for duty back in Saigon in two days time.

"I don't have any gear to pack, sir," Leffanta responded cheerfully. "I donated all my belongings to Cao Dai, and the VC burned-down the office the night of Tet. So if you'll assign me a little corner for my meditation and study materials, I could stay here tonight."

Thus, exactly one month after Aaronson shot himself in the foot, the halcyon days of III Corps as a cohesive, harmonious unit, came to an abrupt end.

"Mr. Hood?" Shimazu called from his office.

"Gone to lunch, sir" Mulcahey called back.

"Mr. Rosenzweig?"

"Gone to lunch with Hood, sir."

"Where is everybody?" a perturbed Major Shimazu whispered to himself.

Braxton Hood had arranged the joyful reunion of Rosie and Sang at Dong An, the eatery a block from III Corps, by parking her there with Mad-dog then coaxing Rosie into leaving the office to help him "move some furniture". They fell into each other's arms at once, crying openly and shouting explanations in front of a dozen startled customers: "Our apartment was rented to strangers! Our furniture all gone, sold off, missing! What was I to think, Zachary?" and "I was under arrest! Thrown into jail by my enemies and I lost my income! How could I afford the rent?" Hood was deeply moved by their love for each other and it endeared the couple to him. He promised himself he would help them in any way he could.

Two days later he invited them to lunch, his treat, at The Caravelle's rooftop restaurant. With the first round of drinks, he drew from his briefcase a two-year lease, fully paid in advance, on an apartment a few blocks from III Corps. "Consider it a loan," he told them, "until you can get on your feet." Rosie was broke even before his demotion, Hood knew, but this $3600 hardly put a dent in the piles of money Monroe had left him and he didn't know how to get rid of the rest.

From where Braxton Hood was sitting, he could see down the whole length of the bar. He always faced the entrance wherever he went because too many art and antique dealers and other wealthy residents of the city, not to mention some CIA-types from Saigon Station, had a grudge against him and he didn't want them to see him first. The briefcase he carried had a loaded .45 in it too, in case it came to that, along with the keys to his Citroën, since the day Aaronson and Mulcahey had shown him why he should never leave them in his desk drawer. Now he snatched up a menu and raised it to his eyes because he recognized the man heading toward a bar stool as Major Cardenas, in civilian coat and tie. Hood preferred knowing more than those around him even before his training at Greyhawk, so he made no mention of Cardenas' arrival to the pair of distracted lovers across from him. Whether Cardenas had recognized him or not was uncertain, along with whether he was meeting someone or not, on assignment or off-duty, or indeed, whether he was calling himself "Cardenas" today. So Hood kept a peripheral tab without seeming to notice. As they ordered lunch and talked about the new apartment, he stole glances around the crowded restaurant but identified no one else. Cardenas hardly touched his beer while he read the menu and when this went on for ten minutes, Hood's antennae began to twitch. He attempted conversation with Rosie and Sang, but he found himself completely distracted by the unfolding drama behind them.

He was prepared for about anything except what he saw: Singleton in a beige, tailor-made suit was led by the maître d' to a table far across the room where two Vietnamese gentlemen sat talking. As they rose to greet him, one of them turned and Hood recognized him as Viet, III Corp's Chief Translator. Cardenas took the occasion of Singleton's arrival as an opportune moment to slip a small camera from his coat pocket to his lap, shield it under his menu and click away in Singleton's direction.

The superficial deductions were not complicated: Cardenas already had photos of Viet and Singleton in his files, so the target here was the third man, the animated one in the brightly colored tourist shirt who must not speak English, otherwise Viet wouldn't be needed to translate. And he must be somebody important to draw Cardenas' direct involvement.

Nothing would have made Braxton Hood happier, personally, than to stride over there, reach out his hand and say, "Where in hell have you been, Singleton? We've asked around all four Corps and nobody's seen you or Levesque! We thought you'd got stuck in

Replo-Depot forever!" But the purpose of training is to overcome instinct, so he tried to keep a poker-face.

"Hello, Earth to Hood, over," Rosie was saying. "How's your pork?"

"Oh, fine...."

"Then why aren't you eating it?"

"Sorry...just daydreaming I guess," Hood said and he looked down to avoid eye-contact as the three men stood and headed toward the door. The man in the colorful shirt could be heard saying something in Vietnamese and then, in perfect English, "I'll be right down...need to hit the head." As this man pushed his way into the men's room behind the maître d' stand, Hood recalculated his deductions: If the man in the Hawaiian shirt was bilingual, what was Viet doing there? Was Cardenas gathering evidence against him? Or against Singleton! Singleton was meeting with a double-agent? Singleton WAS a double-agent? Who was Cardenas setting up?

If his head hadn't been spinning, Hood would have seen her at once, the tall, elegant woman in the beautiful ao dai who emerged from a small table behind a column. Bian handed the waiter some money, waved off the change and glided past the maître d'. Hood was sure of it! He had a good mind for numbers and for faces -- hadn't he spotted Sang on a crowded street weeks after their only meeting? Yes, he was positive this was Bian, Monroe's partner-in-crime and none other. But was she here by coincidence or on some mission having to do with Singleton? Was it merely that this room was haunted by ghosts from Hood's past?

"If you're not going to eat your lunch, can I have it?" Rosie asked.

"Sure. Help yourself..." Hood mumbled, the look of a startled deer frozen on his face. "I'll just have another drink."

"How much money?"

"He told me 'gobs and gobs' in those boxes he keeps in the trunk of his car."

"Left behind by Monroe?"

"That's right, but you have to keep it dead quiet, Mad-dog, because there's no way to prove Braxton didn't steal it himself. You mention one word, he could wind-up in the stockade."

Rosenzweig and Mulcahey stood at the edge of the second-story roof-deck outside the office window, holding coffee cups and talking in hushed voices. The clatter of Leffanta's typewriter assured them that he wasn't eavesdropping.

"Lunch was really weird, I'll tell you. Out of nowhere, he hands us this lease, paid-up for two whole years! Then he gives Sang a stack of MPC...500, 600 bucks...and tells her to go find some wicker furniture, cookware, whatever she needs, and when we try to thank him, he turns all sullen and strange on us and we can't get a word out of him, like he was in a trance. He didn't touch his food...not like him, man. Maybe he's sick."

"Major's had him in there over an hour," Mad-dog said. "Wonder what that's about."

When the door of Shimazu's office popped open, Hood squeezed out and joined them on the deck, where they looked down at Shimazu and Captain Kearny as they emerged from the stairwell and drove off in the new burnt-sienna jeep.

"Eee-ya what's up, doc?" Mad-dog asked in his Bugs voice.

"Major says with Leffanta here, we're top-heavy. The map room is overcrowded, and he's not happy with Babineaux's production, so he's sending me to Vung Tau."

"*Oh, Just Great!*" Mad-dog shouted, "I'm *really* screwed now! Rosie's gonna be with Sang every night and weekend, you're leaving for paradise, and Louie fuckin' Leffanta spends every spare moment kneeling in his prayer-niche with his goofy translator-friend." They paused to see if Leffanta had heard the insult, but his typewriter never missed a beat. "So what am I supposed to do for kicks? Go shopping by myself all day?"

'You could take up reading," Hood offered.

"I'm an *English major!*" Mad-dog howled. "I joined-up to get out of the library!"

"How about Sang fixes you up with someone?"

"Terrific idea, Rosie! Your life has been a roller-coaster-to-hell since you got mixed up with a girl!"

"A woman, you mean!"

"Yeah, OK...a sixteen-year-old 'woman'!"

Hood stepped between them before Rosenzweig could grab him. He dropped his voice, glad that Leffanta was still pounding away. "Listen, we have a more pressing problem to deal with. I was gonna handle this on my own, but I won't be around, so I'm counting on you guys...." And he described in detail the skit that acted itself out at the Caravelle that day.

"I told Mulcahey you seemed lost in space," Rosie said. "You should have tipped me."

"How could I? Sang doesn't know what you do. And I don't even know what I saw."

"Monroe's lady, really?" Mulcahey said. "What was she doing there?"

"Anybody's guess. She just happened to be there or, god-forbid, she was tailing me. Anyway, do this for me: I was gonna take a book and stake out the lobby over there, someplace obvious, out in the open so Singleton gets to make the call, come up and say 'Howdy' or sail on by. If he avoids contact, I was planning to tail from a ways back and see where he goes. 'Til we know how much trouble he may be in, we can't help him. Don't say anything to Viet but keep an eye on him. He may be doubling up on us. There's two of you and Bian's never seen you, so maybe it works-out better this way. Keep in touch on this and keep me informed. Meantime, if you need any, money is no object."

The three of them leaned on the deck rail and gazed down at the damaged Citroën.

"I'm very proud of you men," Shimazu said and not without reason. Belmont wore a clean shirt without a cigarette pack bulging in the pocket and he sat up straight in his chair. And Dodd was in shirt and pants, not saffron robes. "MACV has commended Khap Noi Station in the March report, citing you for timely and accurate intelligence. And you have extended your tour-of-duty without taking any leave-time, Mr. Dodd."

"Thank you, sir," Belmont said. Dodd said nothing.

"I'm accepting all your recommendations for increasing your budget and expanding the network and I've spoken with CP-C, who is extremely pleased with the job you're doing."

"CP-C is a patriot and a man of courage I've learned a lot from him," Belmont said. Dodd said nothing.

"The truth is, I didn't think the Khap Noi operation could be salvaged, but you men have done it. Congratulations."

"Thank you, sir," Belmont said. Dodd just sat there.

Shimazu placed his folded hands on the Khap Noi file folder and rested his hooded eyes on them for a silent moment before saying, "May I speak with you privately, Mr. Dodd?"

When Belmont had cleared the room, Shimazu said, "I think I can understand how you're feeling, Mr. Dodd."

"You could not possibly," Dodd enunciated.

"When I was your age, we blasted our way up the Italian boot. Villages, farms, whole cities in the way of the fighting were turned into rubble and many civilians were injured and killed. I saw it with my own eyes."

"If I had been doing my job, I could have warned them," Dodd said. "Many people saw the VC crossing the river and starting down the road to Khap Noi, but none of them were hired field agents because I didn't recruit any. My people had no warning. Many of them died because I was too busy playing a monk to do my job."

"Perhaps," Shimazu said, "Perhaps not. No one expected an all-out attack until after Tet was over. Surprise has always been a weapon of war."

"It won't happen again," Dodd promised. "I'm extending my tour of duty and will save them next time."

"Good, timely intelligence could save them, you're right. In the meantime, Mr. Dodd, take advice from an old veteran: Save yourself too. Give their basketball coach back to them."

Shimazu left Dodd alone in the tiny office so he could cry himself out in privacy.

John Francis Mulcahey was a fish out of water after Braxton Hood departed for Vung Tau March 6th. He called the rest of March "forty days and nights wandering the desert," although it was fewer than that and Saigon is no desert. The new, revised Leffanta was a typing and filing maniac who shouldered the flow of paperwork single-handedly, but he spent the remainder of his time huddled in his study corner, learning about Cao Dai. Rosie could walk to the apartment in ten minutes so he was more often there than in the office. His cot in the map room was empty every night. Just as he had predicted, Mulcahey did all the shopping by himself. And even the evening meals, though the food was elaborately prepared, were depressing for him, with Rosie anxious to be excused from the table so he could walk "home," Leffanta in his white robe smiling vacantly with his mind a million miles away and the two officers carrying on a lively discussion as they developed a warm friendship that did not include Mulcahey.

Solitude was in no way his natural state and his tentative hold on sanity began to seriously fray during this period.

Two weekends in a row, he sat in the lobby of the Caravelle, as he promised Hood he would do, reading *Ulysses*. But Singleton failed to show, so he marked the page where medical students were getting drunk while Leopold Bloom was sober and lonely, and gave up the vigil.

There was no joy in going to the pool or shanty-town by himself and solo bar-hopping was too risky for a light-weight who couldn't, he had to admit, hold his booze. So his only solace and companion became the bicycle he paid too much for on the day they shot hell out

of the blue jeep, for no reason at all. He chained his bike to a street
sign outside the Caravelle for two Saturdays and Sundays; he took a
spin on it through heavy noontime traffic most days, just for the thrill
of defying death in the fleet shadows of trucks, jeeps and taxis; and
every night, when the dishes were done, he said good night to Papa-
san and launched off to explore the dusty alleys and backstreets of
the Asian capital, often with his SLR camera, mounted with a flash.
He once bought a soft drink from a merchant who lived in his shop
and ended up getting to know him and his family, returning there
often to sit on the dirt floor with the children, watching Vietnamese
shows on an ancient black-and-white TV, laughing with them at sight-
gags and improving his pidgin English. One whole, long night, he
spent feeding sticks to a fire with a Filipino soldier, picking up a few
words of Tagalog from him. Wherever GIs and girls gathered, he
could count on finding a cat-house full of friendly young women and
fellow soldiers, with beer and snacks for a price, full of happy chatter about which girl he should choose to go upstairs with. Bah-me-
bah in hand, he would say to a couch-full of girls, "Teach me talk
Vietnam-ee." One of the girls would point to her shoe and give him
the word. When he tried to repeat it back, they would howl with
laughter and tell him, "No! That word mean 'pig'." He sometimes
picked-out a girl who caught his fancy, but more often he only satisfied his greater need, to be around people and engage in laughter
and teasing, the sustaining bread and butter for a social animal like
Mad-dog Mulcahey.

These nightly excursions often involved his being lost, unable to
find any familiar street or landmark, but he was unworried about
it because he was blessed with the great illusion of youth -- that terrible things happen only to other people. By dawn, he always managed to make it back to III Corps, where Papa-san welcomed him in
and where Leffanta answered the phone and polished off the typing
while he caught a few hours sleep.

On Saturday, March 23rd, this "wandering the desert" chap-
ter ended and a new one began. It was the first weekend he was

not staking-out the Caravelle and he rode his bike downtown, taking photographs of anything he found interesting. He stopped at the park beside the great mountain of bricks called Notre Dame Cathedral to snap a pedi-cab driver using his pith helmet as a bucket to wash his bike-cab with water from a leaking fire hydrant. As Maddog pantomimed for permission to take the picture, he heard odd, high-pitched music between the sounds of passing traffic. Allergic to religion, he had never been inside this looming structure, but now he chained his bike to a tree and went to find the source of the singing.

In front of the communion rail, thirty-or-so boys in three rows were practicing chants in Latin. The conductor would prompt them with a line of litany and then cue their response. Mulcahey hoped his film was sensitive enough to get a picture of them without the flash, but as he stepped into a pew, he caught his foot on a kneeler that had been left down and fell, camera-in-hand, with a clatter. As he struggled to dig himself out of the narrow crevice between pews, Levesque whispered to him, "Are you all right?" They stared at each other, thunderstruck, until Levesque glanced around the church and seeing no one else said, "Are you free to talk?"

The boys were sent with their supervisor back to the orphanage next door and the two friends sat together in the pew for over an hour, catching up on the high-points of the half-year they'd not seen each other.

"If I didn't already know you're a liar," Mad-dog laughed, "I wouldn't believe a word you've told me, Brother Andre."

"Well, I've done more work for the church than for SIC...just ask Cardenas. As an intelligence asset, I've been worthless. Since Tet, I've been assigned to the Cathedral because the Bishop thinks it's too dangerous for a French-speaking Westerner to be out in the parishes. But I don't think the Bishop trusts me anymore. Cardenas insists that I stay here and try anyway. He and Singleton and I meet every Monday at SIC Central."

"Singleton! You and Singleton work together?"

"Not together, but we're both special projects Cardenas is responsible for."

Levesque was able to throw light on some of the Caravelle mystery described by Hood. The noisy man in the tourist shirt was a Cardenas-run agent named Duke -- but what was Viet, the III Corps translator, doing there and why was Cardenas taking pictures of them? Had Hood merely mistaken this third man for Viet? Or was Hood right and Viet was a double-agent, working both sides? And what would Monroe's lady-friend have to do with it, if anything?

"Singleton reported the plantation owner had a daughter named Bian, but I doubt she's the same person," Levesque said. "It's probably a common name."

Then, admitting it was all too complicated to grasp, they got down to serious business.

"That piano over by the pulpit work?"

"That's not the pulpit," Levesque corrected. "That's the lectern. And yes, it does."

"And could you use a volunteer pianist to accompany your choir?"

"Now there is a scary idea if ever I heard one," Levesque said. "It's been touch-and-go building up my Brother Andre identity. I'd lapse into English with you around."

"Hell, you're Canadian!" Mad-dog pointed out. "All Canadians speak some English."

Thus did it arise out of Levesque's boredom and Mulcahey's recklessness and the loneliness of both that the boys' choir would gather 4:00 to 5:30 every day to learn secular songs in English -- a wonderful job-skill for the orphans -- which reminded both young men of "Going My Way".

"Shall I call you Father O'Malley?"

"Better not!" Levesque answered, sure that, unlike the movie, this was going to end badly.

30

6 - 26 March 1968

BRAVO, JULIET !

Without the stress of being with Monroe, Bian and Diem this time, Braxton Hood was free to let the full magnificence of the Vung Tau coastline wash over him. He drove past the hotel where he had stayed on New Year's Eve, following written directions to the address of Field Station E. He arrived before 11:00 and was impressed with how effective and convincing Mark Babineaux's operation was: The "office supply" cover appeared in every aspect to be an actual store, with aisles of displayed products, even furniture, and real customers paying a woman at the counter for actual supplies. How Babineaux managed to keep all this going and still find time to run an intelligence network -- but then, Shimazu had complained that it wasn't much of a network. He waited his turn in line before asking the counter-clerk for Babineaux.

"He no here," she informed him.

Feeling like he was back in Cu Chi on that first day, asking for Monroe, Hood pointed at his watch and said, "When does he come back?"

The dour, dark-complexioned woman spoke to a child in sharp Vietnamese bursts and the little boy took Hood's fingers in his grasp and pulled him toward the door. Never letting go, the child tugged him along like a pet ox through twisting streets and over the sill of an open doorway, through a busy room full of women, mostly young, and into a small courtyard where Babineaux stood before an audience, a dozen women and children on rows of benches.

"I wake up at 6:00," he enunciated slowly and they echoed back his words.

"I drink my tea from a cup." He raised a teacup to his lips while they echoed him.

The little boy stood beaming up at Hood, two open palms just below his smile until, catching on, Hood put a $5 note in his hands. The boy's eyes and mouth popped open in surprise and he ran for the door before this big man could change his mind.

After ten minutes of patient drilling, Babineaux released the class and came over to Hood, who suggested "Let's go somewhere we can talk."

"Can't, I have one more class," Babineaux told him, "Teaching is how I earn my rent for the bungalow...long story."

So it was after noon before the two friends settled into an outdoor cafe across from the teeming beach, beers and menus between them, ready to conduct business. "He wants them all gone for good and not replaced," Hood said, "All the shrimp dealers and nuoc mam salesmen and all them-all. He wants you to get back to the whore-agents you had in December, when you generated all those high-quality IRs and put out the White Paper. He thinks you just got discouraged because MACV didn't roll-over for you then, but he thinks you were on the right track and he wants you back there."

It was hard to know by the smirk on his face how Babineaux was taking this urgent message from the major. He took a long pull on his bottle of Tooheys and asked through his crazy-Cajun grin, "Braxton... have you ever painted yourself into a corner one little brush-stroke at a time and looked around to find there was no way out?"

The ghost of Frank Monroe danced through Hood's vision so it took him a few seconds to respond, "I guess I have."

"You need to realize that Vung Tau isn't Vietnam, man. It's Shangri-La. It's that island of Bali Ha'i Mulcahey used to sing about.

There's a hurricane raging all around you, but here, you're in the eye. It works on your brain. You get disoriented...."

"Truth is, I spent a few days here in late December, and something like that happened to me then, so I think I follow what you're saying," Hood admitted.

"Let's take a walk after lunch and I'll introduce you around, then we can hash-out what to do about operations. But OK," Babineaux said, "We'll start by firing the dead-wood agents."

After lunch, Babineaux led him to a clothing store specializing in beach wear and tourist shirts, all sewn in the back room by three full-time employees working on sewing machines and cutting tables. The owner was a stunningly beautiful teenager named Hang and she embraced Babineaux warmly and kissed his cheek. "This big man is my friend Hood," Babineaux said, "He's coming to live in Vung Tau with me for awhile."

Hang hid a smile with her fingers, blushed visibly and laughed, "Your twins will like that."

As they strolled toward the hospital, Babineaux told him all about Qui, the Olympic athlete who had carried him over the sill of death's door and about Ngon Bich, whom everybody called "Itty Bitchy". "She's probably not of our species," he explained, "She's a raw force of nature or some demon-spirit from mythology. Weighs about a hundred pounds, the best business-mind you'll ever see, and if you back her into a corner, she's got a machete that she's not afraid to use. She set me up to live with Hang, my hired help and bed-mate, until I really got into her like a bee knee-deep in honey, then she snatched her away, used the money I paid her to start that clothes shop and saddled me with a sour-puss old lady."

'You should have told her that you...." Hood began.

Babineaux exploded in laughter and stopped walking. "I told you, she's a force of nature! Try telling the China Sea it's not time for high tide! Look, she owns half this town and is after the rest. That warren of buildings where you saw me teaching? All hers, and the three dozen women you saw scurrying around there? Her army of minions. They look busy? That's because every one of them has a long to-do list from their queen bee. Hang runs that store, makes a living, but Bich owns the building. She owns the bungalow where I live and the office-supply store and...."

"What?! No!" Hood gasped, "SIC pays the rent and expenses to run that store as a front for your network."

"Sweet deal for Ngon Bich, eh? The little woman is a genius. That sour-puss old lady she stuck me with moved in, took the store off my back...which I thought was OK at the time...then turned it into a monster with five full-time workers and daily supply runs to Saigon, something I couldn't have taken back even if I wanted to, and that old lady, Ly, didn't need me."

"The woman I saw behind the counter?" Hood said, "She's not old, maybe 30, late 20's?"

"After you sleep with Hang for three weeks...." Babineaux explained, "Anyway, Bich bought me out, fair-and-square."

"You could get in a lot of trouble for this," Hood warned, knowing more, himself, than he had ever wanted to about stealing from the Army. "How much did you get?"

"Not enough. She drives a hard bargain. And I'm pouring it all into my bar business."

"What bar business?"

"The bar business Itty Bitchy has promised me." They walked a ways in silence before Babineaux added, "It does sound like I'm getting screwed here, doesn't it."

When they found Qui, she was tending babies in the nursery. Babineaux introduced Braxton, who immediately recognized the superb athlete he'd been told about in her powerful hand-shake and quick, lithe movements. She was beautiful and very friendly as she shared the news of her boy-friend, an ob-gyn specialist from Sydney. "I be sure to invite you to wedding," she told Babineaux, delivering a buddy-punch to his shoulder that landed with an audible smack.

They walked uphill into the heart of the town from there, Hood with the briefcase that never left his side, Babineaux kneading the bruise in his left shoulder with his right hand. They stopped-in briefly at a large rice-wine store with a half-dozen workers operated by a woman named Loan, then a foundry that stamped-out jewelry managed by a woman named Khanh, and a silk-worm operation with eight employees run by a woman named Hanh. "All these places got started when Ngon Bich set these women up with seed-money investors...Australians and Americans like me...who divvied-up six dollars a day until they had enough to start up and then she guided them on how to grow the business. She created hundreds of jobs for widows and orphans in this town, but she still owns all the real estate they operate in."

"And she rakes-in a fortune in rents," Hood assumed.

"Hardly!" Babineaux said, "She's broke...worse than broke! She's mortgaged up to her ass, but the war keeps sending her more widows and orphans. They stream into this island of peace grasping her name and address like a life-line. And eventually, she finds a situation for them."

"All right, I get it," Hood said, "You've got all caught-up in this situation and slept with some real beauties, but when we get to your place, we have to talk about your operation."

"We are talking about it," Babineaux said grimly, "I'm showing you my operation." There was a long silence as they climbed the steep, narrow streets toward the bungalow, then Babineaux stopped walking, turned to Hood and asked, "Did Shimazu show you my report to MACV?"

"Sure did. He's very proud of the work you did...wants you to produce more like it."

"Do you happen to remember the code-names for the three principal agents?"

"I do...yes...I see! You used *their* names, your girl-friends' names, to cover the agents."

"What agents?"

The well-grounded mathematician solved for "x" in a relatively short time, but that only increased his surprise. "There were no agents," he said, matter-of-factly, "So you made the whole thing up?"

"Before you start getting all harsh and judgmental on me, Braxton, just walk with me through the rest of my story here. I'm not a strong man! Itty Bitchy used all that youth and beauty to bend me to her will! The hag! The fiend! Wait 'til you see the rest of what I'm suffering through! You won't believe it!"

The bungalow did not have a sitting room. The open space where it used to be was a cramped but elaborate pub, with two twenty-foot bar-sections wedged kitty-corner across each side of the room, a few tables in-between, a candle on each, designer lighting, a full comple-ment of beer, wine and liquor along the glass shelves behind the twin bars. And behind each bar, a petite twin in matching purple ao dais, moving pertly. "Babineaux's Lounge," as the sign over the door iden-tified it, had every element needed for a thriving and profitable en-terprise except one: Customers. There was little space for them, had there been any -- and they would have had to climb seven steep blocks up from the beaches, by-passing a half-dozen other such establish-ments along the way. Though Phuong and Long were cheerful and energetic -- polishing glasses, cutting limes, restless as sparrows -- a pall of sadness and defeat hung over the place, like a Thanksgiving table heavy with turkey, potatoes and gravy but abandoned by the family.

"Go ahead!" Babineaux challenged, as soon as introductions were made, "Any drink you can think of."

"How's about a Tequila Sunrise, Co Long?"

"OK. That's Phuong, but they're used to that. I still can't tell one from the other and we've worked and slept together since December."

Hood looked at the nimble little duo and said, "I can see you've suffered terribly."

"I did at first, but I've gotten used to it," Babineaux said seriously. "We can talk freely. The only English they know has to do with mak-ing drinks...they're like parrots."

And just that quick, a perfect cocktail -- dark red grenadine on the bottom of a tall glass with orange juice fading into crushed ice above it, a floating meraschino, a slice of orange poised on the rim -- was placed before Hood by Co Phuong, who enunciated, "T'at whiw be eight dowah, pweez!" Hood put $10 on the bar and waved off the change, which won him a big smile. He used the long-handled spoon Phuong had placed on his paper napkin to stir the ingredients together, took a sip and lifted it in tribute to his bar-maid. "So this *is* your operation," he said to Babineaux, "I'm looking at it?"

"Shimazu wants high-level intelligence, emphasis on strategic and political? Well *this* is how you get it. Top people...theirs or ours or third-party...do not shop for office supplies. You need girls and booze and the hottest night-spot on the beach. You need big-shots who are on a bender. I've been busting my hump and sinking all my own money into getting SIC what they want and I'm *this* close!" Babineaux held finger and thumb a quarter inch apart. "There's a big villa for sale at this end of the beach that I've been hammering on Itty Bitchy to invest in. It's enormous! It's beautiful! It's all I need and I'm ready to move all this stuff down there and start reeling in the big fish. But Bich says she's leveraged out by the flood of refugees coming in since Tet. I told her, 'Half the women you've taken-in already work as hookers! Why not give them a real business-address, Babineaux's Lounge? I'll look after them like a father and they'll make more money! All I ask is they help me gather useful intelligence'."

"You *did not* tell her that!"

"No reason not to, my friend. She knew who I was and what I was doing here on Day One. Nothing happens in Vung Tau she doesn't know about. She introduced two local CIA agents to me on the beach, told them I was the new guy with SIC. She knew who they were. Vung Tau is a small town, and our translator, Duong, knows everybody, is related to half of them, and leaks like a sieve." Babineaux asked Phuong for a Tooheys, which she poured for him with just the right head on it into a frosted stein. "T'at whiw be fo' dowah, pweez!" she said and Hood pushed another $5 across the bar. Babineaux took a sip and said, "OK, so I cut some corners back in December, I admit."

"You did *way* more than cut corners," Hood corrected him.

"But my report was based on a series of interviews with Australian Army and Navy officers who've been here since the mid-60's, so it was really just the sources I cribbed on, not the substance." He spun his bar-stool around, put his elbows on the bar and smiled across at Long, who was straightening wine glasses on a shelf. She broke into a big, happy smile in return. "The bottom line, Braxton," he sighed, "Is that Shimazu was about to close-down the station, and I couldn't stand the thought of losing all this and getting thrown into a combat zone. This, my friend," he said sleepily, "is the Garden of Eden."

"Yeah, with two Eves."

"With as many Eves as you have the strength for."

Braxton Hood had been paying very close attention to Babineaux's account of things and his reasons for doing what he had done. Because it reminded him so sharply of his own half-year in Vietnam, his compromises and rationalizations, the powerful attraction of comfort and safety, the corners he had painted himself into, brush-stroke by brush-stroke, he felt in no position to judge Mark Babineaux. When he spoke, it was not on impulse. He had made up his mind.

"What do you say we go into business together, Mark? We'll buy a place on the beach... the villa you have in mind, if that works out, or some other place. We'll put it all in Ngon Bich's name, so long as she puts in writing that we manage it our way for six months. We'll load the place with beautiful women from her corral and serve great drinks, mixed by your twins, hire a bunch of locals, ship money home to our parents, and gather a ton of high-quality intelligence from our agent-whores, Hang, Ly and Qui."

Babineaux was staring at him quizzically, his head cocked to one side, the crazy-Cajun smile across his face. "Nice idea," he said, "but first you'll have to find a way to pound fifty or sixty thousand bucks out of Itty Bitchy."

"Not," Hood uttered distinctly, savoring the last of his Tequila Sunrise, "necessarily."

He walked Babineaux to the Citroën, cut the tape on one of the two boxes in the trunk and told him, "You're not the only one who's

been painted into a corner by people wiser and older than you are."
He felt a tremendous sense of personal relief when he pulled the flaps
back, drank-in Babineaux's predictable astonishment, and was finally
able to tell someone, a friend, "Probably $100,000 I would guess, and
I've got a check in my briefcase for another $30,000 and change. It's
not really mine and I'm looking for a way to leave it in-country...for
widows and orphans, maybe."

And so it came about through two days of tough negotiations
with Bich and her attorney, and with Hood conceding to Babineaux
that the tiny, wizened Itty Bitchy was the toughest human being,
pound-for-pound, on the planet -- that the genius and generosity
(if that's what it was) of Frank Monroe came to good use. Braxton
and Mark were guaranteed exclusive management of the company
through 25 September 1968, their DEROS, after which all property, assets and rights reverted to Ngon Bich who, by the time she
finished squeezing them, worked well all around because she could
not tolerate property sitting idle, and so she recruited armies of
carpenters, electricians and others to make sure the establishment
opened by March 25.

Given how deep Braxton Hood's pockets were and how willing he
was to dig into them, it was no surprise that Co Bich was soon able to
convert a private mansion into a public establishment with lighting
and furnishings that would make it the showcase night-spot on the
Vung Tau beach road. Physically, everything would be ready for opening night, but behind the scenes, there was a problem with "naming
rights".

"She can call it whatever she wants after September," Babineaux
growled at Hood as they strolled the beach across the way, watching
teams of workers crawling like ants over the mansion. "Until then,
goddammit, it's going to be Babineaux's Seaside Lounge!"

"I've got to side with her on this," Hood countered, "It's bad business to change names a few month after it opens. She's probably OK
with 'Seaside Lounge'. It's the 'Babineaux' part she doesn't want to
be stuck with after we're gone."

They leaned on opposite sides of a palm tree, arms folded, watching the walls being torn down on the veranda to leave an open deck for tables and chairs.

"It was my dream, not hers," Babineaux muttered.

"It'll be hers soon enough," Hood reminded him.

Two military types, maybe still in their teens, walked by them on the side of the road, buzz-cuts, tight physiques, brand new civilian clothes, black shoes highly shined. As they passed the palm tree, their way was blocked by two excited young girls in the peasant uniforms of white blouses, black slacks, sandals, conical hats. The taller girl laid a gentle hand on the forearm of the blond soldier and said, "This my good-luck day! I look for you long-time, GI."

"Is that right?" he said smiling, amused.

"You, your friend, take us home you. We dance for you, make you happy."

"What kind of dance?"

The girls giggled, covering their laughter behind delicate fingers. "We can-do foxtrot."

"I'm not sure I know how to foxtrot," the blond trooper said.

The girls exploded in uproarious laughter, not entirely free of mockery: "OK, GI," the taller one said, "same-same you talk in phone: Foxtrot, Utility, Charlie, Kilo. You know *that?*"

The young men turned away and held a whispered discussion, their heads together. After a full minute had gone by, the taller girl grew impatient and interrupted: "OK, you no have time for us, cheap charlie? How about Bravo Juliet back-seat taxi-cab?"

The epiphany was immediate and simultaneous as Babineaux and Hood exchanged looks of revelation.

On 25 March, in the nick of time, the huge gold and vermillion sign arrived, was mounted on the veranda roof and fitted with spotlights. By sundown, "Bravo, Juliet!" opened for business: The tiny twins, resplendent in gold and vermillion ao dais, were training their new assistants to the high standards their beloved Babineaux had set for them, a dozen lovely women who had been widowed by war but found protection under the wings of Ngon Bich wafted in flowing silks of rich colors through the rooms, up and down the stairs, orienting themselves to the possibilities now of being a waitress, trained to ask "What's your poison?" in Vietnamese, English and French, or of making more money as a hostess, the carefully chosen few, all named "Juliet," who had been tutored by Babineaux and Itty Bitchy in how to identify and exploit sources of useful intelligence in the seclusion of the upstairs bedrooms.

The first wave of paying customers were Royal Australian Navy personnel, friends of Babineaux and a rowdy but warm-hearted bunch who knew how to party and spend money freely. Walk-in customers stayed if they found the atmosphere and the company of pretty women justified the highest prices on the beach-front, or had a drink and left.

Twelve hours later, the rising sun greeted their last departing guests and Babineaux stumbled home on the arms of his indefatigable twins, exhausted but elated, while Hood locked up then dropped into the only unoccupied upstairs bed, much relieved that two-thirds of Monroe's legacy had been put to good use.

31

29 March - 1 April 1968

APRIL FOOLS

"**T**ell Dodd he can afford to take one damned day off to honor the major," Mad-dog screamed into the phone. He listened for a moment, then told Rosie, "I don't think they can hear me. It's breaking up." He put the phone back to his head and screamed, "Repeat what you said! Wait! Wait! We've got choppers over us!" He dropped the handset on the desk and for the next two minutes loudly cursed Tan Son Nhut Air Base, The Army Air Corps, The Signal Corps, Ma Bell and Igor Sikorsky while a flight of Hueys flew over one-by-one, shaking the whole villa. He shouted "Hello!" into the phone a few times before concluding, "I lost 'em."

Rosie and he had enjoyed his Dinners, lived in a comfortable villa with a hot-water shower instead of the crowded enlisted compound, and had received dozens of bed-time dessert trays from a CO who, though not outwardly expressive, showed great respect and affection for the young men he commanded. It was the least they could do to see him off with a first-rate party. That idea had been kicked around the office for weeks, but when Babineaux and Hood told them about a rich nightclub owner in Vung Tau who would spring for it, that sealed the deal. They put the paperwork through for every man in III Corps to receive an in-country R&R leave from 30 March through 2 April -- every guy except Beatific Louie Leffanta, who had no interest in life on the 68th planet, although he conceded it may be intelligent.

"I don't think Belmont and Dodd are going to make it," Mad-dog said. "If they show up, we'll improvise, but Dodd refuses to leave Khap Noi and Belmont won't come without him. So we should tell Hood we need seven rooms, five for all four nights and two for just April first. You and I, Singleton and Levesque can all double-up, Viet says the Translator's Pool needs three, make sure the major gets the best room and Captain Kearney needs one."

"Plus one more for Major Cardenas," Rosie said.

"Is he coming?"

"Singleton and Levesque had him sign-off on the R&Rs and they mentioned the farewell party for the major. He said he wouldn't miss it. So we'll tell Hood we need three rooms for big-shots on 1 April and five for all four nights."

"Rosie...invite Sang. You know you want to. Otherwise, you'll keep me up all night blubbering in your pillow."

"That's a scary idea...for all kinds of reasons."

"C'mon! You're a trained intelligence operative...you can pull it off. It's a party with all your friends...everything is paid-for by a super-rich guy. She should be there to meet everyone."

"You're right. Thank you, Mulcahey. I'll invite her."

"OK then. Tell Hood eight rooms, 'cuz I'm sure as hell not bunking with you-two."

The weather was perfect -- because in mid-dry season the weather was always perfect -- for the reunion, the festival and the farewell party known forever-after as "The Whale Days". The whole time resembled a square dance, with various pairings and combinations of friends sunbathing and swimming, tumbling in the high waves of the South China Sea, eating and drinking together deep into the night, sharing the adventures of their first half-year in Vietnam and, although these stories were exchanged outside of Sang's presence, Rosie's beautiful girlfriend came to be adopted as the mascot of Greyhawk's ES-3 class of 1967. Sang's loss, however, was missing those exotic tales told in her absence: Of society and intrigue in a plantation mansion, of kidnapping at gun-point, of physical mauling of a superior officer in defense of a woman's honor, of a self-inflicted gunshot wound, of midnight bike rides through the back alleys of Saigon, and of clerical cover in church settings. ("You actually dress up like a priest!" Mad-dog said. "I don't dress up like anything," Levesque responded coldly, "I *am* a deacon in the Church and I dress accordingly...like you would if you wore a fright-wig and a bulb-nose.") At the end of their time together, only Braxton Hood had kept his cards face-down, listening carefully, revealing little.

Mr. Viet and seven other members of the Translator's Pool were also having the time of their lives, once they confirmed the rumor that their rooms and drinks at Bravo, Juliet! were being paid-for by the wealthy owner of the establishment, a friend of Hood's.

By sheer dumb-luck, 30-31 March coincided with the Vung Tau Whale Temple's annual pageant, a surprise treat added to their special weekend. During the parade, the open veranda of Bravo, Juliet! featured, left-to-right: Braxton Hood with Rosie and Sang, then three young women who were typists, Mr. Viet with four other men who were translators (all of them related to the sprawling Pham clan, though the Americans didn't know that), then Mad-dog sandwiched between Rene Levesque and Rick Singleton, and on the right wing, Mark Babineaux with an identical twin under each arm. This festive bloc of partiers clapped, waved and cheered lustily the columns of men in deep blue and burgundy costumes who marched to honor the Whale God, the mythic protector of Vung Tau. Women in pink and red robes preceded the Whale Float, a deep-blue replica of the leviathan itself but scaled down to the size of a school bus. When the parade was over, the whole group walked over to the temple to view for themselves the bones of the actual creature which had washed up on the sands of Vung Tau a century earlier. There he was, glowing under colored lights, massive, immutable, unforgettable, bare bones -- the thing itself.

Monday was to be the pay-off for all the planning Rosenzweig, Mulcahey, Hood and Babineaux had done: April Fool's Day, 1968. The officers arrived mid-morning, Captain Kearney behind the wheel of the burnt-sienna jeep, the guest-of-honor at his side and Major Cardenas in the rear. Their bags were carried for them to the last vacant rooms upstairs in the Shakespeare-themed nightclub, which meant the hostesses -- all of them named Juliet -- had the night off. Hood had paid them a bonus in lieu of lost earnings. The younger men tried to disguise their amusement when the middle-aged officers appeared in shorts and sandals, with milk-colored legs that never saw the sun. While final preparations for an elaborate lunch were made, the three senior men enjoyed a long walk on the strand, talking about whatever career-men talked about.

The luncheon was held at the best sea-food restaurant in Vung Tau and between courses Viet, speaking for the Translators, and each of the enlisted men took turns raising glasses of beer, wine and mixed drinks in tribute to Major Shimazu. The final toasts were made by his fellow-officers, then Shimazu ended the lunch with a brief speech, typically understated, expressing appreciation for everyone in turn, last of all Braxton Hood. He raised his glass in Hood's direction and said, "I'm sorry your friend, our sponsor for this event, was not able to be here and that he prefers to remain anonymous. I'd like to have thanked him in person for all this generosity."

Hood raised his glass and answered, "I'll convey your words to him next time I see him."

Of those present, only Babineaux and Hood -- and perhaps Shimazu himself -- fully understood this exchange.

Mad-dog rose to remind everyone to arrive well before 6:00 for the major's party because, he said, "It's going to start with a bang!"

By mid-afternoon, Phuong, Long and the waitresses had Bravo, Juliet! ready to go: Helium balloons rose on strings toward matching gold and vermillion streamers and a banner that read "Sayonara,

Major Shimazu". The bus from Saigon arrived at 4:30, in plenty of time to get the thirty youngsters of the Notre Dame Boys' Choir something to eat, changed into their white shirts and black slacks, and in their places with their music folders. Mad-dog sat at the upright piano and ran them up-and-down scales until he felt they were ready to perform.

By 6:00, all the invited guests had walked around the sign that said "Closed Tonight for Private Party" and were in their places: The Translator's Pool circled a large table next to the stairway, Mad-dog at the keyboard and the choir in three rows, under the direction of Brother Andre in clerical garb, Hood and Babineaux behind the bar to assist the twins, wait-staff in place, all expecting, momentarily, the descent of the three officers.

Then, as promised, the party started with a bang. The first shot from Bian's Lugar (stolen from a German officer by her late husband when he was a young boy in France) shattered a full-length mirror on the stairway landing. Every head swiveled toward her in shock. The second and third rounds were better-aimed, closer to her target, and sent splinters of wood flying from the banister and newel post. They also sent thirty little boys screaming in every direction, other guests and staff ducking behind the bar, under tables and behind the piano. Bian strode the length of the bar with purpose, shouting in Vietnamese, "You murdered my parents and took over their estate, Minh, you rotten pig, and now you will pay with your life!" She stopped firing long enough to ask, "Where is that snake Gia Trang?"

By then she stood directly in front of Mr. Viet, the Lugar aimed between his eyes. He said to her with calm born of desperation, "Madam, I have never met you before and I know no one named Gia Trang. You have mistaken me for someone else." Pham Viet knew precisely whom she had mistaken him for, so he repeated what he had told her, this time in fluent English.

This caused the assassin to pause -- since she had been told that Minh spoke only Vietnamese. "But I have been following Mr. Michaels and you, waiting for Gia Trang to show."

"My name is Viet and my work has kept me in Saigon six days every week for months. Rarely do I leave the city. You can ask any of these people if that is not so...." But when he turned, there was no one to be seen. A voice from under the table was heard, however, to say, "That is true. Mr. Viet works in Saigon with us every day."

Knowing he had but one chance to live, he remained facing the table, his back turned on his assailant, and he tipped his head forward, as one does for the barber. With her free hand, Bian Guignon ran her fingers across the nape of his neck, across the spot where Pham Minh's jagged scar descended from his hairline. She stumbled back two steps, scanned the room for the young black man, Mr. Michaels, then strode out the open doorway.

Braxton Hood shouted to her, "Bian! Bian!" but she seemed not to notice and he thought better of chasing her into the street, an angry woman with a gun. He did, however, get a clear look at her getaway driver, Frank Monroe, standing on the steps of the veranda with an assault rifle at Present Arms. Leaning out for a better look, he stumbled, catching himself on the edge of the bar, or he would have landed right on top of Rick Singleton. "What are you doing down there?" Hood asked.

"Is she gone?" Singleton whispered.

"She left. Come up out of there!" Singleton peeked over the bar to check for himself then stood up. "Now where do you know Bian from?" Hood asked. "I caught her tailing you at the Caravelle last month, when you met with Viet."

"Who's Viet?" Singleton asked, brushing dirt from the knees of his beige suit. "Look, all I know is the plantation owners I told you about...they disappeared during the Tet Offensive. Bian is their daughter. So I figured she was coming after me, blaming me for what happened. She went after your interpreter and I can see her point. He really is the spitting image of one of the VC agents I met up there, a guy named Minh. But hell, a lot of them look alike to me and the one I met speaks no English at all, I'm fairly sure." Singleton studied

Viet's profile across the room and added, "Different haircut, maybe.
And the other guy has a scar."

"When you met Bian," Hood wanted to know, "was she with
anybody?"

"Yeah, her fiancé...tall, lanky guy with piercing blue eyes...art
dealer from Boston."

"We need to talk sometime," Hood said, feeling sure he would
need paper, pencils and a good amount of time to solve this problem.

When the three officers made their descent, their trepidation was
obvious. Blue smoke and the smell of cordite hung in the air and
shards of glass crunched underfoot as they came down the stairs. But
the crowd cheered them warmly and the enthusiasm of the little boys
who butchered the lyrics of "You're The Top" to Mad-dog's energetic
playing, put the party back on track. The chorus did much better
on the simpler words to "Bali Ha'i" and "Happy Talk". Their show-
stopper was "Oklahoma" and though they again massacred the lyrics,
they sang the title-line with such joy that all the company joined in
and rattled the wine glasses of Bravo, Juliet! Then the choir was led
off by their chaperones to a sleep-over at Duc Me Bai Dau church.

After two more hours of hors d'oeuvres, drinking, laughter and
mixing, the major announced that it was his bed-time. He stood
half-way up the stairway and made his farewell speech to a subdued
room. He thanked everyone who had made the last tour of duty of
his long career "so memorable" and for such an elaborate retirement
party. "The camaraderie," he said, "the little boys in the choir who
sang so...." and he stopped, too moved to trust himself for a moment.
Then he asked Mr. Viet to mount the steps and translate for him. He
paid a special tribute to all the women in the room and throughout
Vietnam. "The beautiful bar-tenders and waitresses who tend to us
with such kindness. I want you all to remember this: When men
go to war and nations fall on hard times, as Vietnam is suffering
through now, it is the women who keep society alive...who preserve
the nation's identity and culture...civilization itself. So that when the
fighting is over, we will have homes and communities to return to.

You, ladies, you keep sanity and decency alive for all mankind." As Viet translated his remarks, Major Shimazu snapped them a crisp salute, turned and was gone.

Mulcahey took advantage of this quiet moment to raise his own clear tenor rendition of the song that had been their anthem since they first met in the City of Brotherly Love:

> You have to look for the silver lining
> Whenever clouds appear in the blue.
> You know that somewhere the sun is shining
> And it's the right thing to do to let it shine for you.
>
> A heart full of joy and laughter
> Will always banish sadness and strife.
> So always look for the silver lining
> And try to find the sunny side of life.

32

2 April 1968

CASTING THE HOROSCOPE

The major's party dissolved quickly after the guest-of-honor retired, but the night was not over for the Greyhawk Six, who would go their separate ways tomorrow. They hauled a case of Tooheys across the street, to a spot on the wide expanse of sand near the water's edge. Quiet waves lapped rhythmically at the beach. Magnitudes of stars filled the black sky over the sea. They sat down in a half-circle around the case and passed bottles and an opener hand-to-hand.

For a long time they sat in silence, sipping cold beer in the embrace of the night and of friendship, until Braxton Hood's soft baritone opened the bidding with, "Did y'all know we met each other one year ago exactly? First week of April, 1967."

"That's right...I remember. Levesque had Mad-dog in an uproar because he was packing to go to Canada."

"I almost did."

"I'd'a kicked your ass."

"I remember Mad-dog mockin' my Southern drawl and I seriously thought about punchin' him out, then and there."

"You should have."

"I never mocked you-all's goofy accent!"

"You snickered. Same thing."

"What I remember is you guys all stood up for me when that pack of racists tried to throw me out of the Greyhawk Inn because I put Lou Rawls on the juke box."

"I'd'a kicked their asses."

"Why is it you're always pickin' fights when you weigh, what, maybe 140 pounds?"

"Who's Lou Rawls?"

"Oh for chrissakes!"

"No need for blasphemy."

"When do you stop being Brother Andre?"

"I'm not Brother Andre, and there's still no need for blasphemy."

"First time I met Babineaux, I took one look and knew he was a crazy man."

"Hey! You're one to talk about crazy, you lunatic!"

"My favorite time was when Levesque came waltzing in as a nun!"

"Sister what-was-it?"

"Sister Philomena."

"That pretty bar-girl dragged this big, tall nun over to our booth...."

"Linda."

"Who's Linda?"

"Screw you."

"Blasphemy!"

"Screw you is not blasphemy."

"Why should it bother you if I don't happen to remember her name?"

"It's Linda."

"My favorite was watching Hood walk those two Hounds up and down the aisles of that supermarket. Watch! We'll get back to The States and they'll still be standing there like statues!"

"There's a plaque in that store: Here lie two C.I. tails who died staring at this spot."

"What do girls talk about when they sit around like this?"

"Where do you come up with stuff like that?"

"I'm just wondering."

"They talk about us, exclusively."

"They talk about the same things we do."

"How do you know that?"

"I have it on the best authority, my mother."

This last word shifted the axis of their thoughts toward families and homes. For a long spell they stared toward the unseen horizon where the blackness of the Pacific Ocean ate up the star-light. Then Hood shuffled and re-dealt the conversation: "You and Levesque did a great job with that choir of orphan-boys, Mulcahey. They really sang well. So five years from now, you think you'll be teaching music?"

Unlike him altogether, John Francis Mulcahey took a moment to think before he answered. "I wasn't sure what I wanted to do back home until this morning. Did you-guys see the papers? LBJ says he's not going to run for re-election. Bobby Kennedy started his campaign two weeks ago and ran Johnson off 'cuz he knows he can't beat him. First thing I do when I get back in September is, I'm going to work for Bobby's campaign. I was in high school when they shot President Kennedy, so here's my chance to express how I feel about the only Irish Catholic to be president getting cheated out of his chance by whoever did it. I've read every biography there is on JFK and the family and I feel like I know them all personally. I have Bobby's book in my room, *Just Friends and Brave Enemies*, if anybody wants to borrow it. Then if I work hard enough for the campaign, maybe I can get a job with the administration when I get out of the service, or politics on the local level, I guess. Wherever they can use someone with advanced skills in high-level espionage. But I'll guarantee you one thing: Bobby Kennedy will be the best president we ever had, even better than Jack."

"How about you, Babineaux? Where you think you'll be five years from now?"

"Oh, yeah! Well, as you know, I'm screwed. I sleep 'til lunch, read on the beach all afternoon, then work in the hottest night-spot on this beautiful strip. Then I go home to a bungalow where I pile-in with two adorable young ladies who can mix any drink I want, any-time day-or-night. I can't tell them apart, but nothing's perfect. So my plan is to stay right here and live exactly as I am now and if the day comes I'm forced to leave, I'll hang myself. It's the only career-move that would make any sense for a man in my position. Otherwise, where would I end-up that isn't a living hell, compared to where I am now? There is, on the other hand, a friendly old granny here named Ngon Bich and maybe I could hire myself out as her care-taker, push her wheelchair through town for her, cook and clean. Naw, forget it. I'm buying a length of rope tomorrow and tying it over a rafter at Bravo, Juliet!"

"Good. A sensible plan. How's about you, Levesque? Think you'll stay in church work?"

"Well, truth is…and please, no wise-cracks from all you cynics…I've never been happier than these last few months, helping troubled peo-ple, sick people, orphans. I feel called to it and my family raised me that way. My mother and aunts would really celebrate it if I entered seminary. But celibacy? Man, that's a deal-breaker for me. I'll tell you a secret. After months of doing so-called intelligence work, it's the only secret I've got to tell. I write a letter every single day to Linda, the girl at the Greyhawk Inn."

"Oh! *That* Linda!"

"Shut up, Mulcahey. Yes, that Linda. And she's written every day to me. Her letters come in bunches. And we've reached what my mother would call an 'understanding' about when I get back. If it comes down to Linda or the collar, the collar loses. She thinks we should turn Episcopalian so I could be a married priest, but if I did that, my mother and aunts would beat Babineaux to the hangin' tree. They'd sooner I was an atheist. Anyway, I'm probably as anxious to get home as any of you-guys. I was only with Linda a few times, formal dates, and all the rest has been through letters. Once we're together and can talk it out, we'll figure some way to minister to folks who need us without my having to give her up to do it."

"Hey! I've got a question! Are Mark and Rene the same species?"

"Shut up, Mulcahey."

"I reckon there's no need to ask Singleton where he'll be in five years. We'll all be lined up on Broadway to buy tickets to see him."

"Maybe someday, if I'm lucky. I've got the same calling to theater Rene has to ministry. But for the next few years, my father's got a different plan for me. I know you-guys don't follow this stuff the way 'we' do, but Reverend King is organizing a Poor People's Campaign all across America and my father is deeply involved in it. They want to take the momentum of the Civil Rights Movement and turn it toward closing the gap between rich Americans and poor Americans. And since there's a whole lot more poor whites than poor blacks, it could unite both races at the grass-roots level. They've been played-off against each other by politicians and business interests since forever...but if Reverend King can get them to see how much they have in common, that could attack segregation and racism from the bottom up, instead of by top-down Federal laws. Anyway, my father's deeply committed to it and has known Reverend King and his family for many years, so I've got a position waiting for me when I get out of the Army, and it's something I can start working on as soon as we get back."

"Sounds exciting, Rick, but promise me you'll steer clear of those sheriffs with the dogs and clubs down my way."

"Those days are over," Singleton assured Hood. "The times, they are a-changin'."

"None of our business, Rosie, but I'll admit there's been gossip about you. We're dyin' to know if you and Sang have plans."

"Absolutely! Like Rene and Linda, we've reached an 'understanding'. Hadn't been for you, Braxton, we'd probably never have found our way back to each other and I'm never going to forget that, man. We owe you all kinds of ways. Back in my room, there's a letter from Major Shimazu. When I paid my respects to him at the party, he asked if I knew I needed my CO's permission to get married in this man's Army. He handed me a folder and said, 'Now you have it.' Besides the letter, he had the documents guys create a new Vietnamese birth certificate for Sang. I was surprised to learn she was actually born in 1949, not 1952 like she thought. Viet made sure her name was spelled correctly, with all the marks on it, in both Vietnamese and English copies. So I guess tomorrow morning, I'll take her for a walk on this beautiful beach and pop the question. Major Shimazu is one of the greatest human beings I will ever meet in my life. That he would care enough about some enlisted guy's problems to just...I don't know...just hand me those documents out-of-the-blue. I was trying to thank him without getting all worked up...I knew that would make him uncomfortable. But he told me that I remind him of someone he met when he was young...someone he owed a favor to. He even said that if Sang and I decided she wasn't comfortable back home in Nashville, he would set us up to live in Los Angeles where there's lots of Vietnamese coming to live and we could have jobs in his restaurant until we found something we liked better. Tell the truth, I don't know why he's taken such a liking to me...but it's pretty overwhelming. He said it was just 'karma'. I don't even know what that means!"

"I believe it's a car."

"Shut up, Mulcahey!"

"Yeah, shut up, Mulcahey."

"Shut up your own selves! If I think it's a car, I've got every right to say so. It's a car."

"That leaves you, Braxton. If you manage to survive the beach and the women and all the cocktails my twins can mix for you, where you gonna be in five years' time?"

"Well, my friends. I don't have any specific plans for the future, like y'all do. All y'all are settin' about to do some great things...in politics, for humankind and your families. Maybe I'll just sit on this beach and dream. Y'all see those four big, bright stars straight out, low on the horizon? Well, that's the Southern Cross. You never get to see those from The States. We're too far north. But I'll bet you our children's grandchildren will get to visit those stars someday, and I would really love to be a pioneer for them. By the end of the year,

NASA plans to shoot some astronauts around the moon and back. And then, shortly thereafter, they'll land some on the surface and bring 'em back alive. The first time a man will ever have stepped foot on a different world than this one, our home-planet. And the way things are goin' with computers, things'll just accelerate from here on out. In our lifetimes, gentlemen, we're gonna witness some *amazin'* stuff comin' our way. Take my grand-pappy, who rode horses to school and didn't see a car until he was ten or twelve. He lives in Florida now and rides jet planes all over the place. You think he saw some awesome stuff? Nothin' compared to what's comin'. I'll tell ya' what I'd like. I'd like to see if they could use a man at NASA who's handy with mathematics, to help along the process. They'll be reachin' for those stars and who knows what else? Curin' all the diseases and growin' plenty of food for everybody on earth and maybe endin' this old habit of fightin' wars with each other. Good, solid science will lead the way and I guess I'd like to be some small part of all that."

A sea breeze blanketed them in warmth and the waves clapped like a heart-beat marking the slow progress of their private thoughts then. And even Mad-dog Mulcahey was at peace on this perfect night.

ABOUT THE AUTHOR

 Raised in northern Indiana, Jack Nolan worked for a time for US Steel at Gary Works, as did his father and grandfather.

Graduated cum laude with an undergraduate degree by Ball State University, Nolan served three years with army intelligence. Between 1967 and 1970, he was stationed first at Fort Holabird and then with bilateral operations in Can Tho and Saigon before returning stateside to train others.

After his service, Nolan obtained a doctorate in history from Columbia University and taught advanced placement American literature and European history to college-bound students at University High School, Tucson, Arizona.

Nolan lives with his wife, Patricia, in Providence, Rhode Island. He's always happy to receive e-mails from his readership, former students, daughters (Kathleen and Heather), and grandsons (Ian, Ben, and Django) at Vietnam.Remix.1968@gmail.com.

Made in the USA
San Bernardino, CA
13 April 2017